I hope you  reading my book.

Gillian James
x

Phoenix and Rosa

Gillian James currently lives in Southampton with her husband, daughter, one cat, two ferrets and three guinea pigs. Although she has northern roots she spent most of her childhood in Guilford, Surrey.

While she has been writing fiction since the age of twelve this is her first work to be published. Although she has degrees in Geology and Oceanography, she has most recently been employed in social care, which she finds more rewarding than academia.

Gillian James

Phoenix and Rosa

Olympia Publishers
London

www.olympiapublishers.com
OLYMPIA PAPERBACK EDITION

A CIP catalogue record for this title is
available from the British Library.

ISBN: 978-1-84897-346-6

(Olympia Publishers is part of Ashwell Publishing Ltd)

First Published in 2014

Olympia Publishers
60 Cannon Street
London
EC4N 6NP

Printed in Great Britain

For Richard

Acknowledgement

Thank you to Ann Graham for additional proof reading.

Part 1

The Man behind the Mask

Island Nation Magazine
Saturday 11th May 2115

REFLECTIONS ON ROSA
Simon Chandra

She was beautiful, of that there is no doubt, but there was more than that. More than just her beauty that made people pay over a week's wages or queue in the streets for hours to see her perform. There was something uniquely captivating about her. The first time I saw her live I was just a boy, a spotty thirteen year old and as yet un-awakened to the appeal of the opposite sex. When the other boys at school lusted over dirty pictures and talked endlessly of breasts I never really understood what the fuss was about, not until that evening. Sitting beside my mother in the packed theatre I watched her swing and fly from the trapeze with such sensuous grace and I felt that I was in love.

Of course now it seems ridiculous that there should be so much excitement over someone who was basically just a circus performer. What Rosa did was not particularly new or original. The apparatus she used and the tricks she performed had been around for centuries. Her popularity was part of a renewed love of the circus which prevailed at the turn of the century. It was because the world was such a grim and dreary place back then that we longed for a little glamour and excitement to brighten our lives.

When I saw her perform live in 2103 she was already celebrity in her own right and the mistress to President Bryant. My mother was then editor of a women's magazine so frequently received free tickets to plays and shows. On this particular occasion my father could not accompany her as he had work commitments of his own, so as a reward for good behaviour and to the great displeasure of my sister, I went in his place.

Live entertainment was such a costly luxury in those days that although I had lived in London all my life it was the first time I had been to a West End theatre. The whole experience was incredibly exciting; the grandeur of the building, the high gilded ceiling, the lights, the music, the cheering and laughter. The whole show was spectacular but it was seeing Rosa which left the most lasting impression. Looking back now I cannot clearly recall any of the other acts, but she is as fresh in my mind as if I had seen her yesterday. Naturally at that time we had no idea of what she would go on to become, how her life would change and how she would completely change ours.

It is now almost ten years since she died and although so much has already been written, or perhaps because so much has been written, I feel I know very little about her. Many entirely contradictory accounts of her life have been published. Did she seek fame or did she find it by mistake? What of the men in her life; did they use her or was she using them? Did she choose the course her life took or was she controlled by others? And of course there are still so many questions about her death.

So I have made it my mission to find some answers. Through interviewing as many people as possible who knew her personally and who took part in the events that so fundamentally changed this country, I hope to piece together the truth. I have already contacted several significant people who have agreed to talk to me and each week I shall publish an account of my progress. As far as possible I shall try to keep to a chronological approach, talking first to the people who knew her as a child and so on, but I may occasionally digress as new information emerges.

I close this week's column with an appeal for your help. If you ever met her or know someone who did then please contact me. I am anxious to hear any details of her life regardless how trivial they may seem. I am hoping that I can gather enough of these seemingly insignificant threads to weave together a tapestry of her life.

Thursday 1st March 2103

Rebecca was worried about her new costume. White and silver had seemed such a good combination when she had initially chosen the fabrics but under the dressing-room lights it looked pale and drab. She was not sure about the asymmetric cut either. The leotard had one long sleeve on the left but only a narrow strap over her right shoulder, on which was fastened a red silk rose. About her hips hung a small skirt of sheer, metallic fabric, which came halfway down her left thigh but her right was exposed. It had looked striking and dramatic when she had sketched the design but now it just looked odd. She did however like the tights as they gave her long legs a shimmering, pearly sheen.

She sat down in front of the mirror so her dresser, Ami Reed, could add another silk rose to her dark hair which was tied up in a bun. With a small sponge Rebecca applied pale foundation to her face and examined the results critically.

"Too much white," she complained, "I look like a ghost."

"Not at all," Ami replied. "The contrast with your hair is perfect. It looks fantastic under the stage lights. Wait till I've done your eyes and lips then you'll get a better idea of the full effect."

Ami dusted and powdered with practised ease and applied a heavy rim of eye-liner. Then she painted Rebecca's lips bright scarlet.

"There, you look like an angel," said Ami.

Rebecca stood up and examined the results before the full-length mirror.

"I'm still not convinced, but it is too late now."

She tried a few stretches.

"It still feels all new and stiff," she complained. "It should have loosened up after the dress rehearsal."

"I wouldn't worry. I've never yet known you to like a new costume."

"True, I guess it is just nerves."

The green light by the door flashed a few times then faded, a yellow one taking its place.

"Time to go," said Rebecca.

"Yep, I'll see you later."

Rebecca descended the stairs to the auditorium, going through the routine in her head. She was greeted in the wings by one of the stage-hands.

"Are you ready Miss?" he asked.

"Yes, I'm ready," she replied.

"You look great," he remarked.

"Thanks. How is it going?"

"Brilliant, they're loving Martin."

"I'm not surprised."

She looked out towards the crowd. It was a full house but in the darkness she could only make out the first few rows. The two large rings standing upright in the centre of the stage ignited into orange flames to gasps from the audience. This meant Martin was about to commence the final part of his act.

"I still can't watch!" complained Rebecca looking away.

"Why not?" asked the stage-hand, "It is no more dangerous than your aerial work."

Martin launched himself from the springboard, performed a forward somersault through the first blazing ring, another across the floor, then dived through the second ring, ending with a third somersault before springing neatly back to his feet. Though Rebecca had looked away she knew he had completed the sequence successfully from the thunderous applause and wild cheering.

There was even louder applause as Martin performed his second passage through the hoops. He paused to acknowledge the house's appreciation before readying himself for the third and final stunt. Rebecca closed her eyes and did not open them again until the yelling and clapping informed her that the act had ended. The lights went down, the burning hoops were extinguished and Martin joined Rebecca in the wings, accepting a towel from the stage-hand to wipe the perspiration from his face.

"How was that?" he asked.

"I don't know, I had my eyes closed," Rebecca replied.

"Honestly Becky! I don't know why you are so scared of a few flames!"

The stage-hands removed Martin's apparatus while a single spotlight illuminated the Master of Ceremonies, who went by the grandiose name of Randolph Rochester, in the centre of the stage as he delivered Rebecca's introduction.

"Ladies and Gentlemen, the climax of our show fast approaches but fear not, for the final performance you shall see tonight is truly breathtaking. Prepare yourselves to be amazed by the gravity defying feats of aerial dexterity… "

"He's milking it a bit," Rebecca whispered to Martin.

"… Ladies and Gentlemen, the sensational Miss Rosa!"

She made her entrance waving and blowing kisses to the crowd. Her act began with just a single rope hanging down vertically in the middle of the stage. She climbed slowly, moving in time to the music. The several metres drop to the ground did not bother her; she was more worried about forgetting the routine. Halfway up she wrapped one leg around the rope, extended the other in front of her and leaned back with arms outstretched so that her body was horizontal. She was vaguely aware of applause but now her concentration was solely on the rope and the next move.

She climbed higher, gripped the cord with her feet and hung upside down. Then she caught the rope with her hands and flipped over. Now each move was flowing on seamlessly from the last and she no longer feared forgetting the routine. She began to enjoy herself as she swung back and forth. She released the rope and caught it again, the crowd gasping with amazement and delight. A second rope was lowered and she flew between the two twisting, spinning and flipping.

Pausing for a moment close to the ceiling, breathing heavily, she looked down on the upturned faces. The music was building to a crescendo as she went into another spin, swung off from one rope, somersaulted in the air and caught the other. Now for the final part. She hung by her feet, released, caught with her hands, then she swung out into the middle of the stage and let go the rope one last time. She turned a double somersault and landed on her feet, acknowledging the wild whoops and cheers with a smile and a wave. She made a bow and retired to the wing as the MC returned to the spotlight.

Ami was waiting with a towel and the rest of the performers were assembling for the grand finale. Rebecca wiped the sweat from her face and neck then Ami touched up her make-up. The band was playing the 'Circus Britannia' theme and the audience was clapping in time as each of the acts entered in turn: first the jugglers, then Hannah Hula, then The Tumbling Troop and many more. Each had a few minutes centre stage before moving aside for the next. All were dressed in white, silver and red. Martin, who had just completed a swift costume change into a silver one-piece, backflipped into the spotlight and danced on his hands.

Then it was Rebecca's turn. The rest of the cast parted to form an aisle down which she walked. She reached up and grasped the bar of the trapeze, which was raised until she was swinging above the heads of the rest of the company. She pulled herself up so she was sitting on the bar then hung beneath it by her knees while the acrobats cartwheeled beneath.

Three small pyrotechnic charges around the edge of the stage threw up sparks and streamers. She righted herself and stood up on the bar. Holding on with only one hand she caught a club tossed up by one of the jugglers. After throwing the club back down she performed a handstand on the bar then swung and looped about it. Above the bar she released, turned and caught it again. Then to a drum roll she swung up high, let go of the bar, executed a double somersault and landed as more pyrotechnics exploded to produce clouds of coloured smoke.

Randolph Rochester came forward to make his closing speech and the performers lined up to take a bow.

"… And now our show is at an end," said the MC, "but before we depart let us salute our most illustrious guest who has honoured us with his presence tonight. Ladies and Gentlemen please show your appreciation for President John Bryant."

The audience rose to its feet and applauded. The artists turned towards what was still known as the Royal Box and bowed. The band played 'Rule Britannia' and both cast and audience sang at the excruciatingly slow tempo produced by many people singing not quite in time and many not in tune. Rebecca always regretted being stood next to Martin at moments like these as he frequently sang his own words and she found it almost impossible not to laugh. Then there was more applause, more bowing and several curtain calls until at last they were free to retire to their dressing-rooms.

Tired after her exertions, Rebecca would gladly have gone home to watch TV and crawl into bed, but tonight she was obliged to attend an after show party. She showered, dressed and repainted her face. She put on a short, figure hugging scarlet dress and dangerously high heels. Her athletic physique was accentuated with a well padded brassiere. She wore her hair down but with similar dark eye make-up and red lipstick to her trademark stage look.

The theatre was just a single part of the vast, sprawling Newman Grand complex which contained a hotel, a nightclub, three restaurants and a number of bars. Rebecca took the lift up to the Skyline Suite where the VIPs were assembled and her fellow performers were beginning to arrive. President Bryant was talking with Samuel Newman and the show's director Nikolai Luchenko.

Bryant was a large man; tall, broad shouldered and portly. His hair was thick and dark, although receding slightly at the temples. His eyes were bright and full of humour. He had a large mouth almost constantly drawn up in a smile displaying perfectly white teeth. His laugh was loud and infectious. It shook his whole frame and caused his double chin to wobble. He was fashionably dressed in a dark suit with a long jacket over a colourful patterned waistcoat and cravat.

Rebecca made her entrance, striding confidently and swinging her hips exactly the way she walked on stage.

"Here she is," Newman announced, "our very own superstar."

"My dear you were wonderful," said Bryant kissing her on both cheeks.

Although it was widely known that Rebecca was the President's mistress he never kissed her on the lips in public.

"Thank you, I'm so glad you enjoyed it," she replied.

"As ever you look ravishing," said Bryant. "Let me get you a drink."

Although they were drinking from champagne glasses, the beverage was just cheap wine mixed with soda water. Rebecca had only ever once tasted real champagne, the night she first slept with the President.

They chatted about the show and as Bryant said how much he had enjoyed Martin's act Rebecca called him over.

"Martin, come and meet the President. John, this is the Marvellous Marti, more commonly known as Martin Ashdown."

Bryant shook the young acrobat's hand and congratulated him on his performance. To say that Martin was good-looking or even handsome would be a ridiculous understatement. Martin was beautiful. He was slender with long delicate fingers, strong cheek-bones and perfectly proportioned features. His hair was long and blond, his eyes two deep pools of blueness in which you could drown.

While Martin was talking to the President, Rebecca did her duty and mingled with other dignitaries. As well as five Cabinet ministers and their extensive PR staff, several executives from the Independent Media Corporation were present along with some famous names and faces from broadcasting and publishing. All were keen to talk to Rebecca and she spoke to each in turn, trying hard to remember names, to sound sincere and not to look bored. She soon exhausted her stock of small talk but most of the guests were satisfied if she just nodded and smiled.

Finally the party began to break up and the President summoned his car.

He drew Rebecca aside and said, "Listen sweetheart, I'm feeling pretty run down and I've got a meeting early tomorrow. Would you mind if I just dropped you home?"

"Not at all," she replied with relief, "I'm exhausted too."

"The meeting should be finished by twelve so we could meet for lunch before I leave for Chequers."

"That would be great."

"Are you ready to go?"

"I just need to get my bag from the dressing-room."

"OK, I'll leave first and meet you at the back door."

Bryant did the rounds, saying farewell to the other guests, shaking hands and still smiling broadly, then departed. Rebecca wished Martin and Luchenko goodnight and slipped out more discreetly. Her dressing-room was full of flowers, mostly roses, which Ami had carefully arranged in vases after the show. Rebecca paused briefly to admire them. Though they looked beautiful there was barely a hint of fragrance from any of them. As Rebecca put on her jacket her eye was caught by a vase of pale pink and yellow tulips. These had a lovely delicate perfume and looked so soft and natural compared with the stiff, uniform roses. There was no card attached to the flowers but a piece a paper lay on the table beside them.

She picked it up and unfolded it. It was a handwritten letter.

Dear Rosa,

After seeing you perform tonight I felt compelled to attempt to put into words my admiration for you. Watching you fly through the air with such elegance and grace made me feel as though I were flying with you. You inspired in me a sensation of freedom which I have not experienced in many years. I am certain that I am not the only person who feels this way. People love you because while they are watching you they are able to forget the cares and hardships of their lives. Your boldness and daring bolsters their own courage and helps them to face this harsh, uncaring world.

I know that you receive much adulation and I am aware that my poor offering looks very meagre in comparison to the other bouquets in your dressing-room, but I hope you will accept both my flowers and my inadequate words trusting they are sincere. If in this letter I have managed to convey some small fraction of my esteem please believe that my true regard for you is many times greater.

Your humble servant
The Man Behind the Mask

Rebecca read the letter twice over. It was beautiful, not just the content but the elegant script. The paper was of good quality but had a ragged edge as though it had been torn from a notebook. She stood puzzled, wondering who it could possibly be from, until she remembered that the President was waiting for her. She grabbed her bag and hurried down to the stage door where Bryant's car was sounding its horn impatiently.

"Where the hell have you been?" Bryant demanded as she joined him on the back seat.

"Sorry darling I got distracted. Look at this. It was in my dressing-room."

Bryant took the letter and exclaimed, "Handwritten!"

"Yes and very well written too, not with a biro I'm guessing."

"So who is it from?"

"I haven't the faintest idea."

Bryant instructed his chauffeur to drive on and read the letter as they proceeded. It was well after midnight so the roads were deserted apart from a few late-night licensed taxis.

On finishing the letter Bryant remarked, "The language sounds very old-fashioned, perhaps he copied it from a book or something. I mean, 'Your humble servant,' that sounds practically Victorian."

"Yes it is a very strange thing to say."

"What about the flowers? Were they nice?"

"Very nice, pink and yellow tulips."

"Tulips! What sort of an idiot would buy you tulips? Your name's Rosa not Tulipa!"

"Perhaps someone who thought I might be bored of roses."

"There's gratitude! If I'd known you were bored of roses I'd not have bothered wasting my money."

"Oh no darling, I'm not bored of roses really, especially not yours. They were lovely, really lovely. It's just that the tulips were quite nice too."

The President was silent as they drove down The Strand. Rebecca wondered if perhaps he was sulking but as they turned off towards the embankment he suddenly spoke.

"I think I know who the letter is from. My new speech-writer James Hutchens, I bet it was him. He's a young chap, Cambridge graduate and former Etonian, studied literature. He's rather eccentric. At meetings he's always scribbling notes in his little book with a fancy fountain pen. The other day I asked him if he would prefer a goose feather."

Bryant laughed loudly and Rebecca tittered politely.

"Was he at the theatre tonight?" she asked.

"Oh yes. He didn't make it onto the guest list for the party but I'm pretty sure he got one of the tickets. Newman gave me about a dozen so I spread them around my staff. He will be at the meeting tomorrow. We can ask him about it afterwards."

By this time they had reached Savoy Place, the luxury development where Rebecca had an apartment. She wished the President goodnight and his chauffeur took him home to Downing Street.

ROSA
The Man Behind the Mask

She rises like a plume of smoke,
Soaring with effortless grace
She escapes the tyranny of gravity.
Seeming oblivious to the wondering crowd,
She performs with sensuous ease.

I watch, breath held, transfixed, mesmerised,
Forgetting everything but her slender form.
The world recedes, becomes irrelevant,
I am alone and free to worship her,
Though I am but one of the pilgrims here.

The danger is part of the beauty.
That she could fall is what holds us entranced,
Yet I long to fly as she does,
To leave the dull, weary, plodding Earth,
Or just my dull and weary self.

She is Liberty though her breast is clothed.
Freedom has always taken female form,
Because the pleasure of woman's beauty
Is something no despot can take away.
She is my hope, my joy, my future.

ROSA'S CHILDHOOD
Simon Chandra

Since both her natural parents and her brother are dead there are few people who can tell me about Rosa's early years. Her half-sister, Kate Taylor is believed to be either in Africa or South America and as this is the nearest I can get to an address I think it unlikely that I will be able to arrange an interview. Her stepfather, Graham Taylor, still lives in London and I eventually managed to persuade him to meet me. I say eventually not because he was reluctant to be interviewed but because he originally asked for a rather large fee which I could not possibly agree to. It was only once he was told that Ellen Clayton had already agreed to talk to me that he decided to waive the fee, on the condition that the interview took place in an expensive restaurant.

I succeeded in securing a table at Anton Blanco's strictly on the understanding that I would write about the wonderful meal we had. The food and wine were both indeed exquisite and well worth the eye-watering bill, over which I am still in a dispute with our accounts department. It would seem that our illustrious editor is of the opinion that since this is my pet project I should be solely responsible for my expenses, thanks a lot Mum!

Before I recount my meeting with Graham Taylor I should perhaps supply a little background information. I have entitled my column "Rosa's Childhood" but this is of course erroneous. She did not acquire the name Rosa until she was an adult. The name on her birth certificate is Rebecca Eleanor Clayton. She was born in Kings College Hospital at 6:10 am on 1st September 2080. Her mother, Marian Clayton, and father, Anthony Jones, were never married but had cohabited for a few years and already had one child, Daniel Clayton, born on 7th June 2078. In those days it was common for unmarried couples to have children. The first Marriage and Parenting Bill was not passed until 2089.

By the time Rebecca was born Anthony Jones was in North Downs prison for drugs related offences. North Downs was one of the controversial, so-called "Modern Prisons" built during the 2020s to relieve the shortage of prison places but by the 2070s they were synonymous with outbreaks of contagious disease, overcrowding, understaffing and poor management. Jones was killed in a riot on

19th February 2081. Marian Clayton married Graham Taylor in October 2083 and their daughter Kate Taylor was born the following March, but the couple separated in the late '80s and in 2090 they divorced.

My first impression of Graham Taylor was that he put a great deal of effort into looking scruffy, the sort of man who goes to great pains to give the impression of not caring about his appearance. He is tall and reasonably slim with craggy, weathered features. His hair is grey and although thinning on top he wears it long, almost down to his shoulders. When I met him he was dressed entirely in black with a kind of cultivated, stylish shabbiness. It took a while to work him around to the subject of his stepdaughter. He spent the first twenty minutes complaining about the weather, the underground, the price of beer and so on. After several of my questions had achieved only monosyllabic answers I eventually succeeded in persuading him to recount how he met Marian Clayton.

"It was in the early '80s," he told me, "I was working for a mate of mine, an electrician. He had a contract with Brixton Council. This was just before all the Borough Councils started going bust and central government had to bail them out. I don't think Phil ever got paid for half the jobs he did for them. Anyway, we were fixing the lift system in the block where Marian lived. We both fancied her, Phil and me, but he was already married. She was hot stuff back then, bright red hair and gorgeous legs. She was coming up the stairs with her shopping bags and me being a gentleman I offered to carry them for her. She didn't have the kids with her at the time or I might not have asked her out. I wasn't much keen on children at the time, but you know, I kind of got used to the idea."

"So when did you first meet the children?"

"I can't remember exactly, it wasn't long after Marian and I started going out."

"How did they take having a new Dad?"

"They were both pretty spoilt, especially Rebecca. They were used to having their Mum to themselves. They had a few tantrums to begin with but they got used to having me around."

"What was Rebecca like growing up? Did she do well at school?"

"She was OK, not super smart but not dumb either. My Katie was the clever one. The one the teachers thought would go places. She was the pretty one too. I mean, Rebecca was a nice enough looking little girl but Katie had the blonde curls and the blue eyes. It was Katie everyone said would grow up to be a real looker, and she did I suppose, just she never got famous."

"Kate is a nurse isn't she?"

"That's right. She is working for the Red Cross. I had an email from her a while ago saying she was in Bolivia or Borneo or somewhere."

"Botswana?" I suggested.

"Yeah maybe, somewhere beginning with B anyway. Lord knows why she took that job, the pay must be lousy."

"Did Kate and Rebecca get on well together?"

"Not at all. Dan and Becky used to pick on poor Katie all the time."

"I expect they were jealous, seeing as she was the baby of the family and your own child."

"Maybe."

"Do you know much about their Father? Did Marian talk about him?"

"No, hardly ever. They split up long before he got himself killed."

"Didn't Daniel or Rebecca ever ask about their father?"

"I expect they did when they were older, but not while I was around."

I asked a great many questions hoping to form a picture of Rebecca as a child but Taylor's recollections were vague at best. He confirmed that she had attended dance and gymnastics classes which she enjoyed but he couldn't tell me what her favourite subject was at school, who her friends were, what games she played or even what she liked to eat.

"Was she happy?" I asked.

"Happy? I don't know. Life was tough back then, for everyone. I did my best for Marian and the kids. There wasn't much work but I did what I could to put food on the table. I don't think they ever really appreciated how much I did for them, how hard I had to work just to keep them from going hungry."

"Was that why you separated?"

"There were lots of reasons. Marian had problems. She always liked a drink but it got out of hand. Things got ugly. If I came home late she'd be pissed out of her head and screaming like a banshee, accusing me of all sorts of things. I just couldn't take it anymore."

"So you weren't having an affair?"

"No I wasn't."

"But when you left Marian you moved in with Jean Laker who you later married, is that not right?"

"Jean was a good friend. She was someone I could go to when things got too much at home, but it wasn't an affair. Jean and I only got together when it was clear Marian and I had no future."

"How did the kids cope with the separation?"

"They were OK."

"They must have still been quite young. Rebecca was what, about ten?"

"Yeah, she and Dan weren't too bothered. I think Katie found it the hardest. She spent quite a bit of time with Jean and me but I didn't see much of the other two."

"When did you last see Rebecca?"

"I'm not sure but I think it must have been at Marian's funeral. I don't think she spoke to me though. She was with her Aunt Ellen. Ellen never liked me and delights in bad mouthing me at any opportunity so I dare say she'd done her best to make Rebecca think it was all my fault. Of course once she was famous Rebecca didn't bother having anything to do with me. I don't think she ever once mentioned my name in all the times she was interviewed. She could have given me some credit; after all it was me that paid for those gym classes."

Friday 2nd March 2103

Arriving at Downing Street shortly after twelve Rebecca was informed that Bryant's meeting was overrunning. She was shown up to the small sitting room within the President's private suite. Number 10 had undergone a major refurbishment while in the hands of Bryant's predecessor. The President of Great Britain did not occupy a flat in the attic like the last two centuries of Prime Ministers but had many grand rooms for his personal use. Though the Cabinet and staterooms had remained unchanged many of the offices had been relocated to allow for the redevelopment. It was Harry Clarkson's wife who had insisted on the addition of a private garden enclosed by high walls. It was this garden which the small sitting room overlooked and Rebecca was at the window admiring it when Bryant finally arrived.

"Here at last my darling," he announced loudly as he strode into the room. "So sorry to keep you waiting."

He grasped her about the waist and kissed her, but only briefly as he was not alone. Following the President and dwarfed by Bryant's large frame was a young, sandy haired man wearing round glasses.

"This is James Hutchens who I mentioned yesterday," Bryant thrust the young man forward with one of his massive hands. "Now James, you haven't met the lovely Rebecca yet have you?"

"No I haven't had that pleasure," Hutchens replied, elaborately performing a ritual of taking Rebecca's hand and kissing it. "Delighted to meet you, simply enchanted my dear lady."

Both his gestures and eccentric mode of speech convinced Rebecca that Bryant was correct and that this was the writer of her mysterious letter, but in person there was something rather awkward and fake about his gallantry quite unlike the unforced eloquence of the letter.

"I was telling James about your anonymous fan mail," said Bryant.

"Yes, it sounds most intriguing," replied Hutchens, "I would very much like to see this letter."

Rebecca produced the letter from her handbag and gave it to him without comment.

"A fine hand and well worded," Hutchens remarked.

"And who do you suppose would write like that?" Bryant prompted.

"I cannot say. I know of no present day, real life masked men though there are numerous examples in literature: highwaymen, The Man in the Iron Mask, The Phantom of the Opera, Batman."

"Batman?" Rebecca queried.

"A fictitious character popular early last century, originally from a series of comic books, later developed for television and cinema. He was a superhero, one of many similar characters who assumed a disguise in order to fight crime."

"Why did they wear disguises if they were the goodies?" asked Rebecca feeling slightly bewildered.

"Essentially they were vigilantes, which is why they were censored and abolished."

"I see, but that doesn't help us to deduce who might have written this letter," said Rebecca.

"No I'm afraid I cannot shed any light on the author's identity," replied Hutchens.

"Come on, James! There's no need to be shy," coaxed Bryant. "You can own up, I won't be cross with you."

"You think it was me!"

"Who else would write by hand when there are so many easier ways of communicating?"

"Alas my writing is not as elegant; see, this is my poor hand."

Hutchens produced his notebook and displayed the illegible scrawl.

"Good Lord!" exclaimed Bryant. "Can you actually make any sense of that mess?"

"I usually manage. It does have the advantage over type in that it is utterly indecipherable to anyone other than myself."

"You're an odd chap, James. Thanks for coming up anyway."

"Not at all, it was most interesting and a great pleasure to meet Miss Clayton. I am only sorry I could not be of more assistance."

"I will see you on Monday. Have a good weekend."

"Thank you sir, and good day to you both."

Hutchens departed leaving Bryant shaking his head in baffled amusement.

As he sank into one of the leather armchairs he remarked, "I still think it was him though. I bet he can write neatly when he wants to."

"But why make such a secret of it?" asked Rebecca.

"Probably just for his own amusement."

"Perhaps. Anyway, I'm hungry, are we going out for lunch?"

"No, I thought we would eat here today, have some privacy for a change. I've ordered something special."

"Oh?"

"Sirloin steak with all the trimmings."

"Real beef steak?"

"Of course, you know I never touch the fake stuff unless it's absolutely necessary. In fact we were talking about cultured foods in the meeting this morning."

"Why was that?"

"It would seem there is some stuff about Mega Meals in the underground press. It's nothing new. The report they are quoting from was written four years ago so God knows how they managed to get hold of it now."

"What's in the report?"

"Only the bleeding obvious! Some clever dick scientist saying Mega Meals' foods are not as healthy as they claim to be and contain additives which can be harmful in large quantities. Well most things are harmful in large quantities and how nutritious can something made from fungus and algae grown in a vat actually be? But as usual the underground press is making a fuss about conspiracies and corruption."

"We ate loads of Mega Burgers when I was a kid. There's nothing too toxic in them is there?"

"Of course not! You're healthy enough aren't you? Perhaps you should do some commercials for Mega Meals. I'm meeting the Chief Executive next week; I could suggest it to him then."

"No thanks. Commercials aren't really my thing."

The kitchen staff had brought the lunch and they adjourned next door to what was called the family dining room. There were two other dining rooms among the staterooms which Bryant used when entertaining but this small room was more comfortable and convenient. Bryant sampled the wine and declaring it acceptable, dismissed the attendants. The steaks were thick and juicy, surrounded by piles of chips, onion rings and salad. Rebecca tucked in with relish. One of the benefits of spending so many hours training and performing was that she did not put on weight.

"This is delicious," she said. "Even better than Mega Burgers."

"I don't know how anyone can eat those things!"

"Your trouble John is your taste buds have been spoilt. You are too used to luxury. If you have never had the real thing the fake stuff doesn't seem too bad. If you have never had real beef, a Mega Burger tastes OK."

"Quite true my dear. You see there are many things that people are better off not knowing. There would be no point in everyone knowing how good this steak is when not everyone can have it. Just like most people will be happier not knowing what additives go into Mega Meals so they can carry on eating them without worrying."

"What are you going to do about this report then?"

"Sue Marsden is holding a press conference this afternoon along with a few of our scientific advisors. They'll just say that the report is a complete load of bollocks which is why it was suppressed four years ago and what was reported in the unlicensed media was just scaremongering and anti-democracy propaganda. I expect the whole thing will be forgotten by Monday."

Bryant poured himself another glass of wine but Rebecca declined as she was performing that evening.

"Are you going to have a busy weekend?" she asked.

"Busy but dull as shit. Caroline has got a load of her do-gooder charity friends coming to Chequers later. Tomorrow I'm going to some sports club for disabled kids, then on Sunday some magazine or other is coming to see what a lovely family we are. You know the score, photos of me playing football with the boys and smooching with Carol in the garden."

"Oh God, how nauseating!"

"I know, but part of the job. Caroline is threatening to come up to town next week. I will try to dissuade her but if I can't I don't know when I'll next have a chance to see you."

"We'd better make the most of this afternoon then. When are you leaving?"

"Not until after four. We have a bit of time yet. There's your favourite chocolate cheesecake for dessert."

After dessert and coffee they retired to the President's oak panelled bed chamber where they made love until Bryant's car was waiting. Then they went their separate ways, Rebecca to the theatre and the President to Buckinghamshire where his family awaited.

ELLEN CLAYTON
Simon Chandra

Ellen Clayton was Marian Clayton's elder sister. She has never married or had children of her own. She was a teacher at Stockwell Park School. After Marian's death in 2095 she became Rebecca Clayton's legal guardian. Ms Clayton now lives in Edinburgh and I met her at a small café on Prince's Street. It was a quaint little place with floral tablecloths, tea served in a proper pot with matching cups and saucers and a dinky milk jug. The walls were decorated with views of the city dating back to the earliest days of photography. Just stepping inside was like being transported two hundred years back in time. We talked over Earl Grey tea and sponge cake. I began by asking Ms Clayton how long she had lived in Edinburgh.

"It must be seventeen years now," she replied. "It doesn't seem that long to me but it was summer '98 that I moved up here."

"What made you leave London?"

"I would have thought that was obvious, after so many unpleasant things had happened there."

This rather stern rebuke made me feel like an errant pupil who had not done his homework. Had I been asked to guess Ellen Clayton's profession solely from her appearance I would have said teacher, if not headmistress. It is something about the way she raises her eyebrows enquiringly and studies you over the top of her glasses that gives it away. She is a slim woman of average height with grey hair cut in a neat bob. The day I met her she was smartly dressed in a navy blue trouser suit and sensible shoes.

"Did you have much contact with Rebecca after you left London?"

"No, we had a bit of a falling out. She was a bright girl and I had always hoped she would go to college and get a decent job. When she announced that she was leaving school to join that travelling show you can understand how upset I was. I mean who heard of anyone running away to join the circus in the twenty-first century? It just seemed crazy at the time."

"It must have been quite a shock to see how famous she became."

"Quite a shock indeed! She was such a quiet little girl, not the attention seeking sort. Yes, she always loved her gymnastics but she wasn't one of those little prima donnas who always want the lead role in the school play. Her sister Katie was the poser. She was the one who would dress up in her mother's clothes and make-up and dance around in front of the mirror."

"From what Graham Taylor said, I gather there was some jealousy between Katie and the older two."

"Some jealousy! Katie was spoilt rotten. She was Daddy's little princess but Graham had no time at all for Becky and Dan. Marian never stood up to him. If she had taken my advice she would have kicked him out long before he started carrying on with that Laker woman."

"Taylor told me that he and Miss Laker were not having an affair."

"Well he was always a liar so there's no reason to expect him to start telling the truth now. Jean Laker wasn't the first. There were plenty of others before her. The fact is Graham Taylor was a terrible husband and a lousy father. He may have doted on Katie when she was small and cute but as soon as Jean was pregnant he completely lost interest in her. He showed the same lack of commitment in all his relationships. His marriage to Jean didn't last very long either. They were already separated by the time Marian died."

"What about Anthony Jones? What was he like?"

Ms Clayton gave a snort of derision, "No better, that is for certain. He was a real Jekyll and Hyde character. I don't know if that was because of the drugs or if he was ill. The first few times I met him he seemed nice enough; good tempered, funny and generally pleasant. Later on he seemed depressed and didn't speak much, then at other times he would be throwing temper tantrums like a two year old. He and Marian were regularly splitting up and getting back together until he went to prison."

"Did you ever talk to Rebecca about her father?"

"Of course, I told her pretty much what I just told you. I know they say you shouldn't speak ill of the dead but I didn't see any point in lying to her."

"It must have been difficult for her to lose so many of her family at such a young age."

"Very difficult. She was utterly devastated when Daniel died, we all were. She adored her brother. It was such a senseless waste."

Daniel Clayton was killed in 2093. He was taking part in a demonstration outside parliament against the government's contraception and abortion policies. He was shot dead by police when the protest turned violent.

"Daniel was what, sixteen when he died?"

"Only fifteen. I had no idea he was involved with that Pro-Life movement. He wasn't a Catholic or anything. They were cunning, manipulative people running those groups. They deliberately recruited the young and impressionable to do their dirty work for them."

"So you blame the Pro-Life campaigners for his death and not the police or the government?"

"I do. It was the protestors who started the violence."

"You don't feel that it was the President's hard line policies which provoked the violence?"

"Certainly not. President Clarkson was tough because he had to be. This country, in fact most of the world was in a hopeless mess. The Tories and Labour had been dithering for years but weren't prepared to take action; Clarkson was. If it hadn't been for Clarkson and the Phoenix Party, Britain would still be in the same chaotic state as mainland Europe."

I did not want to get side-tracked into a political discussion so I changed the subject.

"Taylor suggested that Marian had a drink problem. Is that true?"

"She did drink, but I think that was a symptom and not the heart of the problem. She wasn't well, poor woman. She needed help and support but whenever she went to the doctor they just gave her more pills. Towards the end she was taking dozens of different drugs but none of them were doing any good. She did try to sort herself out, she really did. After Graham walked out she went through a really bad patch. She went into hospital and the children had to live with me. But she got better. She stopped drinking, got a job and started taking proper care of the kids, but then Daniel died. After that she just gave up.

"She spent weeks alone in her flat, hardly ever going out and rarely eating, just drinking. She wouldn't be helped. I went there nearly every day but she wouldn't let me in or even answer my calls. By the time social services got involved it was too late and she died a few months later."

"Do you think that more should have been done to help her?"

"Perhaps, but there is no point trying to find someone else to blame. Marian knew she was drinking herself to death, she just didn't care."

"How did Rebecca react to the loss of her mother?"

"She took it very calmly. I think she knew it was inevitable and had prepared herself for it. Ever since she lost her brother she had become very quiet and withdrawn. Whereas before she would happily chat to me about school, her gym classes and things, she suddenly stopped talking. I suppose that is why I had no idea what was going on until she suddenly announced she was leaving home."

"So it wasn't that she walked out after an argument or anything?"

"No not at all. It was completely out of the blue. We were sitting having dinner and she just said, 'I'm not going back to school next term; I've decided to go away for a while. I've been offered a job with a travelling theatre company and I'm going to take it.' I was horrified. I tried to talk her out of it but next thing I knew she was packing her bags. In the end I let her go because I thought she would be home as soon as she came to her senses. But she never came back. She called a few times and we argued. The last time we spoke I said a few things I shouldn't have. I was angry, I told her not to come home because she wouldn't be welcome. I regret that but it is too late to do anything now. I don't believe in nursing regrets. You have to get on with your life."

"So that was the last you saw or heard of her?"

"Until she started appearing on TV and all over the papers, yes."

"But she never got back in touch?"

"I don't think she ever gave me a moment's thought once she was rich and famous. She certainly didn't talk about her family much."

"No, she seems to have quite deliberately cut herself off from her childhood."

"I suppose I can't blame her for that after all she went through."

I thanked Ms Clayton for her time and headed for the station wondering if this project of mine was destined to fail before it had even begun. Although Ellen Clayton had provided some valuable information about Rosa's early life she seems as much a mystery as ever. At what point did she decide to shun the prospect of college and a stable career for a life in the perilously fickle world of show business? Was she seeking fame or just an escape from her unhappy childhood? Did she share her Aunt's political views or did she blame Clarkson's government for her brother's death?

For those readers who like me are too young to remember the early years of Clarkson's regime I have included a link to an article outlining his achievements. Although this is not what you would call a balanced and unbiased piece of writing it does perhaps explain why even now many people still have a great respect for the first President of the Great British Republic.

The introduction to "Phoenix Rising", the memoirs of Charles Adams, senior political advisor to Clarkson during his first five years in office.

The sea was rising, oil wells were running dry, wars were raging, governments were falling and contagious disease was killing both livestock and humans. It was hardly surprising that people were talking of the apocalypse. This was the situation in the latter half of the 21st century.

In Britain the population had been decimated by two major black flu pandemics and the National Health Service was stretched to breaking point by the resurgence of infections such as TB and the emergence of new ones like the mutated HIV strain. Food and fuel were scarce and the economy was in not so much a depression as a gaping crevasse. The threat from terrorists was constant but our military capability had been exhausted by decades of fighting over the few remaining fossil fuel reserves. Since the Buckingham Palace bombing the whole structure of government was in a state of confusion.

Both Labour and the Conservatives had completely failed to tackle any of these problems. After years of impotent, cowardly government the people were impatient for change. To begin with only a small number of politicians, mostly Tory back-benchers, were bold enough to speak out and demand drastic action. It was Henry Clarkson, then a junior minister in the Department of Security and Justice, who united these few. Together they formed the Phoenix Party.

The feature which characterised the Phoenix Party's successful 2085 election campaign was honesty. They made no empty promises of how they would solve the country's problems overnight, instead warning there would be hard times and sacrifices ahead. Clarkson knew that not all his policies would be popular but had the courage to stand by what he believed was in the best interest of the country.

As soon as they were in office Clarkson's government took radical steps which halted Britain's decline and began the recovery. They withdrew all British troops from their so-called peace keeping duties abroad leaving the USA, Russia and China to compete for whatever meagre amounts of fossil fuels could still be exploited. The armed forces could then be dedicated to internal security and countering terrorism. All ports and airports were closed to immigrants and many asylum seekers and foreign nationals were deported. This not only decreased the threat from international terrorism but also restricted the spread of disease and reduced pressure on social services.

The government then brought in a system of rationing food and energy thus ensuring fair distribution. Grants for new technologies and the scrapping of restrictive regulations meant domestic food and energy production were increased by many orders of magnitude. Much of the strain was removed from the health service by transferring non-essential services and non-urgent treatment to the private sector.

Previous governments had been pouring vast amounts of money into futile measures to hold back the rising sea. Clarkson abandoned these defences and allowed the land to flood, generously compensating those who lost their homes using money previously being spent on hand-outs for immigrants and asylum seekers.

In spite of all these achievements, Clarkson's government will probably be remembered mainly for the social and constitutional changes it enacted. After the death of the King and all immediate heirs, the monarchy had been left in limbo for over a decade with considerable doubt over who should succeed to the throne. No Prime Minister was prepared to dissolve such an ancient institution nor were they willing to find the money needed for its restoration. Clarkson not only abolished the monarchy but many of the other anachronistic institutions that went with it, such as the House of Lords.

Some of Clarkson's most controversial policies were those concerning marriage and families. Clarkson was forward-thinking and realised that the future welfare of Britain depended on the population remaining below the threshold level determined by domestic food production. He also recognised that many of the country's social problems related to family breakdown. It was for these reasons he took measures to limit the birth rate and reduce the number of single parents.

After just five years in office he had achieved what his opponents had insisted was impossible. He had rescued the economy, restored law and order, saved the NHS and laid the foundations for a prosperous future. While the rest of the world was gripped by famine, disease, economic collapse and war Britain had began its first steps on the road to recovery. As the previous superpowers were consumed by civil war, Britain assumed its present position of political and economic dominance.

Thursday 8th March 2103

Rebecca did not give much thought to her mysterious letter over the next few days as she was more concerned by what she had learned about Mega Meals. Shortly after her meeting with the President she had looked up the story on the Real News Network, the uncensored and therefore illegal current affairs website, and read the report Bryant had spoken about. The research suggested that regular consumption of Mega Meals products over a period of ten years increased the risk of getting certain cancers by up to 20 percent.

The government's scientific advisors all dismissed this claim but that was not very reassuring since Rebecca knew that several members of the Mega Meals board were Phoenix Party donors. She at least had the comfort of knowing she was not the only victim. Mega Meals completely dominated the cultured foods industry and had contracts to supply schools, hospitals, prisons, residential care homes and just about every other state run institution.

Rebecca had not discussed the issue any further with the President as she did not see him again for over a week. Caroline had not been talked out of her plan and came up to London on Monday. Rebecca found the separation no great hardship and felt not the slightest hint of jealousy or resentment towards her lover's wife.

On Wednesday evening she received the second letter. It was again left in her dressing-room accompanied by a beautiful, fragrant bouquet of spring flowers. The strange thing was that the front desk had no record of their arrival and Ami was certain they were not among the flowers she had brought up to the room. Whoever had left them must therefore work at the theatre and have access to the dressing-room. This would rule out the President's speech-writer, unless he had an accomplice among the security or cleaning staff.

She had read the letter several times and was still pondering it the following morning while she was sitting in the Courtyard Café of the Newman Grand complex waiting for a friend.

Dear Rosa,

Since I saw you last week I have been unable to get you out of my mind and so had to come again to watch you perform. This second occasion has affected me just as profoundly as the first and I am in awe, I am bewitched and enchanted by you. I leave these flowers for you as they were grown in the open air. Their beauty, like yours, is wholly natural, unlike the glasshouse roses. I hope you will appreciate them even if they are not as costly or as lavish as the bouquets from your other admirers.

I hope that you do not take offence at these declarations of my deepest admiration for you. I flatter myself that you may have some pleasure in reading them. It is the least I can do in gratitude for the ray of sunshine that seeing you casts into my dark world. I shall write again soon, but for now farewell.

Your devoted friend
The Man Behind the Mask

This was written in the same elegant script as the last but this time on a sheet of high quality, watermarked paper and had been enclosed in an envelope. She was reading it yet again when Monica Chandra arrived. She put the letter aside and greeted her friend.

"Hi Becky," said Monica, "I hope you haven't been waiting too long. I've been having one of those mornings where I just couldn't get out the office. Every time I was about to leave there was a call or someone wanted to ask me something."

"It's OK, I was just sampling one of these herbal teas which are supposed to be so beneficial for your complexion, or so I read!"

Monica Chandra was the editor of Amber Magazine and it was to one of their articles that Rebecca was alluding.

"Yes they are miraculous, positive elixirs of youth," Monica assured, "and of course it is a complete coincidence that we have just signed a lucrative advertising deal with the manufacturer. Still, at least they won't do you any harm."

"I'm glad to hear it. I think I've consumed quite enough carcinogens for one lifetime."

Monica lowered her voice and replied, "I know what you mean, but we'll talk about that later." Then loudly she asked, "Have you ordered anything to eat yet?"

"Not yet. I fancied the smoked trout linguine, what about you?"

"I'll have the chicken salad."

Monica was a tall, slim, attractive woman who although she was over forty could easily pass for thirty-five or younger. She was of mixed race with café au lait skin and ebony hair.

Once the waitress had taken their orders Monica asked, "What was that you were reading when I came in?"

"I was going to tell you about that. It's a genuine love-letter of the traditional handwritten variety, something once common and now almost obsolete. I though you could do an article on the subject."

"That's a great idea. It's a safe subject and if we include references to historical and literary examples it might even be quite interesting. Can I see this letter?"

"Certainly, it's the second I've had in a week, both from the same person."

Monica read the letter then asked, "Any ideas who they're from?"

"The prime suspect is one of John's speech-writers, a young chap called James Hutchens. The jury is still out though."

"The Man Behind the Mask," Monica mused. "I'm certain I've heard that before."

She looked thoughtful then leaning forward across the table whispered, "There is an underground poet who posts on the RNN forum who uses that name, I'm sure of it."

"A poet?"

"Look it up later. It is possible there's more than one person using that nom de plume but it would seem to fit wouldn't it?"

Rebecca wholeheartedly agreed. She began forming the idea that her mystery admirer could be a humble cleaner or night watchman at the theatre, who found an escape from his dull existence by writing poetry. She pictured a handsome young man all alone in the theatre late at night, lost in silent contemplation and scribbling verses dedicated to her loveliness. She much preferred this 'Man Behind the Mask' to the phoney, clownish Cambridge graduate.

The waitress brought their food and while they ate the conversation turned to Monica's family. Chandra was Monica's married name; her husband Rashid also worked in journalism. He was a researcher working for the current affairs department of the Independent Media Corporation, the company dominating the entire media industry in the UK. They had two children, Simon and Amira. Rebecca and Monica chatted for a while about the children's progress at school. Then they talked about Rebecca's work.

After the meal was over Monica casually remarked, "I loved your new costume by the way. I'd really like to have a closer look at it."

"If you aren't in a hurry to get back to the office you could come up with me now and I'll show it to you."

"That would be great."

Monica paid the bill and they strolled out into the courtyard which was surrounded by the theatre and hotel complex.

Once outside Rebecca asked, "So what did you really want to talk about?"

"We've heard rumours that Bryant is planning a Cabinet reshuffle."

"That is no secret. Even IMC News has been saying that."

"Do you know Philip Graysby?"

"Not personally. He's a junior minister isn't he?"

"That's right, in the Department of Food and Farming, but the word is he could be promoted soon. RNN is interested because he was the source of the Mega Meals leak."

They paused in their conversation while they entered the theatre and passed the security desk then continued as they climbed the stairs.

"Graysby has had a number of meetings with the directors of Nature Plus," Monica explained. "It is only a small company by comparison but it is probably the only rival Mega Meals has. It may be that their products aren't any safer than Mega Meals but if the cultured foods industry is open to competition standards will have to improve."

By this time they had reached Rebecca's dressing-room. She scanned her thumbprint and punched in the access code. Monica took the chair by the window while Rebecca sat by the dressing-table. They knew it was safe to talk there as Rebecca regularly checked the room for listening devices.

Soon after she had commenced her relationship with the President his security staff had given her an anti-surveillance scanner to ensure she was not snooped upon by journalists of political rivals. She had also invested in equipment of her own to protect her privacy from Bryant's staff. Within the first month of their affair she had removed four bugging devices from her dressing-room and three from her apartment, but recently they had turned up less frequently. The spies were either losing interest or getting more cunning.

"What we would like to know is," continued Monica, "does Graysby's desire for a competitive marketplace only extend to the cultured foods industry or is it a wider philosophy? If it is, and if Graysby has supporters, we could in future see him challenging Bryant."

"I'll keep my ears open and perhaps ask John a few discreet questions next time I see him."

"Don't get me wrong, I'm under no illusions that this Graysby is a champion of liberty and human rights or anything, but he may just possibly take the country a few steps in the right direction."

"Provided that Bryant doesn't suspect him of being a potential rival."

Monica shrugged and replied, "That will depend on how smart Phil Graysby is."

"We shall see."

"Anyway, I suppose I'd better take a look at this costume of yours while I'm here. It will give me something to talk about when I get back to the office."

Rebecca retrieved it from the wardrobe saying, "I don't know how you manage juggling two jobs like this. It must be exhausting."

"It isn't that hard," Monica responded while admiring the shimmering fabric. "Most of the stuff I do for Amber I could make up in my sleep. For example, when I get back to the office I'll spend about ten minutes writing about silver being this season's colour but I'll pretend to take at least three hours over it when really I'm writing an article for RNN."

"Does no one ever suspect?"

"What, the vapid air heads I work with! No, I've taken great care to employ the sort of people who actually seriously care what this season's colour is. What about you? What are you up to this afternoon?"

"I'm meeting Martin. We are working on some ideas for a routine together."

"Oh yes, Marvellous Marti. He's incredible isn't he? I was on the edge of my seat watching him last week."

"He is a great performer. Amber should do a feature on him some time."

"No doubt we will. I had better get back to the office. I'll see myself out." They hugged and Monica said, "Take care of yourself Becky."

By the time Rebecca had changed into her training kit it was almost three. She went down to the large rehearsal room on the ground floor, expecting to find Martin already there as he was usually punctual. She was surprised to find the room empty, but thinking he would arrive soon she spread the mats out and began her warm up. After stretching and loosening up she commenced her repertoire of floor exercises. First a simple handstand into a forwards roll, then a few cartwheels, then putting the moves together in combinations. She finished with a series of backflips followed by a somersault in the air and landing neatly on her feet.

While pausing to catch her breath she glanced at the clock and saw it was half past three. She decided to give Martin a call to find out where he had got to. As she had left her mobile in the dressing-room she headed back towards the stairs and almost collided with him in the corridor.

"Becky, I'm really late, I know. Shit! I'm so sorry."

He looked flustered, his face red and his hair dishevelled.

"Don't worry about it," Rebecca replied. "Are you OK?"

"Yes I'm fine. Come on let's get on with it."

As he pushed his hair away from his face she saw his eyes were bloodshot. She took hold of his arm.

"Marti, what is it? What's wrong?"

He let out a long sigh and answered, "I've been dumped."

"Oh Marti, I'm so sorry. Forget training for the moment. We'll go upstairs and I'll put the kettle on, then you can tell me about it."

"Yeah OK, thanks Becky."

They ascended to Rebecca's dressing-room and Martin slumped in the armchair while she made camomile tea.

"So what happened?" she asked.

"Jason is getting married."

"What? To who?"

"Some girl he works with. He's been worried about his job, about what his colleagues are saying, afraid that rumours concerning his sexuality will ruin his chances of promotion."

"So he's sacrificing you for his career."

Rebecca found herself thinking that if Martin were hers she would not sacrifice him for anything, but rapidly dismissed these thoughts as being utterly ridiculous.

"I can't blame him for wanting a decent job, a nice house and a normal life."

"Does this girl know she is embarking on a sham marriage?"

"I don't think so. I thought about finding some way of warning her, but it is too risky and I couldn't do that to Jason."

"He doesn't actually think that this is going to make him happy does he? Living a life of deceit like that could only make him miserable."

"We are all living a lie. I'm sick of it. I hate having to hide who I really am. Some nights I long to go out on stage and yell out to the whole theatre, 'I'm Martin Ashdown, I'm gay and I'm not ashamed!'"

"You wouldn't do it though, would you?"

"Why not? What have I got to lose?"

"Your freedom Martin. You do it and they'll either send you to prison or worse, one of those rehab or re-ed centres or whatever it is they call them now. I read they are experimenting with aversion therapy again. They wire up electrodes to your genitals and show you gay porn while they zap you."

"You shouldn't believe everything you read Rebecca."

"Maybe not, but they will lock you up and you've done nothing wrong."

"That isn't what your boyfriend thinks."

Rebecca greatly disliked that term being applied to Bryant. Not only did it seem ridiculous to call someone over fifty a boy but the implication of possession was inappropriate for her relationship with the President.

"If you are referring to John Bryant I don't think he actually gives a damn about homosexuality. It was Clarkson who brought in the Second Anti-Homosexual Bill and that was just the usual political bullshit. It is the oldest trick in the book, when times are hard you find someone to blame, and once he'd deported all the foreign nationals and arrested loads of Muslims, gays were next on the list."

"Yes I know, just like it was the Jews, the gypsies and us in Nazi Germany. I suppose we should be thankful they haven't brought back the gas chamber."

"Listen Marti, I am sorry things haven't worked out with Jason, but don't give up. You are still young. There will be other lovers, and who knows, maybe things will change. Maybe you will be free to be yourself and not have to pretend anymore."

"What about you Rebecca? When will you be free? When will you not have to pretend anymore?"

"What do you mean?"

"You know what I mean. I mean you and Bryant. You don't love him. Why do you sleep with him?"

"Because he is rich and powerful. Because his influence has helped me to become a star. Because I know that the kind of fame I have achieved is of a very fickle nature and as soon as someone new captures the public's imagination they will forget all about me. I am wealthy now and I have some money put by, but not enough to keep me for very long in the manner that I have become accustomed to.

"John has already opened doors for me and I'm hoping he will open a few more before he dumps me for someone younger and more in fashion. You're from the same sort of background as me Martin. You know what it's like to be poor and miserable without hope of anything better. I have taken every opportunity I could to escape that existence and I won't go back to it. If that makes me a whore then I don't care!"

"You're no whore, Becky," Martin replied, with one of his crooked half smiles which made her go weak at the knees.

She reached out and took hold of his hand, giving it a squeeze.

"We've still got some time if you want to do some work on our routine," she suggested. "It might help take your mind off things."

"Yeah let's make a start. You're a good friend Becky, thanks."

Island Nation Magazine
Saturday 1st June August 2115

CIRCUS BRITANNIA
Simon Chandra

By the 2060s the entertainment and leisure industries were virtually non-existent. The economic collapse, fear of disease and the threat of terrorism had closed down theatres, bars, nightclubs, sports venues, hotels and restaurants. Television and radio continued but through lack of advertising revenue were only pale shadows of what they had once been. The only new programmes being made were the news broadcasts; the rest of the airtime was devoted to nostalgia and repeats. Popular culture as we know it did not exist. No new books were published, no new music recorded, no new dramas performed either on stage or on TV. Even comedy could not survive without an audience.

It was not until the 2090s that the economy had recovered sufficiently to create a market for entertainment. Samuel Newman was one of a few entrepreneurs who had anticipated this and bought a small theatre. Early productions at the Newman Theatre and others like it were strictly light entertainment. Audiences wanted glamour and escapism and government censorship restricted the material that could be performed. Variety shows were popular. Out of this came the revival of the circus.

The first new circus star to achieve national fame was Dimetri Gregorovich. He was all over the newly revived media long before anyone had even heard of Rosa. He was an acrobat and trapeze artist renowned for the dangerous nature of his routines. Now he owns a circus school in Hammersmith and teaches aspiring performers, which is where I met him.

Gregorovich is an impressive looking man, square jawed, tall and muscular. Although in his fifties he is still able to perform remarkable acrobatics. At present the school has just twenty pupils all aged between fifteen and nineteen. Gregorovich tells me he has very strict admission criteria.

"I expect you get loads of young girls wanting to be the next Rosa," I say.

He gives a snort of derision and replies, "Oh yes plenty of them, but to be a really great circus performer you must have it in your blood. There are very few who can ever be truly great. Rosa could have been great but she chose not to be."

"What do you mean? Surely she was the greatest performer of the age."

"The most famous perhaps, but not the most accomplished. I could have taught her so much more if she had let me, but she just wanted wealth and fame. She didn't care about the art."

Although he has lived in Britain since his early teens Gregorovich still retains his accent. His mother was English but worked in the Ukraine where she married and where Dimetri was born. To escape the war with Russia they came to the UK and were allowed to remain on account of his mother's status as a British national.

"You have said in previous interviews that it was you who first recognised and nurtured Rebecca's talent."

"That's right. When I first saw her she was performing in a cabaret show called Nightingales. It was mostly singers and dancers. Rebecca was one of the girls in the chorus line who would dance around with ribbons and maybe do a few cartwheels. I went to see the show with Nikolai Luchenko; we were talent spotting. I don't think Luchenko would have given her a second glance if I hadn't pointed her out to him. I persuaded him to offer her a job with Nick's Circus as we were called then. She accepted and I dedicated myself to teaching her. I even gave her her name. I said she would never be a star with a name like Becky Clayton and I thought of Rosa. It suited her."

"I understand you were also lovers."

"Yes I taught her that too. She was a virgin when I met her. She knew nothing of men except what she learned from me."

"There was rather an age difference wasn't there. How old was she?"

"She was seventeen and yes I was older, but it was always older men with her. She was only ever interested in men who could do something for her."

"Are you saying she used you?"

"She used everyone. She was a devious, scheming little bitch. She pretended to love me but betrayed me at the first opportunity."

"She betrayed you? How?"

"I had an accident during training. I was working on a new routine and missed a catch. It was a bad fall. I broke my wrist and my collar bone. It meant I couldn't perform for months. She must have been working on Luchenko in my absence because when I was ready to come back he told me that Rosa would be at the top of the bill and not me. She had developed her own routine without consulting me. It was her picture that would be in all the publicity and her new solo performance would be the last act before the finale.

"You can imagine how hurt and angry I was that the two of them had been plotting behind my back. Of course they denied there was anything between them and Luchenko came up with plenty of excuses. They must have thought I was a fool. I couldn't stay. I quit and left them to it. He got what he deserved. She dumped him for Newman soon enough, and then she ditched Newman for Bryant. That was the kind of slut she was."

"You can't deny though that it was after Rebecca became the star that the circus became really popular."

"I don't deny it, but that was due to Newman's investment not her. It was Newman who suggested the name change to Circus Britannia. He had the money and the connections to the media which gave it such a high profile."

"So you feel the circus would have been just as successful without her?"

"If Newman had invested in it yes, but perhaps if he hadn't been fucking Rebecca he would have invested his money elsewhere. Luchenko's wasn't the only circus after all."

"No indeed. You joined another after leaving Luchenko."

"That's right, Billy Bravo's."

"Yet Bravo's never achieved the fame of Circus Britannia."

"It would have done had we found an investor but no one was prepared to rival Newman. He had too many powerful friends."

"Are you envious of Rosa's fame?"

"Certainly not! What good did her fame do her in the end? She would still be alive today had she not lusted after fame."

Monday 12th March 2103

The following Monday morning Caroline Bryant returned to the family home in Hertfordshire and to celebrate his liberation Bryant invited Rebecca to dine with him at Downing Street that evening. The theatre was closed both Sunday and Monday so Rebecca was well rested and they had the whole night to themselves. They were enjoying a pre-dinner drink in the small sitting room and Bryant was in full flow, complaining of all the various annoyances his wife had caused him in the past week.

"It doesn't matter how many times I tell her I have more important things to deal with," he moaned. "Once she gets an idea into her head she just won't let it drop. I mean, she is an intelligent woman and comes up with plenty of good suggestions but she just doesn't seem to understand that I can't always act on them immediately. At the moment she wants me to be promoting the arts as it will make me look more refined and intellectual. Nothing wrong with that, but I have more pressing concerns. I haven't time for paintings and Shakespeare when I have a Cabinet to sort out."

"So the rumours of a reshuffle are true?"

"Yes indeed, certain people aren't performing as well as they should. It's time to prune out some of the dead wood and inject some new blood."

Without a speech-writer to help him Bryant had an unfortunate habit of mixing metaphors. Rebecca was used to it by now and rarely smirked.

"So who's out?"

"Sue Marsden for a start. I spoke to her this morning and she will be announcing her resignation tomorrow. We discovered that the Mega Meals report leak came from the Department of Food itself. Of course no one is suggesting old Sue is responsible but if that sort of thing is going on under her nose then she is losing her grip."

"Who will be replacing her?"

"One of her junior ministers, a chap called Philip Graysby."

"Graves-by! Sounds morbid."

"No Graysby, like the colour."

"Oh well that just sounds dull."

"He's certainly not dull. He's a smart young man. Could go far. He has a background in economics so could be Chancellor one day."

"Sorry darling but he really is sounding more boring by the minute," replied Rebecca, feigning disinterest. "You know I start yawning as soon as anyone mentions economics."

"That may be so but it's our economic policies that allow you to earn such a good living."

"So what sort of economist is this Gray-Bee? Is he the 'wealth for all' or the 'wealth for some' type?"

"I thought you said you weren't interested."

"I'm just making conversation."

"There are plenty of others things we can talk about. For a start you can tell me what you have been up to all week."

One of Bryant's domestic staff came to inform them that dinner was served. Once seated at the dining table they talked about the circus and the various interviews and publicity work Rebecca had done since they last met. She could not bring up the subject of Graysby again without arousing suspicion. Besides, it was unlikely she would learn much more from Bryant. She would have to hope for a meeting with the minister himself.

*

Rebecca stayed the night. The following morning was gloriously bright and although not usually an early riser she was awake not long after seven. The birds were singing lustily and it seemed a shame to waste such a lovely spring day lying in bed. Rebecca put on her robe, made herself a cup of tea and stepped out onto the terrace. She was surrounded by blossoming shrubs, which scented the air. Below, the lawn stretched out in pristine greenness bordered by snowdrops, daffodils, tulips, and crocuses. As she sipped her tea Rebecca listened to the trilling blackbirds and caught the sound of the old gardener whistling in harmony.

The President was now up as well and came out to join her.

"What are you doing out here?" he demanded. "It's bloody freezing!"

"I thought it was pleasantly mild. I was enjoying the fresh air and sunshine. You are very fortunate to have such a beautiful garden."

"Caroline likes it, but I can't say as I'm that bothered about plants myself. She is always going on about fancy names, you know, something japonica or Acer whatsname, but it is all gibberish to me."

Rebecca smiled as though amused but she was not really listening. She was watching the gardener pulling up weeds and the courageous, fat little robin which kept him company. The plucky bird perched on a branch of the apple tree, darting down into the border whenever his human friend unearthed a tasty morsel. The gardener was talking to the robin, until he turned and saw that she was watching and went on with his work in silence.

She felt as though she had intruded upon them so turned to face Bryant but continued watching the gardener out of the corner of her eye. Bryant was still prattling about Caroline's love of botany, oblivious to her lack of interest. The gardener stood up and stretched before moving along the border to continue weeding. His shabby jacket had a hole in one elbow and he wore a peculiar, old-fashioned cap pulled down over his brow where it met the top of his glasses. Rebecca suspected there was something wrong with his eyes as he always wore those same dark glasses even on cloudy days.

"Has young Hutchens written you any more love letters?" Bryant asked, beginning to realise that Rebecca had heard enough about his wife.

"There was another letter," she replied, "but I'm not certain they are from him."

"Oh? Is there another suspect?"

"Not yet, but I know that the writer is leaving the letters actually in my dressing-room and not at reception and there is no way Hutchens could do that."

"Sure he could. He just has to pay someone in theatre security to deliver them for him. I reckon I'm not working him hard enough if he has time for these sorts of shenanigans. Someone ought to remind him that trying to seduce your boss's girl isn't too good for your career prospects."

"I would hardly call a couple of letters an attempt at seduction."

"That depends on the letters. I'm thinking of passing a law making it an act of high treason to flirt with the President's mistress."

"That might not be consistent with Phoenix Party policy on marital values."

"Hey I'm President! Marital values are for other people."

"Hypocrite!"

"Guilty as charged, my dear. You must know by now that I am honest enough to acknowledge my own dishonesty. Oh shit is that the time! I'd better go and get ready. There's a meeting starting in half an hour. I'll call you later and perhaps we can arrange to meet for lunch tomorrow."

He kissed her and went back inside, leaving her to enjoy the sunshine. The gardener had worked his way around the lawn and was now at the bottom of the steps up to the terrace. It seemed rude to continue to ignore him now that he was so close.

"Good morning," she called down to him, "it's a beautiful day."

The gardener slowly raised his head and looked up at her and though it was hard to judge his expression behind the glasses, he seemed surprised or perhaps confused. Rebecca wondered if he was hard of hearing or mentally retarded, but then he touched his cap respectfully and replied.

"Good morning Miss Rosa, it is indeed a lovely day to be outdoors."

Not wishing to disturb him further she went back inside where the staff had laid out breakfast for her. While sitting by the window eating her croissant she saw the gardener cross back over the lawn and through the archway leading to the pond. As she watched him go it occurred to her that the man was not quite as elderly as she had first thought. Though his face was lined the coarse, uneven stubble on his chin was still black and he walked without stooping.

She sipped a glass of fresh orange juice and contemplated having a garden of her own one day. When she was a child she had helped her Aunt Ellen to grow vegetables in her tiny backyard. Maybe in the future she would do the same with her own children, but it did not seem very likely, the way her life was at present.

*

On returning home the first thing Rebecca did was email a brief cryptic message to Monica Chandra.

It said, "I have been examining John's wardrobe and Gray is definitely in this season and could be around for a while. I'm not sure about cut or style yet but I will let you know."

She read some of her regular fan mail and looked through the various requests for interviews and offers of TV appearances forwarded by her agent. She sent a reply saying which interested her then made herself some lunch. After she had eaten she went onto the RNN forum to see if there were any more poems posted by the Man Behind the Mask. After her conversation with Monica she had studied his work in detail and was convinced it was the same man who had written to her.

Later that afternoon the circus company had their usual beginning of the week meeting. As she had arrived at the theatre a little early Rebecca went up to her dressing-room first, hoping there would be another letter for her. She was not disappointed. The envelope lay on the table beside a vase containing sprigs of cherry blossom. Excitedly she tore it open.

My Dearest Miss Rosa,

Yet again I feel this compulsion to write to you. I must express what is in my heart or else it might explode. You no doubt think I exaggerate and perhaps I do, but indulging my passion for you in this way brings joy to what is otherwise a frankly dull life. I fear my adoration for you is becoming an obsession but I cannot believe there is anything unhealthy on unnatural in that. Thinking of you gives me such pleasure; how can it be wrong?

I saw you leaving the theatre on Saturday night in the company of young Martin. You were talking and laughing as you got into a taxi together and I wondered if perhaps you and he were lovers. You looked far happier with him than I have ever seen you with the President. Though I confess I felt envious of him I hoped it was so. It is right that you should love and be loved in return.

Forever yours
The Man Behind the Mask

She read the letter twice over, smiling with delight. She was not surprised that the mysterious writer had seen her with Martin. They had indeed left the theatre together on Saturday night and had been seen by several other members of the cast and crew who were leaving at the same time. They also would have been observed by numerous fans hanging around the backstage door seeking autographs and by the security guards preventing them from harassing the performers.

Martin had in fact gone back to her apartment and they had spent much of the next two days together as Rebecca had not wanted him to be alone brooding over the break up. The Man Behind the Mask was probably not the only one who had got the wrong impression of their relationship but under the circumstances it was not a bad thing. Yet for reasons she could not justify, not even to herself, Rebecca wanted her mysterious admirer to know he was wrong. She decided to reply to his letter.

Since the Man could access her dressing-room all she had to do was leave a letter for him. She searched though the top drawer until she found a pen, discarding several which failed to write. She had no paper so used the reverse of his sheet.

"Dear Sir," she wrote.

This sounded ridiculously formal but better than "Dear Man Behind the Mask", which was long-winded and awkward.

I wish to tell you how much I have enjoyed reading your letters. You are very generous in your praise and I am flattered. In your last you mentioned Martin Ashdown. I would like to assure you that he is not my lover, just a close friend.

I am curious about you. I want to know who you are. Can I meet you?

Yours Sincerely
Rosa

When she had finished she realised that her writing was sloping diagonally down the page and the size of her characters varied immensely. Each line began with large bold script which rapidly shrank and became squashed towards the right hand edge of the page. She also vaguely remembered something from school about the correct use of "Yours sincerely" and felt a nagging suspicion that this was not it. Since she had no paper she could not begin again and the meeting would be starting soon. She slipped the letter back into the envelope, crossed out her own name and wrote, "The Man Behind the Mask." Then she left it where she had found it and went downstairs.

ROSA'S LOVERS
Simon Chandra

After my interview with Dimetri Gregorovich was published I was surprised to receive the following email from Nikolai Luchenko...

Dear Mr Chandra,

I have been reading your column with interest but I wish to set the record straight on a number of points. Firstly, there was never anything either romantic or sexual between Rebecca Clayton and me. Secondly, it was never Rebecca's wish to replace Dimetri as the star of the circus. She only agreed to become the headline act after he was injured, even though I had suggested it several times previously. Dimetri's popularity had been waning for some time and the whole company knew she was the better performer, but she was concerned for his feelings. She would not take on his role until circumstances forced her to do so. Once Dimetri was able to perform again we practically begged him to remain with us but he refused.

I believe much of what Dimetri said to be based on jealousy, and though I am no longer greatly concerned about my own reputation I feel I ought to speak for Rebecca since she cannot defend herself. I hope you will bear this in mind as you continue your quest for truth.

Yours sincerely
Nikolai Luchenko

I say that I was surprised because Luchenko has been rather reclusive in recent years. In particular he has endeavoured to avoid media attention, which is only natural considering some of the material which has been written about him. Not only has Dimetri Gregorovich given a number of similar interviews to the one I published last week, but in Felicity Faversham's book, "Rosa – Her Tragedy", Luchenko is portrayed as a black hearted villain of devilish magnitude.

Though a best seller, Faversham's book is wildly inaccurate. She paints a fantastical picture of young Rebecca being forced to leave school and join the circus or else face starvation. She devotes many pages to the love affair between Dimetri and Rebecca and accuses Luchenko of scheming to break up their relationship in order to steal Rebecca for himself. Faversham even includes lurid suggestions of rape, followed by Luchenko acting as a pimp and forcing her to become first Newman's, then Bryant's mistress.

I replied to Luchenko's email and requested an interview. He at first declined but I persisted, explaining that I would give him the opportunity to tell his own story and refute the allegations against him. Finally he acquiesced.

Luchenko still owns rights to Circus Britannia but takes a less active role in the production nowadays. He lives with his partner Olivia Kendal, a former nurse, just outside Windsor. I met them at their home; a comfortable, modern house which although larger than average is not what you would call grand or stately. Olivia answered the door. She is a short and slightly plump, dark haired woman of about fifty. As she showed me into the hallway I paused to admire a rack of ornately carved walking sticks.

"Niki collects them," she told me. "He has loads more upstairs."

Nikolai was waiting for me in the front room, which although comfortable was that little bit too clean and tidy, the sort of room for receiving guests but not friends. Nikolai is of average height but slim and wiry build. Though receding, his hair has kept its reddish blond colour and his beard contains only a few streaks of grey. His face is unnaturally smooth for a man of sixty-two, no doubt a result of the extensive reconstructive surgery he underwent after the Newman Grand bombing. I had learned from my research that his left arm is prosthetic but would not have known this from looking. Though I studied them carefully, both of his hands appeared identical to me.

I introduced myself and we shook hands. I tried to break the ice with a few compliments on their home but he was not interested in making small talk. Olivia retired to the kitchen to make tea. Nikolai stared at me coldly.

"So what do you want to know?" he demanded.

"You could start by telling me about how you met Rebecca," I suggested. "Dimetri said it was he who spotted her potential and persuaded you to hire her. Is that correct?"

"It is not quite how I remember it. I could be mistaken but I thought the idea to approach her was entirely mine."

"But Dimetri was her teacher?"

"She learned a lot from him yes, but he was never a very good teacher. He was impatient, demanding and frequently bad tempered. I even saw him hit her once."

I was shocked and exclaimed, "He beat her!"

"No it wasn't like that. He wasn't a complete monster! I just remember watching them training together one time. She was hanging from the trapeze and he was supporting her and trying to get her to position her legs the way he wanted. 'Higher,' he was saying, 'higher and straighten it.' Then when it still wasn't right he slapped her on the leg and said, 'Straight you stupid girl, straight!' I mean, he didn't hit her hard, but you just can't do that sort of thing. You wouldn't dare raise a hand to anyone you worked with would you? I certainly wouldn't. But she didn't complain. I suppose she was prepared to tolerate it because she loved him."

"You believe she was in love with him then?"

"I know she was. She was crazy about him. In her eyes he could do no wrong. He was not an easy man to work with. He was frequently moody and rude, but she always defended him."

"If he was always so bad tempered and unpleasant why did she love him?"

"How should I know? Back then he was a handsome devil and a brilliant performer. I suppose he had charisma, that was what made him a star."

"But you said in your email that his popularity was waning didn't you?"

"That's right. While Rebecca was learning new skills and her showmanship was getting better and better, he was getting old and slowing down. His routines were becoming repetitive and the critics didn't hesitate to point this out. They loved Rosa though, as did the audiences. Dimetri knew it; he was just too proud to admit it. He became bitter and resentful and started behaving worse than ever, especially towards poor Becky. I asked her if she would take his place at the top of the bill but she refused. She still loved him in spite of his temper tantrums and would not hurt him. Only after he was injured would she take his place.

"For a while the show had not been doing so well. The reviews had been mediocre and frequently we were playing to half empty theatres, then as soon as Rebecca took the lead the critics were bursting with praise, boosting ticket sales and filling every seat. Just putting her name and picture on our publicity made a huge difference. Then she started doing TV interviews and photo shoots. She was beautiful and sexy, but also witty and amiable. What Dimetri said to you was all just rubbish. She made my circus the success it was."

"Your affiliation with Samuel Newman was the major turning point though wasn't it? It was his investment and influence which made Circus Britannia a national phenomenon."

"Of course, but Newman would never have been interested in an ordinary circus. He didn't want old fashioned family entertainment. He wanted something new and exciting with sex appeal. That was Rosa."

"It has frequently been suggested that your contract with Newman came about solely because she was his mistress. Is there any truth in that?"

"I am ashamed to say it, but I believe that is true. Newman had expressed an interest in the circus and arranged an informal meeting at the main restaurant of the Newman Grand. Rebecca and I went together. It went really well. I told him my ideas for the future of the show and he had a number of his own. Rebecca flattered and charmed him with great delicacy and I felt sure we had an agreement, but once the dinner was over he said that he'd consider my proposal and in the meantime would Miss Clayton come up to his suite for a drink.

"It was pretty obvious what he was suggesting and I was shocked that he was so brazen. I confess I was lost for words, but before I could recover Rebecca had said she would be delighted, and off they went. The next morning I had a call from Newman's PA, to arrange a formal meeting to discuss the details of the contract."

"But you never asked her to do it?"

"What, asked her to sleep with Newman? God no! I saw her later that day and I told her 'You didn't have to do that. We could have found another investor.' I remember the way she smiled at me and replied, 'Don't be so naïve! Newman has more wealth and influence than anyone else in the industry. He can make us all rich and famous.'"

"Was that what she wanted then, money and fame?"

"That was what she said she wanted."

Olivia brought tea and some delicious homemade fruit cake. I devoured a slice before asking more questions. Olivia sat beside Luchenko but said nothing.

"How did Newman take being dumped for Bryant?" I asked.

"I don't think he was dumped," he replied. "Bryant and Newman were firm allies. They had many mutually beneficial arrangements. Newman donated money to the Phoenix Party in return for tax breaks or legislation which helped his business. I think Rebecca became Bryant's mistress as part of a gentleman's agreement between them."

"Are you suggesting that Samuel Newman exchanged Rebecca for some favour from the President?"

"Quite possibly. It was Newman who introduced her to Bryant. Then she started seeing the President regularly and stopped spending time with Newman. There was never any quarrel or falling out. She just moved on from one man to the other."

"But why did she go along with it? Didn't she object to being traded like a horse?"

"I don't know. She never talked much about her feelings, at least not to me. I guess she just saw Bryant as an opportunity. Newman had done all he could for her, perhaps becoming the President's mistress was a type of promotion."

"You make her sound very cold and calculating."

"Perhaps she was, or perhaps she was just more honest than most people are. She never claimed to perform through love of her art, she admitted to wanting fame. It was the same with Newman and Bryant. She didn't profess to love them, only to want what they could do for her."

"She was capable of love though. She had loved Dimetri. Did she ever fall in love again?"

"It's no use asking me. I was never her confidante, we just worked together."

"But you must have a unique insight into her character. She was part of your circus for nearly six years. You must have watched her grow up, change from a girl to a woman."

"She didn't change that much. She was always old for her years. Even at seventeen she knew what she wanted and was prepared to make sacrifices for it. She wasn't like some other young performers who expect show business to be exciting and glamorous. In the early days there was hardly any glamour at all, just hours and hours of training, rehearsing and travelling. The places we performed were decaying heaps, shoddily refurbished and put back into business. The dressing-rooms were always cramped and usually stinking. Our lodgings were basic at best, but she never complained. She remained focused on her ambition. Even once we were making good money, and she had a luxury apartment and her own dressing-room, she was still as dedicated."

"Then her fame didn't change her?"

"Superficially it did. She became more confident, but it never went to her head. She was never arrogant or extravagant. She turned up to meetings and rehearsals on time and she treated everyone in the company with respect. Most importantly she accepted the fickle nature of fame and knew it couldn't last."

"Fame is very fleeting," I agreed. "The whole entertainment industry has changed completely. After Rosa, Circus Britannia never achieved the same popularity again, did it?"

"I thought we agreed this interview was to be about the early years. About her rise to success, not about what came after."

This was true so I did not press him on the matter. Luchenko obviously felt he had answered enough questions and was growing impatient for my departure.

I thanked him for his time and suggested, "Perhaps I could talk to you again another day and get the rest of the story?"

"We'll see," he replied.

Olivia showed me out and I thanked her for the tea and cake.

"That's quite all right," she replied, "I just hope you won't keep pestering him."

I promised I would not and left them to their quiet domestic routine.

Friday 16th March 2103

For the next three days the envelope remained on Rebecca's dressing-table untouched. Ami Reed had seen it and commented on it, but otherwise it went unnoticed until Friday night. Entering her dressing-room before the show Rebecca found her letter was gone and a brief reply was left in its place.

Dear Rosa,
Meet me in the basement stores tonight, after the performance. I will be waiting most anxiously to see you in person. I beg you to come and not to disappoint me.

Yours expectantly
The Man Behind the Mask

Excited at the prospect of finally discovering the identity of her secret admirer, Rebecca was impatient for the evening's performance to be over. She found it difficult to sit still while Ami styled her hair and applied her make-up. She was picturing how she hoped the man might look; young and dark with intelligent, soulful eyes. Then she thought how disappointed she would be if he were old and fat. She was forced to put these considerations aside while she performed her routines, but as soon the curtain fell her thoughts returned to the meeting.

She hurried back up to her dressing-room to shower and change. She wished she had some other clothes than the loose trousers and old sweater she had arrived in at the theatre that evening. After putting on her lipstick she examined her reflection critically. She was not looking her best but it would have to do. She descended the stairs. Most of the company were leaving and she said good night to several of them as they went.

Just as she was about to go down to the stores she paused, having second thoughts. Suddenly entering the basement alone and late at night to meet a strange man did not seem like a wise idea. Instead she went to the security desk where Alistair McKay was on duty. McKay was as Scottish as his name suggested, a Glaswegian. He had been with the Newman Corporation for many years, first in his native city then moving around as job opportunities emerged.

"Evening Miss, what can I do for you?" McKay asked as she approached.

"Hi Mac, has anyone been down to the stores tonight?" she asked.

"Not tonight," he answered checking the security log on his computer terminal. "No one has been down there since a couple of the technicians this morning. Why?"

"I was just wondering if Marti had been down to get the silks we were thinking of using in our new act. I'll pop down and get them now. If I leave it until tomorrow I'm bound to forget all about it."

"Do you want a hand?"

"No, it should only take a few minutes to find them and they aren't heavy."

Rebecca thought that since her mystery man was not already in the basement waiting for her he perhaps was not going to show up at all, unless he was nearby and intended to follow her down. Either way she felt safer now that she had spoken with McKay. He knew she was going down to stores and would be expecting her out again shortly. If she was detained he would come to look for her.

She scanned her thumbprint and typed in the code to open the door. Not only would this show up on the security console but there was a camera above the door also. She flicked on the lights illuminating row after row of boxes, shelves and racks. The stores consisted of two large, low chambers. The first in which she was standing was the smaller of the two, containing mostly costumes and props. The larger one beyond contained hardware and fixtures for lighting, ropes and rigging for the trapeze, devices for deploying pyrotechnics as well as various tools and miscellaneous pieces of equipment.

Rebecca often enjoyed looking around the stores. She sometimes found inspiration for a new act after rediscovering apparatus which had not been used for a while. But usually she came down during the day when the technicians were rattling up and down in the lift, busy fetching the charges and smoke canisters they needed for the night's show. Now the whole basement was eerily silent and as the light at the far end was not working, partially in darkness.

She decided she would walk slowly to the far wall and back and if there was no sign of her mystery man when this was done she would go. She felt a strange need to prove that she was not scared, though prove it to whom she did not know. As she approached the darkest part of the basement a shadow moved and formed a figure. She was startled and almost screamed, but tried to disguise her discomposure.

"The Man Behind the Mask I presume?" she said.

She had been trying all week to decide on something witty to say when she finally met her secret admirer but this was the best she could come up with.

"I am," replied the figure as he slowly approached her.

As he moved towards the light she saw that the mask was not a metaphor. Apart from his mouth and chin his face was completely covered. Rebecca studied him in silence. He was tall, dressed entirely in black with a hood covering his head. Even his hands were gloved.

"How did you get in when McKay said there was no one down here?" she asked eventually.

"I have my ways," he replied.

He spoke softly and slowly, perhaps trying to disguise his voice.

"You're not going to let me know who you are, are you?"

"Neither my name nor my face would mean anything to you."

They were standing close now and she was trying to make out his eyes through the holes in the mask but they were in shadow and barely visible.

"Why did you wish to meet me if you weren't going to reveal your identity?" she asked.

"Just to see you and to hear you speak, that was all I desired."

"I hope I live up to your expectations. Now you see me close up and in the flesh I hope you aren't disappointed."

"Not at all. You are very beautiful."

"But it's too dark down here, you can hardly see me."

"I see you well enough. I see more clearly than most people. I observe what others don't."

"Is that what makes you a poet?"

"You have read my poetry?"

"I have and I like it."

"Then you must have been reading the Real News Forum?"

"It is not illegal to read an unlicensed web page, but it is to contribute to one. Is that why you are hiding your identity?"

"One of the reasons."

"Suppose I gave you my word that I won't tell a soul, would you let me know who you are?"

"Why does it matter? If you have read my work then you know more about me than you could learn from my name."

Rebecca was struggling to find an answer when she was startled by a noise from the far end of the stores.

"Miss Clayton," McKay's voice called out, "do you need any help?"

The masked intruder disappeared among the shadowy mass of lighting rigs and dust sheets. Rebecca hurried back across the basement towards the stairs.

"I can't see the silks I want," she told the security guard as she re-entered the costume and prop store. "One of the lights needs fixing; it's too dark over there to find anything. I'll look again tomorrow."

"I'll let the electrician know," McKay replied.

As they climbed the stairs Rebecca asked, "There isn't any other way into the basement is there?"

"There's the lift of course."

"I mean, no one could get in without security knowing could they?"

"Certainly not. Why do you ask?"

"Oh don't worry I must be getting paranoid, you know, seeing things in the shadows."

"I'm sure no one could have gone down there without me knowing about it but I'll go and have a look round if you would like."

"No, I'm sure it was just my imagination. It's nearly eleven; I'd better go if I'm going to get home before the curfew."

"Why? You're exempt aren't you?"

"I am, but whenever I get stopped by a patrol they always want autographs and pictures, then it's would I sign something for their mum, and their gran and Great Aunt Betty and so on and so forth."

"I suppose that is the down side of being famous."

"Indeed, there are several major disadvantages to being a celebrity, but I'm not complaining. The pay is pretty damn good and the perks of the job more than make up for the inconveniences. Good night Mac, I'll see you tomorrow."

"Good night Miss, sleep well."

Rebecca hailed a taxi just outside the theatre and as it carried her home she pondered her meeting with the Man Behind the Mask. Either McKay was the Man's accomplice, which seemed highly unlikely, or there was a secret way into the basement. She asked herself why she had not alerted McKay to this blatant breach of security. Why had she stopped him from searching the stores? The only answer she could find was that she was enjoying this mystery too much to risk spoiling it.

She tried to focus on what she had learned from the encounter. The answer was not a lot. The Man had been correct in saying that his poetry revealed much about him. From reading his work Rebecca knew his political views. He was opposed to practically every Phoenix Party policy. He was liberal in his attitudes to race, religion and sex. The theme of freedom was a major feature of his work; free speech, freedom of the press and freedom of choice. Yet though the cry for freedom was often the mantra of terrorists he abhorred violence and eloquently argued its futility. From the skill with which he wrote she could assume he was well educated. Also, he had a sense of humour as many of his works were satirical and amusing.

By the time she reached her apartment Rebecca had drawn up a mental list of everything she knew about the mystery man. Though she knew about his politics, his intelligence, his eloquence and his sensitivity there were some most unsatisfactory gaps in his profile. What was his name? How old was he? Was he married? Where did he live? What was his job? Most important of all, why was he so obsessed with her?

A GLIMPSE OF HAPPINESS
The Man Behind the Mask

Today I had a glimpse of happiness,
For today she spoke to me.
I was rescued from my own insignificance
And saved from melancholy.

I should like to preserve the moment,
Distilled, bottled and hidden away,
To keep it safe for a time I will need it,
Like pennies saved for a rainy day.

The rainy day will come soon, I fear,
The clouds are gathering as I write.
Yet trying to cling to a joyful moment
Is like trying to catch a shaft of light.

But there may be a ray of hope,
For I may see her again.
With this thought I'll make an umbrella,
To shelter me from the rain.

Part 2

Phoenix

REAL NEWS NETWORK
Simon Chandra

In the two recent biographies, two completely opposing views of Rebecca Clayton's character have been put forward. In last week's article I mentioned "Rosa – Her Tragedy" by Felicity Faversham, which portrays the young Rebecca as an unwilling victim manipulated by others and forced onto the path to stardom. Faversham then describes a kind of awakening when Rebecca turns against the evil men around her to fight for what she believes in. The rest of her life is a selfless battle ending in martyrdom for her cause. Daniela Rhodes's book "The Rise of Rosa" tells her story from an entirely different perspective. In this account it is Rebecca who does all the manipulating. She ruthlessly pursues her ambition seeking wealth and fame. Rhodes argues that she was completely cynical, switching her allegiance from the Phoenix Party to the opposition purely as a means of her own advancement.

From the interviews I have conducted so far it would appear that the truth about Rosa's rise to fame lies somewhere between the two accounts. She was not a victim, nor was she as ruthless as Rhodes would like us to believe. There is no doubt in my mind that she wanted the wealth and celebrity status that she achieved, but once she had it, did it make her happy? What about her relationship with Bryant? I do not believe that she loved him, but she must have had some opinion of him, both of his character and his policies.

These things are hard to determine as in those days people rarely talked openly about politics. Such conversations were not conducted in bars or in the workplace, only in privacy amongst family or close friends. People were afraid to criticise the government. Even the mildest of complaints against the authorities could be misinterpreted as sympathy with terrorists and extremists and result in questioning by the security services.

My next interviewee is one of the few people who were in Rebecca's confidence so has vital insight into what she really thought and felt. Unfortunately, as this lady is the very busy editor of a popular current affairs magazine she has little time to spare and arranging a meeting was extremely difficult. When I finally managed to persuade her to give an hour of her time she spent the first fifteen minutes criticising my interview with Luchenko. A word of advice to any would-be journalists out there: don't ever try to interview your own mother and never, ever attempt to interview mine.

Before relating the substance of what Monica Chandra told me I should write a little of her background. Her maiden name was Monica Grant. Her parents were fairly well off; her mother a doctor and her father an engineer for a solar-energy technology firm. Although their relative wealth helped them through the hard years of the 21st century they were not entirely immune. She had a brother and a sister both die in their infancy of black flu so grew up an only child. She was privately educated, took a degree at St Andrews University and became a journalist. She married a colleague, Rashid Chandra in 2088. They are still married and have two children, me and my younger sister Amira.

In the 2080s both Monica and Rashid were working in news journalism, which was a very small industry with very limited scope at that time. In 2089 Monica got into trouble with the government censors after broadcasting a report on police brutality towards homosexuals and Muslims. She was forced to resign and was out of work for the next five years. Rashid remained as a low paid researcher for over a decade, constantly missing out on promotion, labelled as a Muslim, a rebel and untrustworthy. He is not nor ever was a Muslim, he would best be described as agnostic but from a Hindu family.

Angry at the government's control over the media they banded together with like minded individuals and founded their own uncensored and therefore illegal current affairs website, the Real News Network. Like other members of the so called "underground media", they had contacts in the Republic of Ireland which was not subject to such intense internet censorship. The RNN website could easily be accessed using a proxy server.

The Phoenix government devoted a great deal of time and money attempting to control illegal websites but with little success. The IT industry had been in decline for years and there were few people with the skills and knowledge required to engineer sophisticated software. Unfortunately for the government, the country's best remaining IT professionals were believers in free speech and so collaborated with the underground media.

Although RNN took up much of my parents' time they never made any money from it. Mounting debts forced my mother to seek paid employment in the resurgent market for fashion and lifestyle journalism. She eventually secured a job with a new women's magazine "Amber", and as she dealt entirely with non-political and uncontroversial subjects she was soon promoted to feature editor. After six years with the magazine she took over as editor, but the whole time continued in secret as a reporter for RNN. It was in her role as a journalist for "Amber" that she first met Rebecca Clayton.

"I don't really remember much about our first few meetings," she told me. "It was before she achieved major stardom and before she began her affair with the President. She was just a circus performer, who I was supposed to interview.

I expect we talked about how much training she did, her diet and how she styled her hair, the usual sort of "Amber" rubbish. It was only a year or so later, after I was editor and after she started screwing Bryant that I got interested in her."

We are in the kitchen of my parents' house. Part of the deal to get her to do this interview was that I made her breakfast.

"It was RNN that broke that story wasn't it?" I asked. "How did you find out?"

"There was a big party at Downing Street for the rich and famous. I was there on behalf of the magazine to write about what everyone was wearing. Rebecca arrived with Newman, but she didn't leave with him. When I later spoke with one of Bryant's domestic staff I learned that she had stayed the night, and not in a guest room."

"Do you think Newman knew about it?"

"I'm sure he did. It was like Luchenko said; Newman traded her for tax breaks or something. That was the way men like those behaved. They felt themselves superior to the laws and morals that govern the behaviour of normal people. Just look at the way Bryant treated his family. Most of the time he acted as though they didn't exist then every so often he would produce them for a photo opportunity."

"So once she was the President's mistress and the most famous woman in the country, that was when you started to take an interest?"

"That's right. I hoped that while I was interviewing her for "Amber" she might accidentally let slip something of interest about Bryant which I could use for RNN, but she never did. She was much too smart. We were rather alike in many ways. We both had our public faces and were accomplished in the art of hiding our true opinions. In fact she was even better at it than I was, as she saw through me long before I penetrated her disguise."

"What do you mean by, saw through you?"

"I mean she realised I was not the person I was pretending to be. I remember that meeting quite clearly. It was April 2102, I was supposed to be talking to her about her new act but I had other things on my mind. It was the run up to a general election and three Liberation Party candidates had been arrested for homosexuality. When Liberation Party supporters tried to protest the police responded as aggressively as ever and several demonstrators were killed. Then of course the government used this violence as an excuse for even stricter curfew enforcement.

"Naturally all this was of much more interest to me than Rebecca's latest routine so while she was telling me all about it my thoughts were wandering. She had been explaining the symbolism behind the act and the significance of the music, something like that. As I was recording what she was saying I wasn't really listening but I got a shock when she suddenly said, 'I wouldn't have spent so much time making this crap up if I'd known you weren't interested.' Of course I tried to bluff, saying I was fascinated, but she wasn't fooled. 'We're both wasting our time here,' she said. 'You know as well as I do that there is no meaning behind my routines. I just do what looks good. Why don't you ask me the stuff you really want to know?'

"I switched off my recorder and said, 'If I did, the censors would never let me print it.'

"She replied, 'The censors don't always succeed though do they? Some things still get published without their interference.'

"I asked 'Do you mean the underground press, RNN and such like?'

"'Yes,' she said, 'Have you ever seen it?'

"'I have,' I told her, 'in fact I know someone who I suspect might be working for them.'

"'It's a dangerous business to be in,' she said. 'If this friend of yours gets caught they could face a very long jail sentence.'

"'Right,' I agreed, 'I wouldn't take such a risk.'

"'But if you heard something interesting,' she suggested, 'might you not pass it along to this friend of yours?'

"'I suppose I might,' I said, 'it depends what you mean by something interesting.'"

"'For instance I could tell you that only one of the Liberation Party members arrested is actually homosexual; the evidence against the other two was fabricated by one of Bryant's advisers.'

"'How do you know that?' I asked.

"'I don't know anything,' she replied cautiously, 'I was just suggesting the sort of thing I could tell you that I perhaps overheard Bryant talking about.'

"We carried on like this for weeks, a subtle hint here, a suggestion there, until gradually we grew to trust each other. Then she became my number one source and we also became friends."

"But why was she doing it?" I asked. "What was in it for her?"

"Not money that's for certain. I never gave her any and she had plenty of her own. I think maybe she did it to ease her conscience. I guess she felt guilty about living in comfort and ease while being surrounded by poverty and misery. She had worked so hard to get where she was, to be wealthy, successful and famous with many powerful friends, but once she had achieved all that she wasn't satisfied."

"If she wasn't happy with Bryant why didn't she leave him?"

"Honestly Simon, you always make everything sound so simple! Life isn't black and white like that. People aren't all either heroes or villains and there aren't just two states of being, happy or unhappy. Besides, we're talking about the President, the most powerful man in Europe, you don't just dump a man like Bryant without expecting repercussions. He could be just as unpleasant to people who crossed him in his personal life as he could to his political opponents."

"I just find it hard to understand how she could have a relationship with Bryant when she knew he was corrupt."

"It was a very strange sort of relationship. Sometimes she spoke of him with utter distain, other times it was with indifference, but there were definitely occasions when she expressed an almost indulgent fondness. It wasn't often but now and then she talked about him as if he were a retard or a small child, someone whose shortcomings were to be tolerated because they didn't know any better. The fact is Bryant wasn't as clever as he thought he was. He was never the brains of the Phoenix Party. Though he didn't like to admit it even to himself, he was entirely subservient to the corporations that paid to keep him in power. Rebecca knew that and I think maybe sometimes she even felt a little sorry for him."

"The man was an unprincipled, selfish, ruthless, fascist tyrant! How could she possibly feel sorry for him?"

"Eva Braun loved Hitler and he was worse than Bryant. Worse in that he killed more people. Their relative badness does rather depend on your perspective. You could argue Hitler was the better man because he was doing what he believed in, for the good of Germany and not just for personal gain."

"Getting back to the point, when did things change? When did she go from leaking information to becoming an active supporter of the Liberation Party?"

"I couldn't tell you. You need to talk to her friends in the Party."

"I intend to, but I'm not entirely sure who her friends were."

"Not my problem. Right, I've indulged you long enough. Now I've got real work to do, you know, current affairs journalism. Current as in stuff happening now, not ten years ago."

Sunday 18th March 2103

Rebecca spent the following Sunday with Bryant. The fine weather continued and she would have liked to get away from London, to take a trip out into the countryside or to the coast, but John was in one of his lazy moods. He spent most of the day sprawled on the sofa in his bathrobe, watching old films and stuffing his face with crisps and popcorn. By the afternoon Rebecca was bored. Leaving the beached whale in his semi-comatose state, she escaped to the garden.

Today there was no gardener and she had the whole place to herself, but she still found the enclosed space oppressive. She fondly remembered the outings with her Aunt and Daniel. They would take the train out into the countryside and walk for what seemed like hours, usually climbing to the top of some hill while she and Dan complained bitterly. Then they would eat their picnic lunch on the top looking down over the patchwork of green, yellow and gold fields and watch the wind turbines turning lazily in the breeze.

Once, while toiling up a lane between fields of brilliant sunflowers they had come across dozens of dead birds. She had been frightened, but Aunt Ellen explained that the sunflowers were GM crops producing vast numbers of oil rich but toxic seeds. The birds were pests which damaged the crops so had to be controlled. Rebecca had understood but still found the absence of birdsong unnerving. That night she had dreamt that the plants were chasing her, their roots scuttling like crab legs. She never liked sunflowers after that.

Bryant's voice called from the terrace and interrupted her reverie, "Becky, have you forgotten that we've got guests tonight?"

The President had showered, shaved and was dressed in a purple silk shirt and black trousers. He looked far more respectable than the crumpled slob she had left on the sofa.

"I hadn't forgotten," she replied, "I'm just coming."

She hurried inside and changed into a short, black skirt and low cut gold top. Even though it was to be an informal dinner she knew Bryant would prefer her not to wear trousers. He liked to admire her legs and it gave him satisfaction to see other men doing so with envy. The guests were some of the government's new, young talent. Philip Graysby was to be one of the company and after all that Monica had told her Rebecca was anxious to meet him.

James Hutchens was first to arrive with Clarissa Derby, Bryant's image consultant. Clarissa was the type of woman Monica pretended to be, obsessed with fashion, clothes and hairstyles. Rebecca thought her the most boring person she had ever met. Unfortunately Clarissa adored her, or at least she claimed to.

As soon as she was through the door of the White Drawing Room, Clarissa latched onto Rebecca's arm and lavished praise on her clothes, her complexion, her hair and her figure. While pretending to listen, Rebecca was watching Hutchens out of the corner of her eye. She was now completely certain that Hutchens was not The Man Behind the Mask. Even leaving aside all the other arguments against him, he was too short.

While Clarissa was still in raptures over Rebecca's shoes one of the newly appointed junior ministers, Sonita Gupta, arrived. In the licensed media much had been made of Ms Gupta's promotion. The fact that she was the first Asian woman to rise to such a position since the Phoenix Party came to power was being hailed as evidence of Bryant's open-mindedness. Rebecca however suspected Gupta was merely a token, a gesture towards diversity in a mostly white, male government.

Gupta herself was entirely unremarkable. Though she had come to dinner wearing a sari, her political opinions were just as conservative as the rest of the party. Her career as an MP had so far consisted entirely of agreeing with the President. She had vocally supported him in the latest round of mosque closures, frequently spoke of the link between Islam and terrorism and was passionately opposed to reopening the borders.

Philip Graysby was last to arrive, but although she was introduced to him Rebecca did not manage to escape from Clarissa long enough for any kind of conversation. Graysby was at least ten years younger than Bryant and several kilos lighter but he had considerably less hair. He made no attempt to disguise the bald patches, the rest of his head being neatly and closely cropped.

Tonight the meal was served in what had always been known as the Small Dining Room, even though it could seat up to twelve guests. When they sat down to dinner, Rebecca found herself between Clarissa and Hutchens at one end of the table while Graysby was with Bryant and Gupta at the other. It soon became apparent that Hutchens's conversation was little better than Clarissa's. Between complimenting and flirting he tried to talk about poetry, but his affectations and pretensions to being an intellectual were utterly nauseating. After a while Rebecca completely gave up listening, turning her attention to the discussion between Bryant and Graysby.

"Just imagine the market-place like a big pond," Graysby was saying, "where every company is a fish. There used to be lots of fish but the big ones ate all the little ones so now there are only a few left."

"Right just like nature, survival of the fittest," replied Bryant.

"But now we have a pond full of overfed, big, fat, lazy fish who just sit on the bottom doing nothing. Isn't it perhaps time we let a few more little fish into the pond for them to chase?"

"But those big fish are our party's major donors. We shouldn't bite the hand that feeds."

"Well you see, that's part of the problem," replied Graysby with a laugh. "Firstly, fish don't have hands and secondly we have become far too dependent on a small number of donors. We do far more for them than they do in return and they abuse their power over us. Just look at the situation with Mega Meals."

"There wouldn't be a Mega Meals situation if it wasn't for the underground press. We've tried everything to block that damned RNN but nothing works. OK, I don't know anything about computers, but we pay large amounts of money to people who do. Why can't they shut the fucking thing down?"

"Even if you were to succeed in abolishing RNN some other pirate network would just take its place. You'll never completely eradicate the free press."

"I thought maybe if we caught the bastards and strung them up by their balls it might dissuade others."

"God no! The last thing we want to do is create martyrs. That's the best possible way to unite the opposition."

By now Clarissa and Hutchens had realised Rebecca was taking no interest and had ceased their prattling. Sonita had been silent but decided that at this point it was safe to venture an opinion.

"We certainly don't want united opponents. So long as the opposition parties all hate each other more than they hate us we are secure."

"Right," agreed Graysby. "The Muslims hate the Catholics and the Catholics hate the Muslims and they both hate the queers so these days we don't even have to worry about rigging elections."

"Good Lord Phil!" exclaimed Bryant. "I hope you're not suggesting we would ever stoop to that!"

Then he roared with laughter. The other toadies joined in while Graysby smiled and chuckled politely then waited until they had finished.

"Seriously though," he said, "I think it is definitely to our advantage to open up some industries to competition and cultured foods would seem as good a place as any to start."

"I understand what you are saying," replied Bryant. "It's an interesting idea and I will certainly give the matter some thought. This is why I wanted you in the Cabinet Phil; it's about time we had some fresh thinking."

"I appreciate the opportunity to show what I can do," said Graysby. "You can expect plenty more new ideas from me."

"Good, I'm glad to hear it. So Phil, how ambitious are you? Do you think you could do the top job one day?"

"You mean your job? I think I could do it, one day. I assume you'll want to retire eventually."

"Eventually. I've no plans to leave office for some years yet."

"Of course not. I'm in no hurry."

Bryant then turned to Clarissa, "If Phil wants to be President we're going to have to do something about his image though aren't we? For a start, I've got more hair on my chest than he has on his head!"

Rebecca could have confirmed this but chose to remain silent. Bryant in fact had enough body hair to make a gorilla jealous.

"Actually recent surveys suggest baldness is not a major drawback," replied Clarissa. "Phil actually gets quite a high approval rating for his physical appearance."

"Oh! And how am I doing?"

"Your weight is an issue. The public dislike fatness far more than baldness."

Rebecca was suddenly struck with a new admiration for Clarissa. No one else would dare to speak to the President like this.

"I'm not going on a diet," replied Bryant, "I absolutely refuse."

"Perhaps you could try taking a bit more exercise," Rebecca suggested.

"Or maybe I could just get IMC to announce that being fat is now fashionable."

*

The following day Rebecca arranged a meeting with Monica Chandra and told her all she had learned about Philip Graysby, which was not much but she could at least confirm the rumours RNN had already received. Afterward she went to the theatre to rehearse her new routine with Martin. When she arrived McKay was on duty at the security desk and told her she had a delivery.

"What sort of delivery?" she asked.

"A big one. It is still in the mail room as it was too big to take up to your dressing-room. We've checked it out thoroughly and it's quite safe. Come and see."

She followed him into the mail room and he showed her the item in question. It was indeed large, a fifty centimetre square container planted up with delicate alpine flowers. On a stone in the centre the words "Rosa's Garden" were painted. There was an envelope taped to one end of the container. Rebecca opened it and read the message.

Dear Rosa,

It was a great pleasure to finally meet you in person. I hope you like my gift. With a little water and plenty of sun these little flowers should bloom for you for many years. May this garden be like a lasting relationship rather than the brief affair with cut flowers which are doomed to wither after only days.

Since you expressed a liking for my poetry I enclose an invitation to an event which may interest you. I would be honoured if you would meet me there.

With Love
The Man Behind the Mask

There was a second piece of paper in the envelope, the invitation to which the letter had referred.

You are cordially invited to
The Tertiary Romantics Masquerade & Cabaret

At the Crown and Sceptre Public House
Palace Place
London SW1E 5QZ

Sunday 25th March
From 8:00pm

Handwritten across the top of this printed sheet were the words, "Come in disguise." Rebecca was studying the invitation when McKay interrupted her thoughts.

"Who's it from?" he asked.

"Oh, it's from my secret admirer."

"A green fingered secret admirer by the look of it. This really is rather nice. My wife is a keen gardener. She'd be able to tell you the names of all these plants. Do you have a balcony or somewhere to put it?"

"Yes I have a large balcony. I've always been intending to get some plants for it but never got around to it. It's almost as if he knew."

Later, after they had finished rehearsing, Rebecca told Martin about the gift from her mystery man and showed him the invitation.

"Do you think I should go?" she asked.

"Of course, why not?"

"You don't think I might be taking a risk? I mean I have no idea who this man is."

"You'd be meeting him in a public place, at this pub, that would be safe enough."

"But what sort of pub? And who or what are these Tertiary Romantics?"

"I've heard of them. They're a group of musicians, poets, comics and the like who perform anti-government material. Of course they've been labelled as anarchists, terrorists and so on but they are harmless. Gay blokes writing poetry aren't going to bring down the government."

"You don't think my poet is gay do you?"

"I wish he was. He sounds hot."

"Do you want to come?"

"I'm not invited, besides I don't want to be the gooseberry."

"What if this guy turns out to be some kind of pervert? He could be the sort of freak who likes to chop women up into little pieces and dump their body parts all over London."

"Or he could be just some hopeless romantic with a huge crush on you. If you don't go you may never find out."

"I'm supposed to go in disguise. How the hell do I do that?"

"That's easy. Go as yourself then no one will ever suspect it's you!"

*

After spending most of the week trying to decide whether or not to accept the invitation, when Sunday finally came Rebecca made up her mind to go. The President was spending the weekend at home with his family so she had the evening free. She took Martin's advice regarding her disguise. Earlier that afternoon she had retrieved an old costume from the theatre basement, a yellow and purple harlequin patterned one-piece bodysuit with an eye mask trimmed with feathers. She felt out of place putting it on at home and it took rather longer than usual to do her hair and make-up without Ami's help. She painted her face white and her lips bright red as she would to go on stage.

As she examined the results in the mirror she started to have second thoughts. This was such a ludicrous idea. She was bound to be recognised. If the press were to hear of secret meetings with a subversive organisation it would be the end of her career, never mind the trouble she would be in with Bryant.

The porter called to say her taxi had arrived and she did not like to send the driver away without a fare so she put on her coat, put the mask in her bag and went down trying to think where she should ask him to drive her. In the end, as she could think of no other destination she asked the man to take her to the Crown and Sceptre.

"Palace Place?" asked the driver, "As in Buckingham Palace?"

The man obviously recognised Rebecca and thought it odd that she should be going to that part of town.

"That's right," Rebecca replied, "I'm going to a party."

"Strange place for a party."

"It is a strange sort of party, very exclusive, no press."

This satisfied the driver as he expected celebrities to have eccentric habits. He drove without making further enquiries. He only spoke again when they had passed the crumbling burnt out ruin which remained of the Palace. He tutted and shaking his head said, "What a mess."

Once they arrived she gave him a large tip and thanked him for his discretion. As she got out of the car she put on her mask. From the outside the

Crown and Sceptre looked like a completely ordinary public house although the surrounding buildings were mostly vacant and boarded up. It had a slightly scruffy and rundown look and would benefit from a coat of paint, but obviously still had regular trade as there were boards with menus and special offers and posters for a band performing the following week. The only thing out of the ordinary was a sign on the front door saying, "Closed for a private function. Entrance by invitation only."

Rebecca felt very conspicuous standing in the empty street. She wished she had not sent the taxi away. She was reaching for her phone about to call for a car to take her home again when two young women dressed completely in black approached. One carried a guitar case.

"Are you here for the Masquerade? Of course you are. Love the costume," said one.

"Come on in, don't be shy," said the other who wore a peculiar old fashioned hat with a veil, the sort of thing an old lady would once have worn to a funeral.

They ushered her inside where they were greeted by an eighteenth century bar wench with a lace cap and impressive cleavage.

"Evening ladies," said the wench and to Rebecca she said, "You must be Rosa. It's incredible, you look just like her. Do you have your invitation?"

Rebecca produced it from her handbag.

The woman glanced at it and said, "Go on up, The Man is waiting for you upstairs."

"We'll show you," said the woman in the veil, "this way."

Rebecca followed the two young women up to the function room on the first floor. There was a bar at one end and a stage at the other. Between were tables and chairs where numerous strangely dressed characters were assembled. The lights were low and among the many masked and veiled faces she could not pick out her man.

"Are you performing?" asked the pretty girl with the guitar.

"Performing? No I'm supposed to be meeting someone."

"Yes The Man. There he is!"

Another masked figured had just emerged from behind the stage curtains. He too was dressed in period costume with a black cloak, black boots, breeches and gloves and a white lace fronted shirt. His face was hidden by the same black mask she had seen in the theatre basement but his head was uncovered, revealing a mass of dark curly hair.

"Hey Man, your date's arrived!" called out the veiled woman.

He approached them and took Rebecca's hand and pressed it to his lips, but unlike Hutchens he did it without ostentation. To him gallantry came naturally and was not assumed. Enough of his face was visible to see he was smiling.

"I'm so glad you came," he said, "you look beautiful, as always. Let's find a table. Can I get you a drink?"

"Thanks," replied Rebecca looking at the bottles of cheap, brightly coloured spirits lined up behind the bar, "I don't suppose they have any wine?"

"They have excellent wine. Take a seat; I'll be just a moment."

Rebecca sat down at a small table while the two women in black seated themselves nearby. Observing their body language she concluded they were more than friends. In fact most of the tables were occupied by couples but it was extremely hard to determine gender in many cases. The lady in the red dress at a table near the stage had very large hands and a prominent Adam's apple while a man in a suit and tie standing at the bar was wearing high heeled shoes.

The Man returned with a bottle and two glasses. He poured the deep red wine and Rebecca tasted it. It was slightly sweet but intensely fruity.

"That's very nice, is it English?"

"Of course, its blackberry wine."

"Blackberry?"

"Yes the landlady makes it herself."

"So what exactly is a Tertiary Romantic?" Rebecca asked.

"We are the third group of people to call ourselves the Romantics. First there were the original Romantics; artists and the great poets like Keats, Byron, and Shelley, then in the 1980s there were pop musicians called the New Romantics, now there's us. We are a mixture of writers and musicians and this is our chance to exhibit our material. In fact I will be reading some of my work shortly, so if you will excuse me I'll make sure everything's ready."

He left her and disappeared behind the stage curtains again. Although there were at least thirty people in the room the atmosphere was subdued and conversation conducted in low voices. As the lights dimmed the audience instantly fell silent and the wench from downstairs stepped into the spotlight.

"Good evening ladies and gentlemen," said the wench, "Welcome to the Masquerade Cabaret. Before we begin a few formalities. For the benefit of any newcomers or those of you with poor memories, the rules. No photography, filming or recording of any kind. While you are here please refrain from using anyone's full name, first names and pseudo names only. I ask you to remember that these events are a celebration of free speech, therefore please respect the rights of others to say what they wish whether you agree with it or not. No heckling, no interruptions and absolutely no bad manners! If you fail to obey any of these rules you will be asked to leave and not invited back.

"Thank you for listening. I hope you enjoy the show. Now I have the pleasure of introducing what would be a familiar face, had we ever seen it. Ladies and gentlemen, The Man Behind the Mask."

There was applause as the masked man stepped into the spotlight. He began by reading a poem entitled "The Death of Democracy", which Rebecca knew form the RNN forum. He followed it with other political poems, some serious, some humorous. Each was well received by the appreciative audience. As he recited his works Rebecca found herself listening as much to his voice as to his poems. It was soft yet powerful, having an almost hypnotic quality.

"I would like to finish tonight with a new piece," he said. "This is called 'Rosa'."

Rebecca was glad of her thick make-up as she could feel herself blushing beneath it. The poem was passionate and sensual, a tender and deeply personal expression of desire, his desire for her. The conclusion was met with loud applause and he thanked the audience.

He introduced the next act saying, "Ladies and gentlemen would you please welcome to the stage Miss Eve."

The young woman with the guitar went up and seated herself on a stool. The Man patted her on the shoulder as he left the stage, a gesture Rebecca recognised as an experienced performer encouraging a nervous beginner. As he returned to his seat the girl began to play and sing. She had a sweet voice and performed a love song, no doubt written for the woman in the veil, who was visibly moved, dabbing her eyes with a lace handkerchief. The singer performed two more sad songs and by the time she had finished her repertoire her partner was not the only one of the audience moved to tears.

The next act was a young man who read out a short story he had written based on the experiences of a friend coerced into having an abortion. He was followed by another poet, an Asian man whose work was on themes of racial and religious oppression. After him the wench returned to the stage to announce there would be a short interval.

"So what do you think of the show?" asked the Man, pouring Rebecca another glass of wine.

"It's very good, but pretty depressing," she replied.

"Yes I'm afraid we can be a rather melancholy bunch at times, but the second half usually has a few more laughs."

The woman in the veil was returning from the bar and stopped by their table.

"I loved your new poem, Man," she said, "but was it about the real Rosa or this one?"

"Both of course," he replied and winked at Rebecca.

As the veiled woman returned to her companion Rebecca remarked, "Is 'Man' what they call you around here?"

"Generally Man or The Man, yes. When I first started coming I didn't really have a name so I was just The Masked Man or The Man in the Mask. It was when I started publishing stuff on RNN that I started signing myself, The Man Behind the Mask. It sounded better. Since it's a pretty long name people tend to shorten it. I like it, The Man, it makes me sound important."

"Are you important? Is that why you read first?"

"No. In show business you save the best till last don't you?"

"I think you're being modest. I think you should tell them you want your name at the top of the bill and your own dressing-room with a big star on the door."

As The Man had promised, the second half of the show was in a much lighter vein. It opened with woman impersonating an IMC news reader breaking increasingly dire stories but desperately trying to spin them in the government's favour. For example, the deaths of three hundred children poisoned by school meals became a successful operation to eliminate potential terrorists. This was followed by a stand-up comic who was less funny but did some good impressions of Cabinet ministers.

The final act was by far the best. The curtains opened and a man wearing a costume similar to Rebecca's own was sitting on a swing. His face was painted with her trademark dark eyes and red lips. A man in a suit padded out with cushions waddled onto the stage.

"Rosa, where are you?" he demanded.

"Up here darling," replied the He-Rosa in a silly high pitched voice.

"Come down," ordered the fat man, "I want to make love to you and my wife will be here in half an hour."

"OK," she replied squeakily, "but what do you want to do for the other twenty seven and a half minutes?"

The audience laughed loudly, including Rebecca. There were several more dirty jokes and the sketch ended to hearty applause and cheering. The wench returned to the stage to thank the performers and spectators. There was more clapping and she made a curtsey. The house lights came up and The Man helped Rebecca into her coat. He took her arm and ushered her out the door, seeming to be in a hurry.

"What's the matter?" she asked.

Once they were a little distance from the pub The Man stopped and turned to face her.

"I'm really sorry," he said, "I had no idea they would be doing a sketch about you or I would not have invited you."

"Don't be ridiculous!" she replied, "I do have a sense of humour you know." She laughed and repeated the line, "'What do you want to do for the other twenty seven and a half minutes?' Alarmingly accurate actually!"

"Then you're not mad at me?"

"Of course not."

"Good, but I think you will be in a moment."

"Why is that?"

He pulled her towards him and kissed her passionately. She could feel the strength in his arms as he embraced her and the strangely erotic sensation of his leather mask pressed against her face. He released her.

"So are you mad at me now?" he asked.

She felt she ought to be but she was not. She was excited and aroused. She was feeling a little light-headed and it took her a moment to find her voice to answer.

"No, I'm still not mad at you."

"Then can I see you again? How about tomorrow night?"

"I'm sorry I can't tomorrow."

"What about after the show on Tuesday? Meet me in Hyde Park by The Fountains."

"Are you crazy? Even I can't go wondering about Hyde Park after curfew."

"Of course you can. There is a great big hole in the fence near Clarendon Gate and Curfew Patrols are lazy. They stick to the places where they know they will find people."

"But what about the several hundred CCTV cameras watching the whole city?"

"The virtue of CCTV is that there are so many cameras recording so many hours of film, no one can ever be bothered to look at any of them unless there's a murder or something serious. I regularly take a midnight stroll and I've never once been arrested."

Even though her common sense told her it was complete insanity to do so, Rebecca heard herself agreeing to meet this masked stranger in a lonely place after dark. He kissed her again but this time their lips only touched briefly. Then he hailed a taxi and she returned to her apartment, still asking herself if she had gone completely mad.

WHEN I FOUND YOU, I FOUND ME
Eve

I've learned so much with you by my side
You are my friend, my teacher and my guide
You showed me the world and took me by the hand
You gave me your strength so now I understand
I've learned the truth and I see
When I found you, I found me

I was so tired of being on my own
I was scared and confused to be so alone
I thought I was the only one who ever felt this way
Didn't even know what it meant to be gay
I've learned the truth now I see
When I found you, I found me

Though we still have so much that we fear
I feel safe just to know you are near
And though our love is a secret we must hide
I will wear it in my heart with pride
I've learned the truth and I see
When I found you, I found me
I've learned the truth and I see
When I found you, I found me

Monday 26th March 2103

The President had called Rebecca twice the previous night and was unreasonably annoyed that she had not answered. No sooner had she arrived at Downing Street than he demanded to know where she had been and what she had been doing.

"I was at the theatre working with Martin on our new routine," she replied, "I thought I told you."

"But why weren't you answering your mobile?"

"We were busy. Acrobatics require quite a lot of concentration you know. I turned the phone off so we wouldn't be interrupted."

This did not appease Bryant as he disliked the fact that Rebecca had been spending so much time with an attractive young man recently and he felt he had the right to disturb whatever she was doing.

"I would have thought Martin had better things to do on a Sunday night," Bryant complained. "Doesn't he have a girlfriend?"

"He recently split up with his partner," Rebecca replied.

"Men don't have partners any more. They have a girlfriend, a fiancée or a wife."

"And perhaps a mistress," suggested Rebecca.

Bryant ignored her comment, carried away by enthusiasm for his own diatribe.

"A woman isn't a man's partner unless they are in business together and any man who voluntarily works with his wife must be completely mad. I have enough trouble trying to keep my wife out of my business. She is still trying to persuade me to promote art and culture. I keep telling her no one has more respect for our cultural heritage than me. I wouldn't be working so hard to get the money together for the restoration of Buckingham Palace if I didn't care about culture."

"Once you and your family are settled at the Palace perhaps you could arrange an official residence for your mistress because I quite fancy Hampton Court."

"What makes you think you'll still be around then? I might have traded you in for a younger model."

"Then you had better hope that the Phoenix Party doesn't do the same with you."

Bryant regretted the unkind remark as he said, "You know I was just kidding sweetheart. I wouldn't trade you for anything. Just look at you, you're stunning. No other woman has a body like yours."

She thanked him for the compliment but asked, "You don't think this dress is too revealing do you?"

She was wearing a short, clingy, black lace number as they were going out to dinner.

"No way, you look great. Anyway, Carson will be bringing his latest assistant and you wouldn't want to be outdone in the glamour stakes."

Dennis Carson, whom they were meeting at a very expensive restaurant, was the top man in the UK nuclear energy industry. The table was booked for eight, but it was already ten past. Carson had been late for his last meeting with the President who intended to keep him waiting in return.

Bryant looked at his watch and said, "I suppose we may as well be on our way."

They descended to the car and arrived at the restaurant shortly after eight thirty. Bryant was annoyed to learn that Carson had only just arrived. Rebecca need not have been concerned about her attire as compared to Carson's scantily clad "assistant" her lace dress was positively demure.

For the rest of the evening Rebecca was bored rigid while the two men talked business and the other woman hardly said a word. Rebecca knew that on occasions like these her job was to be seen and not heard. Bryant preferred to bring her to meet with major party donors rather than his wife, partly because of her value as arm candy but also because, unlike Caroline, she could be trusted not to venture her own opinions.

As a result Rebecca spent much of the evening thinking about The Man Behind the Mask. Though she knew it was unwise to keep her appointment with him the following night she was determined to do so, hoping that this time she would learn something about him. So absorbed was Rebecca with her own thoughts that she completely missed hearing any of the details of what was agreed between Bryant and Carson. Judging by Bryant's mood in the car on the way back to Downing Street the conclusion was more than satisfactory.

On reaching his private sitting-room on the second floor Bryant poured himself a large whiskey.

"You can wake up now Rebecca," he said, "the business is concluded for tonight and I feel like celebrating."

She knew what that meant and after dwelling for so long on thoughts of her passionate stranger in his tight breeches and leather boots the prospect of Bryant's sweaty, panting form seemed utterly revolting. Then she remembered the joke about the other twenty seven and a half minutes and almost laughed out loud. As a refusal would result in a quarrel she submitted to his usual clumsy fumbling and lay back and thought of England while he grunted and groaned.

The whole process took slightly longer than the alleged two and a half minutes, but not significantly so and soon the President was snoring. Rebecca lay awake beside him, again thinking of her mystery man. When eventually Bryant's snores subsided enough for her to drift off to sleep, erotic fantasies surfaced in her dreams. As she was disturbed several times in the night by the cataclysmic upheaval of Bryant rolling over she clearly remembered the dreams in the morning and flushed with guilt and embarrassment at what her subconscious had produced.

*

The day passed excruciatingly slowly. It rained for most of the morning but by late afternoon the sun was out and it stayed dry into the evening. She knew she had not performed at her best during the show that evening as she was too distracted but the audience applauded and cheered just as loudly as ever. She took a taxi to Clarendon Place, telling the driver she was having supper with friends there, although she did not actually know anyone living in that part of the city.

As The Man had promised there was an entire collapsed section of fence with just a length of tape barring access to the park. She reached their rendezvous without encountering a single curfew officer. He was waiting for her between the still pools where there had once been fountains, seated on a blanket spread out on the grass and illuminated by candles. He was wearing a long black coat and his now familiar black mask and he was leaning against a large wicker basket.

"Rosa my love," he greeted her, "come and sit with me. I have another blanket if you are cold."

"Why do you always call me Rosa?" she asked as she sat down, "you must know it isn't my real name."

"Would you rather I called you Rebecca?"

"I don't mind, but I would like to know what to call you."

"You may call me whatever you like. Now, I hope you are hungry, I have elderflower wine, cucumber sandwiches, artichoke salad and apple tarts for dessert."

He opened up the hamper and spread out the banquet.

"Wow, this lot must have cost you a fortune," said Rebecca.

"Not really. I grew most of the vegetables myself."

"Do you have a large garden?"

"Not at all, but you would be surprised how much you can grow in just a few containers."

"So people keep telling me. I really should make better use of my balcony; I just don't know where to start."

"Try growing a few pots of herbs," The Man suggested. "They look good, smell great and do wonders for your cooking."

"I rarely cook. Even when I have the time I can't be bothered."

"I love cooking, especially baking. I made these tarts."

This put a comical image into Rebecca's head of the masked man dressed completely in black as he was at present, including the black gloves, wearing a flowery apron and rolling out pastry.

She hid her smirk by taking a sip of elderflower wine and said, "So you are a cake baking, vegetable growing poet who wanders around the city in the middle of the night. Does that leave any time for a day job?"

"I do have a job but it is very dull."

"You're not going to tell me anything that might reveal your identity, are you?"

"No I'm not. You wouldn't be here at all if your curiosity had not been aroused by the mystery. If you knew the truth about me you would not be interested at all. I am not rich and influential like your other lover."

Feeling that she was being judged Rebecca replied, "That may be true but this mystery won't hold my interest forever. You run the risk that I will get bored of this game and go back to Bryant anyway, because as you say he is very wealthy and powerful, and he is also extremely generous and charming."

This was not a complete lie. Bryant was capable of both great generosity and charm he just had not exhibited much evidence of either lately.

"But he doesn't love you," said The Man, "not the way I do."

"Now you are being ridiculous. How can you possibly be in love with me? You hardly know me."

"I know you better than you think. I know about your background, your family, how you lost your brother and your mother."

"So what? You read "Amber" Magazine. That doesn't mean you know me."

"I know what a perfectionist you are. I know how hard you train and how many hours you spend rehearsing in order to get your routines exactly right. I also know that sometimes you make mistakes on purpose to make the routine more exciting. You fake a fall or a near miss."

Now Rebecca was surprised as this was something only Luchenko and a few of her fellow performers knew.

The Man continued, "I know that you love animals. You stop to stroke cats and to watch squirrels and birds. You are also utterly fascinated by little creepy-crawlies you find under leaves even though you have no idea what they are. You love plants as well, and not just flowers. You aren't content to just look at them, you like to smell and touch them. Sometimes you take off your shoes just to feel the grass between your toes."

Rebecca set down her glass and replied coldly, "So you've been spying on me."

"Not exactly spying, just admiring you from a distance."

"From a distance! You've been inside my dressing-room!"

"Only to deliver my letters."

"Well please don't deliver anymore," she said, getting to her feet.

"What's the matter? I thought you liked my letters."

"I did, but that was before I realised the kind of dangerous obsessive you were."

The Man slowly stood up and replied, "Obsessive maybe, but I'm not dangerous. You know I'm not or you wouldn't have agreed to meet me here tonight."

"You're right; I shouldn't have come at all. I don't know what I was thinking."

"I don't understand Rosa. On Sunday you let me kiss you but tonight I tell you that I love you and you are angry."

"I am sorry, I should never have encouraged you like this, it was completely irresponsible. From now on I want you to stay away from me. I don't want any more letters or gifts. I want you to leave me alone."

She tried to turn away but he caught her arm and demanded, "Just what is it I have done that has so upset you?"

She shook herself free and answered, "There's a word for what you have been doing, it's stalking. If you don't realise what you have been doing is wrong then you have a problem. You should get help. I am really sorry that I allowed this to get so out of hand but it ends now."

This time she did turn away and hurried back across the park. He followed and tried to stop her.

"Rosa please! Let me explain."

"No, this has to stop. Don't follow me. Don't speak to me. If I ever see you again I will call the police."

He gave up, watching her go. As she headed towards the gate she glanced back over her shoulder and saw he was still standing where she had left him. She hoped he had heeded her warning but she knew her last threat had been an empty one. She could come face to face with The Man the next morning but without his mask she would never recognise him.

Once out of the park she turned east down Bayswater Road, hoping to hail a passing taxi. The pre-curfew rush was over so it was likely that a few late night licensed cabs would be around. If she did not find a taxi she would call for one once she had put some distance between herself and The Man. She was far more anxious to get away from the masked freak than she was to avoid curfew patrols so when she saw a police car approaching she walked straight towards it. She was even relieved when it pulled up and the passenger side window opened and a brash voice rudely addressed her.

"Alright darling, stay where you are. Do you know what time it is?"

As the officer heaved his bulky frame out of the car she looked at her watch and replied calmly, "It's eleven twenty-five officer."

He shone a powerful torch in her face and said, "You're in luck sweetheart, 'cause before midnight I'm open to negotiations. What are you gonna do for me?"

"Do for you? I'm afraid I don't understand what you mean."

The officer took a step closer and studied her face more carefully.

"I've seen you before haven't I? Sorry bitch, your luck just ran out. I don't give second chances. In the car."

He grabbed her and forced her roughly into the back seat. She made no protest or effort to resist.

"Let's see your ID then slag."

She took out her wallet from her bag and was opening it when the officer lost patience and snatched it from her. He got back into the front of the car, read the ID, checked the number with his computer, checked it again then handed it to his partner in the driving seat.

"Oh shit!" he swore.

The driver turned to look at Rebecca then back at the ID.

"You fuck wit! You must know who she is."

"I thought I recognised her face, but she looks different to how she looks on TV."

"Is there a problem officers?" Rebecca asked.

"No problem at all ma'am," replied the fat patrolman. "Your ID is in order and you have a valid curfew exemption."

"I know that," replied Rebecca, "I would however like to know what you meant earlier when you spoke of negotiations."

The fat man's face fell, then he forced it into a sickly smile.

"That was just my little joke ma'am."

"I did not find it very funny. You called me a bitch and a slag and you hurt my arm while manhandling me into the car. If I'm injured and can't perform tomorrow night Mr Newman will want to know why."

"I am very sorry ma'am, I didn't know it was you."

"That is no excuse. You should have established my identity before physically and verbally abusing me. I'm sure President Bryant will be extremely unhappy when I tell him about this."

"Please ma'am, I really am sorry."

"Perhaps we should see you home," the driver suggested. "It is late and it isn't safe for you to be out alone."

"That would be very good of you. I have had a rather unpleasant evening and I'm very tired."

They drove through the empty streets passing only a couple of black cabs and another patrol car. The two officers remained in chastened silence throughout the journey. Secretly Rebecca was glad to have met with corrupt and incompetent officers. Had she been stopped by a more dutiful patrolman she would have been obliged to find an excuse for being alone in that part of town. Also the gratification of seeing their faces when they discovered who she was had been worth the slight bruise on her arm. She had worked hard and made many sacrifices for the small amount of power she possessed and exercising it over these two officers, who no doubt regularly abused their own authority, gave her some pleasure.

Her satisfaction did not last long however. As soon as she returned to her own apartments her mood began to sink. The Man's letters were still lying on the coffee table. She tore them to shreds and tossed them into the bin. She crossed to the window and looked out, searching the shadows for the masked man. She did not see him but that was not enough to convince her he was not there. She checked the locks on each of the doors and windows twice over.

She made a cup of tea and tried to relax, but she could not. From what the masked man had said it was evident that he had been watching her closely for some time. She could easily alert the theatre security and Bryant's protection officers but to do this she would either have to lie or admit how foolish she had been. Though The Man made her nervous she was not as angry with him as she was with herself. Whoever he was he was probably some kind of inadequate unable to form normal relationships so had become obsessed with her. It was not as though she had never encountered this kind of behaviour before. The only difference was that this time the stalker had written beautiful, eloquent letters instead of semi-literate or obscene emails.

Before finally going to bed she reached a decision. If The Man heeded her warning and she received no more letters or gifts she would not mention him to anyone. If however he did write again then she would alert theatre security and tell them just as much as was necessary to prevent him from having any further contact. Hopefully this way she would not even have to lie, just withhold certain facts.

In spite of forming this resolution she still slept badly. The next morning she felt tired and depressed and her head ached. The weather was sunny with a light breeze so she took a walk in the hope that fresh air would make her feel better. She strolled aimlessly at first along The Strand towards Trafalgar Square but then decided to head for Martin Ashdown's flat in Soho. Martin had recently moved from his old abode in Clapham to luxurious and fashionable rooms in a newly refurbished block. His rent was only marginally less extortionate than her own as he lacked the view over the Thames.

Martin was not an early riser and although it was after ten, when Rebecca arrived he still was not dressed. However he did not mind Rebecca seeing him in his underpants so invited her up. He served strong black coffee for them both and attempted to assemble the ingredients for breakfast. He had cereal but no milk so converted some stale bread into toast.

"I thought gay men were supposed to be good with domestic stuff," remarked Rebecca.

"That is just one of the many pieces of crap that people say about us, you know, like us all being child molesters and having Aids."

Rebecca scraped the mould off the top of the jam then spread some on her toast.

"Have you heard from Jason at all?" she asked.

"No but I hear on the grapevine that he has set the date for the wedding. It's probably best that I just let him get on with it, try to keep it as clean a break as possible."

"Yes I expect that will be best."

"You didn't come over to talk about my love life though. What's on your mind?"

She told him all about her meeting with The Man Behind the Mask on Sunday night and about the previous evening. She told him that she was frightened now that she knew The Man had been stalking her and how angry she was with herself, how ashamed she was of her own foolishness and how afraid that others might learn of it. Martin listened but his response was not what she had been expecting.

He shrugged and replied coldly, "When you are dating two men at once it is bound to blow up in your face."

"I wasn't dating him."

"I doubt Bryant would see it that way."

"Since when have you cared about John Bryant? I seem to recall it was you who persuaded me to go on Sunday."

"I just encouraged you to do what you wanted to do. Don't blame me if you don't like the consequences."

"I'm not blaming you. I just want to know what you think I should do."

"Do about what?"

"About this masked freak who has been spying on me. Haven't you been paying attention?"

"Honestly Becky! We are all being spied on; at work, walking in the streets, our computers and phones are being monitored and even our neighbours, colleagues and friends are being encouraged to watch us to make sure we are behaving ourselves. And you are worried about one man!"

"One creep who is completely obsessed with me."

"You have something in common then."

"What?"

"You are completely obsessed with you. There are so many bad things happening in the world and you only care about your own trivial little problems."

"Well I'm sorry I bothered you. I didn't realise you were busy saving the world or I wouldn't have dreamed of disturbing you."

"Save the sarcasm, just watch this."

He retrieved the TV remote from down the back of the sofa and played a recording of an interview with Harriet Jacobs, the Minister for Social Reform.

"Changing the laws on homosexuality has done a great deal both to control disease and preserve moral values," Jacobs was saying, "but we still have much to do in order to eradicate sexual perversion entirely."

"Why are you showing me this crap?" asked Rebecca.

"Just listen," Martin instructed.

"The problem we have now is that sexual deviants have been driven underground but are continuing their selfish and socially damaging behaviour, just in a less obvious fashion," Jacobs continued. "We need to have the courage, as a nation, to say we will not accept this and we will take action to prevent it. These people need to know that if they break the law they will be found out and punished."

The interviewer asked, "But how are these people going to be found out if they commit crimes in secrecy?"

"We will be relying on members of the public to come forward with information," replied Jacobs. "There will be people watching this programme now who know of sexual deviants in their neighbourhood or at their workplace. What the government is trying to do is make it easier for those people to speak out. At present people remain silent out of fear and ignorance. There are certain attitudes that are a hangover from last century, a general feeling that we must tolerate behaviour we do not like so long as it happens behind closed doors. This is simply not true. We all have the right and the duty to speak out against what we know is wrong."

"Do you want to hear her plans to encourage snitching or shall I turn it off?" Martin asked.

"I've heard quite enough thank you," Rebecca replied. "Please turn it off, that woman makes me feel sick."

"So you see Harriet the Hatemonger wants us all to spy on each other now."

"You're not worried are you?"

"Of course I'm worried. You have no idea what it is like to live your life in fear, hiding who you really are, terrified that a careless word or action could give you away."

"Oh Marti," she said, reaching out to embrace him.

He pushed her away answering, "Don't 'Oh Marti' me! Do you think a hug and a few kind words are going to make it all better?"

"No I don't, but what can I do? Believe me, if there was anything I could do I would do it."

"Yeah anything so long as it involves no risk or inconvenience for you."

"If that is what you really think Martin then I might as well go."

"Yes do. You didn't come to hear about my problems, just to whine about yours."

"I'm sorry I disturbed you but I made the mistake of thinking we were friends. I'll see you later."

Martin did not even say goodbye as she walked out. The earlier sunshine had disappeared and the sky was becoming greyer by the minute. When she was almost home it began to rain, a light drizzle at first but steadily becoming heavier. Rebecca was so deeply engrossed in her thoughts that she hardly noticed the weather and by the time she had made it to her building she was soaked through.

Once inside her own living-room she gave way to the depression that was engulfing her. She collapsed onto her sofa, buried her face in her hands and cried. There were very few people in the world she considered real friends but she had thought Martin was one. His accusations of selfishness hurt her, particularly because she knew there was some truth in them.

Rebecca very rarely cried. She hated the way it made her head ache and her face go red and blotchy so never allowed herself to indulge in tears for long. She was soon drying her eyes and washing her face. She made a cup of tea and tried to decide what to do with the rest of the day. She knew that if she stayed at home brooding over her stalker and the quarrel with Martin she would make herself even more miserable. She made up her mind to spend the afternoon at the health club. She would go for a long swim then have a massage and a manicure.

She carried out her plan and although it did not completely take her mind off her problems it at least kept her from dwelling on them. She went to the theatre that evening feeling a little better but on entering her dressing-room she saw she had received another letter. This time there were no gifts or flowers, just the envelope lying on her dressing-table.

She tore it open and read.

My Dear Rosa,

I am so very sorry to have upset you. I assure you I am not a stalker and would like to explain how I know so much about you. Would you please agree to meet me again? Leave a reply for me here if you consent. I beg you to give me the chance to acquit myself of the crimes with which you have charged me. Do not be so cruel as to allow me no defence. Don't break my heart.

Yours forever
The Man Behind the Mask

Without giving the contents of the letter a moment's thought Rebecca took it down to the security desk.

"Mac, who has been in my dressing-room since I left last night?" she asked.

"Just the cleaner, why?"

"Someone keeps leaving these letters for me."

She thrust the paper in McKay's hand.

"You found this in your dressing-room?"

"Yes and there have been several before this."

"But apart from you and Ms Reed only security and the cleaning staff have access to your dressing-room."

"I know that Mac. Either the cleaner or someone from security is doing it."

McKay checked the entry log for her dressing-room on his computer.

"Are you sure it was since last night?"

"Yes I'm certain. It wasn't there when I left and it was on my table when I arrived a few minutes ago."

"It's just that they only person who has been in since you left yesterday evening was Mrs Bridges the cleaner and I doubt she would be writing to you."

"Then someone else must have given her the letter. I would like you to have a word with her. I didn't mind at first, they were just letters, but it has become apparent that the writer is stalking me. I want you to check the basement as well, because I know he's been down there."

"I remember you saying something a few weeks ago about seeing someone in the stores, but didn't you decide it was just your imagination?"

"That was what I thought at the time but now I am not so sure. This guy is a complete psycho and I want him stopped."

"I understand. I'll speak to all the security staff and cleaners. I'll search the basement personally and I'll put up a camera right outside your door. Does that put your mind at rest?"

"Yes, thank you Mac."

MY CONDITION
The Man Behind the Mask

If you knew how you infect my brain
You would doubtless pity this poor invalid.
In wakefulness I strive to cast you from my thoughts.
I labour and strain and sweat and toil.
For some brief space of hours I may succeed,
But on lying down my weary form
My sleepwalking mind goes in search of you.

Thursday 29th March

The next day Rebecca was relieved to find no more letters. McKay assured her he had searched the basement and found no signs of an intruder. He had also warned all the security guards and cleaners to look out for The Man, and threatened anyone who was helping him with disciplinary action. Rebecca sincerely hoped this would have the desired affect and The Man would leave her alone, but she remained anxious and depressed.

On Friday she met Bryant at the Courtyard Café of the Newman Grand for afternoon tea. The President was leaving for his constituency shortly but would be back again on Sunday night. Bryant was still in the same high spirits as he had been on Monday evening; he was so busy talking and joking that it took him a while to notice that Rebecca was not equally cheerful.

"What's the matter with you?" he eventually asked, "we hardly ever get to spend time alone together and here you are sulking."

"I'm not sulking."

"You've hardly said a word. It isn't easy for me to find time to see you between the demands of my work and my family. When I do you could at least make an effort to be pleasant company."

"I'm sorry. I've got a few things on my mind at the moment."

"Like what? What to wear for your next TV interview!"

"No, like this weirdo who has been stalking me."

"What weirdo?"

"The one who writes the letters. You remember, the ones you thought that James Hutchens was writing. Well I'm certain it isn't Hutchens. This guy is unbalanced. He's obsessed. He's been watching me and following me."

"When has he followed you? Where has he been watching you?"

"I don't know."

"Then how do you know he's doing it?"

"Some of the things he said, stuff he knew about me, he could only know it if he had been stalking me."

"You've told theatre security about this?"

"Of course."

"Then I'm sure there's nothing to worry about, but I could have a couple of my guys keep an eye on your apartment if you would like."

"Thanks but I've spoken to the building manager and regular security patrols are on the lookout so it probably isn't necessary."

"I'm surprised that you are letting this get you down. You've had stalkers before."

"I suppose it is just because this man's letters seemed so nice to begin with. I'm disappointed that he turned out to be just another creepy freak."

"Honestly, women! You are all such suckers for a bit of romance."

"And what is wrong with a bit of romance? It isn't illegal is it? Or does craving romance make one a sexual deviant nowadays? Perhaps you ought to report me."

"You saw the interview with Harriet Jacobs then?"

"I did. You're sinking pretty low aren't you? Encouraging people to tell tales on their neighbours and work colleagues is going to open up a whole can of worms. Every time someone is pissed off with their boss or fed up with the noise next door they'll just call up the hotline and cry sexual deviant."

"I agree with you entirely. This wasn't my idea, it was all Jacobs and her office."

"But you must have approved it."

"Correct. People like having someone to hate. They need a healthy outlet for their frustrations."

"You call queer bashing a healthy outlet?"

"No one is going to be bashing anyone. I'm just going to let Harriet get everyone worked up about sexual deviants, then after a few arrests and a few high profile trials society feels better. Making people feel better is why I went into politics."

"No it isn't!"

"Well perhaps not, but it is what I like to tell journalists."

*

On Saturday afternoon, Rebecca arrived at the theatre to prepare for the matinee. She and Martin had barely spoken a word to each other since their falling out, so when she saw him in the corridor while on her way to her dressing-room she was going to walk straight past him. She was surprised when he stopped her.

"Becky have you got a minute?"

"Yes I suppose. What's up?"

"For a start I would like to apologise for the other day. I was upset but I know that is no excuse. I let Horrible Harriet get to me and I shouldn't have taken it out on you."

Rebecca was more than ready to forgive him and replied, "It's all right. I shouldn't keep bothering you with my trivial problems when I know you have plenty of your own."

"Don't say that. I was completely in the wrong. I was utterly vile to you and I'm really sorry. How are things with the old masked man anyway?"

"Quiet. I'm hoping he's got the message and is going to leave me alone."

"I'm glad. Now we have cleared the air I am just dying to tell you my fantastic idea for the show."

"Go on then?"

"I'll tell you in your dressing-room, you ought to sit down. This is so brilliant it might blow you away!"

Rebecca led him to her room and they made themselves comfortable.

"So what is this idea?" she asked.

"We are all going to be animals."

"Animals! What sort of animals?"

"All sorts. I've discussed it with Nikolai and he loves it. The Tumbling Troop are going to be monkeys, the jugglers, dogs and Hannah Hula a cat. I'm not sure how they will feel about that but they can always change if they can come up with a better idea. We thought Claire could be a rabbit then Anton could pull her out of his hat or something, and perhaps he should be a fox."

"What about Randolph?"

"A lion of course."

"I doubt he would be satisfied with anything else."

"No I'm sure he wouldn't. By the way have you heard the rumour?"

"What rumour?"

"Apparently his real name is Kevin Pratt."

"No wonder he tries to keep that a secret. So what are we going to be?"

"I thought for our double act we could be cats. Not pussy cats like Hannah but leopards or tigers, something like that."

"Brilliant, you could be a leopard and I could be a panther, or vice versa. And for our solo acts?"

"I'm not sure. How do you fancy being a bird?"

"What sort of bird? I'm not being a pigeon for any money!"

"I was thinking a bird of prey."

"That's more like it. A falcon or a golden eagle perhaps. How about you?"

"This is the best part. I'm going to be a snake. Something deadly like a cobra. And I'm going to scare the punters out their seats!"

"Would that involve pyrotechnics by any chance?"

"Hell yes! I've been talking to the experts and we have some fantastic stuff planned. That must be such a great job, blowing stuff up for a living. I'm going to get them to teach me all about it so when I'm too old and creaky to do back-flips any more I will have a whole new career open to me."

"You're a complete pyromaniac Marti! It is possible to do a crowd pleasing routine without setting fire to anything."

"Where's the fun in that?"

Ami Reed arrived to do Rebecca's hair and make-up so Martin departed for his own dressing-room. He left Rebecca in better spirits than she had been in a long time. Not only was she pleased that they were friends again but his ideas for the show had renewed her enthusiasm.

Since Circus Britannia had been based at the Newman Grand they had been constantly changing and renewing the production so that the same audiences would keep coming back to see something new. The show never ran for more than three months without some major changes. The last had been Rebecca's own act and the finale less than a month ago but a complete revamp of the entire circus was planned for the summer. They would close for about a month and then reopen with completely new routines, costumes, music and even some new performers.

When Rebecca first joined the circus she had loved the creative process of redeveloping the show, but as the years went by her enjoyment had diminished. Recently she had begun to feel that she was running out of ideas. Each new routine that she put together was almost the same as an old one and although the critics were not yet complaining she knew it would not be long before they were.

It was exactly what had happened to Dimetri. His performances had become dull and repetitive so Rebecca had replaced him as the star. She fully expected that very soon Martin Ashdown would be succeeding her, but unlike Dimetri she planned to step aside gracefully and give him her support. She did not know when this time would come but it could not be more than a couple of years away.

In the meantime she was looking forward to creating a routine in which she could soar like an eagle. Having this gem of an idea, a piece of inspiration to start from, made the process of inventing something new much easier. Trying to build a routine out of nothing, with no theme to structure it around, was far more difficult than when she knew what she was aiming for. If Martin continued to come up with clever ideas he might have a future as circus director rather than as a pyrotechnician.

*

Bryant had arranged that he and Rebecca were to dine together at Downing Street on Sunday evening. In the morning he called her to say that Philip Graysby would be joining them. Rebecca was glad of the opportunity to find out more about Graysby but she thought it a little odd since Bryant had recently been complaining how little time they had alone together. She mentioned this to Bryant while they were awaiting Graysby.

"There is a little matter I was hoping you could help me with," he explained. "I require your feminine intuition."

"What for?"

"I like Phil, I think he's a good man, capable of thinking for himself and could go a long way, but there is something about him that worries me. He isn't married, and doesn't as far as I know have a girlfriend. He says he is too dedicated to his work and doesn't have time for relationships, but I want to be sure."

"You're worried that he is gay? What has that got to do with me? Why don't you set Harriet Jacobs and her gang of witch-hunters on him?"

"The fact is my dear, I don't give a damn if he's an arse bandit or not, I'm only worried about the potential embarrassment if he is and it is found out."

"Have you tried asking him?"

"He's hardly going to tell me."

"Probably not, but he isn't very likely to confide in me either."

"He doesn't have to confide in you. Just flash your legs at him a bit and if his trousers start bulging we'll know on which side his bread is buttered."

"That doesn't sound like a very scientific method."

"It may not be scientific but it is pretty damn effective."

"Let me get this straight. Your theory is that if any man does not find me so irresistibly attractive that he gets an erection just looking at me he must therefore be gay!"

"That's about it, yes."

"Well I'm flattered John, I really am but I can't help feeling that you exaggerate my sexual magnetism."

"Rubbish. Either he's a red-blooded male and wants to give you one or he isn't. I've arranged to be interrupted by an important phone call after dinner. That should give you the opportunity to do a little subtle probing."

"If your theory is correct and he is not gay then he's the one who will be doing the probing given half a chance."

"I'm sure you can handle him."

"I'm sure I can, but I'd rather not have to."

They were unable to discuss the subject further as the man in question arrived. Bryant greeted him with much handshaking and hearty back slapping, showing his affection in as manly and heterosexual a way as possible. He took Rebecca's hand and kissed her briefly on the cheek demonstrating neither discomfort nor an uncontrollable desire to tear her clothes off.

Graysby first asked after Bryant's family and then they discussed the business of their constituencies over pre-dinner drinks. While they ate Bryant sought Graysby's opinion on Harriet Jacobs's recent interview. Although Graysby did not openly disapprove his praise for Jacobs was decidedly lukewarm.

"It was a very good interview and I think it was well received by the public," he said, "but Harriet's problem is she almost always speaks on the same subject. So far she has done very well in promoting anti-gay sentiment but if she constantly harps on about sexual deviants people are just going to get bored."

"So you think it is time she changed her tune and got another string to her bow," said Bryant.

"Perhaps, or perhaps it's time we stopped flogging a dead horse."

Rebecca wondered if Graysby had deliberately thrown in another metaphor in order to confuse the President. Could Graysby be hoping to give Bryant enough rope to hang himself?

"What would you suggest?"

"I think it is time we were really bold and scrapped the post altogether. We don't need a Minister for Social Reform any more. Society has been reformed. Whatever responsibilities Jacobs has can easily be divided between Health, Education and Justice. There can't be any harm in announcing a victory can there?"

"There are some in the party who feel our social reforms haven't gone far enough."

"I know the people you mean and I confess I haven't much time for them. Since the Phoenix Party came to power we have dealt with the major social issues affecting the nation's prosperity. We have population growth under control, we have drastically reduced the number of single parent families sponging off the state and we have made huge advances in stopping the spread of STDs. I don't see how meddling in people's relationships and policing their morals is going to profit anyone."

"Your problem Phil is that you only think in terms of economics."

"I don't see that as a problem. Successful leaders make their country richer and anyone who tries to tell you that wealth doesn't make you happy has obviously never been really poor."

Bryant obviously could not find an argument to counter this so he changed the subject completely.

"You should get your face on TV more," the President suggested, "raise your profile."

"I'm doing a couple of interviews next week," Graysby replied.

"No one watches those serious political shows you do. Do a bit of light entertainment, you know, a guest spot on a cookery show or that gardening programme."

"I don't feel I'm cut out for that sort of thing. I'm too boring."

"Then get someone to teach you how not to be boring. Rebecca, you're the expert. You can show him how it's done."

"I don't know about that, but I am doing 'My Kitchen' next month. The idea is that I teach the viewers how to cook my favourite recipe. I did tell the producers that I don't actually know how to cook anything but they said that wasn't a problem, they'll think of something for me. As long as I wear a low cut top and lean forward they will be happy."

"I don't think that will work for me," replied Graysby.

"Go for the sentimental approach," Bryant suggested, "Say you are going to cook your favourite dish from childhood just like dear old granny used to make, then go all dewy-eyed while you reminisce about the halcyon days of your youth."

"I'm not sure I could do dewy-eyed."

"It's easy, just look sad and dab your eyes like this," Bryant said demonstrating. "Dear old Nana. No one can make dumplings the way she did. I still miss her whenever I see a stew."

"That's brilliant," Rebecca replied laughing. "Do you mind if I use that? Both my grandmothers died before I was born and my mum was a worse cook than I am but hey, who's to know?"

"Tell you what," suggested Graysby, "I will study Rebecca's appearance on the show very carefully then I will work on a performance of my own. Speaking of performances, how are things at the circus?"

While they finished the meal Rebecca talked about her work and told them about the ideas for the new show. Although Bryant seemed to be nodding off Graysby appeared genuinely interested. He asked many questions and soon Rebecca was telling him the whole story of her career. Graysby was so interested in all that she had to say that they remained at the table much longer than Bryant had intended. They had only just adjourned to the living-room for coffee when the promised phone call came in. Bryant excused himself leaving Rebecca wondering how to tackle the task he had set her.

"Would you like a drop of something in that coffee?" she asked, hoping a little more alcohol might make her job easier.

They had already had gin and tonic before dinner and shared out a bottle of wine with the meal but Graysby was quite willing to have a generous measure of brandy added to his cup. When she poured a smaller measure in her own she sat on the sofa beside him.

"John says you're not married," she remarked, fearing it sounded like an accusation.

"No I'm not," he replied.

"Have you a girlfriend?"

"Not at present. I'm married to my job and I find most women aren't prepared to come second all the time."

"You must have needs though, certain natural urges if you know what I mean?"

"You mean sex? Is there really an important phone call or is this some kind of test? Has John left us alone together to see if I can be trusted with his girlfriend?"

"Something like that, only kind of the opposite. John is worried you might be gay so left us alone together in the hope that you will prove you are not."

"I see. So all this time that I have been taking great care not to flirt or behave towards you in any way that John might find offensive, I have in fact been incriminating myself."

"You've got it."

"So would a few sexist and offensive remarks about the length of your skirt suffice or do I have to physically throw myself at you to exonerate myself?"

She laughed and answered, "How about I just tell him that we talked and I don't think you're gay?"

"That would be kind of you, but I would not want you to be offended by my failure to make a fool of myself. After all, you are so beautiful you must be used to men falling at your feet. I am quite happy to assume the position."

He put down his coffee and knelt beside her.

"This really isn't necessary," she said, giggling.

"But I'm enjoying myself now!"

He pulled off her shoe and kissed her foot and ankle noisily.

"Stop it!" she protested without the slightest conviction, laughing so much she could hardly speak.

Of course this was the moment Bryant returned to the room. Graysby laughed so much he could not stand up.

When eventually he regained his self-control and got to his feet he said, "John, I am terribly sorry. I wish I could say this isn't how it looks but I'm afraid I can't. I can only excuse myself by saying that I have had far too much to drink and I think it is time I went home."

Rebecca was still giggling tipsily so could say nothing.

"Yes I think perhaps that would be best," agreed Bryant.

Phil shook hands with his host and said, "Thank you for a delicious dinner and a very pleasant evening."

Then he kissed Rebecca on the cheek with far greater warmth and enthusiasm than he had when he had greeted her and said, "Goodnight Rebecca. Thank you very much for not slapping me! I beg your pardon and hope I will see you again soon."

"Goodnight Phil," she replied, giving him an affectionate embrace. "You are forgiven, this time, but don't push your luck!"

He departed, leaving Bryant stony faced and glaring at Rebecca in mute disapproval.

"What?" she demanded, "That was what you wanted wasn't it? Concrete evidence of his heterosexuality!"

"A little too concrete!" Bryant complained.

"I can't help it, I'm irresistible, remember. You said so."

His face softened into a smile and he put his arms around her.

"Right, you are, and I'm the luckiest man alive because I don't have to resist you."

He kissed and caressed her with far more tenderness that he had shown in months.

"I love you," he said.

He did not use the 'L' word very often, but when he did he meant it. Rebecca could not bear to lie to him when he was being sincere so she answered him with a kiss. They went to bed and for once she did not have to fake it. Afterwards, as she lay in his arms she reflected that although he was by no means a good person there were many worse. Perhaps with the help of Graysby he could be a better President and with a little gentle persuasion from her he could be a better man.

Part 3

Circus Britannia

Wednesday 6th June 2103

In the auditorium of the Newman Grand theatre a very select audience was watching the first ever performance of Rebecca's Golden Eagle routine. Her costume was still being made so she was wearing just a plain leotard, but even so she created the illusion of soaring flight as she swung through the air on the trapeze. After executing a final release and double somersault she landed, paused for a moment to catch her breath, then descended from the stage to speak with her audience.

"So what did you think?" she asked.

"Fantastic," said Rajesh of the Tumbling Troop, "I love the contrast between the fast and slow elements of the routine."

"Me too," seconded Hannah. "With the costume it will be even better."

"It's a really great routine," Luchenko agreed, "but it needs a better ending."

"I know," Rebecca answered, "but I want to save some of my best moves for the finale."

"I wouldn't worry too much about repetition," Luchenko said, "most of the audience won't notice."

"I wanted to ask you about the running order," Rebecca said.

"It hasn't been decided yet," he answered, "but I assume you will close the show as usual."

"That was what I wanted to talk to you about. You see, I think my other routine with Marti is much better than this one and perhaps that should be the last act before the finale."

Luchenko turned to Martin who was seated beside him with his feet up on the back of the seat in front.

Martin shrugged and said, "It's up to you, you're the boss."

"We'll try it out when we do the full run through," Luchenko proposed. "If it works we'll go with it."

"Unless you want to put Marti's solo act at the end," Rebecca suggested. "You've seen it now, I'm sure you agree it is really something."

"It is," Luchenko responded, "but you are still our star Rebecca. You are the one most people will have come to see. Any ideas for the finale yet?"

"Nothing much."

Aware that a number of impatient stage-hands were lurking in the wings wanting to prepare for that night's production Luchenko suggested, "How about we all go and brainstorm over a coffee?"

"OK, but I'll shower and change first."

"Me too," said Martin, who had also been demonstrating his routine.

"We'll meet you in the Courtyard then," said Luchenko.

The Circus was now closed while they worked on the new production but the theatre was still in full-time use, staging a new musical about London during the Blitz. Most of the circus artists had to share their dressing-rooms with members of the musical theatre company, but as stars of their show Rebecca and Martin were privileged to still have exclusive use of theirs.

As they were on their way up the stairs Rebecca said, "You were very quiet just now. You think my routine is crap don't you?"

"I don't," he protested.

"Please tell me honestly what you think," she begged.

"I think it is good but not one of your best by a long way."

"And nowhere near as good as yours?"

"I wasn't going to say that."

"You don't have to. It's a fact. That is why I suggested Luchenko ought to move you up the bill, but it seems he's not ready to do that yet."

"I'm not bothered about the billing. What I would like though is to know how it feels to take centre stage in the finale, to have the house on its feet and cheering for me. I would love to find out what that is like, even if it was only once."

"It will happen soon enough I promise you. Just wait until Luchenko sees the reaction to your routine. I bet you a hundred pounds that by the time we go on tour you and I will be taking our bows together, and I bet you anything you like that by this time next year your name will be down as the star act."

Martin did not seem especially pleased with her predictions, perhaps not believing them. His mood had been extremely changeable for the past few weeks. Sometimes he was vociferous and so full of energy he was almost manic, then suddenly he would be morose and gloomy as he was today. Though Rebecca had often asked him what was troubling him he had not confided in her. Perhaps he had difficulties with his love life or maybe it was just the constant persecution of homosexuals that Harriet Jacobs had saturated the media with at present. She hoped the mood swings were not a symptom of anything more sinister, an illness or a drug problem.

She entered her dressing-room and took down her hair. It felt greasy with perspiration as she ran her fingers through it. As she tossed the hair band down on the dressing-table she saw a familiar looking envelope out the corner of her eye. It was weeks since she had received her last message from The Man Behind the Mask and she had almost succeeded in putting him out of her mind.

She reluctantly picked up the letter. It said "Rosa" on the front in The Man's usual hand but underneath in capitals was written "IMPORTANT" and underlined. Had it not been for this she would probably have taken it down to security unopened, but although she was annoyed she was also curious. She read the letter.

Dear Rosa,

Forgive me for writing to you again but I must give you this warning. Your life is in danger. I have heard a rumour of an intended bomb attack on the Newman Grand. I do not know any of the details but I suspect the President is the intended target. If he is to be at the reopening of the circus I beg you not to be present.

Please believe that your safety is my only concern.

The Man Behind the Mask

As soon as she had finished reading she ran straight down to the security desk. McKay was not there and a young man she did not know was on duty.

"Who has been in my dressing-room in the last hour?" she demanded.

"No one," replied the young man looking confused and alarmed.

"Someone must have been in there," Rebecca responded angrily. "This letter was not there when I went in to change just before two but it was just now. Who put it there?"

The security guard checked the entry log and reviewed the footage from the camera in the corridor.

"Apart from you no one has been in or out of your dressing-room and Martin Ashdown was the only other person to pass the door."

Rebecca was furious, convinced the young man was either a part of the conspiracy or just incompetent.

"Get McKay," she demanded, "I want to speak to him at once."

"He isn't here. He won't be in until four."

"Then get him here! No better still, who is McKay's boss?"

"Terry Craven is overall head of security for the complex but... "

"Call Mr Craven and tell him I want to talk to him right now."

"Mr Craven doesn't... "

"Call him now or do I have to call Sam Newman and tell him how useless his staff are?"

The young man was sufficiently intimidated to make the call. Rebecca listened carefully to his half of the conversation, determined that she was not going to be fobbed off.

"Mr Craven, this is Craig Roberts from theatre security. I have Miss Clayton here and she wants to see you immediately... She really wants to see you personally... No I don't think it can wait... She seems very upset... She says she will call Sam Newman... Thank you sir, she'll be over at once."

Rebecca realised she was still wearing only her leotard and dashed back upstairs to put something more decent on. On the way she passed Martin.

"Hey Becky, what are you doing? You aren't even dressed yet."

"Tell the others I'll catch up with them later. Something has come up."

"What's the problem?"

"Later. No time to talk now."

She threw on her linen trousers and sandals and hurried over to the offices at the back of the hotel complex. Terry Craven was in his office waiting for her. His appearance was not impressive. He was short, fat and bald. His suit was crumpled and even though the air conditioning was on full he was perspiring. He held out a limp, damp hand for Rebecca to shake.

"What can I do for you Miss Clayton?" he asked with an insincere smile.

"I want to talk to you about an appalling lapse in security," Rebecca began. "Someone has been accessing my dressing-room on a regular basis and your staff seem completely incapable of stopping them."

"I did get McKay's report on this matter and I understood it had been dealt with."

"McKay assured me it had but today I received this."

She gave Craven the letter and he perused it briefly.

"This is no doubt an empty threat," he said. "There is no way that any attack on the Newman Grand complex could succeed."

"I wouldn't be so sure. This man can get in and out of the theatre whenever he pleases; what is to stop him blowing the place up while he's at it?"

"We have a very sophisticated security system Miss Clayton. As well as security cameras and round the clock surveillance we have highly advanced scanners on every entrance and at several positions within the buildings. They are capable of detecting any kind of weapons or explosives. Any deliveries to the complex are x-rayed and any suspicious packages searched."

"I know all this, but someone is slipping through your elaborate system. What are you going to do about it?"

"It should not be too difficult to determine who is delivering these letters. I'm sure Mr Roberts could have helped you with that. All you need him to do is find out who has accessed your dressing-room in the period... "

Rebecca interrupted angrily, "Mr Roberts denies that anyone has been in my room and yet still this letter appeared! Either this man has some other way of getting in or Mr Roberts is lying. You had better find out which, and find out quickly because the circus reopens in three weeks and President Bryant will be attending the opening night."

"The President has a highly competent security staff of his own who have always been completely satisfied with the safety of this venue."

"We shall see about that."

Rebecca knew she was getting nowhere so walked out without wasting any more breath. She returned to her dressing-room and called Bryant himself. He was not immediately available but she left a message for him and by the time she had showered and dressed he returned her call. She had expected him to be angry with her for disturbing his work but he was extremely sympathetic. He listened patiently as she explained the problem and put her in touch with Chief Inspector Andrew Steel who was responsible for the President's own security. This set wheels in motion and the following morning she attended a meeting with Steel, Craven and McKay.

Andrew Steel was square jawed with grey crew cut hair and a neck so thick he must have to have his shirts made to order. Although strictly speaking he did not have any authority over Craven he was used to being in charge and dictated the agenda without any objection from the others. He began by asking many technical questions regarding the camera and scanner systems, then he questioned Craven about his staff and whether he could be certain of their loyalty.

Rebecca listened without interrupting. She felt reassured by Steel's thorough and competent approach but she was still afraid that they were not taking the threat seriously enough.

"Don't you think we ought to postpone the circus's reopening?" she asked.

"Newman will never agree to that," replied Craven. "He has invested too much money to postpone now."

"Perhaps Bryant should not come then?" Rebecca suggested.

"Bryant will be there," Steel answered. "There is a principle at stake. We can't allow ourselves to be bullied by terrorists. If we respond to this threat it will encourage them to threaten us again. Besides, I agree with Terry that this Man Behind the Mask does not represent a real danger. He is probably just some desperate, attention seeking loner."

That evening Rebecca met Bryant for dinner. Perhaps he was becoming more sensitive with age because when she arrived he said nothing about himself but asked about her problems.

"How did the meeting with Steel go?" he asked.

"Not bad," she replied. "He is going to personally search every inch of the theatre from the basement to the roof and he's going to check up on the staff as well. Wherever the breach is he should find it."

"Good. I hope that puts your mind at rest."

"Sort of."

"Why sort of? What is still worrying you?"

"I don't really know. It's just a nagging feeling that something bad is going to happen."

"That's understandable, you were pretty upset when you called yesterday. Try to put this business out of your mind. Let Steel and Craven worry about it, it's what they are paid for. Concentrate on the new show, because from what you've told me it sounds like it is going to be fantastic."

"You're being awfully sweet tonight John. What's got into you?"

"I'm a sweet kind of guy, aren't I?"

"Not always. Sometimes you are brash, arrogant, insensitive… "

"All right, no need to go on," he interrupted. "Yes I know I'm a pigheaded beast some of the time, well actually most of the time. Let us just say I am putting in a little effort to prevent you from being stolen away by one of my younger rivals."

"What younger rivals?"

"There's Phil Graysby for a start. Or have you forgotten already about the whole toe sucking thing?"

"He wasn't sucking my toes, don't be disgusting! We were just rather drunk and messing about, and anyway the whole thing was your idea."

"I'm not accusing you of anything. I'm just saying that other men are bound to find you attractive and it is possible you may prefer one of them to me."

"It is possible, but you are President, Graysby isn't."

"He could be one day. I'm just hoping it won't be for another ten years or so, when I'm ready to retire. He's a smart man and an asset to the party, but I want to keep him on my side, not on the side of my enemies."

"How do you plan to do that?"

"By making sure he has more to gain as my ally than my rival. I've let him know I have high expectations for him, I can only hope he doesn't get impatient. I'm giving him a leg up, I don't want him to turn round and stab me in the back."

This time Rebecca could not stop herself from laughing.

"What's so funny?" Bryant demanded, oblivious of the image his words had created.

"Nothing, I was just thinking how similar our positions are. We are both going to have to concede our position to someone else, me sooner than you."

"What do you mean?"

"I mean that I don't think I am going to be the star of Circus Britannia for very much longer. Soon I shall be passing the baton on to Martin Ashdown so that he can run with it. At least I don't have to worry about him stabbing me in the back though."

"Martin Ashdown could never be the star. Blokes come to the circus because they want to see a beautiful woman in a skimpy costume, not some guy in tights!"

"Not all of our audience is male."

"No but our friend Newman is, and I don't think Martin will appeal to his taste as much as you did. Face it he only signed the contract with what's his name, the Russian bloke, to get you into bed."

"I don't think that is completely true and Luchenko isn't Russian. His father was Serbian and his mother's English."

"Don't change the subject. Newman knows sex appeal sells tickets."

"Martin has plenty of sex appeal."

"Not to me and not to Newman. Trust me Becky, you will be the star of Circus Britannia for a while yet. If you are going to be replaced it will be by someone with tits."

"Tits are a distinct disadvantage on the trapeze you know."

"But a major advantage on the billboards!"

"They usually doctor the pictures of me to make mine bigger."

"Standard practice, most pictures of me have had a few of the wrinkles airbrushed out before they are released. Clarissa thinks I should have collagen injections but that seems a bit, what's the word?"

"Narcissistic?" Rebecca suggested.

"I was going to say pansified."

"Is that a word?"

"It is if I say it is."

"Speaking of pansies, could we dine on the terrace?"

"With a plague of flies and wasps buzzing around! No thank you!"

"But it's lovely out there, the roses are in bloom, the air smells sweet and the birds are singing. What is the point in having such a beautiful garden if you aren't going to use it?"

"All right, a compromise. We dine inside but have our coffee on the terrace. Will that make you happy?"

"It's a deal."

Friday 29th June 2103

Although Chief Inspector Steel carried out a thorough inspection of the theatre complex as promised, he found nothing of significance. Rebecca received no more messages from The Man Behind the Mask. She wanted to believe that Steel was right and that the bomb threat was just a desperate bid to get her attention, but could not entirely convince herself. She had spoken to Steel several times since the meeting and he assured her that he was taking every precaution and there was absolutely no possibility that a bomber could penetrate the theatre's security.

The opening night was to go ahead as planned. The President and a number of Cabinet ministers would all be in the audience and would attend the VIP party after the show. Rebecca was always nervous during the last couple of days before the first performance of a new show, but this time her nerves were more on edge than usual. She was at the theatre early the morning of the big day. She wanted to check everything: her costume, her make-up, the apparatus and the lighting. She also wanted to speak with Steel one last time, just to be certain every aspect of security was covered. He was overseeing a last search of the complex but was happy to take time out to reassure her once more.

After this she was to meet Bryant for lunch. She took a taxi to Downing Street and arrived rather earlier than she was expected. The President was still at the House. As it was a beautiful day she said she would wait for him in the garden and asked for some tea to be brought out for her. She hoped a stroll among the plants would help calm her nerves and take her mind off the performance.

The gardener was there again today, deadheading the roses. As ever he seemed oblivious to her when she passed him by. She walked to the pond and back, by which time her tea had been brought. Sitting in a shaded corner of the terrace she sipped it and watched the gardener at work as he snipped his way methodically along the bushes. She grew fidgety sitting still and even though she had not finished her tea she decided to walk again. After a few more circuits around the lawns and pond she heard Bryant's voice calling her.

She crossed back over the grass and ascended the stone steps to the terrace. The gardener had now worked his way around the bushes at that end of the lawn and was up on the terrace removing the faded blooms from the trellis. He seemed just as unconscious of the President standing in the doorway as he had been of her presence. She passed close to him at the top of the stairs and was about to bid him good morning, but he stepped back suddenly and collided with her. He lost his balance and fell against her. She slipped and fell down the steps.

She landed hard, jarring both her wrists and banging her knee. For a moment she was dazed and winded. The gardener was trying to help her up.

"I'm so sorry Miss," he was saying, "I didn't see you. I just stepped back and... "

Bryant pushed the old man out the way and lifted Rebecca to her feet.

"Are you hurt?" he asked. "Should I get a doctor?"

"I think I'm OK," Rebecca replied as she opened and closed each of her hands, testing the range of movements. "I don't think I've broken anything."

Bryant began berating the gardener. "You stupid twat. She could have broken her neck. What is wrong with you? Are you blind and deaf as well as demented?"

"It was an accident sir," pleaded the man, "I was busy working, I didn't know she was behind me."

The old man wore a large floppy sun hat and dark glasses which obscured most of his features but it was evident from his voice that he was greatly distressed. He had a strong accent, possibly Irish.

"Leave him alone John," said Rebecca, "he didn't mean to do it. Let's go inside."

Once in the living-room Rebecca inspected the damage. She had gashed her knee on the edge of the step and there was blood on her cream linen trousers. One of Bryant's domestics was summoned as the duty first aider. She cleaned and dressed the cut and fetched some ice to keep down the swelling.

"I'll have that idiot sacked at once," said Bryant.

"Please don't, it really was only an accident."

"That freak wanders around in those dark glasses without the faintest idea of what is going on around him. The man is a liability."

"He is a good gardener though. No one else in the city has roses like yours. Please don't fire him."

"All right I won't, but I'll be having words with him later. Are you sure you're OK?"

"Yes, just a few bumps and bruises, I'll live."

"What about the show tonight?"

"I think I will still be able to perform. I might need a few painkillers though."

"Newman would go mad if you'd broken something. He'd probably sue me. No use suing the gardener, he won't have any money."

They had their lunch as planned and later that afternoon Rebecca returned to the theatre. She cautiously tried out a few moves and found she could perform without too much pain. She kept a good supply of analgesic and anti-inflammatory drugs in her dressing-room as she was used to performing with minor injuries. She took a few of these then went through her breathing exercises which helped her to relax and focused her mind.

At six o'clock the performers and backstage staff assembled in the auditorium and Nikolai gave his opening night pep talk to the cast and crew. Rebecca barely listened to a word as it was practically the same speech he had given dozens of times before. After he had said his piece, Newman had a few pearls of wisdom to bestow upon them, none of which sparkled with any originality. These formalities completed they separated, the artistes going to their dressing-rooms to change.

As Rebecca's act was not until the end of the first half Ami was attending to some of the others before helping her. While she waited she checked her email and read a little of "Amber" magazine. There was a rave review for her appearance on the cookery show suggesting that if she retired from the circus she could have a promising career as a TV chef.

Ami arrived and seeing the article open on the computer screen remarked, "I thought you said you couldn't cook."

"I can't," Rebecca replied, "but I can pretend and that is all most TV chefs do these days."

"I tried making the bean casserole that you did. It was quite nice actually."

"Perhaps I should give it a go sometime. I've had a set of knives sitting in my kitchen unused since I moved in. I bought them because I thought a kitchen ought to have knives, but they really should have another purpose than decoration."

"Does the President cook?" Ami asked.

"No, he's worse than me. He couldn't even manage tea and toast without the aid of his domestic staff."

As Ami helped Rebecca into her costume she noticed the bruise on her leg, which was now large and bright purple.

"That looks nasty, what happened?"

"I fell down some steps this morning."

"That was bad luck. Is it painful?"

"Only a little, I'll survive. Fortunately it won't show through these tights."

She put on her gold tights and leotard then Ami helped her into the flowing cape, which was shaped to represents the eagle's wings.

"Marti will be on soon," Rebecca remarked, glancing at the clock.

"I saw him getting ready earlier. I don't think I've ever known him so excited."

"Have you noticed he seems… "

Rebecca was about to ask about Martin's recent mood swings but she was interrupted by the blaring wail of the fire alarm.

"Oh Lord! Not tonight!" exclaimed Ami, but her words were inaudible above the siren.

Rebecca followed Ami out the door and towards the stairs. Just as Ami pushed her way through the fire doors, which opened onto the stairwell, someone grabbed Rebecca from behind. She screamed but the doors had already swung closed and her friend could not hear her. The figure in black dragged Rebecca away from the stairs and along the corridor in the opposite direction. She struggled but he clung to her arm so tightly that she could not break free.

Then the whole building buckled and heaved. The floor rose and fell like a breaking wave, the corridor fractured in two and a gaping fissure opened. Before she was even aware she had fallen she was sliding towards the mouth of the crevasse. She could hear nothing but the excruciating ringing in her ears. The Man had hold of her arm again and was pulling her to safety. All the lights had gone out; the only illumination coming from the small glass panel in the door to the stairwell, which flickered with an orange glow.

She was soaking wet and water was pouring down upon them from the sprinklers. The Man was speaking to her as he helped her to her feet but she could not hear what he was saying. He had a torch and guided her through the mess of rubble strewn over the uneven floor. At the far end of the corridor he had to throw himself against the door to force it open. The walls were bending inwards and the door was jammed in the deformed frame.

Eventually the door yielded, opening onto the back staircase which led up to the Skyline Suite. They climbed as quickly as the treacherous stairway would allow. It was slippery with water and littered with ceiling tiles and fragments of the light fittings. The banister had collapsed and steps were fractured and warped. All the time they ascended The Man kept hold of her arm. Frequently her legs threatened to give way, but he propelled her onwards, up and up until they emerged among the wreckage of what was to have been the after show party.

Tables and chairs were upturned and scattered. Broken glass crunched underfoot. She followed The Man as he picked his way across the room. He forced open the door and they stepped out onto the roof terrace. It was not yet fully dark and there was still a rosy glow in the western sky. As the ringing in her ears began to subside, Rebecca could hear sirens coming from the streets below. The Man led her to the edge of the roof. The theatre adjoined the hotel buildings but there was a three storey drop down to the neighbouring rooftop.

"I'll lower you down," said The Man.

Before she could protest he had lifted her over the wall which surrounded the roof terrace and lowered her down the other side. He held her by her arms stretching down as far as he could.

"Ready?" he wheezed.

He let go and she fell. Fortunately the automatic responses programmed by years of aerial acrobatics took over and she landed painfully but without injury. The Man followed, lowering himself over the wall by his arms then dropping. He struck the roof hard, knocking the breath from his lungs. Rebecca stood staring, utterly bewildered as he recovered. She remembered Ami going through the door just moments before the explosion and the sinister orange glow that had followed. She thought of all Craven's and Steel's promises that there was no way anyone could bring a bomb into the complex. She thought of The Man who could enter the theatre without detection and had known that the attack would take place.

"You bastard!" she exclaimed, knowing the word was completely inadequate to describe what he had just done. "You sick bastard. Why?"

Her voice was shrill and close to hysteria.

"You think I did this!" replied The Man Behind the Mask.

"You knew about it. You must have been part of it."

"I told you I heard a rumour, that was all. I did not know who was responsible or how they would do it until moments before the bomb went off. It was me who set off the fire alarm. They were beginning to evacuate just before the explosion and the fire doors were closed. That should have given some of them a chance to get out."

"But who did this?"

"It was Martin Ashdown."

"No. It couldn't have been."

"I worked it out just as he was about to go on stage. No one could get an explosive device past all the scanners but there were huge quantities of explosives in the theatre already, most of them for use in Martin's act. They were all wired to go up at once, taking the whole theatre with them."

"I don't believe it."

"Well, at least you will live to find out the truth."

"Do you want me to be grateful to you? You may have saved my life but you let Ami and god knows how many others die."

"There was nothing I could do."

"You didn't even try to help her."

"What was I supposed to do? Run into the fireball after her? I tried that once, I couldn't do it again."

He pulled off one of his gloves and showed her the mass of scarring on his hand. Even in the dim light she could see he must have been seriously injured sometime in the past.

"I don't just wear this mask to hide my identity you know."

He scrambled stiffly to his feet. Rebecca could find no words. She felt sick with shock and was becoming aware of a throbbing pain in her head and an agonising ache in her wrist.

"We should go now," said The Man. "You're shivering, take this."

He removed his leather jacket and put it around her. He led her to the door which allowed maintenance staff access to the roof.

"Go straight down the stairs and follow the signs to the exit," The Man instructed. "I'll find another way; I don't want to have to answer any questions."

Once inside the building she was deafened by the continuous shrieking of the fire alarm, but the sprinklers had not activated in this part of the complex and there was no evidence of any bomb damage. Her legs were so weak she had to cling to the banister while she descended. She stopped frequently, fearing she would black out. All the time the pain in her head was getting worse and her vision was becoming blurred.

Had it not been for the illuminated signs she would never have found her way to the exit. She came out into the central courtyard somewhere behind the hotel laundry. She was found by a couple of men in uniform but her senses were becoming so indistinct she was not sure if they were security, police or fire crew. They were asking her questions but their words seemed distorted like sounds heard underwater. She allowed her eyes to close and leaned on them for support. She was vaguely aware of being helped into a car. There were sirens and flashing lights, but she kept her eyes shut tight, trying to block out the pounding in her head.

When she opened her eyes again she was at the hospital surrounded by nurses. As she drifted in and out of consciousness they were constantly asking her the most ridiculous questions.

"Do you know where you are?"

"Do you know what the date is?"

And most bizarre of all, "Who is the President?"

After x-rays, scans and tests she was finally allowed to rest. When she woke she was lying in bed in a bright, fresh smelling room, surrounded by flowers. At first she could remember nothing and did not know where she was. Her right arm was in plaster between the elbow and wrist. This must be the hospital. Her mouth was dry and she reached for the water on the bedside. As she did so she caught the heavenly scent of the gorgeous bouquet of pink roses positioned closest to the bed. There was a card with them.

It said, "To Rebecca. Get well soon. Love from John."

It certainly lacked the poetic sentiments of The Man Behind the Mask but if the flowers were from Bryant then he must have survived the blast. She was immensely relieved. She remembered what The Man had told her about Martin being responsible but could not believe it. Where was Marti now? What had happened to him?

While she was trying to comprehend all that had happened a nurse entered.

"Good you are awake," she remarked. "How are you feeling this morning Miss Clayton?"

"My head hurts," Rebecca replied.

"You have a slight concussion. I have some painkillers for you. The doctor will be in to see you shortly."

Rebecca swallowed the tablets and the nurse checked her temperature, pulse and blood pressure. The doctor arrived a few minutes later, a middle-aged woman with grey hair and a reassuring smile. When she had looked in Rebecca's eyes, asked various questions and tested her reflexes and hand eye coordination she pronounced there was no serious harm done.

"We'll keep you in for another night just to be certain but you should be able to go home tomorrow," said the doctor. "The police are waiting to ask you a few questions but I can tell them to come back another time if you don't feel up to it."

"I'll talk to them," Rebecca answered, hoping they might be able to tell her exactly what had happened.

It was not just any constable waiting to take Rebecca's statement. Superintendent Patrick Hunter of MAT Force, the specialist Metropolitan Anti-Terrorism division, had come in person. Rebecca had met Hunter a couple of times before at dinners held by the President. He was someone who rarely smiled and his forehead was creased into a permanent frown, thick black brows partially obscuring his eyes. His remaining hair was dark and his nose was large and crooked. He was accompanied by a female detective, something of a rarity in the police force these days.

Hunter began with a few polite questions about her state of health but small talk was not one of his strong points.

"How much do you remember of what happened last night?" he asked coming to the point.

"I'm not sure," Rebecca replied, "it's all a bit hazy."

"Could you talk us through what you recall from the time you went up to your dressing-room?"

"OK. It was a bit before seven when I entered my room. I was alone for about half an hour until Ami arrived."

"That is your dresser Ami Reed?" Hunter interrupted.

"Yes," answered Rebecca, wondering who else she could possibly mean. "She did my hair and make-up and I was just putting on my costume when the fire alarm sounded. We headed toward the exit. She was in front, I was following."

"You went towards the stairs leading to the ground floor?"

"Yes of course, that is the fire exit."

"Then what happened?"

In gratitude to The Man for saving her life Rebecca decided to say nothing about him unless it was completely necessary.

"That was when the explosion took place."

"You had not yet entered the stairwell?"

"Ami had, I hadn't. She is dead isn't she?"

"The identities of the fatalities are yet to be released."

"She is dead, I know it. There were flames on the other side of the door."

"So the door between you and the stairs was closed, protecting you from the blast?"

"Yes."

"So then what?"

"I couldn't get out down the stairs so I went the other way to the stairs at the far side and up to the Skyline Suite."

"But it must have been pitch black after the bomb took out the electrics. How did you find your way?"

"I'm not sure. I think I just felt my way along the walls."

"And you managed to climb up several flights of stairs in the darkness in spite of the bomb damage?"

"I must have. I don't remember the climb, only arriving in the Skyline Suite."

"Were you alone? Did you see anyone else?"

"I think I was alone."

"By the time you could have reached the Skyline Suite the lower floors of the theatre were engulfed in flames. How did you get out?"

"I went out onto the terrace and jumped down onto the hotel roof."

"That's a long drop!"

"Yes, about the same distance as falling from the trapeze but without a crash mat. I wouldn't recommend it to anyone who does not have acrobatic training."

"So then you came down the back stairs of the hotel?"

"That's right and out into the courtyard where they found me."

"That is quite an incredible escape."

"I suppose so."

"Earlier that evening did you notice anything unusual or was anyone acting strangely?"

"I'm not sure, could you be a bit more specific?"

"Was Martin Ashdown behaving at all suspiciously?"

The mention of Martin's name seemed to confirm her worst fear. She was thinking of what The Man had said and did not answer the question.

"Were you aware that Martin Ashdown was homosexual?" persisted Hunter.

"No I had no idea," Rebecca lied, fearing she did not sound very convincing.

So many thoughts were whizzing around her head, she could not concentrate on what she was saying. She had to clear her mind and focus or she could get herself and others in serious trouble.

"Had you noticed him taking a particular interest in pyrotechnics lately?" continued Hunter.

"Martin has always loved fire in his acts, ever since he first started performing."

"But recently he had been showing an interest in the technical side of how these devices actually worked, is that not so?"

"Yes I suppose he had."

"Had Mr Ashdown seemed depressed or anxious at all in recent weeks?"

"Perhaps. What happened? Is Martin dead?"

"I'm afraid we cannot tell you anything at the moment."

"You wouldn't be asking all these questions if you didn't think he was responsible."

"I think you have told us all that we need for the present. No doubt we will be in touch with you again in a few days. We will leave you in peace now and hope you have a speedy recovery."

As soon as they were gone Rebecca found the TV remote and switched on the news channel. The bombing of the theatre was the only story but solid facts were in short supply. The number of fatalities was yet to be confirmed and none of the dead had yet been named. It seemed that all the VIPs in the audience had escaped unharmed. Bryant had given a speech that morning condemning the attack as cowardly. She was watching a recording of this when the man himself arrived.

"Oh turn that old wind bag off!" he said as he entered her room.

He grasped her left hand and kissed her on both cheeks several times.

"I'm so sorry I wasn't able to come earlier," he apologised, "I had to talk to the police and the press, the usual crap. How are you?"

"I'm OK; I should be out of here tomorrow."

"Good, I'm so relieved that you are all right. After the blast it was total confusion. They knew people were still trapped inside but couldn't get to them. I was so afraid that you were still in there, then the police told me you had been found and I could have wept with joy. How on earth did you get out?"

"I'd rather not talk about it now. I'll tell you some other time. I've just been talking to the police and I'm tired."

"Of course my love. I won't stay long, but I had to see you. Is there anything you want? Some grapes perhaps?"

"I want to know what happened. The police kept asking questions about Marti but they wouldn't tell me anything."

"It will all come out when the investigation is complete."

"Please just tell me, is Martin dead?"

"Martin Ashdown was on stage when the explosion took place. As the blast originated from the stage we can assume he did not survive."

"And the police believe he was responsible?"

"As I understand it, that is the present line of enquiry."

"It must be a mistake. I don't believe Marti would have done this."

"We'll know more when the forensics are completed. Try not to worry about it now. You need to rest sweetheart. I'll come back later if I can."

*

By the following morning the death toll was announced as forty-six while at least a hundred casualties were still being treated. Among the fatalities whose names had now been released were Ami Reed, Anton the magician and his assistant Claire, the young woman known as Hannah Hula and the jugglers Paul and Jake. Also named were the six musicians who performed the circus's musical score, several stage-hands and two other dressers. Martin Ashdown's death was also confirmed but as yet there was nothing on the news to suggest he was a suspect.

Some further details had been released. The fire alarm had been activated exactly forty-seven seconds before the blast, though by whom and why was as yet unknown. Evacuation commenced immediately and the fire curtain between the stage and the auditorium automatically began lowering and was almost closed when the explosion took place. The VIPs seated in the boxes and upper circle had the shortest escape route from the auditorium. Most reached the foyer before the detonation and those who were still inside were screened by the fire curtain. Those seated in the stalls were less fortunate as the force of the bomb was channelled beneath the lowering curtain.

Again for the people backstage it was those few vital seconds between the alarms sounding and the explosion which made the difference between life and death. The artists with ground floor dressing-rooms had time to reach the fire exit while those on the floors above were either caught in the blast or trapped in the burning building. Being partially contained by the fire curtain, the explosion had ripped through the backstage area, taking out several walls and the flames had been funnelled up the stairwell.

Within minutes of the detonation fire crews had gone into the theatre to rescue those trapped but they had been forced to abandon the search as the structure was unsafe. About twenty minutes after the explosion the rear part of the building had collapsed and what had been Rebecca's dressing-room fell through onto the floors below.

Nikolai Luchenko had been pulled from the wreckage just moments before the collapse. As soon as she had been discharged by the doctors Rebecca went to see him. He was conscious and had been moved from intensive care to a private room, but he was completely immobile and every inch of his skin was swathed with bandages. Even his eyes were covered and as his hearing had also been damaged the only way Rebecca could communicate was to lean in close and almost shout.

"Hey Nik, how are you feeling?" she asked.

"Like I've been blown up," he replied speaking overly loud. "Do I look like Tutankhamen's big brother or what?"

"We both had a lucky escape."

"I don't feel very lucky just now. I've lost an arm and an eye so far. Lord knows how much of me there will be left by the time these butchers have finished."

"But at least you are alive."

"I suppose you heard about Martin?"

"The police seem to think he was responsible for this."

"He was. Fuck knows how long he had been plotting this right under our noses."

"No, Martin would never do this. He was our friend."

"I'll tell you exactly what I saw and why I've ended up in this state and you judge for yourself. All right, picture the scene: its opening night and I'm watching the show from the wings. Anton and Claire have just finished their first set and have gone up to change. Randolph goes on stage to do his song while the stage-hands prepare everything for Martin's act. Martin comes down and stands beside me. He tells me he's really excited and can't wait to go out there. Randolph does his big finish, lots of applause and he launches into Martin's introduction. Martin runs out onto the stage, waves, turns a cartwheel and just at that moment the fire alarm sounds.

"The house lights come up, the recorded announcement goes out over the tannoy, the fire curtain starts coming down and the punters are all getting to their feet and fussing. Randolph and all the tech guys head for the door but Martin just stands there right in the middle of the stage as if he is frozen to the spot. So I shout at him. I go out onto the stage and I call to him. He turns around and smiles at me and something inside just screams that I'm in danger. That smile, that look in his eyes, I knew it wasn't a sane man I was talking to.

"As I turned and ran for the door he said something to me but I didn't hear it. I made the mistake of stopping and looking back. I should have carried on running. It was as though nothing had happened and he was just going ahead with his routine. He ran up to the springboard and launched himself into the air. Then that was it! Boom and the whole building was collapsing around me."

"But why?"

"Don't ask me. You knew him better than I did."

"I thought I knew him. It seems I did not know him very well at all."

*

The next day Patrick Hunter made the official announcement. Martin Ashdown had planned and carried out the bombing with help from the theatre's pyrotechnics expert Roger Drayton. They had worked together on the plans for the routine. In their proposal the springboard was to have been wired up to a switch which was supposed to ignite a ring of flame around the stage which would burn for the duration of Martin's performance. Instead the switch had been wired up to detonate the entire gas supply for the ring of fire as well as numerous other charges which had been intended for use later in the routine.

Had the evacuation not already begun and the blast not been partially contained by the fire curtain it is likely that most of the audience would have been killed.

As Drayton had been seen heading for the back door even before the fire alarms had sounded, he was one of the first people to be questioned by the police. He confessed to rigging the bomb but insisted the idea had all been Martin's. A search of Martin's apartment had produced an array of incriminating evidence as Martin had no desire to hide his guilt. He had even left a suicide note saved on his computer, addressed to the police.

The authorised media did not publish or broadcast Martin's final message as it has designated "terrorist propaganda" but it was somehow leaked to RNN who printed it in its entirety. It read:

Dear Police Officers,

I beg you to spare a moment to consider why a young man with a promising career in show business would take his own life and at the same time the lives of so many others. The answer is desperation. President Bryant must die and this seemed the only way to achieve that. As you have no doubt discovered by now I am gay and under the laws of this country I am condemned as a sexual deviant and a criminal. The frustration of my love leads me to hate. To hate the man who has taken away our freedoms and destroyed our democracy. For these crimes he must die.

As for all those innocents who must also die I can only hope that I am releasing them to a better place. May their sacrifice not be in vain and may my actions force upon this country the change we so painfully need.

For myself I will not ask forgiveness as I know I shall not receive it, but perhaps one day, in a better future, I will be vindicated.

Martin Ashdown

Reading this in the privacy of her apartment caused Rebecca to scream aloud in anger at the young man who would never again hear her.

"You stupid, stupid, fool!" she yelled at the walls, "you idiot."

She knew that even if he had killed Bryant, someone just like him, or perhaps even worse, would fill the vacancy. By committing this act of terrorism Martin had justified the government's oppressive regime and given them ammunition in their persecution of homosexuals. The part of his letter which enraged her most was the reference to releasing his victims to a better place. She was certain there was no better place. This dirty, shitty, dying world was all there was. Beyond it was nothing, oblivion. Forty-five people, many of them her friends, had been robbed of their one chance of existence and why? He had achieved nothing.

Rebecca threw herself onto the sofa and pounded the cushions with fury. She replayed in her head all her recent conversations with Martin, looking for some sign that she had missed of what he had been planning. The strangest thing was, in the midst of her anger she bitterly missed him. Though she wanted to hate him for what he had done, for murdering her friends and almost killing her, she could not. She kept seeing his brilliant blue eyes, his crooked smile, hearing his voice, thinking of all the times they had laughed together, the secrets they had shared, the love she had felt for him. Yet their friendship had meant nothing for he had been intending to do this terrible thing and not spoken a single word of it to her.

It hurt so much. Her chest felt as though it was crushing in on her organs and her guts wrenched with misery. She felt so lost and alone that she hardly dared to move from the sofa. She was small and vulnerable in a vast and hostile world and even the smallest task, like going down to the shop on the corner for some milk, seemed too great an ordeal. So she remained without even the comfort of a cup of tea, watching mindless rubbish on the television, trying not to think.

ON READING TOO MUCH TENNYSON
The Man Behind the Mask

On either side the river lie
The GM crops that make birds die,
The lark no longer sings on high,
You have no permit to pass by
You cannot go to Camelot.
Up and down the policemen go
They'll lock you up if you show
An iota of desire to know
The Lady of Shallot.

Faces whiten you start to shiver
Fear of disease makes you quiver,
So down some booze, goodbye liver.
Just who wants to live forever?
There is no Camelot.
Close the borders, shut the ports,
Throw out the nasty foreign sorts
We don't want any impure thoughts
Despoiling our Shallot.

Stone the Muslims, shoot the gays,
Go back to our old-fashioned ways,
The family life of former days
Tolerance was just a phase
To Hell with Camelot.
In tower blocks high are empty rooms
Full of relics, silent as tombs,
In damp corners mildew blooms
Long gone the Lady of Shallot.

Forget freedom and live in fear,
The terrorist threat is present and clear,
Don't think too loud the police are near,
Beware for they might overhear
Foolish dreams of Camelot.
The Utopian Dream is a false ideal
Virtue and justice were never real,
We have no pity left to feel
For the Lady of Shallot.

EVE
Simon Chandra

It may seem odd that I chose to do this interview since the subject never even met Rosa. However, as she knew both The Man Behind the Mask and Martin Ashdown she has vital insight into Rosa's story. Though she now uses another name she used to be called Evelyn Collins. To The Man Behind the Mask she was known as Eve, which was the name she used when she performed at the Tertiary Romantics' Masquerade. She was a singer and songwriter. We met at the Crown and Sceptre which is still regularly used as a venue for similar cabarets and is the place to see new talent. The only difference is that now the shows are well publicised and open to all and not shrouded in secrecy. To begin with I asked her about her music.

"I was very young when I first started writing songs," she told me. "I was one of those solitary children who didn't have many friends at school. I didn't get on with my parents either. I felt like I didn't fit in anywhere. I spent most of my time in my room alone, listening to music, playing my guitar and eventually writing my own songs. I suppose I was trying to figure out who I was and writing songs helped me to do that."

"When did you start performing?" I asked.

"It was after I met my first girlfriend. I had known I was different for a long time of course, but it wasn't until I was eighteen that I acknowledged that I was gay. No one else knew about my songs. It was only once I fell in love that I dared to share them. My partner persuaded me to come to the masquerade with her and I finally found the courage to get up on stage."

"And it was at the masquerades that you met The Man Behind the Mask?"

"Yes but I already knew his poetry from the Real News Forum."

"Did he always wear a mask?"

"Always."

"What was he like?"

"He was kind. He was very supportive and encouraging. He had been performing his work for a couple of years when I started so I appreciated his advice."

"How much did you know about him?"

"Very little, almost nothing. I never knew his real name, where he came from or what he did for a living. We were always careful when we talked not to reveal too much. We talked about music and poetry, and about politics, but not about anything personal."

"How did you meet Martin Ashdown? Did he attend meetings of the Tertiary Romantics?"

"No, it was Roger Drayton who introduced me to Martin. My partner was a member of the Liberation Party and we often went to political meetings together. She introduced me to Roger, who was also a party member, and had been a close friend of hers but in recent years they had grown apart. My partner recognised that his views were becoming increasingly radical and warned me to avoid him. She was a little older and a great deal wiser than me and I should have taken her advice, but I was young and arrogant and thought I knew better. By that time Roger had split from the Liberation Party and was talking about forming a new party of his own.

"He was a brilliant speaker. There were plenty of people frustrated with the Liberation Party's lack of progress and they were the people he appealed to. He promised action. Being young and naïve I was easily convinced. I thought he had all the answers. My partner of course knew that his kind of answers meant violence and death. She begged me not to get involved. I said she was a coward. We argued and our relationship ended. She was right of course. I had only known Drayton a few weeks before he began talking of bombings and assassinations. At the time I believed him when he said it was the only way we could achieve change.

"For all Drayton's tough talk he was really a fraud. He wasn't prepared to die for what he believed in but would gladly persuade others to do that for him. I didn't know the details of the Newman Grand bomb plot but I knew Roger and Martin were planning something major. Roger had prepared a series of press releases which were to be submitted to RNN after the bombing took place. I don't know where he intended to go but Roger planned to do a runner and go into hiding after the attack. He entrusted me with the press releases with instructions for when each was to be issued, but the instructions had all been written assuming the President had been killed or at least seriously injured. As Bryant escaped completely unharmed the attack was a complete failure and I erased most of the documents. The only thing I did pass on to the underground press was Martin's final letter.

"Drayton's escape plan was a complete failure also. He was arrested before he could even hail a taxi. Then he revealed his true colours. If he had kept silent he would have faced the death penalty, but like the coward he was he chose to save himself at the expense of others. He confessed the whole plot but tried to place the blame on Martin and he gave the police my name along with some of his other supporters. I was arrested, charged and given a life sentence."

"That was harsh considering you were so young."

"They believed in tough punishments in those days. Had the political climate not changed so profoundly I would never have been released. Being young is no excuse though. I was nineteen; I was old enough to know that innocent people would die. I'm just thankful that Drayton's plan did not succeed as then I would have so many more deaths on my conscience."

"You feel the blame should lie with Drayton not Martin Ashdown."

"Yes I do. Martin was like me, young and foolish enough to believe he could change the world by one violent act. He was seduced by Drayton's fine words just as I was. The only difference between us was that Martin was so desperately unhappy that he was prepared to take his own life."

"What were Drayton's reasons for hating the government? He must have had some personal motives which turned him to violence."

"I'm sure he did. I think he may have been Catholic, but I'm not certain. He was religious and passionately opposed to the government's family planning policies. He had been married but had gone through a messy break up a few years before I met him. Shortly after they filed for divorce his wife discovered she was pregnant. Whether she willingly had an abortion or was coerced into it by the authorities I don't know, but I know Roger was very bitter about the whole thing."

"Do you ever wonder what would have happened if Drayton's plan had succeeded?"

"Frequently. If Bryant had been killed he would no doubt have been replaced by a prominent member of the Cabinet. The Phoenix Party would have remained in power and would probably have introduced even harsher measures to crack down on terrorism. At best it would have achieved nothing, but suppose Rosa had not survived?"

"I understand she was very lucky to get out. Her dressing-room was in a part of the building which was completely destroyed."

"Exactly, if she had died that night things would have been very different for us."

Wednesday 4th July 2103

After remaining for a couple of days alone in her apartment with only grief and anger for company, Rebecca was attempting to put back together the pieces of her life. Her arm was still in plaster but otherwise she was well, physically at least. She visited Luchenko at St. Thomas' Hospital. His hearing had recovered and the bandages removed from his remaining eye, making communication much easier. He had told her that Sam Newman had been to see him the previous day. On the night of the bombing Newman had been seated in the box with the President so had escaped without a scratch.

"He said that the whole theatre will have to be pulled down and rebuilt," Nikolai told her, "so it will be some time before the Circus Britannia will be performing there again. In the meantime he is prepared to find us another venue, that's if we can scrape together enough performers to put on a show. It is a generous offer from him. Do you think we can do it?"

"Sure we can," Rebecca replied with more confidence than she actually felt. "I'll be back at work as soon as my arm is healed and we still have Randolph and the Tumbling Troop. As soon as you get out of here we can start auditioning new acts."

"They were some very talented people who died that night. You don't really think we can replace them that easily?"

"No of course not, but there are more skilled performers out there and nurturing talent is what you are good at. It will be a few years before we have a circus as good as the one we have lost, but we will get there so long as we don't allow ourselves to be defeated."

"You sound like Bryant!"

"I know, it's contagious. But we can't let this finish us. After all the work we put into the circus together we can't give up now. We owe it to the memory of our friends to carry on, to keep it alive."

"Actually I think that little speech was even better than Bryant's. Have you thought of going into politics?"

"I'm serious Nik. Promise me you'll fight for us."

"I'm not sure I have much fight left in me."

"Oh come on Nik, I've known you for a long time. You've always been ready to battle with whatever fate threw at you."

"That was when I had the full use of all my limbs."

Rebecca could think of no suitably encouraging response so she changed the subject.

"The police still haven't released Martin's body you know."

"I can't imagine who will go to the funeral when they do."

"I will."

"You're joking! He tried to kill us all. The only reason I would go to his funeral would be to spit in his fucking coffin."

"Please don't talk like that. Whatever madness drove him to do what he did he was still my friend once."

"Did you know he was queer?"

"I'm not going to answer that."

"Then you did. I had my suspicions but I wasn't sure."

"I'd rather not talk about it."

"I keep seeing him standing there in the middle of the stage, the smile, that crazy look in his eyes. I expect I'll go on seeing that for the rest of my life. You had a pretty miraculous escape though didn't you? How did you manage to find a way out?"

"I don't know. It's all a blur. I'd prefer it stayed that way."

"I envy you. I can recall it all far more clearly than I would like."

"I'm afraid I have to go now. I'm meeting John for lunch. I'll come again tomorrow."

"You don't have to. I realise I'm not great company at the moment."

"I want to. I need a reason to drag myself out of bed in the morning or I'd just lie there festering all day."

"Have a good lunch."

"I'll try to."

"I'm sure whatever you are having will be better than the food in this place. Still, I suppose I should be thankful that I'm alive to eat it."

"I'll bring you some fruit tomorrow. What would you like?"

"Stuff the fruit. Bring me a large bar of chocolate and a bottle of vodka."

"I'll see what I can do. Bye for now."

"Goodbye Rebecca, thanks for coming."

She took a taxi to Downing Street and found Bryant waiting for her in the garden. The scorching summer weather was continuing, turning the greenery of the city brown. Only a few private gardens like that of the President remained lush and verdant through constant irrigation while everywhere else the grass, trees and shrubs were shrivelled and parched. Bryant was sweating profusely even though he was seated in the shade. He had sacrificed the comfort of his air-conditioned dining room to eat outdoors as a favour to Rebecca, knowing how much she loved his garden.

They ate poached salmon and salad beneath the rose covered pergola on the terrace. Rebecca struggled to make conversation, not wanting to talk about the bombing but finding it impossible to think of another topic. Bryant talked about his colleagues, about a feud which was brewing between Phil Graysby and Harriet

Jacobs. She tried to take an interest, offering a remark or two, but political wranglings seemed so trivial.

There were raspberries and cream for dessert, the raspberries grown there in the garden. They tasted sublime so at least Rebecca could comment on these.

"They are delicious aren't they," Bryant agreed. "Which reminds me, did you like the roses I sent to the hospital?"

"I did. They were beautiful and had such a wonderful scent."

"They were from the garden too. In fact it was that crazy old gardener's idea. I was just going to send you the usual dozen red roses from the florist, but the funny fellow came to see me early that morning. He said I should send some from the garden as he was sure you would like them better. He was ever so concerned about you. Probably still felt guilty about pushing you down the steps the day before. Perhaps he should have pushed you a little harder. If you had been in hospital with a broken leg you wouldn't have been at the theatre!"

"That's not funny."

"No, sorry. Well, I'm glad I didn't sack him after all. There he is now."

The gardener came into view crossing the lawn with a bundle of canes under his arm.

"He must be roasting working out here in this weather," Bryant remarked.

"What's his name?" Rebecca asked.

"His name? Now what was it? I did ask. It's an Irish name. Was it O'Connor? No O'Brien, that was it."

"Is he Irish?"

"Possibly, he has a funny accent."

"I think I might go and speak to him, thank him for the roses."

"OK, but I'm going inside before I melt."

Rebecca descended the steps from the terrace, walked over the lawn and through the archway towards the pond. She found the gardener kneeling in the midst of the border partly obscured by foliage and tying sweet peas to the canes. He had not observed her and was intent upon the fiddly task. Her gaze rested on his hands and forearms. They were strangely mottled with patches of red and lines of silvery white. She remembered seeing something very similar only recently. In fact not similar, the same.

She cleared her throat and called to him.

"Mr O'Brien, may I talk to you for a moment?"

He left his work and extricated himself from the border but remained a short distance from her. He buried his hands deep in his trouser pockets and stood with his head down and shoulders slouched. As ever he was wearing dark glasses and a sun-hat and his chin was covered with three or four days growth, but even so she could tell that the face was not the lined and wrinkled face of an old man as she had thought but the face of a young man lined with scars.

"I wanted to thank you for the roses," she said.

"Don't mention it Miss," he muttered.

"It is polite to take off your hat when you are talking to a lady."

The man reluctantly removed the hat to reveal a mass of thick, dark, curly hair.

"And stand up straight please," she ordered.

"To be sure I am standing up straight Miss," he argued with such a heavy dose of the Emerald Isle she knew it was phoney.

"No you aren't, you're stooped over like an old man. Take those glasses off too; I want a proper look at you O'Brien."

She spoke his name loudly as though binding a demon with an enchantment.

He dropped the accent and replied in the familiar soft, deep voice, "So now you want to look at me. How many times must you have passed by me working here, without so much as a glance?"

He straightened his back and stood at his full impressive height. Slowly he removed the glasses and looked her in the eyes. There he was, tall, muscular, and horribly scarred. His face seemed partially paralysed on the left as the eyelid drooped slightly and his mouth moved less on that side when he spoke. One cheek was discoloured and a mass of dark furrows and raised silver lines criss-crossed his forehead. His eyes were a cold blue-grey and they stared at her intently.

She flinched under his gaze and looked away but then she looked back and finding her voice she said, "Give me one good reason why I shouldn't run to the house and tell Bryant, the police, hell everybody, who you are."

"I saved your life. Is that reason good enough?"

She thought about this for a moment then replied, "All right. I'll keep your secret but only if you promise to abide by my terms."

"And what are they?"

"Stay away from me. Don't write to me, don't speak to me and don't spy on me. Do you understand?"

"I understand perfectly. You are to carry on with your comfortable, little life and pretend I don't exist. Fear not, I am used to being invisible. Ignore me and I shall just fade away into the background."

"Then we have an agreement?"

"I will agree to your terms if that is what you want, but you cannot stop me from thinking about you."

"No I cannot. Perhaps you should get psychiatric help for that."

"You think a doctor could cure me of my love for you?"

"That's enough. I won't listen to any more of this madness. Just promise me that I won't hear from you again."

"Will that make you happy?"

"Do you promise, yes or no?"

"Very well, you have my promise. Run along then, no doubt Bryant is waiting for you."

She turned back towards the house, knowing that his eyes were still upon her as she walked away. Crossing the lawn she felt all the misery of the past few days well up inside her and by the time she ascended the steps to the terrace tears were stinging her eyes. She entered the living-room where Bryant was sprawled on the sofa reeking of sweat.

"Finally!" he said. "I thought you were going to be out there all day. You know what this place needs? It needs a pool. Not that I'm much bothered about swimming but you always feel cooler when you're lying by the pool. Still, you like swimming don't you Becky? Becky, are you here or did the aliens abduct you?"

"I'm sorry John; I'm not feeling very well. I expect I'm just tired, I should go home."

"If you're tired why don't you have a lie down; you know where the bedroom is."

"I'd rather go home."

"All right, I'll call a car. I'm pretty busy tomorrow but we could meet for dinner."

"I don't know. I'll see how I feel."

IN THE GARDEN
The Man Behind the Mask

The blood-red petals of the dying rose
Fall like the tears I will not weep,
I am not wounded by your words
But your cold steel eyes cut deep.

Barbed thorns pierce my heart
Their poison drips, I shall not heal.
Yet for this agony I am thankful
It reminds me I still can feel.

By the time she arrived home Rebecca felt completely exhausted. She ought to have been relieved to have discovered The Man Behind the Mask's identity and to have secured his promise to leave her alone, but she felt no relief. She felt empty and terribly alone.

The following morning she kept her promise to Nikolai but found it impossible to raise his spirits when her own were equally depressed. She did not stay at the hospital long as it was the day of Ami Reed's funeral, the first of several funerals taking place over the next couple of weeks. Sitting in the stale, recirculated air of the crematorium chapel she was unable to cry, much as she would have liked the release that tears would provide. Though Ami had been her friend as well as her dresser, her own grief seemed insignificant compared to the agony of Ami's poor parents and the young man she had been going to marry.

Bryant had tried to call during the service and had left a message asking if she would be coming to dinner. She called his office but did not bother asking to speak to the President, just told his secretary that she would not be seeing him that day. She could not face Bryant now. It was his government, his policies, that had driven Martin to kill.

John Bryant called many times over the weekend but she would not answer. To begin with his tone was concerned and sympathetic.

"Hi Becky, I just thought I'd call to see how you were. I understand you probably don't feel up to much at the moment but just give me a ring and let me know you are OK."

By Monday his compassion was giving way to impatience.

"Becky, could you return my calls please, it is only polite. I know you have been through a rough time recently but sitting around moping isn't going to help."

On Tuesday night what little patience he had was exhausted and he delivered an ultimatum.

"You know I'm a busy man Becky and I don't have time to mess around. I am up to my neck in security briefings and anti-terror legislation but I can free up a couple of hours tomorrow evening. You can either come over to Downing Street at seven and we can have dinner or you can forget seeing me at all until Parliament is in recess. Even then I can't promise anything because Caroline will want me to spend time with the boys. It's your choice, but don't say I didn't warn you."

The tone of this message roused Rebecca from her apathy. She left a message with Bryant's secretary to say she would be there. The following evening she ordered a taxi and arrived at Number Ten a bit before seven. She waited for the President in the small sitting-room. He arrived at ten past. Her obedience to his summons had reduced his anger and he was ready to forgive, but his pride had been hurt by her refusal to return his calls so he would not make the first move towards reconciliation.

"Well Rebecca, here you are at last," he said, greeting her more coolly than usual. "Where have you been since last week and couldn't you call and let me know you were all right?"

"I'm sorry; it's been a tough few days. It was Ami's funeral last Thursday, Jake's on Monday and Anton's this morning. I've been in a bit of a state and it's taken me a while to get my head together."

"I understand sweetheart, I just wish you'd phoned, I've been worried. Anyway, do you want to go out for dinner or shall we stay in?"

"Can we talk first? There's something important I want to say."

"Oh dear, if this is serious talk we need a drink. What will it be? Gin and tonic?"

"Yes, anything."

She sat down and waited until he had finished fiddling about with the bottles and ice. He had helped himself to a very large whisky and served her a drink containing almost as much gin as tonic. While he sipped she took a deep breath then began.

"The thing is John, I've been thinking and I've decided I want to end this."

"End what?"

"Our relationship. This affair."

"Why?"

He was still sipping his drink calmly and did not appear to be taking her words very seriously.

"Many reasons, for a start I'm sick of being the other woman."

Now he put down his glass and gave her his full attention.

"Oh I see. I know what this is about. You aren't the first mistress I've had Rebecca. I know there always comes a point when women start making demands. This is the old 'leave your wife and marry me' pitch. Well sorry but it isn't going to happen. I'm not divorcing Caroline so there's no point in arguing."

"I don't want to marry you! I want to leave you!"

"There's another man then? Who is he? I hope he's rich."

"There is no other man. This is just about us. I'm not happy with our relationship any more so I want to end it."

"You're not happy, after I've lavished my time and money on you! What more do you want?"

"I'm not happy because I don't love you. God damn it John, I don't even like you. In fact for what you have done to this country I hate you. You've sold our freedom and destroyed democracy and yet you sit there completely oblivious to the utter misery you've caused."

"Who the hell have you been talking to? Where are you getting this fucking crap from?"

"I haven't got it from anyone, it is the truth. You are corrupt and dirty and I don't want any more to do with you."

"Do you realise what you are saying? Have you any idea what you are doing? You dare to speak to me like this! Have you forgotten what power I have?"

"How could I forget, you abuse it freely enough."

"You will regret this! I've helped you up to the dizzy heights of wealth and success and it's a long way back down to the gutter where you came from. You won't find it very easy to climb back up now you've burnt your bridges."

She stood up saying, "No doubt you will make me regret it but I've made up my mind. Goodbye John, give my regards to the family."

As she turned to leave he called after her, "There are plenty more whores out there Rebecca. Don't imagine you will be difficult to replace."

She paused and turned back but it did not seem worth wasting her breath to make any reply. She shrugged off the pathetic insult and walked out with her head held high. She knew that this action would have consequences but she felt better than she had done in a very long time. She felt as though her life finally belonged to her again. For the first time in over a week she slept soundly and woke feeling refreshed and ready to face the world.

The world did not wait long. Just as she was finishing breakfast Nikolai called her from the hospital. He asked her to come to see him immediately and sounded upset. She already had suspicions as to what the matter was but agreed to come straight away. She found him sitting up and watching for her, drumming his fingers on the frame of the bed anxiously.

"I'm here, what's the problem?" she asked as she took a chair beside the bed.

"Sam Newman was here this morning. You can guess that for him to come to see me at half-eight in the morning it must have been more than a social call."

"Right, so what did he have to say?"

"He wanted to talk to me about you Rebecca. He said some rather worrying things. He says you've been mixing with political radicals. Please tell me that you didn't have anything to do with the bombing."

"Of course I didn't."

"What is all this Newman was telling me then? Since when have you held extremist views?"

"Relax Nik! Let me explain. Last night I ended it with John. He was pretty mad so no doubt he has been bad-mouthing me to Newman and coming out with all kinds of crap."

"I'm sorry Rebecca but Newman was very explicit. He said that as long as you were in the show he would be having no further dealings with the circus."

"I see, well consider this my resignation. I'll put it in writing later and send a copy to Newman."

"Dear God Becky! What sort of a circus are we going to have without you?"

"I don't know, but without Newman's backing you won't have a circus at all. I'm sorry I've got you involved in this mess but you do realise what has happened? I pissed John off so he got straight on the phone to Newman and called in a few favours. Newman comes here and tells you I'm a lunatic or a terrorist sympathiser or whatever and threatens to ditch the circus, all to satisfy the whims of that petulant brat who got himself made President. I was expecting something like this."

"I wish I could tell Newman where to stick his backing but he owns more than half the theatres in the country."

"I know, I understand. I wish you all the best for the future Nik. I look forward to seeing a new and better Circus Britannia."

"Who are you kidding Becky? It isn't going to happen. The circus is on its way out. According to Newman musical theatre is the next big thing. We're a passing fad, yesterday's story, old news. All we have to look forward to now is touring ever smaller venues and scraping in a little cash until no one wants to see us anymore."

"Don't talk like that Nikolai."

"You know I'm right."

Rebecca recognised there was probably truth in what he had said and could not bring herself to lie. Instead she was vague in her reply.

"We can't see what the future holds can we? Who knows what may happen next year or even next week. I certainly don't, but if I can I will come and see you again soon. Unless you think it is better that I don't."

"I'm not so weak that I will let Newman bully me into shunning you completely. Good luck Becky."

"You too and thanks."

"For what?"

"For so many things. For spotting me in the Nightingales all those years ago and recognising my potential. For all the support and encouragement. For being a good man."

She walked back over Westminster Bridge in order to save the taxi fare. Now that she had officially resigned from the circus her income would be significantly reduced and although she had some savings she would not be able to maintain the lifestyle she had become accustomed to. As she walked along the embankment she contemplated her future. She paid a hefty rent for her luxurious rooms and would have to make arrangements to move out before long.

When she entered the foyer of her building the police were waiting for her. They had a warrant to search her apartment and although they did not place her under arrest they were quite insistent that she accompany them back to the MAT Force Headquarters in order to help with their enquiries.

The Metropolitan Anti-Terror force had facilities almost opposite New Scotland Yard in what had been the premises for the Department of Trade and

Industry. On her arrival Rebecca was met by Chief Inspector Andrew Steel and another man whom he introduced as Detective Sergeant Dale. Dale was slight of stature compared to Steel but had overly large hands which he never seemed to know what to do with. He was constantly putting them in his pockets, pulling them out, scratching his head and resting them on his hips.

Steel seemed rather embarrassed at meeting Rebecca again under these circumstances. He showed her to an interview room where she took a seat. He and Dale sat down on the opposite side of the table. As yet Dale had not spoken and seemed content to allow Steel to do the talking while he looked on with a grim expression.

"I am told, Miss Clayton," Steel said, "that you made some rather alarming comments during your last conversation with the President."

"Alarming in what way?" asked Rebecca.

"You accused President Bryant of having 'sold freedom and destroyed democracy', is that not right?"

"I don't remember exactly what I said but as it was a private conversation between the President and myself, I have no desire to comment on it."

"It was the President who reported your words to me. He is very concerned that you should be expressing such views. You must realise how serious it would be if someone as close to the President as yourself were to be revealed as a terrorist sympathiser."

"Perhaps the President did not tell you that he and I are no longer close."

"It may be too late. The damage may already have been done. You have in the past been in the President's confidence. Have you ever betrayed that confidence?"

"Never," Rebecca lied.

As she had not yet been formally arrested and charged she could refuse to answer Steel's questions, but if she did not cooperate the arrest would soon follow and there was no right to remain silent under the anti-terror laws. It was easier to lie now and hope to avoid a full interrogation.

"Then you have never passed on information about the President or other members of the government to the unlicensed media or to anti-government organisations."

"No."

"But we have seen from your computer that you have been visiting the RNN site rather frequently."

"I was not aware that it was illegal to visit that site."

"It isn't illegal, but it is inadvisable. You do know that RNN is an unlicensed broadcaster so the information on the site is frequently inaccurate, if not outright lies."

"That is why I like to keep track of what they are saying, in case it concerns me. They have been responsible for spreading gossip about me in the past."

"Is that the only reason you visit the site?"

"It is the main reason."

"Have you ever contributed anything to the RNN site?"

"No certainly not. That is illegal."

"But you have been reading the discussion forum?"

"Reading it yes, joining in, no."

"There are some pretty extreme views expressed on the forum. Several people have published comments saying they were sorry more people were not killed in the theatre bombing. How do you feel about such comments?"

"How do you think I feel?"

"Could you answer the question please Miss Clayton?"

"It makes me angry, naturally."

"Then you do not in any way sympathise with such views?"

"Of course not. I was almost killed, remember."

"Do you know any person or persons who may be working for the unlicensed media or a terrorist organisation?"

"No, at least I hope not. I knew Martin after all, but I didn't know his secret."

"Then he never said anything to you which aroused suspicion?"

"Never."

"And you maintain that you were unaware that he was homosexual?"

"No, I had no idea."

Steel seemed to have exhausted his own list of questions so Dale stepped in.

"I find it incredible that you escaped from the theatre after the bombing. No one else who was trapped inside made it out. Perhaps you could tell us some more about what happened that night."

"I'm sorry, I have already told everything I remember to Detective Superintendent Hunter. I have nothing to add."

"It was you who first received the warning that the bombing was going to take place?"

"That is correct, but Chief Inspector Steel already knows all about it." She turned to Steel and said, "Perhaps if you had taken the warning more seriously, forty-six people need not have lost their lives."

"That is a very good point," replied Dale with a sneer.

"I acted on the information I had," answered Steel. "It is not my fault the intelligence was deficient."

There was evidently some bad feeling between the MAT Force detectives and the President's chief protection officer. No doubt both wished to blame the other for failing to prevent the attack.

"Has the Man Behind the Mask made any further attempts to contact you?" Steel asked.

"No," Rebecca answered truthfully, but not adding what she had learnt about him.

"Yet someone using that name is still contributing terrorist propaganda to the RNN forum," remarked Dale.

"If I receive any more letters from him I will let you know immediately," Rebecca answered.

Dale let out a grunt of impatience and said to Steel, "Have we wasted enough of our time yet? You do realise this fishing expedition is utterly pointless?"

"I am acting on instructions which came directly from the President," Steel replied.

Dale stood up and said "Well you can tell the President that we at MAT Force would be glad to carry out his personal wishes had we not more pressing matters of national security to deal with."

"I will certainly pass on your message," answered Steel as Dale left the room.

"You don't really have any evidence against me at all do you?" demanded Rebecca. "This is all just because John Bryant wants to make my life difficult."

"Let us just say that the President was very concerned by some of the remarks you made and I would recommend you are very careful about making such statements in future. I would also advise that you avoid the unlicensed media."

"Thank you for your advice Chief Inspector. Now am I free to go?"

"You are."

He ordered a patrol car to take her home. Her apartment had been turned inside out but she felt she had got off pretty lightly under the circumstances. Had Bryant really been intent on revenge he could have easily arranged for the police to find something in her rooms. She well knew that such malice was not beneath him.

Before setting to work tidying up the mess Rebecca first scanned her apartment for listening devices. There were none in the rooms but she would be very careful about who she called or emailed. Once reassured that she still had her privacy she started picking up all her clothing which had been scattered over the floor and putting it away in her drawers and wardrobe. She had a lot of clothes, all from expensive designer boutiques and many items had only been worn once. It was not that she really cared about fashion; it was just that her lifestyle demanded a new outfit for every party.

She suspected the police officers had enjoyed searching through her underwear drawer and was vaguely annoyed to fine several articles were missing. She had a disturbing image enter her head of some fat, ugly constable jerking off while fondling her black lace knickers, which made her feel slightly ill. Still she was used to such things. Her photograph had made it into the bedrooms of many a male adolescent and had been drooled over by many a man old enough to know better.

While tidying her clothes away she came across a battered black leather jacket which did not belong to her. It was a man's jacket. At first she was puzzled but then she remembered it had been in the bag she had brought home from the hospital. It was The Man's jacket. At least now she knew who he was she could return it to him. She would package it up and post it to Mr O'Brien, Gardener, 10 Downing Street. She could tell from the smell that it was real leather so he would probably be glad to have it back. In fact it smelt rather good, a musky man scent.

She put it to one side and concentrated on cleaning up the mess the police had made of her cosmetics. Make-up and bottles had been tossed carelessly all over, spilling their contents and staining the carpet. Then there were her books and ornaments to put back on the shelves. Several pieces of glass and china had been broken but looking around at her possessions there were very few things she was truly attached to. All these things she had accumulated were just clutter. There were things she had bought just because they were expensive and she could afford them. There were gifts from Bryant and from Newman before him. She could gladly dispense with most of it.

She cleared up the kitchen last, putting all the pots, pans and utensils which she never used back into the cupboards and drawers. This apartment was not really a home. It was just somewhere she slept or passed a few idle hours in front of the TV. She had taken the rooms furnished. The décor was stylish, modern, sterile and completely impersonal. She had a cleaner who kept the rooms spotless and as she never cooked there was rarely any mess. She had occupied the rooms for over two years and yet they were completely unlived in.

It had taken her all afternoon to clear up and between visiting Nikolai at the hospital and being dragged in for questioning by police, she had forgotten to have lunch. While tidying the kitchen she realised how hungry she was. Feeling reckless and radical she threw open the cupboards and rooted around inside until she found a bag of pasta, a tin of tomatoes and a jar of anchovies. Tonight she would cook.

In spite of her enthusiasm the resulting dish was not a complete success. The tomato sauce was rather lacking in flavour and would no doubt have benefited from some garlic or herbs. This reminded her of the conversation with The Man Behind the Mask when he had talked about growing herbs in containers. She wondered why it had not occurred to her that he was a gardener by profession. Also now that she knew who he was his knowledge about her did not seem quite so sinister.

He had talked of her love of plants and animals and the way she sometimes took off her shoes to feel the grass between her toes, all things he could have observed while going about his daily work. However his profession did not explain his access to the theatre, particularly not how he was able to get into her dressing-room without being recorded on camera. Still, she should be thankful he was able to enter the theatre since he had saved many lives on the night of the bombing, including her own.

Thinking about The Man Behind the Mask, or O'Brien as she now knew his name to be, reminded her of the container of plants he had given her. Although she had destroyed all his letters she had forgotten about the rock garden and it was still sitting out on her balcony. She had not watered it in weeks so it must be completely dead by now. She stepped out onto the balcony to take a look.

The sun was low in the sky and turning the windows of the neighbouring buildings a beautiful rose gold. She was delighted to see her plants were thriving. Even though she had completely neglected to mention the plants to the cleaner the conscientious woman had been watering them. There were even some delicate little pink and purple flowers swaying in the evening breeze. Rebecca decided that when she moved out she would take her garden with her.

She did not often sit out on her balcony but this evening she stayed there until after the sun had set, just gazing at the tiny blooms and daydreaming. She was thinking about where she would go, where to live, what to do with her life. Her musings produced few sensible plans for her future but it was pleasant to contemplate the freedom she now possessed.

After dark when the air was turning cool she went back indoors to continue her reflections over a cup of tea. She was thinking of all the parts of the British Isles she had never visited; the half submerged coast of Norfolk, the sparsely populated highlands and islands of Scotland, the hills and valleys of North Wales, all the places which lacked theatres so had not been included in the circus's tours. She was trying to decide which of these places she ought to see first when she was startled by a noise outside on the balcony.

The curtains were partially drawn but silhouetted against them was the shape of a figure. Instinctively she knew who it was and strangely she was not in the least bit alarmed. She opened the doors and there he was, The Man but without the mask.

"How the hell did you get up here?" she asked with a calmness which surprised even herself.

"I didn't get up; I came down from the roof. I started from the top of the shopping centre multi-storey car park, from there onto the roof of the building overlooking yours then down onto your roof."

"And people say *I* have a good head for heights!"

"I realise I am breaking my promise but I was worried about you and wanted to check you were all right."

"Couldn't you have used a telephone or sent an email?"

"I'm assuming your communications are being monitored and if the President's gardener were to start showing interest in your welfare it would arouse interest from parties I'd rather not have dealings with. That is why I came to see you by this rather unconventional route rather than through the front door, which is being watched."

"Do you want to come in? I've checked for bugs so it is safe."

"Aren't you going to yell at me or threaten to call the police or anything?"

"No, but I would appreciate it if you would answer a few questions."

"Sure, ask whatever you want."

She showed him into her living-room and offered him a seat. He perched awkwardly on the edge of the sofa, as though ready to make his escape at any moment. Unlike the last time they had met he was clean shaven, no untidy stubble hiding the scars. There was a prominent line running between his left ear and the corner of his mouth.

"Would you like a cup of tea or perhaps a coffee?" she offered.

"Tea would be great," he replied and he watched her as she busied herself in the kitchen.

"I heard on the domestic staff grapevine that you ditched Bryant," he said.

"I did," she answered.

"Apparently since last night there have been several urgent telephone calls and important meetings so I'm guessing he isn't accepting his fate with dignity and resignation."

"No, the only resignation was mine from the circus. Bryant put pressure on Newman and Newman leant on Luchenko, I'm sure you can guess."

"I read on RNN that the police had you in for questioning this morning. What was that about? Some petty act of revenge on Bryant's part?"

"It was nothing really. The police asked me a few questions and messed this place up a bit, but it was just to scare me. If Bryant was determined to punish me they would have locked me up on terrorism charges by now."

"He's probably hoping you will run back to him in tears and beg his forgiveness."

"He'd love that, but it isn't going to happen."

"I'm glad."

She gave him his tea and took a seat on the armchair opposite. He was beginning to relax a little but still seemed uncomfortable, as though not in his natural environment.

"So, is O'Brien your real name?" Rebecca asked. "And is that who you are tonight since you aren't wearing your mask?"

"The name on my birth certificate is David Michael O'Brien, but whether or not the name defines who I am is more philosophy than I care to contemplate at this time of the evening."

"Then may I call you David?"

"Of course, if you wish."

"So now I have established your name as well as your occupation. This is progress, but from your agility in scaling vertical walls and leaping off roofs I am guessing you were not always a gardener."

"No, I used to be a soldier. Would you like the whole story? Naturally it is a long one but I am prepared to tell it if you are prepared to listen."

"I'm listening."

"Right, where to begin? I'm afraid in order to tell the whole tale I will have to start from my birth. I did warn you it would be a long story."

"Please take your time. I'm not going anywhere."

"All right then, Chapter One, 'I am Born'; my mother, Martha O'Brien, was a secondary school teacher and my father Nathaniel is a doctor. I was their first child and my mother contracted an infection in hospital shortly after my birth. She died. So I was an only child and raised solely by my father who never remarried. However, in spite of losing my mother I had many advantages which you did not. We were fairly affluent, lived in a nice house and my father could afford for me to be well educated. I studied English literature at Cambridge because that was what I had most enjoyed at school and because I didn't really know what to do with my life.

"I always had some boyish ideas about being a hero and some naïve notions about serving my country, so on graduating I applied to Sandhurst. I got in, I worked hard and did as I was told and eventually qualified as an officer. This was the early nineties, after Clarkson had pulled all our forces out of the oil wars and set us to protecting our own soil. I was happy with that at first. We were protecting our borders, preventing the spread of infectious disease and keeping the peace within the country. But gradually protection changed to oppression.

"The armed forces were being mobilised more and more frequently but against fewer actual threats to national security. We were being called on to prevent demonstrations and to shut down unlicensed media broadcasters. There was one memorable occasion when we were ordered to break down the door of a suburban house in the middle of the night and seize the occupants as they were suspected terrorists. It turned out that the fifteen year old son of the family had been researching fireworks for a school chemistry project.

"When I first joined the army it was with my Dad's support, even though he would have preferred that I had chosen a different profession. He realised the way Clarkson's government was going long before I did. He is a practising Roman Catholic, as was my mother, and although as a doctor he was always in favour of birth control he was never happy with the government's family planning policies. He was furious when the army was called in to prevent demonstrations against those policies. He wanted me to resign my commission. I didn't like what I was being asked to do by my superiors but I wasn't prepared to quit after all the work I had put into achieving my rank. My father and I argued, well that is an understatement. We both completely lost it and said some terrible things to each other. We haven't spoken since.

"So after the bust up with my father I carried on, trying not to listen to my own conscience and following orders. Then Clarkson announced his resignation. I was not alone in hoping that after his departure someone more moderate would come to power and some of our freedom would be restored. But of course it was John Bryant with his sterilise-the-poor, gay bashing and book burning policies who sailed into office, sparking off the riots in the North-East. Riots is not really the right word; I should say massacre. That is what tends to happen when heavily armed soldiers go up against civilians.

"It had started with demonstrations, and then there were arson attacks on the Phoenix Party regional HQ and IMC television studios. I remember sitting in an armoured car with buildings burning all around and bodies scattered all over the road. I gave the order for my men to cease fire but someone countermanded it. Anyone who moved was shot, regardless of whether or not they had been involved in the attacks. Then I saw people calling for help from the top floor of one of the blazing buildings. The fire had spread from the Phoenix Party offices to neighbouring blocks. I went in to help them. It was crazy, I had no protective clothing or breathing apparatus and the whole building was collapsing all around me. I didn't save anyone. They all died and I only just survived.

"I spent the next few months in hospital being treated for the burns and post traumatic stress. The army doctors patched me up and helped me to pass for sane, but I wasn't what you would call well balanced. They had to take good care of me though because IMC had decided to make me a hero.

"The riots had plenty of TV coverage but naturally 'Government orders soldiers to shoot hundreds of unarmed civilians' wasn't the angle they went for. Instead it was 'Hundreds killed in anarchist arson attacks' and 'Brave Captain risks his own life to save victims from burning building.' I wasn't really aware of what was going on at the time, I was too much of a gibbering wreck, but I read the reports afterwards.

"Some junior defence minister decided to cash in on the media interest in me and offered to find me suitable employment working for the government since I was to be invalided out of the army. I could have been a driver or chief brass knob polisher or something but since I had taken an interest in growing things during my convalescence I was offered the position of gardener at Number 10. I expect it seems strange to you that I accepted.

"As I said I was not exactly well at the time, mentally speaking. When I agreed to take the job I was meditating on suicidal schemes to assassinate the President. I came quite close to doing it. I had a large knife among my garden tools which I sharpened regularly while contemplating cutting his throat. Once I even approached within a couple of metres of him with the knife in my hand, but my nerve failed. Deep down I knew Bryant's death would not achieve anything. He would be replaced just as he had replaced Clarkson. Though I was 'half in love with easeful death', I could not bring myself to throw my life away so pointlessly.

"So I remained working for him, perhaps just waiting for some better reason to die. I had always written poetry. When I joined the army I fancied myself as a modern day Rupert Brookes although later I inclined more towards Wilfred Owen. Writing was always a sort of therapy, but I never shared my work until I discovered other poets publishing on the RNN forum. I started to regularly submit poems and then I learned about the Tertiary Romantics and began attending their meetings.

"I suppose I enjoy my work, even though I loathe my employers. Between my job and my writing, life was just about bearable, but sometimes after dark, at home on my own, the frustration of feeling so powerless in a harsh and cruel world would eat away at me. I felt so trapped within the four walls of my flat, within my own body, that I just had to get out and do something. I took to exploring the city after curfew, avoiding the patrols by going over the rooftops or under the ground. I was amazed at how easy it is to go anywhere you want if you just avoid the conventional roads and pathways."

He paused to catch his breath after talking for so long.

"How did you get into the theatre?" Rebecca asked.

"I found my way in pretty much by accident," he explained. "There are so many tunnels beneath London, drains and sewers, abandoned underground lines and Lord knows what else. One day I found myself in a bit of disused Victorian sewer which runs right below the theatre basement. The basement is part of the original theatre building which was knocked down when the Newman Grand Complex was built, so it has a manhole which opens onto the sewer below. When they completed the Newman Grand they covered over the manhole when they put down that non-slip rubber material over the concrete of the basement floor, but it is only a very thin layer and I could easily cut through it with a small knife."

"Andrew Steel assured me they that he had personally searched the basement and yet he missed that."

"I was careful to arrange the stack of crates and boxes to conceal my secret entrance. I guess if you didn't know about the old sewer you would not expect anyone to be coming up through the floor so wouldn't know what to look for."

"But how did you get from the basement to my dressing-room?"

"Easily, up the service lift shaft, when not in use of course, and into the air-conditioning system. In fact I never actually set foot in your dressing-room. The vent in the ceiling was too small to climb through but as it was just above your dressing-table I could lower my letters or flowers down through it."

"Or watch me undressing," Rebecca suggested.

"No! Never!" he protested, "I would not do that ever. I didn't go near your dressing-room when I knew it was occupied. I promise I only delivered my letters and gifts when I knew you weren't there. Is that what you thought? That I was a peeping Tom?"

"You could have been. How was I to know?"

He ran his hands through his hair and sighed.

"It is only now that I try to explain all this that I realise how crazy it sounds. I know my behaviour makes me seem like a pervert and a sick freak but I'm not, really I'm not. It all started as a game. Something to pass the time. I found my way into the theatre because I could, because I was curious. I watched you perform from a suitable hiding place in the lighting gallery and I thought you were wonderful. You know what I thought, I wrote it all down.

"I had seen you at Downing Street and on television so I knew who you were, but when I saw your routines live it was inspiring. I became addicted. I had to keep coming back to watch you perform and sometimes to see you rehearse. I wrote to you because I wanted you to know how I felt. I never wanted to frighten you or make you uncomfortable. I realise now how stupid I was and I am sorry."

"It isn't entirely your fault," Rebecca replied. "I behaved badly too. I started playing your game because I enjoyed your letters and it was exciting to have a mysterious admirer. I encouraged you but then I got scared. You wanted to explain all this before didn't you? After our quarrel at the picnic you wanted to meet again so you could tell me all this."

"That's right, but it was too late. You had already decided I was an obsessed lunatic. You were probably right. I am an obsessed lunatic but in my defence I can only plead that I am a harmless one."

"Why didn't you ever talk to me at Downing Street? You must have had plenty of opportunities."

"I lacked courage. I'm sorry about pushing you down the steps by the way. You've probably figured out by now that it wasn't an accident. I didn't know what was going to happen at the theatre that night but I knew it would be bad."

"You knew and yet you were there. You could have been killed."

He shrugged and replied, "I had to try to prevent it."

"Your actions must have saved hundreds of lives but no one knows it apart from me."

"I'd like it to stay that way."

They sat in silence for a while listening to the loud tick of the alleged antique carriage clock on the mantelpiece. Rebecca had bought it from a quaint, rural shop while on tour last year and paid a scandalous sum for it. Examining it after returning home she began to suspect it was not quite as old as the woman in the shop had claimed. For a start, a quick bit of research revealed the type of batteries it took had not been invented in the 1950s.

O'Brien broke the silence, "So now you have resigned from the circus what are you going to do?"

"I have no idea. First of all I'll have to find another place to live. As long as I am here John will have his thugs watching me and can harass me whenever he chooses. Also the rent on this place is astronomical so I had better start looking pretty soon."

"I have a spare room at my flat in Hackney."

"That would be great. It would just be for a few days until I found somewhere else."

He was looking at her, rather startled as though he had not been expecting to be taken up on the offer.

"Oh, you weren't serious were you? Don't worry, I'll find somewhere."

"No I was serious. I would love to have you stay with me for a while; it's just that I didn't think you would, considering my rather deranged behaviour."

"You know what they say, any port in a storm. I'm not comfortable here anymore. It was bad enough when I thought you were watching me but now I know that Bryant's goons are spying on me I feel like I'm living in a goldfish bowl. That and I'm fed up of all of this."

She gestured to indicate her luxurious suite of rooms.

"I'm ready to move on," she explained. "I have no ideas what the future holds for me but I want to make a break. This flat is part of my old life and that is now over. Incidentally, how did you know where I live? Did you follow me home sometime?"

He laughed and replied, "Oh no it was much simpler than that. I just asked Eddie, Bryant's driver. So how soon do you want to move out of here?"

"The sooner the better. There isn't much I want to pack. Most of this crap can be sold, I don't want it. I'll sort everything out with the letting agent after I've gone, then the police won't know I'm planning on leaving."

"Well my place is a typical bachelor pad so it will need cleaning and possibly fumigating before it is fit for habitation. Is tomorrow evening soon enough?"

"That would be great. I have a plan. I'll chuck a few spare clothes into my sports bag and go to the health club. If the police think I'm just going for a workout and a massage they won't pay too much attention. I'll spend the afternoon there then meet you somewhere."

"OK, I'll see you at Hackney Central at six. I finish work at three-thirty so that should give me enough time to get the place sorted."

"Great. I'll be there, and thanks, I really appreciate this."

"Don't thank me yet, you haven't seen my flat. I'll be on my way then."

"Are you going back the way you came?"

"I think so. It's a lovely evening for a walk and the view from up there is wonderful."

"I always think London looks a lot better in the dark."

"It is lovely at night but I like it best by the first light of dawn when 'This city now doth like a garment wear the beauty of the morning; silent, bare.'"

"Is that one of yours?"

He laughed and replied, "No, that is Wordsworth."

"OK laugh at my ignorance. So I'm a philistine, I don't know my Keats from my Shelley or my Shakespeare from my Milton."

"No it isn't that. I was just amused that you mistake the work of one of our greatest poets for something of mine."

"I haven't read much poetry other than yours. I don't know the difference."

"Then while you are staying with me feel free to browse my collection. Goodnight Rebecca, I will see you tomorrow."

"You just called me by my name and not Rosa."

"I thought perhaps you would be leaving Rosa behind now you have left the circus."

"Indeed, Rosa can stay here with all the evening gowns and party dresses I don't need any more. Goodnight David Michael O'Brien, I'm glad to have met you properly at last."

She opened the doors to the balcony and he stepped out into the night. Nimbly he jumped up onto the railing then caught part of the roof above. He swung himself up with almost as much ease as Rebecca on the trapeze. He called a last goodnight back down to her then disappeared over the rooftop. He left her contemplating the complete change in her circumstances that the previous forty-eight hours had produced. Though her future was now full of uncertainty she felt optimistic and was looking forward to the following day.

REFLECTIONS
The Man Behind the Mask

The mirror shows me a man I hate,
He is naïve foolish and cowardly.
The idiot child who grew up too late,
Still in love with boyish fantasy.

The quest for honour made him bold,
He was one of the band of brothers.
He followed orders, did as he was told
And left the thinking to others

Now he writes these appalling rhymes
And indulges in self pity.
He cannot atone for his crimes
And his poetry is just shitty.

Part 4

Liberation

Friday 13th July 2103

At just before six the following evening Rebecca met O'Brien at Hackney Central Station. She carried with her only a single rucksack and was dressed in her gym clothes. Though she had been exercising O'Brien looked considerably more hot and flustered than she did. He was wearing baggy shorts and a grey T-shirt which was wet with perspiration and his hair hung in damp locks over his brow.

"Sorry I'm in such a state," he apologised, "it took much longer than I thought to clear all the junk out of the spare room. I was going to get cleaned up but then I realised the time and had to run straight here."

"It's all right, I hadn't realised I was putting you to so much trouble or I wouldn't have arranged to come so soon."

"It's no trouble. I needed to sort out all my stuff anyway."

Just a short walk from the station they reached the tower block where O'Brien lived. It was a prime example of the ugly, grey, concrete monstrosity school of architecture. They took the lift to the eighth floor and at the end of the corridor was O'Brien's flat. The grim exterior had not given Rebecca high expectations but she was pleasantly surprised when he showed her inside. Though much smaller than Rebecca's apartment it was clean, tidy and homely. The furniture was not stylish or fashionable but it was comfortable. Unlike her bare walls he had shelves everywhere, mostly filled with books and plants.

There were two bedrooms. The larger contained a double bed, the smaller had until recently be used as a study. It still contained a desk but the chair had been removed to make space for a folding bed.

"You can have my room," O'Brien offered, "you'll be more comfortable. I have changed the sheets."

"Certainly not," Rebecca protested, "I'll be fine in here. Is this where you do your writing?"

"Sometimes, but it was mainly just where I kept boxes of books that I hadn't got around to sorting out or putting on shelves yet. I have a serious book habit. I buy old books by the box at auctions and clearance sales and they sit here gathering dust. Speaking of dust, I'm covered in it too so if you'll excuse me I'll take a shower. Make yourself comfortable. Don't be afraid to have a nosey round and find out where everything is."

He disappeared into the bathroom so Rebecca decided to familiarise herself with the kitchen. Though it was spotlessly clean everything had the look of being well used. The wooden spoons and spatula were worn smooth while the chopping board was rough and furrowed. She located teabags and milk and put the kettle on. Above the sound of running water she could hear David whistling as he showered.

She was admiring some of O'Brien's many plants when he came out of the bathroom. He was wearing only his pants and rubbing his hair with a towel. His stomach was almost completely flat and his torso splendidly muscular, as were his arms and legs. He had a little hair on his chest and a neat little tuft just below his navel.

He caught her looking at him and asked, "Are you admiring my scars?"

"No I'm admiring your toned and athletic physique," she replied honestly.

He gave a derisive snort and said, "Yeah right!"

"No I mean it. You have a fantastic body."

"Not bad considering what it has been through; shame about the face though isn't it!"

"For someone so good at making compliments you aren't very good at receiving them. So you have a few scars, you are still a very attractive man."

He met her eye and saw she was in earnest. "Thank you Rebecca, it is very kind of you to say so. I'll put some clothes on then see about some dinner."

He cooked a delicious meal of beans and rice in a tasty, spicy sauce served with fresh green salad grown on the balcony.

"I could get used to this," Rebecca remarked as she helped herself to seconds.

"I thought it was supposed to be the way to a *man's* heart that was through his stomach," David replied.

"If I stay living here for too long I'll get horribly fat, especially since I've just cancelled my membership to the health club."

"You'd still be beautiful even if you were fat and you could always do what I do for exercise and take a stroll over the rooftops. You can come with me sometime, but perhaps not tonight. The forecast is for thunder and even I'm not reckless enough to be up there in a storm."

The forecast was correct. By the time they had finished their meal a distant rumble warned of the approaching storm. They sat together on the sofa drinking coffee and listening to the hammering rain. Feeling relaxed and happy, Rebecca rested her head on David's shoulder.

"I love the sound of the rain," she remarked.

"So do I," he replied putting his arm around her and stroking her hair.

She nuzzled his neck and kissed his cheek. As she tried to press her lips to his he stopped her and pushed her away.

"What's the matter?" she asked, "I thought you liked me."

"You know I like you, I love you, but this isn't what I want. I don't want your gratitude or your sympathy. I want you to feel the way I do. I want you to love me."

Rebecca sat back with a sigh and answered, "That is a lot to ask. I don't think I'm capable of loving the way you do. I'm too cynical for the passionate, self-sacrificing, all-encompassing love you write about in your poetry, but if I could fall in love with anyone it would be you."

This promise was enough for him and he kissed her. They embraced and caressed shedding their clothing. They adjourned to the bedroom. He was full of passion but patient and sensitive. Also he had a great deal of stamina. When finally he was exhausted she lay in his arms feeling utterly satisfied. The rain had stopped and the building around them was surprisingly quiet. Her eyes closed sleepily as he ran his fingers through her hair. He spoke to her softly.

"I'm sorry if I wasn't any good. I'm rather out of practise."

She laughed out loud then hit him with her pillow.

"Ow! What? What did I say?"

"You idiot! I've just had the best orgasm of my life and you're apologising for not being any good!"

"It is very sweet of you to massage my ego like that but I think you are flattering me."

"I'm not. You mustn't believe some of the things you read about me. I haven't had the hundreds of lovers certain journalists claim and I haven't had the wild and varied sex life they suggest. Apart from the two fat old men whom you no doubt know about, I only ever had one other lover before you."

"Then you aren't disappointed?"

She attacked him again with the pillow. He fought her off and rolled over on top of her then kissed her several times.

When he paused for breath she asked, "What about you? Are you disappointed? Now you've seen everything do I live up to your expectations?"

"You're everything I ever wanted you to be and much more."

Now he was aroused again and they made love once more. This time he really was spent and fell asleep grinning like the Cheshire Cat.

*

They slept in late the morning after. David got up to prepare breakfast while Rebecca showered. As she dried herself she could hear him singing "Bring Me Sunshine" as he clattered about in the kitchen. A buzz announced a caller at the front door. David swore loudly. There was a brief exchange on the intercom which Rebecca did not catch followed by more swearing from David.

He banged on the bathroom door and asked, "Becky are you decent?"

She opened the door wearing only a towel and replied, "Not exactly, what's the problem?"

"I completely forgot I was expecting visitors this morning. You'd better put some clothes on."

"What sort of visitors?"

"Just a couple of friends. I'm really sorry, I forgot all about it and now they are here so I can't really tell them to go away."

"No of course not. I'll get dressed."

"Actually you look good like that."

"Thanks but I think I'll wear something a little more conventional."

There was a knock at the door and she disappeared into the bedroom. David went to greet his guests.

"What's this?" demanded a female voice. "Unshaven and only half dressed at ten o'clock. Not like you David!"

"I'm sorry," he replied, "I've been rather distracted, I forgot you were coming."

"Distracted? Have you got a woman here?"

"Guilty!" David confessed.

Another male voice asked, "Anyone we know? I thought the only woman you had eyes for was the lovely Rosa."

"That's right, it is Rosa."

"No seriously," said the woman, "who is she?"

"Seriously," replied David, "she is Rosa, or rather Rebecca Clayton to use her real name. You must have heard the rumours that she has split with the President. Well, they are true. She wanted to get away for a while so she is staying with me."

"Yeah right!" replied the other man in disbelief. "Where is she then?"

"In the bedroom getting dressed." David knocked on the door and asked, "Do you want tea or coffee Becky?"

By now Rebecca was respectable so she opened the door and replied, "Tea please my love."

The looks on the faces of his two friends were priceless. If only they had been captured in a photograph they could have been printed and framed for all eternity. While they stood gaping, David busied himself in the kitchen serving tea and coffee.

"There are croissants in the oven if you are hungry," he said.

"Yes please I'm starving," replied Rebecca.

The two visitors were recovering from their initial shock but were still staring. They were both a little older than her; the woman was an attractive red-head, the man was black, tall and of slender build.

"Are you going to introduce me?" Rebecca asked as she helped David to carry the breakfast things through to the living-room.

"Yes of course, this is Karen Baker and Sean Nichols, they are representatives of the Liberation Party. They are here to discuss the forthcoming by-election."

"What by-election?" asked Rebecca.

"It's not surprising you haven't heard about it," replied David. "Hardly anyone has. With the theatre bombing and everything else not even RNN have taken much interest, but the MP for Hackney, Tony Fincham, recently announced he will be retiring on grounds of ill health. Of course the Phoenix Party regards holding an election as a mere formality so haven't done much to publicise it."

They all sat down around the coffee table, David and Rebecca tucking into croissants while the guests sipped their coffee.

After her first few mouthfuls Rebecca said to David, "You didn't mention you were a member of the Liberation Party. I mean I knew that was where your sympathies lay but I didn't know you were politically active."

"Not very active," David answered. "I pay the membership, get the newsletters and have been to some meetings but nothing more. Although Karen and Sean are here today to persuade me to be more active."

"That could be dangerous," replied Rebecca. "You'd risk losing your job for a start."

"I've been thinking about chucking that in for a while. I like growing things and the pay is reasonable but I don't much care for my employers."

Neither Sean nor Karen seemed inclined to speak for a while. They were no doubt still trying to come to terms with the presence of a celebrity.

Eventually Karen suggested, "Perhaps we should come back later."

"No it's OK," said Rebecca. "If you want to talk to David I'll go out for an hour or so. I could take a walk or do some shopping."

Karen looked relieved but as Rebecca was about to stand up David stopped her.

"I'd rather you stayed Becky. If I'm going to make any important decisions about my future I'll want your opinion. That's assuming you are going to be a part of my future."

"I hope so," she answered, giving his hand a squeeze.

"Then you'll stay and hear what Karen and Sean have to say?"

"Yes of course. If that is what you want."

Now both the visitors were looking extremely uncomfortable.

"Are you sure about this?" Karen asked reluctantly. "Is it wise to discuss Liberation Party business in front of someone so closely connected to Phoenix?"

"But Rebecca isn't connected to Phoenix," David argued.

"She was until very recently closely connected to the President," Karen insisted.

"But that is over now," David said firmly.

"OK, as long as you are sure," Karen relented. She turned to Rebecca and explained the business which brought her and Sean there, "We have asked David to stand as Liberation candidate. If there is to be any point in contesting the election at all we need a candidate who can't be ignored. David may not have much political experience but he is extremely eloquent and his reputation as hero of the North-East riots is something we can exploit. Also, not wishing to be offensive but it is a fact; his face is one people will remember."

Rebecca was shocked that Karen should speak about David's scars so bluntly. She felt angry that Karen had drawn attention to his disfigurement but at the same time she understood the truth in what Karen had said and respected her honesty.

Sean confirmed what Karen told her and added, "Things are going badly for the Liberation Party at the moment and we need to try some new tactics. If I, Karen, or any of the other party stalwarts were to stand we would just be ignored. We desperately need a candidate who will at least be worthy of a few lines in the licensed press."

"I see," said Rebecca, then turning to David she asked, "Are you going to do it?"

"I haven't decided yet," he answered. "Although I would be willing to stand I can think of several reasons against it. Firstly I barely know anything about politics. Secondly we can't make use of my slight fame as The Man Behind the Mask as if I revealed my secret identity I would be arrested for submitting material to an unlicensed website. Thirdly my so-called heroism was so long ago now it has been completely forgotten and isn't likely to be of any PR value. If it is a face you are looking for you should use Rebecca's. Far more people would vote for her lovely visage than for my battered old mug."

"You are the best chance we have," said Karen. "If I stand I would be lucky to even get my picture on the local news site; if you stand you would be on the front page."

"But if Rebecca were to stand she would be the top story on the IMC evening news," said David.

"Could you please take this seriously?"

"I am. You want a candidate who will get noticed. Rebecca would get noticed."

"Rebecca isn't a party member and she doesn't even live in Hackney."

"She does now and she could join the party today if she wanted. What do you think Rebecca? Fancy giving it a go?"

"You really are quite insane aren't you?" replied Rebecca.

"Possibly," agreed David, "but you must know far more about the workings of parliament than any of us. Perhaps now you have left the circus you should consider a career in politics."

"It is an interesting idea," said Karen, "but can we stick to the point. The by-election is going to be held in three months and we need to select a candidate. Sean and I agree you are the best choice but we can't put your name forward until you've made a decision."

"Well I had pretty much made up my mind that I would do it," David answered, "but as you see my personal circumstances have changed rather dramatically just recently and now the decision isn't mine alone to make."

"What does that mean?" demanded Karen.

"It means that I need to discuss this with Rebecca before I give you my answer."

Rebecca was flattered but rather alarmed that David already regarded her as his partner.

"It really isn't up to me whether you stand or not," she said.

"But we ought to talk about it. In fact there are quite a lot of things we ought to talk about."

"We don't need an answer today," said Sean. "This obviously isn't the best time for this discussion."

"Alright," Karen reluctantly acquiesced, "but we can't leave this for more than a week. We have to stop dithering and start fighting if we are to have even the remotest chance of winning this seat."

"I'll call you on Monday," said David, "I should have a better idea where I stand by then."

He bid farewell to Karen and Sean and they departed.

Once they were alone David suggested, "Let's go for a walk, my brain functions better in the fresh air."

It was a beautifully sunny day, warm but with a light breeze. The air smelt fresh after the previous night's rain. They walked in silence for a while. There was virtually no traffic on the roads. The only cars were rusting on driveways or burnt out wrecks abandoned in empty car parks. A number of cyclists were risking the potholes but most people got about on foot. Rebecca remembered the typical inner city gait from her youth in Brixton, the head down, slouching walk with hands pushed deep into pockets. The posture of people who did not need to look up as they already knew what was there and could entertain no possibility of any change.

David took Rebecca's arm and said, "I know when you agreed to move in with me it was only supposed to be for a few days but I'd like it to be longer. Do you think you could make this a long-term arrangement?"

"I don't know," she replied. "Really we have only just met each other. We'll have to just see how it goes, but right now I'd rather be with you than on my own. I don't have many other friends and the few I do have are better off without me at the moment, what with John trying to convince everyone I'm a terrorist sympathiser. You do realise if any of his people find out about us you can kiss your job goodbye?"

"I'll have to pack that in pretty soon anyway. Even if I don't stand in the by-election I plan to take a more active role with the Liberation Party, which won't go down well at Downing Street. I just feel it's time I tried to do something with my life."

"Funny you should say that, it's exactly how I feel."

"What? You're already famous!"

"But I've never done anything important or useful."

"Yes you have. You made people happy."

"I also helped to line the pockets of some very rich and corrupt people like Samuel Newman, not to mention all the publicity I created for the Phoenix Party. No I'm done with that. I'm done with John Bryant; I'm done with Phoenix and all those self-serving, greedy bastards who keep them in power. If you want to stand in this by-election then I will do whatever I can to help."

"Certainly a celebrity endorsement will drastically improve my chances."

"Unless John decides to take it as a personal insult and have us both arrested."

"That is the main reason I am now reluctant to stand. Phoenix only tolerates opposition so long as they are ignored. If a candidate starts to get noticed they are dealt with. Of course I was aware of this before and as the risk was to be mine alone I was prepared to take it. Now I have you to consider."

"If you are prepared to face the President's wrath then I am too."

"We should take some time to think this over. Are you hungry? There's a nice café just over the road. I know it looks awful but they actually make some decent sandwiches and their cakes are great."

David had been right about the café and they had an excellent lunch. They spent much of the afternoon exploring the neighbourhood. David was an extraordinary guide. He had a talent for seeing past the mundane revealing fascinating details which were invisible to the less informed observer. He spotted exquisite tiny flowers among the masses of weeds growing through the pavement. He pointed out a sparrowhawk and a peregrine falcon where Rebecca would only have seen pigeons. He also knew much of the area's history, showing her where there had been gasworks and factories.

Back at David's flat later that afternoon Rebecca helped him to prepare dinner, or rather he instructed her on how to chop an onion without losing any fingers. She was horribly embarrassed by her clumsiness with even a small kitchen knife and was regretting offering her assistance, when the phone rang. It was Karen wanting to know if David had reached a decision yet. They talked for several minutes, David repeating what he had already said that morning.

On hanging up he returned to the kitchen complaining, "I did say I would call on Monday."

"Did you tell her you would stand?" asked Rebecca.

"I said I still wasn't certain but I probably would and if I did you would be supporting me."

They had just sat down to eat when there was another call. Again it was Karen. This time David put it on the speakers so Rebecca could hear what she had to say.

"I've just been talking to Alicia Cain," said Karen. "You won't believe what she said."

"I bet I can guess," replied David. "She wants to know if Rebecca will stand instead of me."

"How the hell did you know that?"

"It's obvious. Liberation needs a candidate who will get people's attention."

"I tried to explain that I'd only just met Rebecca and that she isn't even a member of the party but as soon as I mentioned Rebecca's name Alicia was completely carried away with the idea of trying to persuade her to stand. So I promised to call and ask if there was even a remote chance you would consider it, Rebecca."

"Are you serious?" asked Rebecca.

"I am, or at least Alicia is. She really thinks it could be our big chance."

"And she's right," agreed David.

"I would consider it if it wasn't such short notice," Rebecca answered. "I mean I would like to help the Liberation Party, but this is too sudden. I only arrived in Hackney yesterday. I don't know anything about the place."

"What is there to know?" replied David. "It is an inner city borough full of poor people who the government doesn't give a shit about. Do you think whoever the Phoenix Party nominate will be any better acquainted with the concerns of ordinary citizens? Tony Fincham spent most of the time he wasn't in the Commons at his second home in Surrey."

"If you do want to help Liberation this might be your only chance," warned Karen. "It is four years until the next general election and God knows what might happen in that time. Bryant might crown himself king and scrap elections altogether."

"I doubt even he would dare to go that far," replied Rebecca.

"Perhaps not," agreed Karen, "but who knows. Alicia has practically begged me to ask you both to come to Party HQ on Monday evening. Can I tell her you will come?"

"We'll be there," David answered, "unless you can think of any reason why we shouldn't go, Rebecca."

"No, in fact I would very much like to meet Alicia Cain."

They made arrangements to meet on Monday evening and Karen finally rang off and allowed them to finish their meal.

GRASS ROOTS
Simon Chandra

To anyone used to seeing Karen Baker address hundreds of delegates at the Liberation Party Conference it will be difficult to imagine her making speeches in some run-down social club to an audience of a dozen people or fewer, but this is how most of the Party stalwarts began their careers. In the days when Phoenix was completely dominant the Liberation Party had a constant uphill struggle just to remind people that they still existed. This was a time when political debates rarely featured on television and the media was entirely controlled by the government. In the first years of this century the Liberation Party was so insignificant and inadequately funded that the government no longer needed to use the underhand tactics they had relied on in the past to discredit the opposition.

It was at one of these poorly attended meetings that Karen Baker met The Man Behind the Mask, David O'Brien, and through him was introduced to Rebecca Clayton. I would have liked to talk to her about this but Ms Baker has very little time to spare between her ministerial duties, her constituency and her family. Although she was not available for an interview we did exchange emails. She was kind enough to arrange for a meeting with her husband, Sean Nichols, who is a former Liberation Party MP and was acquainted with both Rebecca and O'Brien.

We met at their London flat. Nichols still works for the party and was in town on business but Karen was travelling the country visiting hospitals at the time. Nichols explained how though they both used the London flat regularly it was very rare that they occupied it at the same time.

"It must have been even more hectic when you were both in parliament," I remarked.

"It was. We hardly ever saw each other. That was why I gave it up. There was no way we could have a family if we were both constantly dashing between Westminster and our constituencies."

"A lot of men would expect their wife to be the one to give up her career."

"They might but we are Liberation Party to the core. We don't hold with the Phoenix idea of traditional family values. To me 'traditional family values' just means sexism and prejudice. Karen's smarter that I am. I accept that and don't have a problem with it."

"I've heard suggestions that she has ambitions to climb even higher, perhaps even take the top job one day."

"I thought you came to talk about Rebecca Clayton, not my wife's career."

"I did, sorry but my editor would never forgive me if I didn't try to sniff out an exclusive. Right, to the point then, were you and Karen already together at the time you met Rebecca Clayton?"

"We were, we got together at university. We were both law students and both politically active. Unfortunately our involvement in a demonstration got us both kicked off our respective postgraduate courses and we were unable to continue our legal careers. I ended up working as a groceries delivery driver and Karen, who had been training to be a barrister, got stuck with a string of menial office jobs. We continued campaigning for the Liberation Party but it was pretty futile until Rebecca came along."

"Just how did that happen? How did she go from President Bryant's mistress to Liberation Party candidate?"

"It was pretty sudden. To this day I don't know exactly how it happened. Originally we had intended that David should stand in the by-election. He had been a member of the Liberation Party for a couple of years and was keen to take a more active role. Then Rebecca appeared."

"You make it sound like she suddenly materialised out of nowhere."

"That's because that is pretty much what happened. We knew David was a massive fan of hers. He talked about her loads and we read the poems he composed about her. Karen and I were among the few people who knew he was the Man Behind the Mask. He had mentioned meeting her while he was working in the President's garden, but had never suggested they were at all intimate. I had not even realised they were on first name terms; until the day he introduced us he never even referred to her as Rebecca, he always called her Rosa. We literally knew nothing about it until we went round to his flat one day and there she was."

"So he didn't tell you about the letters he wrote to her?"

"What letters?"

"He used to write to her as The Man Behind the Mask. She showed some of the letters to my mum but she didn't know who they were from at the time. I wanted to know at what point he revealed his identity to her."

"I'm afraid I can't help you. Of course we asked him how it was that he and Rebecca got together but he refused to say. He never liked to talk about himself. He could talk very eloquently about political issues but personal questions always received monosyllabic or cryptic replies. We only found out how he got those scars by accident. Karen was reading about the North-East riots and came across some of the articles about David. We didn't even know he had been in the army until then."

"So you don't know exactly when or why Rebecca split with Bryant and the Phoenix Party?"

"No I'm afraid not. We only know that she broke up with Bryant shortly after the Newman Grand bombing. In truth though I don't think she was ever a true Phoenix supporter in her heart. Certainly by the time we knew her she hated everything they stood for."

"It has been claimed by some people that she had no political convictions at all, only affiliating herself with the Liberation Party as she saw it as a means to success."

"I don't believe that. At the time she joined us we were at our lowest standing in the polls ever. I don't think anyone could have predicted what happened. If she wanted political power she would have stuck with Bryant."

"Other people have suggested that she was weak minded and was indoctrinated by people around her."

Nichols laughed and answered, "There was nothing weak about her."

"But she was in love with David. Did she stand because it was what he wanted?"

"No. I think he may have been the first to suggest the idea but the decision was definitely hers."

"Did she understand the risk she was taking?"

"Of course. We all understood the dangers and talked about them regularly."

"Some people have said that if David really loved her he would never have allowed her to expose herself to those dangers."

"I can't comment on that. Perhaps there were times when they were alone when he begged her not to carry on, or perhaps he knew it was what she wanted to do and refused to allow his own feelings to interfere. I know Karen and I had long talks about the risks of our campaign. If either of us had ever wanted to walk away we agreed we both would. Of course things were different when there was just the two of us. Now we have children our priorities have changed. I wouldn't now be prepared to do anything which could jeopardise their safety or wellbeing."

"There is just one more thing that I would like to ask you and that is, what was Rebecca like?"

"You mean what was she like to work with?"

"Yes and as a person. Did you like her?"

"Yes I liked her. She had beauty, charm and charisma so she was hard not to like, but I never felt as though we were really close. She kept a lot hidden. She wasn't quiet like David, she always had plenty to talk about, but she didn't share her feelings or confide in anyone other than David. She worked extremely hard. She was tough and she was smart too. She may not have had the best of educations but she had brains."

"What about O'Brien? Are you still in contact with him?"

"We didn't hear anything from him for a long time. He was living a rather reclusive existence up in the Highlands of Scotland. Then last month he suddenly reappeared. Apparently he's working for the Party again, writing some of our literature. I bumped into him at Party HQ. The odd thing is, he still has the scars. I'm sure he could have had treatment for them by now. After all the work Karen has done to revive the Health Service it can't be the cost of the procedure that is preventing him."

For a long time after my meeting with Nichols I thought about O'Brien's scars. Under the Phoenix Party government only urgent and life-saving treatment was funded by the NHS: anything else had to be paid for by the patient. The delicate cosmetic procedure to remove scarring would have been expensive and doubtless beyond O'Brien's means as a gardener. However, since O'Brien has published several volumes of poetry and regularly contributes to a number of publications he must now make a respectable living and as Nichols says, under the Liberation Party the NHS would at least partially fund the treatment for such severe disfigurement. Why then has he chosen to remain so badly scarred?

Perhaps after having the scars for so long he has come to regard them as much a part of himself as any other feature. Or does he choose to keep them as a reminder of his past? Maybe it is because it is the way Rebecca knew and loved him and in honour of her memory he refuses to change. I long to ask him, but although I have made numerous attempts to contact The Man Behind the Mask I have received no reply. He possesses the answers to so many of my questions and without his help this history of Rosa which I am compiling will never be complete.

Monday 16th July 2103

David worked early hours in the garden of Downing Street so it was only just after six when he kissed Rebecca goodbye and left the flat. Rebecca was used to the other extreme and fell asleep again as soon as he was gone. She had had difficulty sleeping the last couple of nights as her mind was filled with thoughts of the forthcoming by-election. When she did get up she spent the morning reading up on the career of Alicia Cain in preparation for their meeting that evening.

The Liberation Party had formed shortly after Clarkson came to power, from a coalition of remaining members of the former main parties who opposed Phoenix's radical policies. Alicia had begun her political career as a Liberal Democrat but the massive landslide victory which brought Clarkson into office virtually annihilated them as a parliamentary party.

When the battered remnants of the old parties had first joined forces using the name The Liberty Party they were a credible opposition with a respectable number of MPs. Clarkson and his government were not prepared to tolerate genuine opponents. They took extreme measures to destroy not only the Liberty Party but the democratic system.

Within a few months of the Liberty Party's formation, several of their MPs were arrested, including the party leader, and charged with various offences such as associating with known terrorists, distribution of terrorist propaganda and withholding information from the security forces. More arrests followed over the subsequent months and years, sometimes relating to terrorism, sometimes to homosexuality, sometimes to financial irregularities. Though only a few of the MPs were ever brought to trial, the arrests were enough to force their resignations. In the resulting by-elections the seats were invariably won by the Phoenix Party but if anyone dared to suggest there had been any interference with the electoral process, they ended up facing charges themselves.

During the first three years of its existence, the Liberty Party went through a rapid succession of leaders. Each one was forced out by allegations of some form of misconduct. Clarkson took advantage of this and called an early election, claiming he wanted a mandate from the people to enact more radical changes. Whether it was down to the constant stream of damaging headlines or whether the voting was rigged, the Liberty Party was soundly thrashed in the next general election and the Phoenix Party returned an ever larger majority.

It was after a second, equally devastating election defeat in 2092 that Alicia Cain took over as leader of the party and the name was changed from Liberty to

Liberation. By now Clarkson's regime had achieved such total dominance that it no longer had anything to fear from its bruised and battered rivals. So long as a token opposition existed they could maintain the pretence of democracy so allowed Cain to remain.

Rebecca admired the fortitude which had kept Cain fighting all these years. As a black woman Cain constantly faced prejudice. There had been plenty of unpleasant rumours about her circulated in the licensed media over the years but she never stooped to the childish name-calling her opponents delighted in, and focused on trying to make her arguments heard. This was not easy when the major publishers and broadcasters were entirely controlled by the government.

David returned from work just after four. Once he had showered and changed he and Rebecca walked to the station where they met Karen and Sean. They took a train to Bethnal Green where the Liberation Party had their headquarters. Rebecca was familiar with the Phoenix Party's London offices and although she was expecting the Liberation Party HQ to be smaller and less grand, she was still surprised by the shabbiness of the building to which she was taken that evening.

Like much of inner London, half the buildings on Bethnal Green Road were boarded up, with "For Sale" or "To Let" signs on display. The property on one side of Liberation HQ had formerly been a fast food restaurant but judging from the faded and peeling paintwork it had been vacant for some time. On the other side was a second-hand clothing shop.

The party offices had bars on the windows and numerous security cameras but these measures had not prevented vandals spraying slogans such as "Lesbo Niggers", "Pakis and Perverts Out" and "Aids Fuckers" all over the walls. Only a single discreet board revealed the owners of the office building and this had been defaced. On gaining access they went up to a first floor meeting room where Alicia Cain was waiting for them. She already knew both Karen and Sean but had yet to be introduced to David.

Alicia Cain was extremely unremarkable in appearance. She was middle aged, average height and average build, black but not exceptionally dark. She was smartly dressed in a grey suit. Her hair was short and neat. There were coffee and biscuits already on the table and they all took a seat.

After Karen had made the introductions Cain addressed Rebecca, "So the rumours are true, you have split up with Bryant."

"That's right," she replied.

"And you have split from the Phoenix Party also?"

"I was never really with the Phoenix Party," Rebecca answered. "Any publicity work the circus did for them was just a job and I never was a member of the party. In fact I've never even voted for them. Last election I voted Liberation."

"Karen tells me you now wish to take an active role in supporting the Liberation Party. That you are prepared to publicly back David should he wish to be our candidate."

"That is correct."

"I think Karen may already have told you this, but it is my opinion that we would stand a better chance of winning the seat if you stood yourself. I'm not going to lie to you. I'm not going to tell you that I think you will be a fantastic politician and a champion of the people. You may be, I don't know, I don't know you. As Party Leader I want you to stand because frankly we are desperate. If you ask people on the streets about the Liberation Party and what our policies are they haven't a clue. Many people don't even know we still exist. If we could get a talking duck to stand we would. We would do anything to get ourselves heard."

Rebecca was not offended at being compared to a talking duck. She appreciated Cain's honesty. Had Cain attempted to flatter her she would have been less inclined to take the proposal seriously.

"If I were to stand how do we know it will be a fair contest? I know Bryant well enough to know the kind of dirty tricks Phoenix has resorted to in the past."

"I'm afraid I can't give you any guarantees," replied Cain. "We can only hope that since they already have such a large majority they will be prepared to lose Hackney. In general it is in Bryant's interest to keep up the illusion that he is not a dictator and allowing his opponents an occasional victory is a good way to do this."

"Suppose I do stand and win; since, as you say Phoenix has such a huge majority, what could I actually achieve?"

"We have to keep fighting for every seat or we may as well give up all together, besides your fame and popularity would be a major asset to the party. For instance you would stand a better chance of getting on TV than any of our other MPs. IMC are more likely to want you in for an interview than me or anyone else in the party."

"Only until the novelty has worn off."

"Perhaps, but like I said we are desperate."

They talked for some time about the Liberation Party in general, what the job of MP would actually involve and the benefits to the party of a high profile victory. Throughout the meeting Cain addressed herself almost entirely to Rebecca and seemed to have forgotten that David was also a prospective candidate. Now that they were beginning to comprehend the possibilities having Rebecca as their candidate would create, Karen and Sean also began to look favourably on the idea and added their support to much of what Alicia said. They even began to make suggestions for her campaign.

Eventually Cain asked, "So will you do it?"

"I still need to think about it. How soon do you need a decision?"

"By Friday at the latest."

"Then I promise I will let you know by then."

"And if Rebecca does not stand will you do so?" Cain asked, finally addressing David.

"I will," he agreed, "but I realise I'm a poor substitute."

*

Much later that night Rebecca was lying awake mulling over all they had discussed. David had hardly spoken since they had left Liberation Headquarters; no doubt he too had been deep in thought. Though he had been the first to suggest the idea he now seemed reluctant to give an opinion on whether or not she should stand. After lying awake for over an hour she got up and went to the bathroom. Getting back into bed beside him she saw that David was awake also.

"I'm sorry, I didn't mean to disturb you," she apologised.

"It's all right, I wasn't asleep."

"Too much on your mind? Me too."

"Still trying to decide?"

She sighed and answered, "I want to help the Liberation Party, I really do. If I thought that being arrested and thrown in jail would help to bring about the end of Phoenix Party tyranny then I wouldn't hesitate to do it. I'm just not prepared to risk my life and my freedom in order to achieve nothing."

"I understand that," David agreed. "Too many people have thrown their lives away for nothing. I almost became one of them. But Cain is a smart woman with a lot of political experience. I'm sure she wouldn't ask you to do this if she didn't believe there would be some benefit. What concerns me though is that benefit may be all the Liberation Party's and the sacrifice all yours."

"I wouldn't mind that. I would happily suffer slander and the ruin of my reputation or even spend a few years in prison if I thought it would help bring an end to the sort of misery and desperation to which poor Martin was driven. The problem is that I know Bryant too well. Cain is right about John Bryant trying to maintain the illusion of democracy but I know him and he is a cunning bastard.

"No doubt he would allow me to win the election and take my seat in parliament. Then after a few months in the House of not doing anything spectacular, when people are starting to lose interest in me, unpleasant rumours about me will start to circulate. Eventually I'll either have to resign in disgrace or else I will be arrested. Then there would be another by-election and Liberation would be in an even worse position than before, as Bryant will be able to say to the electorate, 'I told you so! The Liberation Party can't be trusted.'"

"That does sound like an all too probable course of events. You had better talk to Cain and tell her that you won't do it."

"But you have said you will stand if I don't."

"Someone has got to."

"Then it will be you that risks ending up in prison."

"It will only be a very slight risk for me. Far more likely I will just be ignored, Phoenix will win and nothing will change."

Rebecca glanced at the clock. It was after midnight.

"You should be asleep," she said. "Don't you have to be up before six?"

"I do, but don't worry. I can take a nap in the potting shed. I frequently do when I've had a busy night. No one ever disturbs me. You know Bryant hardly ever ventures further than the terrace."

"He's a fat, lazy git."

"Indeed. Let's talk about the election when I get back. Then we can call Cain and tell her what we have decided."

"OK, now let's try to get some sleep."

OLD LONDON
The Man Behind the Mask

The city wears a veil of mist
To hide its cankerous pock-marked face
Nature's own brand of cosmetics
To hide neglect, ruin and disgrace.

Heavy silence stifles my breath
Mouldering dampness seeps under my skin
Weeds invade through cracks in the pavement
The wilderness is creeping back in.

Once there were crowds, noise and traffic
Fumes of petrol poisoned the air
Now there is a canvas of nothing
But loneliness, isolation and despair.

Where greed once ruled, apathy reigns
It is futile to strive against the decay
One can only stand in dignified silence
And watch old London crumble away.

Tuesday 17th July 2103

The following day was showery and Rebecca spent the morning lolling about the flat, still thinking about the election. At lunch-time Karen Baker phoned, wanting to know if she had made a decision yet and to share some ideas for the campaign. Rebecca refused to discuss any details, insisting that she still had to make up her mind. Karen reminded her several times how little time there was before the by-election but Rebecca was determined she would give no definite answer, at least until she had spoken to David that evening.

In the afternoon she went out to do a bit of shopping, mainly just to pick up some toiletries and feminine articles to clutter up David's bachelor bathroom. She was back at the flat before David returned from work. He arrived around four and while he showered and changed she made a pot of tea. They sat down together as perfectly at ease as if they had been married for years.

"How was your day?" Rebecca asked.

"Quiet, I spent most of it keeping out the rain in the potting shed and yes I did have a siesta in there. The household staff were pretty busy as Bryant is having a dinner party tonight, but they generally just leave me to my own devices. How about you? What have you been up to?"

"Not much, buying shampoo and body lotion. Karen called earlier. She has all sorts of plans for my election campaign. She will be horribly disappointed if I don't stand."

"But I thought we pretty much decided last night that Bryant was unlikely to let you keep the seat if you won it so there would be little point in you standing?"

"That's right, but I've been thinking about it all day and it occurred to me that there could be a way that I could stand without Bryant interfering."

"How?"

"I could resort to a few dirty tricks of my own. I could convince him that I'm really on his side and not a proper Liberation supporter at all. It would have to seem like it was his idea, but if he thought I was his mole working inside the opposition he would allow me to enter parliament."

"Do you really think you could fool him?"

"I'm fairly confident I could. I know how he thinks."

"It's too great a risk. If he found you out you'd lose a lot more than your seat."

"But think about it, with Bryant's trust I could not only get into parliament but I might even be able to do something once I'm there."

"We should talk to Cain and the others about this."

"No I want to tell as few people as possible in case there are leaks. Also what I'm planning is essentially dishonest and Cain has a reputation for honesty which I wouldn't want to sully."

"You're really serious about this aren't you?"

"I am. Now that I have had the idea I don't think I can let it go. I have to try it. I know it could go horribly wrong but if I let this opportunity to make a difference pass me by I know I will regret it forever."

"It's your decision. If you think you can do this and you are certain it is what you want, then I will do whatever I can to support you. I will help you in your campaign, I will take care of your personal safety to the best of my ability and if it comes to it I will even try to break you out of prison, but I can't promise that I will succeed."

"I hope it won't come to that. If it does then just remember I chose this course of my own free will. Not you, Karen, Sean or even Alicia Cain are to blame if anything happens to me."

"So, what is our first move?"

"Tomorrow I go and talk to John, then it all depends on him. If I succeed with him then I call Alicia Cain and tell her I will stand."

*

Rebecca was awake much earlier than usual the following morning. She was up before David had left for work but as she knew that Bryant was not an early riser she waited a couple of hours before setting out on her mission. She arrived at Downing Street shortly before nine, causing many eyebrows to be raised. She was admitted to the reception area and asked to wait rather than being allowed up to the President's private apartments as she would previously have been. After waiting for over half an hour she was finally shown to the President's study.

Bryant stood as she entered but didn't bother to greet her.

"You've got a nerve turning up here after all you said the other day," he said.

"I know," she replied, "I've come to apologise."

Bryant laughed humourlessly, "You don't think you can just walk in here and say sorry and everything will be as it was before do you? What makes you think I'll want you back? Besides, I've heard some worrying reports about your behaviour over the last few days. I'm told you've been attending meetings with Alicia Cain. If that is the kind of company you are keeping now you can consider yourself unwelcome here."

"I'm not expecting you to take me back and I don't want to return to how things were, but I want to explain. I want you to know that I regret all the stupid things I said and that I understand now how foolish I was."

"All right Rebecca, sit down, I've got a few minutes to spare and for old time's sake I'll listen to what you have to say."

He slumped in his chair, resting his elbows on the desk while she took a seat opposite. After taking a deep breath she began.

"You know how upset I was by what happened at the theatre. I blamed you and the Phoenix Party for what Martin did. I understand now how stupid that was but I was angry. I suppose you know that the police questioned me and searched my flat?"

"It is hardly surprising after the sentiments you expressed to me. The things you said sounded like terrorist propaganda. I may have repeated your words to certain other people; they chose to act as they thought best."

"Yes of course, I realise that. It was just that after the police had been to my apartment I wanted to get away for a while so I went to stay with a friend."

"Would this be a male friend?"

"Yes but he's nobody special," she lied. "He's just a guy I met at the theatre. Anyway, this friend happens to be a Liberation supporter. He told me all the usual stuff about how much better the country would be with Cain in power and at first I was ready to believe it all. I wanted to put my faith in a miraculous solution to all our problems. I wanted to share his conviction that the Liberation Party had all the answers. That is why I went to meet with Cain on Monday."

"And does Cain have all the answers?"

"No of course not! She hasn't got any at all. I realised after talking to her and some of her colleagues for just a few minutes that they are a pathetic bunch of idealists and dreamers. They live in some kind of fantasy utopia, completely out of touch with reality. We talked about the Newman Grand bombing and they confidently promised that if they had been in power it wouldn't have happened as they would legalise homosexuality. So I asked what they plan to do to prevent the spread of diseases like New Aids. They said they will educate people to use condoms, but that has been tried before. Even if people know they should use a condom they don't. They forget, or they're too drunk, or they just can't be bothered."

"This is true. People cannot be trusted to do the right thing unless they are forced to do so. They will always choose their own immediate gratification and ignore the future consequences."

"Exactly, I tried to tell them that but they wouldn't listen. It is the same with family planning. They say under a Liberation government everyone would be allowed to have as many children as they want whether they are married or not. I asked who is going to provide for all these children and they responded with the usual crap about redistributing wealth. You know, the old Robin Hood policy of taxing the rich and giving to the poor. I attempted to point out that the net result is that everyone ends up poor but I think Cain's grasp of economics is even worse than mine."

"So the rumours I hear about you standing in the Hackney by-election are completely unfounded?"

"Cain did suggest it, shows how desperate they are. I said no but they still seem to be convinced that I'm going to change my mind if they pester me enough. I now understand just how dangerous these people are. If you allowed them to go on television with all their crazy promises of freedom and wealth for everyone then they would certainly get elected. People in general are too stupid to ask how it is all going to be achieved. Then once Cain and her loony lefties are in power and doing whatever they like, everything the Phoenix Party accomplished during the recovery would be destroyed in a matter of months and in its place we'd have poverty, disease and famine."

"So you finally understand what my colleagues and I have stood for all these years?"

"I do, and I'm sorry it has taken me so long. I had to meet Cain and hear the complete pile of bullshit for myself in order to get my head around it."

"I'm glad you've learnt something out of all this and I accept your apology, but I'm afraid I've moved on."

"You mean you have found someone else already?"

"Not exactly, but I have a date tonight."

"That's OK, I didn't come here to try to get back together. I just wanted you to know that I am sorry and that I have a renewed respect for you and what you have done for this country. It is time I moved on too. We had a wonderful time together but I don't want to be the other woman for the rest of my life. At least we can part as friends."

Bryant looked thoughtful for a while then said, "Perhaps as a friend you would have dinner with me tomorrow. There are a few more things I would like to talk to you about but I haven't time now."

"Dinner sounds great. I'll see you tomorrow then. Would you mind if I have a quick wander around the garden before I go? You know how much I've always liked it out there."

"Sure go ahead, but watch out for the crazy gardener. I'm told he's been acting even more strangely than usual. Apparently yesterday he was singing to the plants because it makes them grow better!"

The previous day's rain was long gone and there wasn't a single cloud in the sky. The air was rapidly heating up under the intense glare of the sun which was still ascending. Rebecca found David by the pond clearing out weed his arms streaked with mud and slime. When he greeted her he spoke with the Irish accent he had used before.

"Ah Miss Rosa, good to see you again, so it is."

She took a seat close by him on the low wall which surrounded the pond. The shade of the walled garden was refreshing after the baking heat out on the lawns.

"I've spoken to John," she said softly.

"How did it go?" he asked in his normal voice.

"Quite well I think. I believe I have convinced him of my allegiance. He has invited me to dinner tomorrow, so I will have to tackle the hard part then. Hopefully he will come up with the idea on his own, if not I will have to find a way to put the notion into his head."

"You'd better tell me all about it when I get home. We'll arouse suspicion if we are seen talking for too long."

"Right, I will leave you to your work. That stuff stinks."

"I don't mind the smell. It's just good clean mud with a few dead things in it."

"Yuck!"

"It's how nature works. The rank and rotting feed the fragrant and floral. Nothing is wasted. All this weed will go on the compost heap and will be nourishing the soil in a few month's time."

"Is that a metaphor?"

"No just a fact, but you may take it as a metaphor if you wish."

"I'll see you later. Try not to bring too much of that slime home with you."

"You may joke, but I frequently bring a bag of Downing Street's finest compost home on the tube. How else do you think I keep the plants on the balcony so healthy?"

"You are a very strange man!"

"I try my best."

*

Before going home Rebecca stopped off at her old flat. She wanted to pick up something suitable to wear for dinner with the President. It was very strange entering her old residence. Although she had only been gone for a few days it felt as though she had been away much longer. It was more like visiting someone else's apartment than returning to her own. She realised how much more comfortable she was in David's cosy flat surrounded by all his books and plants.

She pulled out a suitcase from under the bed, the one which had accompanied her on the last tour, and put her red dress inside. She gathered together make-up and accessories then looked through the rest of her wardrobe. Some of the suits might be useful if she was really going to be a politician. She folded them carefully and packed them. She filled the rest of the space in the case with more casual attire, some nightclothes and underwear, then tossed her bathrobe and a couple of towels on top. She retrieved a smaller bag and filled it with a few books, a couple of framed photos and the programmes she had kept from early circus performances.

Deciding she was now officially moving out and would not be back again, she called the letting agent to give notice. Then she called a taxi and asked reception to send a porter to collect her bags. As she was unsure whether Hunter was still having her movements watched and did not want to lead them to David's address she told the taxi driver to take her to Liverpool Street Station. From there she took another taxi to Hackney.

Once back she unpacked her suitcase. There was plenty of space in the wardrobe to hang her clothes and David had emptied out a couple of drawers for her. After finding places for all her possessions she made herself a light lunch and wondered what to do with the rest of the day. She felt she ought to do something useful so would attempt some cleaning.

The problem was that it was so long since she had needed to do any housework of her own she was not entirely sure of the best way to do it. Her mother's approach to domestic duties had not provided much of an example to learn from. She pulled out various bottles of cleaning products from the cupboard. The label of one indicated that it was ideal for cleaning ovens and hobs. She examined the cooker. She was even less familiar with how to clean one than how to cook with it.

The cooker at the apartment she had just vacated had various lights and buttons under the heading "self-clean". Though she had never done anything with them herself she was aware that the cleaner must have, as sometimes sloshing and gurgling noises came from the appliance accompanied by a soapy, citrus smell. David's cooker had no such controls. She decided to research the topic some other time and settled for wiping down the work surfaces with a cloth and some spray and sweeping the floor.

When she had finished in the kitchen she changed the bed sheets as this was something she at least knew how to do, but as she was out of practice it took longer and was more difficult than she remembered. Once she had fluffed the pillows and smoothed the covers she sat down for a rest. Her eye fell on the book on David's bedside table. It was a notebook she had frequently seen him scribbling in, jotting down ideas for his poems. She picked it up but then had second thoughts. It would probably be wrong to read it without his permission.

As she put the book down it fell open naturally at the last page he had been writing on and she could not prevent herself from reading it. Most of what was scrawled there was illegible and there were many crossings out and smudges, but from the few phrases she could decipher she knew he was attempting to write about her.

The graceful joy of the kestrel on the wing
Is nothing to the rapture of holding you

My heart soars higher than the bird
Lost in boundless skies of blue

She thought these lines were beautiful but underneath he had scribbled the words "rubbish" and "cliché". It seemed that while trying to write he had been doodling in the margin of the page as there was a pretty pattern of roses and hearts. Closing up the book and feeling guilty about the intrusion into his privacy, she rested her head against his pillow, contemplating her own feelings for this intelligent, passionate and courageous man. Already she knew that she loved him, yet she still intended to dine with John Bryant the following night and knew how an evening with her former lover was likely to end.

Rebecca had read enough books and seen enough films to think she understood what true love was supposed to be. If she really loved David the way that he loved her, he ought to be her only concern. Her motivations should be purely to make him happy, and yet her head was so full with so many other desires. She realised now just how much she wanted to enter parliament. She not only sought the opportunity to help the Liberation Party but she also wished to prove she was not just a pretty girl who could do acrobatics. If she could be a part of just a few small changes which made Britain a better place to live, it would be a much greater achievement than her fame as a circus performer.

She was still sitting on the bed deliberating these things when David returned.

As he entered the flat he called out cheerfully, "The Slime Monster is back!"

She greeted him with a brief kiss and asked if he would like a cup of tea.

"I'd love one. I'll have a quick shower first so I don't offend your nostrils any further."

Once he was clean he joined her in the living-room and flopped onto the sofa.

"It's hard work being a Slime Monster," he complained, "especially when the weather is so hot. The forecasters are predicting a whole week of this heat. Still if things work out for you I'll probably be chucking in the gardening job anyway. I'll miss the compost but I won't miss being bossed around by people who don't understand the first thing about plants and are terrified of a bit of dirt."

Rebecca had not been paying attention so made no reply. She was gazing into her cup of tea while contemplating what she should say to him.

"You have to drink the tea before you can read the leaves," David suggested.

"What?" she asked, roused from her reverie.

"I thought you were trying to divine the future from your tea leaves. It was something people used to do a long time ago. I think the art was lost with the introduction of teabags."

"I'm sorry David I haven't the faintest idea what you are talking about."

"Hardly surprising, you were miles away. Is something wrong?"

She put her cup down and said, "I have a confession to make, well, more than one. I can't work your washing machine, I don't know how to clean a cooker and I read your notebook."

"That's all right. You are entitled to read it, most of it is about you! Has something I wrote upset you?"

"No, it's not that."

"Then what is the matter? The meeting with Bryant went well didn't it?"

"It did but I've been thinking about tomorrow night. I know John, I know what he is like. If I have dinner with him he'll want to sleep with me and if I say no any chance of our reaching an agreement will be gone. He is petty and pathetic like that. He isn't so much a man as a massive ego with a dick!"

"Or possibly vice versa," David suggested.

"Well it boils down to either I sleep with him or the whole thing is off."

"I see the problem."

"No you don't. I knew this as soon as I talked to him. I even went back to my old apartment to pick up my little red dress and sexy undies. I've slept with him before to get what I want. That is the kind of slut I am and that is the problem."

"You are not a slut."

"If you ask me not to do it I won't. I'll call Alicia Cain and tell her I won't stand."

"I can't do that. I won't ruin Liberation's chance, your chance, of winning this election just because of trivial sexual jealousy."

"But if I do this will you hate me?"

"Hate you? How could I? I loved you before when you were his mistress. I will love you even more if you can go to him but come home to me."

"Do you mean that? Can you promise me you will never reproach me if I fuck him for Britain?"

"I swear it."

She flung herself into his arms and clung to his neck so tightly he could barely breathe.

"Hey steady on Becky!" he protested, "I should like to die in your arms but not tonight."

*

Wearing her sexy red dress, killer heels and black stockings, Rebecca arrived at Downing Street on Wednesday evening. This time she was allowed straight up to Bryant's apartments where he was waiting for her in the sitting-room.

"You look gorgeous as ever," he said, kissing her on the cheek.

"Thanks, you are looking very well too. How is work?"

He poured her a gin and tonic and answered, "Oh you know, busy, busy. I've been in talks with Sam Newman. His insurance policy for the Grand doesn't cover acts of terrorism so he wants the treasury to loan him the money to rebuild."

"Poor Sam. Are you going to help him?"

"Of course. Sam and I are old friends and we can't afford to let a company like Newman Enterprises go under. Not after all that he has done to help rebuild this country."

"Luchenko seemed to think Newman was losing interest in the Circus. He said something about musicals being the next big thing."

"It's hardly surprising after what happened. With so many performers lost in the bombing Circus Britannia is never going to be the same again. Even if you were to go back to them, and I'm sure you could now we have sorted out that little misunderstanding, it wouldn't be anything like the show it was."

"That is true. I'm not even sure I want to go back to the Circus. After what I've been through I feel I need a change."

"I can understand that. And you're right about Newman's interest in musical theatre. He brought some of his rising stars to dinner here the other day. He was anxious to demonstrate that the Grand would still have a future even if the Circus doesn't."

"And were you convinced?"

"Absolutely, Newman knows how to spot talent. Have you heard of a young lady called Sophie Andrews?"

"Of course, she has been on TV loads in the last couple of weeks and she was playing the lead in the production at the Grand last month. I've also heard some rumours that she is Sam's latest mistress."

Bryant shrugged and replied, "They may have had a brief fling, but as it happens it was with Sophie I had the date last night."

History was repeating itself. Newman had found an attractive, talented young woman and helped advance her career in return for sex. Then when he needed something from the President he had traded his protégée for, in this case, the cash to rebuild his theatre. Bryant had no doubt mentioned Sophie in the hope of making Rebecca jealous, but failed to achieve the effect he desired. Rebecca only felt a little sorry for Miss Andrews.

"How did it go?" she enquired, purely out of politeness.

"Very well I think. I certainly enjoyed our evening together and she has agreed to see me again. She has also agreed to sing at the Phoenix Party Conference."

After Clarkson came to power the Party Conference became increasingly less of a conference and more of a party. Speeches took second place behind entertainment until the event was basically a variety show organised by the government and sponsored by their corporate supporters. In previous years

Circus Britannia had taken part in this extravaganza, usually as part of the grand finale after the President's speech.

"Will she be leading the national anthem?" Rebecca asked with a slight smirk.

"I expect so. This year we'll make sure we have the words up on big screens or something."

Ever since the death of the monarchy there had been a certain amount of embarrassment about the national anthem. Clarkson instated 'Rule Britannia' but with variations to make it more up to date. The problem was no one could remember the new words and a large proportion of the population did not even know the tune. Generally, whenever singing it was required, there were a few loud 'Rule Britannias' with lots of indistinct murmuring in between.

Suddenly the memory of Martin Ashdown singing his own unique versions of the anthem came into her head.

She must have been smiling at the thought because Bryant demanded, "What's so funny?"

"I was just wondering what would happen if someone put up some alternative words on your big screens."

"I'd hang them for treason, that's what. Are you hungry? Dinner should be ready now."

Once they were seated in the dining room and the entrée was served, Bryant asked, "If you aren't going back to the circus have you any idea what you will do?"

"None at all," Rebecca replied. "Cain and her cronies still seem to be convinced I'm going into politics."

"You wouldn't be the first celebrity try it. You do realise you could easily win the Hackney by-election? The Phoenix candidate is some boring old biddy without the slightest hint of wit or charm."

"You aren't suggesting I stand are you? We both know Liberation is a bunch of fantasists who need to wake up and face reality."

"Indeed, the problem with the Liberation Party is they think that giving the people what they want will make them happy, but that isn't true."

"No it's complete rubbish," Rebecca agreed enthusiastically. "People are always saying they want less rationing but if you let them they would eat a month's food in a week and then go hungry and blame the government."

"Sometimes the best way to make people happy is just to let them think they are getting what they want. I mean, suppose you were to stand for Liberation. You'd be elected to parliament and it would give the great unwashed something to feel good about."

"But I'm not sure I want to be involved with those lunatics. If I were to stand shouldn't it be for Phoenix?"

"As a Liberation MP you could be a moderating influence. As an elected representative of the people you would have power over some of the more radical factions of the party."

"I hadn't thought of it like that."

"It's your decision but I believe the best thing for the country would be for you to stand. Phoenix can afford to lose one seat, even a London one, and by losing we restore public confidence in the electoral system."

The staff came to take their plates and serve the main course, which was roast lamb. Bryant probably ate more red meat in a week than the average family consumed in a year. While they ate Bryant chattered about the restaurant where he and Sophie had dined the previous night. Rebecca tried to sound interested but now the real business was concluded she just wanted the evening to be over as soon as possible. By the time dessert was served Bryant had consumed the best part of a bottle of wine on top of the large whisky before dinner and was entering the boozy, euphoric state of unbearable smugness which was all too familiar to Rebecca.

They adjourned to the living-room for coffee and as soon as Rebecca took a seat on the sofa, his bulk flopped down beside her and a heavy arm was thrown around her shoulders. Stinking of alcohol and cologne, which failed to disguise the body odour beneath, he utterly repulsed her. She tried to recall how she used to tolerate him.

"You are looking incredibly sexy tonight," he said, in what he thought were seductive tones but sounded more like a throat infection.

"I thought I would make an effort, for old time's sake," she answered.

He put his sweaty hand on her thigh and slid it up her skirt.

"And wearing stockings you naughty girl! You know I can't resist you!"

He pressed his lips to hers, almost suffocating her with his liquor laden breath. She shut her eyes and allowed her mind to drift away while he got on with his clumsy groping. She was thinking that on an MP's salary she and David could buy a house with a garden. David would have his own room, perhaps in the attic where he would not be disturbed, somewhere to read and to write. Maybe they could have a pet. She had always wanted a cat when she was younger.

He dragged her to the bedroom and fumbled with her clothing. She assisted him so as not to prolong the unpleasant business. She made some appropriate noises in answer to his grunting and groans but in her mind's eye she was decorating her future living-room. It would be cosy with a big, comfy, desperately old-fashioned sofa where she and David could snuggle up together and the cat would have its own armchair.

She was so immersed in these contemplations that she did not realise that Bryant was already asleep. She would have liked to slip out, to run home to her true love but it was after curfew and her exemption was no longer valid. She tried to sleep but could not for Bryant's thunderous snoring. She lay listening to the wind in the trees and the occasional footsteps of the security guards on patrol, longing to be home. Finally she drifted off but woke again at dawn.

Bryant's snores had subsided but he was still breathing heavily and noisily. Unable to get back to sleep, Rebecca wrapped herself in Bryant's copious dressing-gown and went out to sit on the terrace. It was pleasantly cool out of doors and the birds were singing. She had been enjoying their morning concert for a while when she heard another familiar tune. David had arrived for work and was whistling as he crossed the lawn.

"Romeo, Romeo, wherefore art thou Romeo?" she called down to him.

He doffed his floppy sun-hat and bowed to her. She descended the steps and joined him on the lawn.

Speaking in a whisper she said, "It's going exactly to plan. As soon as John wakes up I'm getting out of here, then I'll call Cain and tell her I'll stand."

"Great, I'm going to chuck this job in."

"Are you going to give notice today? What reason will you say?"

"I shan't bother with all that. I'll just get myself fired, it's quicker and simpler."

"Get fired, how?"

"Here comes the great blubber-beast now! Just watch this!"

Bryant had appeared on the terrace in his pants and vest, his hair sticking straight up.

"What's going on?" he demanded. "Rebecca, what are you doing out here at this time?"

"Nothing, I couldn't sleep," she replied. "Mr O'Brien and I were just talking."

"To be sure," said David in his best and most ridiculous Irish tones. "I was just saying what a lucky man you are Mr President to have such a lovely young woman as well as a fine figure of a wife."

Bryant had already been looking displeased at finding his former mistress chatting with the gardener and not in his bed, but at David's words his sagging face fell even further.

"You are impertinent Mr O'Brien, kindly refrain from making such remarks about my personal life."

"I meant no offence sir," David continued shamelessly. "I admire you sir. You must have a great deal of stamina for a man your age."

"That's enough!" Bryant replied angrily.

"I'm sorry sir, I didn't mean to imply that you are old, just that you are a fair bit older than the lady and you must be a lot fitter than you look. I mean not that there is anything wrong with how you look sir. Some women like fat blokes."

"Shut your face you fucking paddy twat!"

"Now sir, there's no call to be swearing, especially not in front of the lady."

185

"I'll swear as much as I bloody well like in my own fucking garden! You can keep your damn mouth shut! Jesus Christ!"

David's mouth fell open in mock horror.

He crossed himself and said, "Mother Mary forgive you sir! There be no need for blasphemy."

"Not one more word from you, do you understand?"

"How am I to say whether I understand or not without saying a word? Shall I just nod me head?"

"Get out of here right now or I'll have you thrown out."

David touched his hat and bowed to Rebecca before retreating out of sight.

"I knew I should have sacked that bloody man weeks ago," raged Bryant. "It was you that stopped me, remember."

"I feel sorry for the poor man," she replied. "He obviously isn't all there, if you know what I mean."

"Obviously, but this is Ten Downing Street, not the insane asylum."

Rebecca was about to ask, "Is there a difference?", but resisted as it would be unwise to provoke the President any more in his present mood.

"When I find out who was responsible for hiring that deranged bastard I'll have them sacked as well. It's too early for this kind of crap. Are you coming back to bed?"

"I thought I would have a shower then head off. There are a few things I want to do today."

"What sort of things?" Bryant demanded.

Even though his relationship with Rebecca was supposedly over he still seemed to feel he had the right to know her every movement.

"I've been thinking about what you said last night and there are a couple of people in the Liberation Party I want to talk to."

"Are you going to stand then?"

"I'm seriously considering it."

"Don't spend too long thinking about it or you'll miss your chance. It isn't like you have to do anything difficult. Just show the voters a bit of leg and tell them you love niggers and queers. I'm going back to bed and I hope when I get up again today will have improved. It can't get much worse."

*

Rebecca travelled home in one of the President's cars. She got the driver to drop her off on the main road as she did not want Bryant to know her exact address. As she turned the corner she recognised David, walking a short distance ahead. Though he had left straight after his quarrel with the President, he had come back by train so she had caught him up. She called his name and ran after him. He turned and smiled broadly, holding out his arms to embrace her. Anyone who observed that meeting would think they were two lovers reunited after a long separation, rather than having parted less than an hour ago.

"I love you," he said.

"I love you too. I love you so much I can't tell you though I wish I could. If only I were able to write the way you do then I could express how I feel, but I can't."

The words spilled out of her and she found her eyes were wet with tears.

He kissed her cheek and stroked her hair replying, "You don't need to write it. If you say that you love me that is enough. It is all I have wanted, what I have dreamed of hearing for so long."

Arm in arm they walked home together, falling into a passionate embrace as soon as they were through the door. He was full of love and desire while she was desperate for his tender caresses to brush away the memory of the other man. For a long time afterwards they lay without speaking, Rebecca winding the curls of his hair about her fingers while he stroked her cheek and neck with gentle fingers.

"I should call Alicia Cain," Rebecca said finally.

"And Karen and Sean," he added.

"After that I guess I'll make use of some of my contacts in the media."

"Right, we'll get dressed and get started. This is exciting isn't it?"

"Exciting and scary."

"You can still change your mind. You can still call Cain and say no."

She shook her head, "I'm not going to chicken out now. I may have stumbled rather blindly onto this road but now I'm going to follow it to the end, wherever that may be."

"I'll be right behind you every step of the way."

Part 5

Democracy

RIVALS
Simon Chandra

Rosa was one of five candidates standing in the 2103 Hackney by-election. The others were Imran Syal for the Muslim Democrats, Colin Peters for the Christian Alliance, Alan Chambers for Moral Justice and Dorothy Lawson for Phoenix. Lawson had worked with Tony Fincham, the retiring member for Hackney, for more than ten years. She was the strong favourite to win the contest until the Liberation Party announced their candidate. In speaking to Mrs Lawson it is clear that she has never overcome this major disappointment.

Dorothy Lawson contacted me some weeks ago when I first began this series on Rosa's life, promising that although she never knew Rosa on a personal level she had plenty of valuable insight regarding Rosa's political career. I was sceptical as Lawson's account of the by-election has already been published more than once. However I agreed to meet her as I confess at present I am rather struggling. Since my brief conversation with Sean Nichols I have been unable to secure interviews with any of the other principle figures in Rosa's story.

Perhaps it was because she reminded me of my maths teacher, but something about Dorothy Lawson made me feel uncomfortable. She has grey hair tied back off her face, which has prominent cheek bones, a pinched nose and a severe expression. We met at her place of work, the offices of the London Planning Authority. Lawson has held various positions with the civil service since Phoenix's defeat in Hackney. Although over sixty she assures me she has no plans to retire. She talks in detail about her work but I am afraid I glazed over after the first couple of minutes. She bombards me with phrases like "resource management", "intelligent drainage solutions" and "adaptable infrastructure", the meaning of which are beyond me.

"Do you ever wonder what you would be doing now if Rosa had not stood against you in the election?" I asked, hoping to bring her abruptly to the relevant topic.

"I'm not inclined to idle speculation. I know that I would have won the election had she not stood and I am confident I would have done a good job as Hackney's MP."

"A better job than Rosa?"

"Certainly. She wasn't at all interested in Hackney. She had only been living there a few weeks before she entered parliament. Her primary concern was never her constituency. Winning the by-election was just a way into politics. She was too ambitious to care about the problems of individuals."

"Yet there are numerous examples of times she helped her constituents."

"Only in the Liberation Party literature. It's true people thought she was wonderful, but that was only because she was famous and glamorous. If you actually looked at how many hours' work she put in on behalf of her constituents or what she did for the community you would probably find she did far less than Tony Fincham and certainly less than I would have."

"It must have come as a shock to you when you found out she was standing against you?"

"It certainly did. I was about the last to know. Of course Bryant knew long before I did. He wanted her to win, that was why he didn't warn me earlier."

"Why would Bryant want her to win?"

"Everyone knows they were lovers."

"As I understand it they split up before she agreed to stand. If they had still been together surely she would have stood as a Phoenix candidate? Why would he want the opposition to win?"

"I don't know the whole story but I have heard that she went to see Bryant just a few days before she announced she was standing. If Bryant had not wanted her to win he could have prevented it. He could have warned me sooner and supplied the money and staff I would have needed to mount a successful campaign against her. Then of course there is her questionable use of the unlicensed media, which everyone including Bryant turned a blind eye to."

"What do you mean by that?"

"I am aware that your magazine has links to the Real News Network but the fact is that at the time any communication with the underground press was illegal. Since detailed articles on Rosa and her policies appeared in the unlicensed press they must have originated from her or her colleagues. I know the Liberation Party does not approve of media censorship but that is no justification for breaking the law."

"Considering how poorly the Liberation Party was represented in the licensed press it is hardly surprising they resorted to using the illegal media."

"She had far more legitimate media coverage than any of the other candidates."

"Somewhat biased though."

"I don't think so."

"She won with quite a significant majority. It has been alleged that her actual share of the vote was even larger than the fifty-four percent announced at the time. Claims have been made that the figures were altered on the orders of the government."

"I cannot comment. No one in the Phoenix Party ever said anything to me on the subject."

"Then you believe that you had thirty-two percent of the votes cast rather than the eight percent suggested by some of the officials involved in the count?"

"I told you I cannot comment. I am aware of the rumours you are referring to but since they can neither be proved nor disproved this long after the event I see no point in dwelling on them."

"It doesn't bother you that members of the party you represented may have interfered in the electoral process?"

"I have said all I wish to on this subject."

I concluded my meeting with Mrs Lawson shortly afterwards. In spite of her refusal to comment on the important question of whether the Phoenix Party manipulated the ballot results, the interview did raise one interesting point. What was Rosa's relationship with Bryant at that time? Rumours that she and the President had quarrelled were circulating weeks before she announced she was standing for the Liberation Party, but as Lawson says Bryant could have done much more to prevent her winning. Considering the actions the Phoenix Party had taken against the opposition in previous elections it does appear that Rosa was allowed to win for some reason. Most likely this reason was connected to her relationship with Bryant but, according to Nichols, by this time she and O'Brien were lovers.

The only logical explanation I can come up with is that she used her relationship with Bryant to persuade him to allow her to stand for the opposition. How she managed to convince him is quite beyond me but she must have had powerful influence over him. Perhaps she knew some secret about him that she used to blackmail him. It is unlikely that simply threatening to reveal their affair would be enough as it was widely known although not spoken of. Certainly there is little doubt that Bryant's wife knew of it. The secret would have to be something far more damaging. Perhaps she had pictures of him indulging in some extreme act of sexual perversion. Since Bryant is unavailable to question I fear this mystery will not easily be solved.

Another interesting topic which Lawson mentioned was the amount of coverage Rosa's campaign had in the licensed media. Her fame as the star of Circus Britannia made her headline news but most of the publicity was less than favourable. I include a sample here for you to judge for yourselves whether or not you believe this to be biased. This report appeared on the IMC homepage, accompanied by a picture of Rosa performing on the trapeze, the day she announced she was to stand.

ROSA TO STAND FOR LIBERATION

Former circus star announces she will stand in Hackney by-election

Rebecca Clayton, better known as Rosa the glamorous trapeze artist of Circus Britannia, has announced her intention to stand in the forthcoming Hackney by-election. Clayton, 23, has no previous political experience and is understood to have moved to Hackney in the last few weeks after residing in the West End for a number of years. As a close personal friend of President Bryant and previous supporter of the Phoenix Party, Rosa's new allegiance to the Liberation has come as a surprise.

The by-election was triggered after Tony Fincham, 72, announced he was retiring from parliament on grounds of ill health. The respected Phoenix MP had represented the constituency since the party came to power in 2085. Rosa's opponent will be Dorothy Lawson, 49, who has been resident in the Hackney area for over twenty years and has much experience as Fincham's right-hand woman. Lawson is married with two children who both attend Hackney Downs Secondary School.

This career change for Rosa follows the bombing of the Newman Grand Theatre which killed and injured many of Circus Britannia's performers. Rosa herself was fortunate to escape with only minor injuries. The terrorist responsible, homosexual Martin Ashdown, was an intimate friend of Rosa's although she denies any knowledge of his sexual deviancy or extremist views.

Liberation Party leader Alicia Cain has issued a statement of support for Rosa. She insists that Clayton is serious about embarking on a political career and denies that her standing is merely a publicity stunt. Victory in this by-election would mean Liberation gaining a forth inner London seat. At present they hold only Camberwell and Peckham, Lewisham and Cain's own constituency of Bethnal Green. The party's current standing in the opinion polls is at its lowest since Cain took over leadership after a string of scandals involving sexual perversion and links to terrorist groups.

Friday 12th October 2103

At the newly commissioned Hackney Liberation Party offices the victory party was in full swing. The official result had been announced just after midnight and because of the curfew no one could leave the premises until the following morning. There was some suspicion over the exact result as their own exit polls suggested their lead was even larger than that given by the returning officer, but that was not important. There was no champagne or even wine as the budget did not extend to such luxuries but there was plenty of other alcohol of dubious varieties.

Karen Baker had been in command of the army of volunteers and had hardly slept in three days. She was exhausted, jubilant and extremely drunk. She was going around the rooms hugging everyone and telling them how much she loved them. Sean Nichols was slightly more sober than his partner but was slumped in a corner surrounded by empty bottles. He had been in charge of communications with the licensed media. Beside him was Stacey Barnes who was generally understood to be Nichols's assistant but the real nature of her role, liaising with the underground press, was known only to a handful of those present.

Alicia Cain was there with the members of her staff who had worked on the publicity materials for the campaign. Cain was completely sober and professional. She was taking the opportunity to talk to as many of the volunteers as possible and thank them for their hard work.

In spite of all the skills and technology available to the party, the lack of access to the licensed media meant much of the campaign had been conducted the old-fashioned way, with Rebecca trying to speak to as many voters as possible in person. While Phoenix could rely on television and the internet to broadcast their message Rebecca had to make speeches in shopping centres, canvass on doorsteps and visit pubs, clubs and workplaces, often having to shout very loud to make herself heard.

Throughout this exhausting process David had been at Rebecca's side acting as chauffeur, minder and personal secretary. He was beside her now as she circulated among the many selfless volunteers who had spent the whole day standing outside polling stations in the rain.

"There is no way Lawson got more than twenty percent of the vote," said one of the pollsters, echoing a sentiment many others had voiced.

"Both Syal and Peters were far more popular than the results show," agreed another. "I wouldn't be surprised if both the Muslims and the Christian Alliance came ahead of Phoenix."

"Moral Justice had a pretty poor showing whichever figures you believe," added a young man just old enough to vote.

"Bunch of dickheads!" said a bearded man as he swigged from a large bottle of vile smelling fluorescent orange liquid.

The debate as to the actual share of the vote which Rebecca achieved continued into the early hours of the morning. It was generally considered to be somewhere between sixty and seventy-five percent although some were suggesting figures in excess of eighty percent. What was not disputed was that the turnout was unprecedented in any election in recent years with over ninety percent of registered voters braving the rain.

By six am Rebecca was so exhausted David almost had to carry her down to the car. Rebecca had purchased the ancient vehicle with some of her savings but as she had no licence, David always drove. It was a fantastically ugly car with numerous dents and scratches on the bodywork. The interior had several stains on the worn upholstery and a lingering, musty odour. It had passed through the hands of many owners in over twenty years on the road but it was reliable with a reasonably efficient hybrid engine.

Rebecca flopped into her seat on the passenger side and yawned until her eyes watered.

"I think it is time the Member for Hackney went home to bed," said David as he started the engine.

"I'm afraid the Member for Hackney is going to be a big disappointment," she replied.

"You won't be," David reassured.

"I fear I will. Everyone has such high expectations. They want me to do something wonderful that will save the world or at least the country. What can an MP for a vastly outnumbered opposition party do to change anything for the better?"

As they pulled out onto the empty road David replied, "Sometimes it is the little things that make all the difference. If you try to tackle all the problems at once you will be overwhelmed. Start small and do one thing at a time."

"I'm sure that is good advice, but which small things should I start with and how do I go about doing them?"

"Later," he answered, "we'll work that out later. At the moment you need to sleep and so do I."

Island Nation Magazine
Saturday 13th July 2115

REBECCA CLAYTON MP
Simon Chandra

From the lack of reports in the authorised media you could be forgiven for thinking that Rosa did not do very much during her first two years as a member of parliament, but the underground press and her own detailed records show a very different story. Her constituents from that period are also quick to defend her. As soon as last week's interview with Lawson was published I was inundated with emails from current and former Hackney residents who wished to refute Ms Lawson's claim that Rosa was not concerned about the people she represented.

All Liberation MPs kept, and arguably still keep, meticulous records of all their official correspondence and meetings. The vast majority of these are available to anyone to look at online. From these records we can see that Rosa held a surgery for her constituents to come to her with their problems, not every month as was common practice, but every week. We know these surgeries were well attended and appointments were filled up several weeks in advance. Although much of the personal information concerning the individuals who sought her help is not disclosed, she kept detailed notes on each case including the action she had taken on the constituent's behalf.

The vast quantity of documents on file for this period shows she was in the habit of writing to certain government ministers on a daily basis. In the case of the Minister for Justice, Adrian Grant, during February 2104 she sent emails three or four times a day demanding information concerning a Hackney resident who had been imprisoned without charge under the anti-terrorism act. Her appointment diary also shows that at the end of that month she spent three hours waiting outside the Minister's office until he finally agreed to see her. Two months later the prisoner in question was released.

Of the material I received during the last week the most compelling story was that of Edward and Mary and their daughter Julie. These are not their real names as they wish remain anonymous. Edward and Mary still reside in the same mid-terrace house in South Hackney where they lived when Rosa won the seat, although Julie has since left the area. I spoke to them in their living-room, surrounded by photographs of their family.

Edward and Mary attended one of Rosa's surgeries soon after she was returned to parliament. In 2101 their eldest child Julie had been arrested on charges of homosexuality. Arrests for so called sexual deviancy were extremely common in the early 2100s but in this case the accused was only 13 years old. Julie was not formally charged but was taken into custody by social services and sent to Croydon Re-education Centre. For two years the parents were forbidden from having any contact with their daughter.

"No one would help us," Edward told me. "We spoke to lawyers, social workers and to Tony Fincham but all we got were expressions of sympathy and being told it was for the best. How could taking a teenager away from parents who loved and cared for her possibly be for the best?"

"Did you have a good relationship with your daughter?" I asked.

"Oh yes," Mary replies, "she was a good kid. Of course we had our quarrels like any family, but she was a smart girl, she worked hard at school and had never been in any real trouble before."

"Was there any reason to believe she was a lesbian?"

"She was thirteen! How could she possibly know what she was? She was a child."

"Then do you know why she was suspected?"

"We think it was one of her teachers who reported her to the authorities," Edward answered, "but on what evidence we don't know. When the police searched the house they took away some books and her diary but we don't know if that was significant."

"So after two years with no support you went to see Rosa."

"That's right," said Mary. "We didn't really believe she would be able to help us but we were desperate and would have tried anything. Thank God we did. We knew from our first meeting that she was taking us seriously. When we told her our story she wanted to know all the details, she was genuinely interested."

"Then the day after we saw her story was on RNN," said Edward. "We read RNN but we never dared to contact the underground press. We assumed our communications would be monitored and getting ourselves arrested wouldn't help Julie. After the story was published, readers responded with messages of support for us and outrage towards the government. It was good to know there were people on our side."

"You had several more meetings with Rosa I believe?"

"Yes many more," Edward replied. "At first she did not seem to have achieved anything but she eventually managed to get the authorities to release some information about Julie. It was not good news. During her so called treatment she had attempted suicide three times. We were terrified that if we didn't get her out of there soon she would succeed the next time."

Edward's fears were well founded in that the number of deaths among juveniles in custody was a scandal soon to blow up in the face of the government.

Institutions were overcrowded, understaffed and staff were poorly trained. There were cases of inmates being given overdoses of medication or the wrong medication, injuries and illnesses were frequently untreated, violence among inmates was common and suicides frequent.

"And you did. You got her out."

"Rosa got her out. She threatened to reveal the catalogue of incompetence of which the Croydon Centre staff were guilty if certain inmates including our daughter were not released."

"It wasn't a very good deal for Croydon Re-ed Centre since the whole juvenile detention scandal broke only a few months later."

"They couldn't expect to cover up something that awful forever," said Edward. "It was bound to come out sometime. Whether Rosa had a part in it or not I don't know but I am convinced she saved our daughter's life and I will always be grateful to her."

"And how is Julie now?"

Much better," Mary answered. "It took her years to get over what she went through in that terrible place but she put her life back together. She went to college and got some good qualifications and has a job in a bank now. She is married, to a very nice man, and we are hoping there will be grandchildren in a few years."

"Then she isn't a lesbian?"

"No, not that we would mind if she was," replied Mary. "Thankfully things are changing."

"There is still a lot of prejudice," I reminded them.

"I think attitudes will change just as they did last century," said Mary. "At least those dreadful places like the one Julie had to endure have been closed down. The way they treated my girl, you wouldn't want that for the most hardened criminal never mind a child. As a Christian I wish I could forgive the people who treated my child with such cruelty, but as a mother I can't. It is the most terrible thing to know your child is suffering. It is our strongest instinct isn't it? To protect our children."

Tuesday 20th November 2103

It had been another busy day and yet again Rebecca was running nearly an hour behind with her appointments. The last person she had to see was Dr Nathaniel O'Brien. Looking at the name on the screen it seemed familiar but that was probably because the surname was the same as David's. It was a pretty common name after all.

Whenever anyone made an appointment for one of her surgeries the receptionist made a brief note, usually just one word, indicating what the discussion was to be about. Under the name of the person who wished to see her it would say "Legal", "Financial", "Health" or "Welfare" to provide a general guide as to the nature of the problem. This helped to see the big picture of what concerned her constituents and also helped her to get into the right frame of mind and have suitable notes in front of her in preparation for seeing the constituent. In the case of Dr O'Brien, under his name was just the word "family".

Dr O'Brien was not a young man but could still be described as handsome. He had a kind, intelligent face with a strong bone structure which was pleasant to look at. His hair was grey and receding but neatly cut. The word "distinguished" would apply far better than old. His face also seemed familiar but she could not remember ever meeting the gentleman before.

"I'm sorry to keep you waiting for so long," said Rebecca as her visitor took a seat. "Dr O'Brien, a medical doctor or another sort?"

"Medical, I am a GP," he replied.

Had she not known she might have guessed that was his profession. His was the sort of face you would want to see when you were ill; friendly, approachable but competent.

"And how can I help you Dr O'Brien?"

"I want to talk to you about my son. I realise it is probably taking a liberty with your valuable time but I wanted to meet you personally as this is a rather delicate matter."

"Please go ahead, tell me about your son. I will help in any way I can."

The doctor retrieved a picture from his jacket pocket and placed it on the desk. It was a photograph of Rebecca addressing shoppers on a Saturday morning in the town centre, taken only a few weeks ago during her election campaign. Dr O'Brien indicated the figure standing behind her in the picture.

"That is my son," he stated.

Rebecca took the photograph and looked at it more closely but she already knew who they were talking about. It was David.

"I am not actually a Hackney resident," Dr O'Brien explained, "but I was following your campaign when I saw this. I had no idea my son was working for you. We quarrelled some years ago and have not been in contact since."

"I know," Rebecca replied.

"I came to you as I hoped you might help me to get in touch with him. I know this isn't really your job but I am desperate. If you could just give me an address or a number I would be more grateful than you can possibly imagine."

"Would you wait here a moment? I will see what I can do."

She went to the office next door. David had completed his work for the day and was reading RNN while waiting for her.

On seeing Rebecca in the doorway he asked, "Are you done already? It isn't even eight o'clock yet."

"I'm almost finished but you might be able to help me with my last appointment."

"Why what's the problem?"

Rebecca leant against the door-frame and looked at her lover. The resemblance to the man she had just left was so strong she was amazed she had not realised at once that it was David's father.

"Your father is here. He wants to see you."

"He's here? You mean in the building?"

"Yes in my office. He doesn't know I am talking to you now. I didn't tell him you were just next door. So far he only knows that you work for me. What answer shall I give him?"

David sat mute, biting his lip and drumming his fingers on the chair arm.

Then he ran his fingers through his hair and answered, "I don't know. God I don't know what to do. This is too sudden."

Rebecca took the chair opposite him and suggested, "Shall we go through the options? Number one, I can go back and tell him you don't want anything to do with him. Number two, I could give him your email address then when he gets in touch you can decide whether or not to respond. Number three, I could tell him you will think about it, and take his contact details so you can call him if you decide that is what you want to do."

"Or number four I can go and speak to him right now," David added.

"Right, pick a number."

David stood up decisively.

"Number four," he said.

"Are you sure?"

"No, so let's go before I change my mind."

The shock was clearly visible on Dr O'Brien's face when his son entered the room. He had come only hoping for an address or phone number and was ill-prepared for a meeting. He stared at David for an uncomfortably long time without saying anything. No doubt he was contemplating how much his boy had changed since last they met, and the mass of scars were a significant change.

It was David who broke the excruciating silence.

"Hello Dad, how are you?"

Slowly O'Brien senior rose to his feet and stood facing David, who had paused in the office doorway with Rebecca close behind him.

"It is so good to see you David," Dr O'Brien said. "I heard what happened during the riots. I tried to contact you then but you never replied. Then I was told you were working for Bryant. So now you work for Miss Clayton?"

"That's right, it is a very long story."

"I was surprised to learn you were working for Liberation. I thought you were a Phoenix man."

"You thought wrong."

"Obviously. It is a long time since we spoke. There must be a lot that I don't know."

"When we did speak you didn't often listen."

"I think we were both guilty of that."

"Perhaps."

While this exchange took place, the physical distance between them remained with David still stood in the doorway as though poised to flee at any moment. Rebecca took charge and shoved him bodily into the room closing the door behind her. She deposited him in a chair beside his father.

"It sounds like you two have a lot to talk about, so you should at least make yourselves comfortable," she said. "Would you like some tea or coffee or something?"

David held her arm to keep her close to him and replied quietly, "Not now, just stay for the moment, please."

"Of course if you want," she answered, slipping her hand into his and giving it a gentle squeeze.

Dr O'Brien glanced towards Rebecca and back to his son observing this intimate gesture and perhaps speculating on the nature of their relationship. After another awkward pause David spoke.

"So how are you Dad?"

"I'm well."

"Are you still in Peterborough?"

"Yes I'm still working at the same surgery and I plan to carry on for some time yet. If I retired I wouldn't know what to do with myself. How about you? Are you well?"

"Yes I'm fine."

"You were badly injured though weren't you? You had to leave the army."

"The damage was mostly cosmetic," David replied indicating his scars. "I had to leave the army more because of my mental than physical state, but I am well again now."

"Good. So you are responsible for Miss Clayton's security?"

"That is my job title but mainly I just drive the car and make the tea."

"You liar!" Rebecca interjected, then addressing his father she explained, "David does about a million different things for me. I have a fantastic team. Karen and Sean make all the big decisions about where I am going and what I am doing. David gets me there safely and on time with the right bits of paper, makes sure I know who to talk to and what about. He also helps to write letters and speeches, remembers all the important things I forget and he does make a very nice cup of tea."

"Wow, sounds like you are pretty busy then."

"Rebecca is exaggerating. Sean and Karen help her with all the important things; I'm just a general dog's body."

"So how did this all come about?" Dr O'Brien asked. "How did you meet Miss Clayton and when did you start working for the Liberation Party?"

"That will take some explaining and it is time I drove Rebecca home."

"There is no hurry," Rebecca insisted.

"Perhaps not but I'm tired. Can we talk some other time Dad?"

The older man looked disappointed, even hurt by his son's coldness, but he replied, "Yes of course David. I realise it has been difficult, my turning up out of the blue like this, but it is good to see you. I have been trying to get in touch with you for a very long time now. I've missed you. I just wanted to know that you were all right. It has been dreadful not knowing."

"I'm sorry. I got your messages after the riots and I should have replied or at least got in touch once I got my head back together. I promise I will call you soon, when I have time to talk. Is your number still the same?"

"Yes still the same."

"Thanks for coming. I shouldn't have put you to so much trouble."

"It was no trouble."

Dr O'Brien stood up as though preparing to go but he hesitated, unable to leave his only child without some expression of warmth or affection.

He took a deep breath and said, "Listen David, I am really sorry for some of the things I said to you. I was arrogant and stupid. Whatever differences of opinion we have, or may have had in the past you are still my son and I love you more than anything else in the world."

This was all David needed to hear. He too stood and put his arms around his father.

He hugged him tightly and said, "I'm sorry too Dad. I was wrong about so many things. I thought I knew what I was fighting for but then I found out I was taking orders from a corrupt, fascist tyrant. At first I was too proud to admit my mistakes, then I was too ashamed."

Rebecca felt she was intruding and wanted to leave but they were standing between her and the door blocking her escape, so she remained as silent and unobtrusive as possible. When father and son released each other from the embrace, both had tears in their eyes. Rebecca distributed the tissues and made another attempt to go.

"Wait Becky," David said preventing her again, "let's all go back to ours. We can have something to eat then Dad and I can talk while you get some rest. It will be more comfortable than hanging around here all night and I expect you are hungry by now."

"Sounds like a good plan, I am hungry."

They descended to the car park, now empty apart from their aged vehicle. Dr O'Brien chivalrously climbed into the cramped back seat, leaving Rebecca to take her usual place.

"So, you two live together," he remarked.

"That's right," David replied.

"Are you… a couple?"

"We are."

"That's unexpected. I mean it is good, just a bit of a surprise."

"You mean what could a beautiful young woman like Rebecca possibly see in a battered old wreck like me?"

"No that is not what I meant at all. I'm just a little overwhelmed. Meeting Rosa in person is overwhelming anyway but then to find out you are not only working for her but living with her!"

"I know what you mean Dad. Waking up in the morning next to the most beautiful woman in the entire world does take a bit of getting used to."

"Don't be silly David," said Rebecca, blushing. "First thing in the morning I'm a long way from being beautiful and you know it."

"She is always beautiful," David contradicted, "even when she is eating spaghetti and gets the sauce all over her face."

She thumped his arm, "Shut up!"

It was only a few minutes' drive between the Liberation Party Offices and David's block.

"This is where I live now," David told his father as they got out the car. "It looks pretty awful from the outside but inside it is quite nice. It is very quiet as half the flats are unoccupied. There are a lot of blocks like that around here. If anyone had the money they could buy some of the smaller flats and do them up to make nice big ones, but you don't see many investors around."

"It is the same in Peterborough," his dad replied. "There are several houses on our street which have been vacant for years. They just sit there getting increasingly derelict when the land could be put to much better use. There are plenty of families desperate for allotments and gardens."

"I've a meeting with the Urban Planning Committee next week," said Rebecca. "I intend to harangue them constantly on the subject until they agree to part with some money."

When they reached their flat David said, "There's still a large dish of bean casserole in the fridge. I'll heat that up for dinner."

"I'll do that," replied Rebecca. "I'll throw together some salad to go with it. I think I'm just about capable of that."

"OK but don't chop your fingers off!"

She went through to the kitchen and started pulling things out of the fridge while David offered his father a drink.

"It isn't what you would call a proper malt whiskey," he explained, "but at least it won't take the roof off your mouth."

"That will be fine," Dr O'Brien replied. "I'm not quite as discerning as I used to be. While I've been living alone I've rather let my standards slip. When you were at home I had to set a good example and see that you ate properly; now I eat Mega Meals slumped in front of the TV and drink stuff that smells like toilet cleaner."

"I know what you mean. All the domestic chores seem so much more worthwhile when you have someone else to do them for. It's great having Becky living here."

"I bet it is you lucky bastard!"

Rebecca came back through to the living-room to set the table.

"I hope you are hungry," she said. "As usual there is enough to feed a small army."

"I am quite hungry thank you Rebecca," said Dr O'Brien. "It is all right if I call you Rebecca?"

"Of course, Rebecca or Becky. A lot of people still seem to call me Rosa, but that's mainly people who don't know me very well. What about you? Are you Nathaniel or Nathan?"

"Nathan is fine."

She returned to the kitchen to finish preparing the salad. Although she tried not to listen in to their conversation it was impossible not to overhear.

"I see you still love books," remarked Nathan, admiring the extensive shelves.

"Yes well you know who I caught that habit off."

"You are much tidier than I am though. At least yours are on shelves, not piles all over the floor."

"You should have seen this place a few months ago. Before Becky moved in the there were boxes from floor to ceiling and you could hardly breathe for the dust."

"That is exactly like my house. Do you think it's genetic?"

"Nature or nurture, who knows."

"We always were very alike," Nathan remarked with a sigh. "I think that might have been part of the problem."

"Yes we were both convinced we were right and too stubborn and proud to listen to the other's point of view."

"But we are on the same side now aren't we? I mean we are both Liberation supporters now."

"I thought you voted Christian Alliance."

"I did, but I'm getting less evangelical in my old age. I still disapprove of abortion but I understand there are circumstances where it is justified. It is Phoenix's tyrannical contraceptive policies that I really object to. Also I don't support Christian Alliance's policies on homosexuality. I find it hard to believe it is such a terrible sin for a man to love another man."

"I wish we'd talked about all this years ago," said David, "I mean talked properly rather than yelling at each other and name-calling like a couple of children."

"I know. I still cringe when I think of some of the awful things I said."

"I think I said far worse, but to be honest I have trouble remembering. It seems so long ago to me."

"Really? To me it is as clear as yesterday, clearer probably."

Rebecca announced dinner and they took their places around the table. The conversation was rather limited to small talk while they ate, as Rebecca's presence prevented father and son from saying all they might if they were alone. Nathan complimented the food and David explained that he had grown many of the ingredients himself. Gardening was another interest they both shared. Seeing them chatting so easily and comfortably Rebecca found it hard to imagine a quarrel so severe that they had not spoken in years.

After the meal Rebecca left them alone together while she took a bath. By the time she had finished soaking they were deep in conversation and she retired to bed without disturbing them. They were speaking too softly to overhear once the bedroom door was closed and the sound of their voices lulled her to sleep.

She awoke again what seemed only a few minutes later but the clock said 1:27. In the living-room they were still talking and it was a raised voice which had woken her.

"But that is insane!" Nathan was saying. "You would have been killed. It is complete madness."

"Yes I know," David replied, "that is exactly what it was. I didn't ever get a professional diagnosis but I think I can safely say at that time I was not what you would call sane."

"My God! I had no idea!"

"I'm not sure how sane I am now. Unfortunately sanity isn't like temperature or blood pressure. It is hard to measure. Right now I feel OK because I have Rebecca but if she were to leave me I fear I might break down completely."

"Are you afraid she will leave you? She seems very fond of you."

"I don't know. Sometimes I think I just happened to be there when she needed someone. Face it, she could do so much better."

There was a brief pause then Nathan replied in a low voice. Now Rebecca was not overhearing but straining to listen to what they were saying.

"I often wondered the same thing about your Mum. OK, so she wasn't a glamorous superstar like Rebecca, but she was beautiful, clever and so vibrant. She was one of those people who everyone wants to talk to at parties. She had so many funny and interesting things to say and she was so much fun to be with. I often asked myself why a woman as admired as her could love such an average, boring and completely unremarkable man as me. But she loved me, she married me and had my child. If I hadn't had you to live for, her death would have killed me."

"Do you think she is still somewhere watching us?"

"I believe she is. Perhaps I am wrong and there is nothing beyond this world, but I choose to believe that there is and that we will meet again."

"Then I hope this makes her happy, us speaking again, I mean."

"I'm sure it does."

Rebecca rolled over and tried to shut out the conversation in the other room, feeling guilty for prying. Tomorrow she would tell David how much she loved him and promise not to leave him. Now she ought to mind her own business, which was sleeping.

FOR MUM
The Man Behind the Mask

I search my memory for the vaguest recollection of you
Your face, your voice, your smile
But no amount of longing will bring you to me,
You are gone, without leaving a trace on my infant mind.

It seems unfair that though you gave me life
I do not remember you at all,
And yet the sense of loss is just as keen
As if I had known you in my early years.

Is there a world beyond this one of sorrow?
I long to believe that there is,
That when I die we shall meet at last
So I may tell you, though I never knew you, I love you.

DINNER AT THE CHANDRAS'
Simon Chandra

This week I had the most unbelievable stroke of luck. My parents were having a dinner party for some friends to which I was invited, on the understanding that I would be on my best behaviour. One of the guests was Stacey Barnes, editor of a certain rival publication, but perhaps surprisingly a good friend of my parents. I knew that Barnes had been Alicia Cain's head of communications for a number of years but as she does not often talk about her political career I did not know just how closely she worked with Rosa until I had the great fortune to be sitting next to her at dinner.

Before she was Cain's top PR woman, Barnes had worked for the Liberation Party in the highly risky and unrewarding role of liaising with the underground media, which was when her friendship with my parents originated. I knew all this of course, but what I only found out on Wednesday was that she had worked as Rosa's link to the unlicensed press. I asked her why she had never talked before about working for Rosa.

"There's not much to tell," she answered, "everything she did has already been reported. I was just the messenger."

"But you knew her?"

"Only on a professional level. We weren't close friends."

"What was she like to work for?"

"She was extremely polite, people often underrate that. She always said please and thank you. It was one of things she and Alicia had in common."

There is a school of thought that says Alicia Cain owes her political longevity to good manners. The fact that she was always civil even to people she did not agree with means she never upset anyone enough for them to oppose her.

"And was she her own boss or was she just doing what Nichols and Baker told her to do?"

"I don't know. To me it seemed that they all made decisions together. She knew her job better than many MPs I've worked with. Whatever we were discussing she always had a good grasp of the facts and figures and was definitely able to think for herself. Some people I've worked with can't even have a conversation about the weather without detailed notes in front of them."

"Then she did take an interest in her work? It wasn't just a path to fame and power?"

At this point my mother interrupted saying, "For God's sake Simon! Can you not manage one evening without talking about Rosa?"

"Mum, I'm trying to establish some very important facts."

"You are obsessed. You have become a complete Rosa fanatic since you started writing this column. You never met her but you know more about her than I do. You even know her shoe size don't you?"

Size six, in case you were wondering.

"I am trying to build up a complete picture of her as a person," I explained.

"You ought to focus on the important facts and not the trivia," Mum advised.

My Dad was kind enough to speak up in my defence.

"Give the guy a break Monica! You know how popular his column on Rosa has been."

"Yeah," Mum replied scathingly, "popular with the kind of brain-dead morons who are obsessed with what colour pants she wore and what she ate for breakfast."

This, dear readers, is my mother's and editor's opinion of you. Please send all complaints directly to her.

"It is hardly surprising people want to know about Rosa," said Stacey. "She is one of very few political figures who were actually admired and liked. In this country we have her and Winston Churchill, no one else comes close. Unlike Churchill she died before her popularity had chance to decline. At the time I had no idea how important she would be. This is why I don't talk about her. The time I spent with her was all one big missed opportunity. There were so many things I wanted to know but I didn't ask. I always thought, I'll ask next time. I'll find out later, once we have got to know each other better. But then there was no more later. You knew her better than I did though didn't you Monica?"

"Not really," Mum replied, perhaps with regret. "I hardly saw her after she was elected to parliament. Once she was an MP she didn't have time for the leisurely lunches we used to enjoy together and when we did meet, our relationship had changed completely. As a journalist I had to be objective about her and the party and she was much more guarded with me. We were never intimate but before we had been friends, afterwards we were just professional acquaintances."

"It seems everyone I speak to says the same thing," I complained. "Everyone who knew her liked her but no one got really close."

"Apart from David," replied Stacey, "and possibly Alicia Cain."

"But neither of them will talk to me."

"I knew they wouldn't and that was why I advised against this Rosa project," said Mum. "I warned you it wouldn't yield anything new. Don't you think that if the truth about Rosa could be found either Stacey or I would have done it by now?"

"I think Simon has been doing pretty well," Stacey replied, "I've been reading his column with envy. I wish we'd thought of it first. I was particularly interested in the interview with Luchenko. The way he describes her as hardworking, dedicated, but never arrogant and always courteous to her colleagues, that was definitely the Rebecca I knew. To answer your question, yes she did care about the work she was doing. I sometimes think she cared too much. I remember the case you wrote about last week. She really took that poor girl's plight to heart. Fortunately that story had a happy ending but I dread to think what it would have done to Rebecca if it hadn't. She had got so emotionally involved it wasn't good for her."

"Did you ever advise her to be more detached and professional?"

"I didn't, as I said we weren't that close. I know Karen did and possibly Alicia, and David was always concerned about her. I don't know that she ever did learn not to get so involved, but she did at least learn how to make it appear so."

Though I spent the rest of the evening trying to persuade Stacey to tell me more about Rosa she refused to say anything further on the subject. There were other guests she wished to talk to and other topics of conversation. I requested a proper interview but she declined. My Mum got quite cross at one point and threatened never to invite me again. I was disappointed not to leave with a more detailed picture of what Rosa was like to work with but I feel I am at least getting a glimpse of insight into her character. I shall soldier on in the face of my mother's disapproval as I may yet prove my mettle as an investigative journalist.

Saturday 15th December 2103

The Member for Hackney had spent the morning at a children's sports club. Although it was freezing cold and her feet were numb with standing out in a muddy field, Rebecca had actually quite enjoyed herself. The young people were full of enthusiasm in spite of their poor facilities and lack of equipment. There had been some excellent photo opportunities when she had joined in the football game and the kids had all been thrilled to meet her. In fact she had enjoyed the morning so much she was late for her lunch appointment with Monica Chandra.

Monica was supposedly interviewing her on behalf of "Amber" magazine. They met in a secluded corner of a small Italian restaurant near Hackney Town Hall. There was a birthday party going on over the other side of the restaurant, which provided plenty of noise and distraction so no one could overhear their conversation. It was the first time they had seen each other in months and much had happened since they last had lunch together in the Courtyard Café of the Newman Grand. They exchanged greetings and Rebecca apologised for her tardiness. She related a little of her morning to Monica as it was the kind of material she could use in her article.

"How about I ask you all the dumb stuff for "Amber" first and we can get it out of the way?" Monica suggested.

"Sure, go ahead," Rebecca replied.

"Do you miss the circus?"

"No not at all."

"Are you enjoying your new career as a politician?"

"Yes it is hard work but very rewarding."

"What are you doing for Christmas?"

"I'll be spending a few days with my partner and his dad in Peterborough."

"Who will be cooking the Christmas lunch?"

"I don't know. Not me anyway."

"Will you be having turkey?"

"Good God! Is this really what your readers are interested in?"

"I'm afraid so. Pathetic isn't it? Are you all right Becky? You seem tired."

"No I'm fine, it's just been a busy morning."

"From what I hear it sounds like you are always busy. You should be careful you don't overdo it."

"Really I'm fine," Rebecca replied irritably. "Let's get on with it."

"OK if you're sure. Can you tell me a bit about this boyfriend of yours?"

"What do you want to know?"

"What do I want to know or what do "Amber" readers want to know? Because they are two very different things."

"We'll tackle what your readers are interested in first."

Rebecca was feeling rather awkward. Previously Monica had been someone she could confide in, someone she told her secrets to. Now there were things she wanted to conceal.

"My readers would like some slushy romantic story about how you met and got together. I expect they would also like to know if you intend to get married or continue living in sin."

"Can't you just make something up?"

"It might help if I had some facts to base the story on. Was he really Bryant's gardener?"

"Yes he used to work as the gardener at Number Ten."

"And before that he was in the army?"

"Yes."

"And he was among the soldiers responsible for killing hundreds of unarmed civilians during the North-East riots?"

"That isn't one of the "Amber" questions is it?"

"No sorry, that is one of mine."

"Why are you asking me if you already know the answer?"

"I want to know who this man is who is suddenly playing such a major role in your life. It was this mysterious man who first introduced you to members of the Liberation Party wasn't it?"

"It was. Why does that matter?"

"OK Becky I'll be honest with you," replied Monica, lowering her voice to almost a whisper. "There are rumours that you struck some kind of a deal with Bryant in order for him to allow you to be elected. We both know the sort of dirty tricks Bryant is capable of. If he had wanted to prevent you from winning he could have. Now I find it interesting that this boyfriend of yours used to work for Bryant. Is he in on the deal too?"

"I have no comment to make on any of this groundless speculation."

"Look Becky, I think you are a good person so I don't think you would enter into anything you thought was wrong, but are you sure you know what you are doing? Bryant is a dangerous man to have as an enemy."

"Do you really think I don't know that?"

"I'm worried that other people, perhaps this O'Brien guy, have dragged you into something you don't fully understand."

"I'm not quite as stupid as you think Monica. I know how perilous standing against the Phoenix Party is and I know I'm treading a fine line, but it is my choice. No one has dragged me into anything. Now if you want to make up some great romantic epic about me falling in love with Bryant's gardener for "Amber"" then that's fine, but if I read any libellous rumour mongering about him on RNN, this will be our last interview."

Rebecca put her hand to her mouth as she spoke the name of the illegal website.

"So you are certain you can trust him?"

"With my life."

"I hope it doesn't come to that, but you realise it might?"

Rebecca smiled at this remark as already David had saved her life, but she said nothing. That was one of their many secrets. After a brief pause Monica attempted another line of questioning.

"So when was it exactly that you decided to leave the circus and enter politics?"

"I made up my mind to leave Circus Britannia shortly after the bombing. At first I didn't know what I was going to do instead, but after David introduced me to his friends in the Liberation Party I decided to join them."

"It was rather a sudden switch in political allegiance wasn't it?"

"You know it wasn't. You know I never really supported the Phoenix Party, but if you want something for Amber you can say I spent many sleepless nights trying to reconcile myself with Phoenix policies before eventually finding I could not and so was forced to end my friendship with the President."

"What really happened between you and Bryant? I've heard you had a massive row so he got you fired from the circus and set MAT Force on you."

"That's right. I told him what I really thought of him and he didn't like it."

"But I also heard that you have been to Downing Street since the break up."

"I did see him a couple of times after we split but I don't want to talk about it, it's personal. Anyway it is all over now. I haven't seen him in months and he is with Sophie Andrews now."

"I never quite understood why you were ever with him in the first place."

"Like I said, it's personal and I don't want to talk about it. Aren't you going to ask me anything sensible about Liberation policies?"

Monica was forced to abandon her attempts to learn the truth about Rebecca's relationships with Bryant and his gardener so asked about Liberation policies for regenerating the inner cities. She also managed a few more questions about an MP's lifestyle for Amber magazine before Rebecca had to leave for another appointment. They parted somewhat coldly and Rebecca could not help feeling depressed at having lost a friend.

Wednesday 19th March 2104

The long and desolate winter of the Urban Planning Committee had failed to blossom into a productive spring. The lack of any funds from the Treasury prevented any plans being put into action, but still this body of professional circumlocutors met on a weekly basis. Rebecca was not on the committee, which consisted entirely of Phoenix back-benchers, but she had made herself very well known to each of its members. Months of harassing them individually and collectively had yielded no answers to her question of what was to be done with all the derelict property within the inner cities. Now it was apparent that no answer would ever be forthcoming she decided to try a different tactic and made an appointment to meet with the Minister for Food and Farming, Philip Graysby.

Unlike the majority of his colleagues Graysby was happy to fit Rebecca into his schedule. As she entered his office he greeted her warmly, as though they were old friends rather that political opponents.

"It is so good to see you Miss Clayton," he said. "It has been a long time since we last spoke, hasn't it."

"It must have been around this time last year when we met at Downing Street," she replied.

"I seem to remember on that occasion I was rather drunk and behaved extremely inappropriately."

"I wasn't exactly sober myself."

"I haven't had chance to congratulate you. I think perhaps I was rather less surprised by your move from show business to politics than many of my colleagues were. Even while you were still with Bryant I suspected there was a sharp mind at work behind your pretty face. You must have learnt a great deal from the time you spent observing him. It is just a pity you chose to stand for the other side. If you had joined us you could have been in the Cabinet one day."

"I chose my party according to my principles, not the prospects for promotion."

"You and I are that rare breed of politician then, those with principles."

"Particularly rare among the Phoenix Party."

"So what did you wish to see me about?"

"My constituency, like most inner city areas, has a large number of vacant buildings which are unlikely to be occupied at any time in the future. Many of these buildings were originally local authority housing, ownership of which was taken over by central government in the eighties. My recommendation is that they are demolished and the land converted to allotments which can be rented to residents."

"Of course it makes sense to turn housing we don't need into productive land, which we do, but it will require significant initial investment to make these plots suitable for growing food."

"But if these buildings remain as they are they will start costing the government money in order simply to prevent them collapsing."

"Perhaps the buildings could be sold to private investors who could fund the demolition and rent out the plots."

"Phil, you know as well as I that if private investors are involved only the very rich will be able to afford to rent the allotments. I was proposing to provide land for people who cannot afford to buy fresh fruit and vegetables."

"I know what you were proposing but there is no way I could sell that to the Chancellor or the taxpayer. Why should hard-working people who don't have the leisure time for gardening pay so that other people can indulge in a pleasure they can't?"

"Well if the government really isn't prepared to stump up public money to benefit the public, perhaps you could do more to persuade the private investors you mentioned to use some of their cash in places other than the centre of London. Could you not offer some tax breaks or incentives to encourage inner city regeneration?"

"I'm afraid that is beyond my remit. You will have to talk to the Chancellor or the Business Secretary."

"I've tried. The Chancellor is too busy to see me and I had one meeting with Robert Parsons, who has since then taken great trouble to avoid me. He actually ran away from me in the lobby the other day."

"Well I can't promise anything but I will raise the matter with Bob next time I have the opportunity."

"Then if you do come up with a scheme he can take all the credit."

"Certainly not, I'd never allow that to happen. If we were to come up with a workable proposal I shall be claiming the idea was entirely my own! Seriously though Rebecca, my department does have a few things in the pipeline but I'm afraid I can't discuss them with you as they have yet to be approved by the Cabinet."

"If the Cabinet does approve your plans what are the chances of Hackney seeing any of the benefits?"

"I think you already know the answer to that."

"Bugger all chance then?"

"Let us just say the government is always more willing to help out its friends than its enemies."

Realising she had learned as much from Graysby as he was prepared to tell her on this subject, Rebecca did not press him further. Instead she asked,

"Speaking of enemies, how far did you get in persuading Bryant to give old Harriet Jacobs the boot?"

"It would be extremely inappropriate for me to answer that but don't be too surprised if next time there is a Cabinet reshuffle she gets shuffled out."

"And is there a reshuffle imminent?"

"I wouldn't know."

"And I suppose you also wouldn't know anything about the rumours that the Chancellor has ambitions for the top job?"

"If there were such rumours, and such rumours were true, I think Bryant would already know about it and be planning accordingly."

"So if it comes to choosing sides..?"

"I will be on the winning side."

"Of course."

"Tell me Rebecca, have you ever considered challenging Cain for the leadership?"

"I can honestly say I haven't."

"Perhaps you should think about it. The party would be crazy not to choose you."

"Well I have enjoyed this little chat Phil, but I had better be on my way. There are several more people I have to see today."

"Yes, I hear you are a busy woman. I understand Adrian's entire staff at the Ministry of Justice have been living in terror of you for the past month."

"I am glad. I am hoping that the boys and girls at Care and Welfare will soon be equally intimidated."

"Good luck with that," Graysby said as they shook hands.

*

After spending the rest of the afternoon going back and forth between various civil servants at the Department of Care and Welfare, Rebecca managed to achieve a small success. At around five o'clock when the staff were wanting to go home and were anxious to be rid of her, they released copies of five lengthy reports. One of these she was still reading at half past eleven that evening, or at least attempting to read. Her eyelids were drooping and she had been staring at the same paragraph for several minutes without managing to absorb what it said.

She was sitting in David's spare room, which was now her office, where she had been since they had arrived home. A few hours earlier David had brought a plate of food, then later collected the empty plate and delivered a cup of tea. Now he returned and stood behind her chair massaging her shoulders.

"It's bedtime," he suggested.

"I'm almost finished," she replied, not entirely truthfully. "I want to get through this before the meeting tomorrow."

"Surely you don't need to read all of it?"

"Sadly I do. It is a standard Civil Service tactic to hide stuff they don't want us to know somewhere within an extremely badly written, two hundred and eighty page report. They know if they attempt to keep things secret we will keep searching until we find them out, but they hope that if they give us the information this way we will read the first few pages then give up and forget about it."

"Can't someone else help you out?"

"This is only one of the reports I managed to get today. Karen and Sean are already working on the other four. We are determined to get the important facts out of them so we have something to show for ourselves when we see Alicia tomorrow."

"But at this rate you won't be able to stay awake during the meeting. Come on, bed."

"OK I won't be much longer."

He reached over and switched off the screen saying, "No, bedtime now!"

"David! I told you this is important. I need to finish it. Leave me alone and let me get on with it."

"Look Becky, you are too tired to achieve anything useful tonight. How much of what you have read during the last hour has actually sunk in?"

"All right, you win. I'll come get some sleep now, but I'll have to get up early and read the rest before the meeting."

"Better still, I'm usually up early anyway, I'll read it and give you a summary."

"No way!"

"Why not? Don't you think I'm competent enough to pick out the relevant facts and figures?"

"It's not that, I just don't want to exploit you any more than I do already."

"Exploit me?"

"Yes, I live in your flat rent-free, I pay you a pathetically small wage for the hours you work for the party and I don't pay you at all for the cooking and cleaning. I've completely hijacked your life and most of the time I'm too exhausted even to have sex with you!"

"It is a labour of love."

"You'll be rewarded for your devotion one day, I promise."

"You mean I'll have a golden throne and fifty virgins or something when I get to heaven? I thought you were an atheist."

"I was thinking of a more earthly reward. I was thinking twenty or thirty years from now, when we live in a better world and I've learnt to cook, you can lie on the sofa drinking beer while I make the Sunday lunch then we can make love all afternoon."

"It isn't going to happen. Twenty or thirty years from now you will be President of the United States of Europe and will be too busy overseeing the hydrocarbon mining of Jupiter's moons which will fuel the newly constructed pleasure dome on Mars."

"Is that possible, mining hydrocarbons from Jupiter's moons I mean?"

"I don't know, I'm not an astrophysicist."

"I thought you might have read a book about it. I was wondering if it could be a viable alternative to those toxic fields of GM biofuels which kill every living thing for a thirty mile radius."

"Thirty miles is a slight exaggeration. Anyway, I thought we agreed you were going to bed?"

"I am, I'm going. If I were President of Europe you couldn't bully me like this!"

"You think not? You just wait and see!"

SHATTERED ILLUSIONS
The Man Behind the Mask

I used to think I loved you,
But that was only fantasy.
The you I loved was but a dream,
Now it's the real you I see.

In my mind you smelt of roses,
Your skin flawless, marble white,
Your satin hair as black as a raven,
Your sensuous kisses an unearthly delight.

But now it's cold grey morning
And I must drag you from our bed.
Though half closed eyes you barely see me,
Your words are cold, your lips are dead.

You sip your tea in grumpy silence,
As you dress you curse and swear,
Your mousy brown roots are showing
As you drag a comb through tangled hair.

Yet I rejoice in shattered illusions.
Such foolish dreams should not come true.
I never loved that imagined woman,
The one I love is you.

MAKING HEADLINES
Simon Chandra

With my connections to the unlicensed media of the Clarkson and Bryant years I have perhaps been guilty of bias and have overlooked the importance of the authorised media. It is easy to assume that everyone working for the government-licensed media was greedy, lazy and corrupt. It is certainly true that the executives responsible for the Independent Media Corporation (IMC) were an unprincipled group whose sole concern was making huge profits and awarding themselves obscene bonuses, but not all the corporation's employees were similarly motivated. There were a large number of people working within IMC who cared about their work. Many were nostalgic for the days of quality entertainment and real news journalism.

Peter Sheridan was one of these. Considering he was the political correspondent for IMC's news channel between 2098 and 2106 he was never especially well known as news audiences were exceptionally small during this period. Even at their peak, viewing figures for IMC News were less than a quarter of those for the sport, music and light entertainment channels. For those of you who, like me, do not clearly remember what the IMC News channel was like I would highly recommend you follow the links to the archives. The scope and focus is completely different from what we expect of mainstream news now.

Opposition politicians rarely made the headlines and international news was extremely limited. There was a great deal of emphasis on terrorism, particularly the trials of alleged terrorists. Crime was also a major preoccupation, especially crimes of a sexual nature or involving homosexuals. As a matter of course every bulletin concluded with a positive story about the President or a member of his Cabinet, perhaps opening a new hospital or attending a sporting event. There is some fantastic footage of Bryant visiting a mother and baby group and being handed an infant for a photo opportunity. The cute little cherub is promptly sick all over him and the look on his face is just priceless, a mixture of revulsion and impotent rage.

Sheridan still works in television but as a producer not a presenter. We met at Reportage's London studios which used to belong to IMC. Though his once dark hair is now mostly grey Sheridan has aged well. He is still as slim as he was ten years ago and his face is not much altered. He is dressed casually and says not having to wear a suit is one of the things he likes about working behind the camera. I ask him if there is anything he does miss about his old job.

"Only the make-up girl," he answers. "She was a pretty young thing and had such a gentle touch at dabbing on the powder."

"It must have been frustrating working under such rigorous control by the government."

"Frustration doesn't begin to describe it. We frequently had to record an item three or four times over before the censors would approve it for transmission. They took objection to the most ludicrous things as well. I remember once we were told we couldn't use the word 'gay' anymore, it had to be homosexual or sexual deviant. Another time we were forbidden from using the word 'abortion' to describe terminating a pregnancy."

"You can't have enjoyed working under such conditions; why did you?"

"Sometimes I did enjoy it. There were times when I relished the challenge of attempting to report the truth while the censors tried to prevent us. There were occasions when we succeeded."

"Such as?"

"Well, since it is Rosa you are interested in I will give you the major example involving her, but it wasn't the only time. It was April 2104 and reports of the number of deaths and serious injuries in so called Re-education Centres were the top stories in the underground press. Since her election Rosa had taken an active interest in Re-education Centres and had been investigating them on behalf of some of her constituents. Her office regularly released information on the subject to IMC but we were forbidden from broadcasting it. The topic was completely off limits. The censors insisted the issue was too sensitive and would cause unnecessary embarrassment to the families concerned. The usual crap. Even Liberation's own publications were prohibited from discussing the subject.

"As it was well known that this was an issue Rosa was concerned with, when the full scale of the problem did hit the underground press it was assumed that the story originated from her office. There was no evidence against her or she would have been arrested immediately. Instead the government made its usual statements about illegal publications and broadcasts spreading lies and alarming the public. This of course was the angle we had to work with but in damning the underground media for their irresponsibility we took the opportunity to repeat the substance of the story, thus spreading it to a wider audience.

"We also gave the Liberation Party some much needed publicity. We employed the rather old-fashioned technique of ambushing Rosa leaving her home and accused her of leaking the story. Naturally I conducted the interview in a tone of moral outrage at such underhand tactics but I gave her the opportunity to speak on the official TV news, and she was smart enough to make the most of that opportunity."

"Then you believe she was intelligent and politically astute?"

"Extremely. I had met her before she entered politics. At parties, at the IMC studios when she was doing other programmes and a couple of times when we appeared on shows together. We didn't know each other well but I liked her. She was incredibly candid actually. There was a time we were on a quiz show together, back when she was just becoming well known. We were in the Green Room chatting and I asked her if the rumours on RNN were true that she was having an affair with Bryant. She answered that she was without the slightest hesitation. I said 'You ought to be careful about telling journalists stuff like that.' She replied, 'Why? The censors won't let you repeat it.' Which was perfectly true. Bryant's affairs were common knowledge but no one dared speak of them."

Sheridan's interview with Rosa speaks for itself, their exchange is printed below. With hindsight we can recognise this as a major turning point for the Liberation Party after years of being ignored. Rosa is very careful not to directly accuse Geoffrey Hanes, the Minister for Care and Welfare, of either lying or withholding information as this would make her liable to arrest under the much abused anti-terrorism laws of the time. To call a Minister a liar would be considered as distributing terrorist propaganda. Rosa had obviously been warned of the TV crew's presence as although it is only 8:00am she emerges from the block looking immaculate. As usual O'Brien is standing close behind her.

Sheridan: Miss Clayton, would you like to comment on the story in the unlicensed press this morning?

Rosa: Which story would that be?

Sheridan: I'm referring to the false allegations of neglect and mistreatment of patients in Re-education Centres. Did this misinformation originate from your office?

Rosa: Giving any information, true or false, to the unlicensed press is a criminal offence.

Sheridan: Then you deny you were the source of these libellous reports?

Rosa: The only facts I have on Re-education Centres come from the Department of Care and Welfare and therefore I must assume they are accurate.

Sheridan: Then you can confirm that the reports in the underground media this morning are false?

Rosa: I'm afraid I cannot, the articles which I have seen so far this morning are all in agreement with the information that I have.

Sheridan: Yet you still deny that you leaked this story?

Rosa: I have not been in communication with any representatives of the underground press.

Sheridan: But can you be certain that the leak did not come from one of your employees?

Rosa: I cannot and will be investigating that possibility, however it is equally likely that the leak came from the Department of Care and Welfare.

Sheridan: This is not the first time you have been suspected of passing information to the illegal press. Is it not time that a proper criminal investigation was carried out?

Rosa: I would be happy to co-operate with any such investigation if there were any evidence to justify one.

Sheridan: Do you condone this reckless action by the illegal media? Are they right to cause alarm and distress among the public?

Rosa: Many of the people I have spoken to are already distressed by the treatment of their children in so-called Re-education Centres.

Sheridan: Then you support the spreading of unsubstantiated rumour by guerrilla journalists?

Rosa: Certainly not, but so far I have not seen any reports which are not confirmed by the government's own figures.

Sheridan: But the Minister for Care and Welfare has already stated that these allegations are false, are you accusing a Cabinet Minister of lying?

Rosa: I am making no accusations. I wish only to possess the facts. From the reports I have read I conclude the figures stated by the press are approximately correct but look forward to seeing accurate information when Mr Hanes can provide it.

Sheridan: But the Minister has already said that this information is highly sensitive and he does not wish to cause further stress to the families involved by making it public.

Rosa: The parents I have spoken to are desperate to know what happened to their children and would gladly see it made public in order to prevent other parents from having to endure the same ordeal.

Sheridan: Surely if you were the parent of a sexual deviant you would not want the fact to be all over the news?

Rosa: Firstly, there is very little evidence to prove most of these young people are sexual deviants. The majority have been imprisoned without formal charges or a trial. Secondly, an investigation into conditions in Re-education Centres could easily be conducted without releasing the names of the individuals concerned. By making these poor excuses for not disclosing information the Department of Care and Welfare is in danger of making it appear that it is trying to hide something.

Sheridan: It has been suggested that your concern about the treatment of homosexuals is a reflection of your own sexuality. Is this true?

Rosa: Are you trying to ask me if I am a lesbian?

Sheridan: Are you a lesbian?

Rosa: I am not and there are plenty of people who can confirm that, including the President. Now if you will excuse me I have a meeting to get to.

Tuesday 8th April 2104

Alicia Cain was still watching the IMC News channel when Rebecca arrived at her office. David had remained outside with Alicia's PA so they talked alone.

"That was a brilliant interview," Cain said. "You handled Sheridan beautifully."

"I'm not so sure," Rebecca replied, "I have a feeling it went exactly the way he intended."

"But you made it clear that Hanes is covering up the truth without openly accusing him. It was extremely well done."

"Only because Sheridan let me. His attack over the leak was very half-hearted and he let me answer all of his questions without interruption. As for asking me if I'm a lesbian, he must have expected me to allude to my relationship with the President. Has there been any response from Hanes yet?"

"He is meeting with Bryant as we speak, but so far they just keep repeating the same excuses about the issue being sensitive."

"How are the public reacting?"

"They are furious. The Mega Meals scandal was just a minor embarrassment compared to this. People are starting to gather at the gates of Re-education Centres all over the country. There have been a couple of clashes with police already but no serious injuries so far."

"That will change once the police start shooting. What are we going to do? Should we issue a statement urging people to stay home? I don't want to be responsible for getting anyone killed."

"For the moment we wait and see what Hanes and Bryant are going to do. I'm guessing we will be hearing from them before too long."

Footage of some of the demonstrations was now being featured on IMC although not the same pictures as appeared on RNN a few minutes earlier. IMC showed the police calmly holding back a crowd and allowing staff to enter the centre. RNN had a rather blurred and shaky video of police with batons lashing out at a group of women. While they were watching the telephone rang.

Alicia answered it, listened a moment then replied, "Put him through."

She put the call on speakerphone for Rebecca's benefit.

"Good morning Miss Cain," said the voice on the line which seemed familiar to Rebecca. "This is James Hutchens from the President's communications office. I'm sure you are aware of the trouble the illegal media have stirred up. Naturally the President is very concerned by these scenes and is anxious to calm things down as quickly as possible."

"Naturally," agreed Alicia.

"I'm sure you would also wish to prevent any outbreaks of violence. The President will be making a statement for IMC News in about an hour reassuring the public and asking them to refrain from disorderly behaviour. Might we recommend that as leader of the opposition you do likewise?"

"I would very much like to do as you suggest but at present I have no reassurance to give. I cannot make a statement refuting the allegations in the unlicensed press if I am not in possession of the relevant facts."

"Which facts do you require?"

"If I am to reassure the public that these figures for the number of patient deaths are exaggerated then I need the actual figures. The same goes for attempted suicides, errors in administering medication and serious injuries."

"I believe Mr Hanes has already explained that this information cannot be released due to its sensitive nature."

"Mr Hanes has stated that several times but you understand that without the correct information I cannot address the public. I would look very foolish trying to talk about a subject on which I am woefully ignorant at present."

"Could you not simply assure the public that they can trust their government to care for these vulnerable young people?"

"I fear the public would not find such a vague statement very convincing."

"I will consult with Mr Hanes and see whether you can be provided with the information you have requested. I will call back shortly. Thank you Miss Cain."

When he rang off Alicia exclaimed, "Sleazy little prick!"

"What are you going to do when he calls back with a load of made-up figures?" Rebecca enquired.

"I'm not sure, I'm kind of making this up as I go along."

"It's rather reassuring to know that even you have to do that sometimes."

"Don't tell anyone but I do it quite often."

They continued watching developments on both the authorised and pirate news networks until about twenty minutes later when an email arrived from the Department of Care and Welfare, claiming to be the figures Alicia had requested.

Alicia read the brief message and exclaimed, "This is brilliant! Just look at this Becky."

Rebecca glanced at the document on the screen and saw immediately that the government had made a foolish mistake.

"Four deaths!" exclaimed Rebecca. "They don't honestly expect us to believe that do they? I know for a fact there have been four deaths in the Croydon centre alone this year."

"This is perfect. If they had given us sensible figures we may have had to go along with them and at least pretend to believe them but this is just ridiculous. We can prove they are lying."

"What's our response?"

"Let's keep them waiting for a while. Then I want you to talk to Hutchens since you have done all the research. You must be careful though. You must not accuse them of deliberately lying or of making up these figures. Say you just want to clarify a few points, then hit them with what we know."

They allowed half an hour to go by before they contacted Hutchens again. Rebecca went through her notes and made certain she had all the facts laid out in front of her. Alicia's PA, Samantha, brought tea and they watched the TV pictures of growing crowds outside Re-education Centres across the county. In several locations armed police had been called in but as yet no shots had been fired.

More cases of police brutality were being aired on RNN. In Birmingham protestors had attempted to scale the fence around the centre, many receiving injuries from the barbed wire and spiked railings. There was footage of police officers pulling already bleeding demonstrators down from the fence, throwing them to the ground, kicking and beating them.

"OK let's call Hutchens," Alicia said eventually.

Samantha got him on the line then put him through to Alicia.

"Hello again Mr Hutchens," she said, "thank you so much for sending those figures through. I have been looking at them with Miss Clayton, the Shadow-Minister for Care and Welfare, and there are a couple of points we would like to clarify."

"I was not aware that Miss Clayton held the position of Shadow-Minister," Hutchens replied dubiously.

"You could be forgiven for not knowing that. The appointment was made only recently."

Very recently, for it was the first that Rebecca had heard of it. Before now the Liberation Party had not bothered with Shadow-Ministerial titles as they had so few MPs.

"Miss Clayton is with me now," said Alicia. "Would it be all right if she asked you a few questions?"

"Of course," replied Hutchens but he sounded slightly nervous.

"Good morning Mr Hutchens," said Rebecca. "It is a pleasure to speak to you again. It is quite some time since we last met. You have given us a figure for the number of deaths within Re-education Centres during the last year. Is this the figure for all the centres in the UK?"

"Yes, all forty centres," Hutchens replied hesitantly.

"And you are certain this information is correct?"

"Do you have reason to doubt it?"

"I'm afraid I do. I have in front of me the annual report of the Croydon Re-education Centre where one of my constituents was a patient and this clearly states there were four deaths in the last year at that institution alone."

"Then there cannot have been any deaths at any other institutions."

"Except I know that there was a death at the Portsmouth Centre as the father of the victim is also one of my constituents."

"Your information must be at fault for I am certain mine is correct."

"You are probably right but I would like to account for the discrepancies. Bearing in mind I saw a copy of the death certificate for the Portsmouth case and the report from the Croydon centre came from the Department of Care and Welfare, that would suggest a total of five deaths."

"The Croydon report must be wrong."

"It is a fairly horrendous mistake to get the number of deaths in the institution wrong. Don't you find it rather worrying that a government department could make such an error?"

"I expect there is a reasonable explanation, perhaps a patient was taken from the centre to hospital where they then died, while my figures only reflect the deaths actually within the centres."

"That would seem possible, but it does rather throw up the questions about the other figures you have sent us this morning. You state that there were twenty-eight injuries among patients which required hospitalisation. How many of these patients subsequently died? You say that of these twenty-eight only seven were attempted suicides but again the Croydon report would indicate the actual number is much higher. Eleven patients from that institution alone were admitted to hospital after attempting suicide."

"I would have to consult the Minister before I can answer these points since I have not seen the report you are referring to."

"Perhaps you could put me in touch with Mr Hanes directly."

"I shall see what I can do."

As he rang off Rebecca sank back in her chair and let out a huge sigh of relief.

"Do you think that was OK?" she asked.

"It was better than OK," Alicia replied, "it was positively statesman like."

"Do you think Hanes will call in person?"

"I think he will. This is his mess. He'll have to sort it out."

Rebecca had resolved herself for another long wait for the next development but the phone rang again after only ten minutes. Alicia allowed Samantha to answer the call and then to put it through. It was Geoff Hanes and he sounded flustered.

Good morning Miss Clayton. James Hutchens tells me there is a problem with the figures which my department released to you."

"There are certain discrepancies between these figures and those I was given by members of your department several weeks ago."

"Hutchens said something about a report from Croydon."

"Yes, I have documents from several Re-education Centres but the most complete records I have are from the Croydon institution as that is where one of my constituents was until recently a patient."

"Could you tell me which other documents you have?"

"Mr Hanes, I have a great many and it would take me hours to list them all. Since I could not get a comprehensive report from your department containing the information I wanted I have been attempting to piece the facts together from the material I was allowed access to."

Rebecca glanced towards Alicia who gave her a reassuring thumbs-up.

"Surely the information we sent this morning was comprehensive enough," said Hanes.

"Indeed, but it contradicts the previous figures I have obtained from your department."

"Miss Clayton, I assure you that at any other time I would be glad to go through all these documents with you and explain the discrepancies but the present mood of public unrest requires immediate action. We need to calm and reassure the public before anyone is seriously hurt."

"I believe there have already been a number of serious injuries. What do you suggest?"

"Perhaps if you and Miss Cain could support the government's condemnation of the illegal press and urge the protestors to return to their homes?"

Alicia shook her head indicating she was not prepared to make such a statement.

"We will gladly help to end these protests," said Rebecca. "We are anxious to prevent further violence. If I announce that you and I are co-operating in a full investigation into Re-education Centres then I expect the public will find that far more reassuring than simply condemning the media."

Alicia nodded encouraging her to continue on this tack.

"An investigation?" asked Hanes, sounding puzzled and slightly alarmed.

"Yes, you said you would go through the relevant documents with me. That would count as an investigation wouldn't it?"

"Yes, I suppose it could."

"I'm sure you will have no objection to my medical and legal advisors assisting us in our investigations since you will no doubt be calling on the assistance of your own advisors."

"There may be security issues about including other people in our discussions."

"What sort of security issues?"

"Can we finalise the details at a later date? At present we need to deal with the immediate civic unrest."

Out of the corner of her eye Rebecca could see Alicia shaking her head vigorously but she had no intention of letting the Minister off so easily.

"Certainly," she said, "but if I am to announce an investigation to IMC viewers I will need to know something about the nature of the investigation. I need to be able to assure the public that it will be thorough, unbiased and that the results will be published. I also need to assure them that any problem we uncover will be rectified."

"I understand. In that case you may say that the board of investigation will consist of ourselves and our medical and legal advisors plus an independent chairman."

"Who will that be?"

"I will have to consult with my advisers before nominating a suitable person."

"If your department chooses the chairman he can hardly be called independent can he?"

Alicia was on her feet like a sports spectator awaiting the winning goal.

"The same could be said of a chairman of your choosing," argued Hanes.

"Precisely why I was about to recommend we include the other parliamentary parties in this investigation then elect a chairman from among us."

"You wish to involve the radical minority parties in this issue?"

"I wish to involve all parties to ensure openness and fairness."

"You risk the whole process being hijacked by the lunatic fringe."

"I do not believe that is likely. The representatives of other parties whom I have spoken to are all concerned about the welfare of young people in your Re-education Centres and take the issue very seriously."

"Very well, we will include all parties with more than ten representatives in Parliament."

Alicia punched the air in triumph but Rebecca was not satisfied yet.

"Make it ten or more and we should allow the others and the independents to nominate a representative to join the investigatory committee."

"All right," Hanes agreed with evident impatience in his voice, "and you agree that both you and Miss Cain will make a statement to the media to stop the protests."

"We can only ask the protestors to stop, I cannot promise anymore."

"But we have an agreement?"

"We do Mr Hanes. It has been a pleasure talking to you."

"Thank you, now if you will excuse me I have much work to do."

"Goodbye Mr Hanes and good luck."

Rebecca's mouth was bone dry after the long conversation. She poured herself a glass of water and looked towards Alicia who was beaming the broadest smile.

"I wish we had something stronger to drink," Alicia remarked.

"I don't know why you are so excited," Rebecca replied. "OK, Hanes has agreed to an investigation but he will find a way to prevent the truth from getting out."

"Maybe, but this is the first time we've ever managed to force the government into doing anything. This is the greatest success the Liberation Party has achieved. I choose to believe it is the first step on our road to bringing down Phoenix, so please just let me enjoy the moment."

Part 6

Alliances

Island Nation Magazine
Saturday 3rd August 2115

THE BOARD OF INQUIRY
Simon Chandra

In my column last week Peter Sheridan stated that the Re-education Centre scandal was the major turning point for the Liberation Party. There has been much discussion of this on our message board. Many have suggested that the decline of the Phoenix Party began long before this. An in-depth political analysis is beyond the scope of this series but I believe things went increasingly downhill for Bryant and his allies from the moment the scandal hit the underground press. After Rosa and Cain both appeared on IMC appealing for an end to the protests the crowds outside the centres gradually diminished. Some were reassured by the promise of an inquiry but most were probably just aware of the futility of protesting. The inquiry took almost three months to set up and several other events of note occurred in that time.

Geoff Hanes announced his resignation only a couple of weeks after the scandal and a major Cabinet reshuffle followed, among rumours that the Chancellor Anthony Freeman was plotting a leadership challenge. Freeman was removed from the treasury and demoted to Hanes's old job. Officially all rumours of a leadership challenge were denied and allegedly Freeman's transfer was a sign of the confidence Bryant had in his ability to sort out Hanes's mess. Philip Graysby was promoted to the Exchequer, possibly Bryant's biggest mistake.

When the government eventually ran out of delaying tactics the first meeting of the board of inquiry was finally convened on 14th July 2104. The opposition had been forced into making a number of compromises concerning the number of advisors that were permitted in attendance. While Freeman was assisted by five staff from the Department of Care and Welfare the Liberation Party had only three representatives; Rebecca Clayton, Karen Baker as her legal advisor and Dr Brian Phelps, the medical expert. The other four members of the board were not allowed any advisors at all.

Dr Phelps had been a member of the Liberation Party for fifteen years and had been a regular advisor to Cain so was the obvious choice to assist Rebecca. Originally his work for the Party had been voluntary and only when his full time work as a GP allowed, but once he joined the inquiry committee he became employed on a more formal basis.

Now in his late fifties, Dr Phelps has retired from politics and returned to being a GP. We met at his surgery and I asked him about his acquaintance with Rosa.

"I didn't know her at all before Alicia asked me to join the inquiry board," he tells me. "Of course I had heard a lot about her in the media and was curious to know what she was really like."

"And what was she like?" I asked.

"She was extremely attractive, very intelligent and utterly dedicated to her work."

"Did you work closely together?"

"Very. Even before the first meeting we spent hours going through reports and statements with a fine tooth-comb, hoping to decipher what the government was trying to hide. Sometimes the three of us spent hours shut up in a meeting room together at Liberation HQ. We must have drunk several gallons of coffee. My job was basically just to translate all the medical terminology, which is not as easy as it sounds since the reports were frequently deliberately worded to be misleading."

"It sounds exhausting. Did tempers ever get frayed during these long meetings?"

"Not usually but there were a couple of occasions when it became apparent there was a certain amount of tension between Karen and Rebecca."

"Tension?"

"I remember one occasion when a few heated words were exchanged. It was a couple of days before the board's first meeting and we were making sure we were fully prepared. As usual what we thought would take only a couple of hours occupied us all evening. At around nine o'clock David O'Brien came into the room and announced that it was time to finish. I say announced because it wasn't a request or a suggestion; he marched in and said, 'Right it's late, it's time I drove Rebecca home.' I expect she was tired because she didn't argue and neither did I because I had a wife and family waiting for me, but Karen wasn't happy.

"I don't recall her exact words but she questioned what right O'Brien had to decide when the meeting ended.

"He answered, 'You may be able to work for twelve hours straight Karen but Rebecca needs to take a break.'

"To which Karen said to Rebecca, 'You don't have to let him order you around just because you are sleeping with him.'

"Rebecca replied something like, 'He is just taking care of me.'

"Karen went off on a complete rant about gender politics saying, 'That's pathetic! You claim to campaign for equality then you allow yourself to be bullied by a man just because he professes to care about you.' She made several rather offensive personal remarks in this vein but Rebecca was very cool. She just very calmly advised Karen to mind her own business and left with O'Brien. Karen was seething but I didn't hang around to hear what she had to say on the subject. I had no intention of being drawn into the argument and wanted to get home.

"After that there was always a bit of an atmosphere when they were together. They never really quarrelled and it didn't interfere with the work at all but they never seemed to really be on friendly terms. Mind you, Karen wasn't exactly friendly at the best of times. She was very direct and always got straight to business, no pleasantries or small talk.

"So would you say you got on better with Rebecca than with Karen?"

"I suppose, Rebecca was a little easier to feel comfortable with. She always asked after my wife and kids. In fact with both Rebecca and Alicia you always got the impression that they actually cared. Most people ask questions like 'How are you?' and 'How are the family?' just because it is expected, they aren't really interested in the answer. I guess it was the little things like remembering my daughters' names and asking how they were getting on a school that made Alicia and Rebecca popular. I suspect such niceties come naturally to some politicians and others have to learn them."

"Has Karen Baker learnt them since those days?"

"I don't know. I haven't talked to her in a while."

"Anyway, getting back to the Inquiry. Rebecca was elected as chairwoman wasn't she?"

"She was. Freeman nominated one of his staff and naturally all the other members of the department agreed but the rest of the committee was unanimous in voting for Rebecca. She and Karen had got all the other opposition parties on our side by thoroughly briefing them before the first meeting took place. Of course once Rebecca was chair, Freeman could not dictate the proceedings any further. The original agenda was extremely complicated with a whole range of preliminary topics all intended to prevent us from getting to the point. Rebecca's first move was to reject all these. It was put to the vote, carried and a new agenda drawn up.

"It was decided we would look at the reports from each of the forty Re-education Centres and interview members of staff and patients until we had a comprehensive analysis of conditions in each of the centres. We would then make recommendations based on our findings. Freeman and his cronies did everything possible to hinder the process. We were constantly coming up against reasons why we couldn't speak to particular people or see certain documents. This went on for months, but Rebecca never gave up and would not allow any of the other committee members to do so. She continually reminded everyone of the importance of the inquiry."

"On the whole do you think you were successful? Did you get the comprehensive analysis you wanted?"

"By the time we concluded the inquiry and published our recommendations we had seen the majority of the information we had requested and spoken to most of the witnesses. There were obviously still things the government were trying to cover up but the conclusions we reached were damning enough. Freeman was forced to order the immediate closure of five of the centres and major changes to the running of the others. We basically struck a deal with the department that certain parts of our report would not be made public provided that our recommendations were implemented immediately."

"A number of political commentators have criticised this co-operation with the government to suppress the most damning parts of the report."

"It is easy for people to criticise now but they forget how much power the Phoenix government wielded. Had the report been published in its entirety there would have been a repeat of the spring protests, only this time they would have ended in violence and probably many deaths. We had no way to force the government to follow our recommendations but Freeman was anxious for his name not to be associated with another scandal. We had to compromise in order to achieve anything at all. I agree it was not very much for all those months of work, but dozens of young people were released as a result of our actions and conditions for the others improved slightly."

"So you feel it was worthwhile? You did achieve something?"

"Yes I do, but also you have to understand that this small measure of success was part of the bigger picture. It was the first time the Liberation Party had any influence over government policy. At the time it felt like a pretty poor compromise after all our efforts, but with hindsight I see the greater significance."

Friday 21st November 2104

The inquiry was over and David was driving Rebecca home. In spite of their successes she was not feeling triumphant, only exhausted. Running through her mind were all the cases she had researched, the cruel and humiliating treatment so called patients had been subjected to. Children as young as ten had been taken away from their families, locked up and forced to endure invasive, unpleasant and often painful procedures intended to cure them of alleged sexual deviance. Reflecting all the horrific things she had learned during the past few months Rebecca found herself crying.

"Oh Becky!" David exclaimed when he saw her tears. "What is wrong?"

She dried her eyes and sniffed back a sob.

"It's nothing," she replied, "I'm all right, I'm just overtired."

"I'm not surprised, you deserve a rest."

"Yes I think I do. Wake me up on Tuesday."

"Do you want to get away for a few days? It's pretty short notice but I expect we could arrange something, like a couple of days in the country or by the sea. A change of scene would do you good. What do you think?"

"Ask me again tomorrow. I'm too tired to make any decisions right now."

"OK."

They travelled in silence for a while, Rebecca looking out at the grey skies and drizzling rain. Though not yet five o'clock it was already dark and the gloom outside added to Rebecca's depression. David tried to remind her of what she had achieved in the hope of raising her spirits.

"So the Croydon centre is to be closed down then," he remarked.

"Yes," she replied, "and Glasgow, Gateshead, Moss Side and Swindon. Most of the patients will be transferred to other centres. Did I say patients? Bloody Care and Welfare jargon! It's contagious. I meant prisoners. Anyway most will be transferred but some will be released. For a start all children under the age of fifteen will be released unless they actually have a criminal conviction."

"Just think how many families will be reunited thanks to you."

"I didn't exactly do it all on my own. Anyway I can't help thinking about the rest of the prisoners in those other thirty-five centres who will still be suffering. Did you read the method they use to test for sexual deviance? It is crude, disgusting and has virtually no scientific basis."

"I didn't need to read about it. In order to join the army you have to be tested."

"What! Oh my God, I didn't know that. That must have been so embarrassing."

"I suppose it was a bit, but when you sign up you get used to that sort of thing. Dropping your pants and having someone poke your genitals is a fairly common practice. I expect the procedure is more unpleasant for a woman than a man. I mean, for a man all it involves is attaching sensors to your penis to monitor blood flow."

"But it is completely pointless. If you are looking at pictures of naked women and not getting aroused that doesn't make you gay. It just means pornography isn't your thing. And what if you are looking at men and suddenly start thinking about your girlfriend? Then they lock you up."

"I know. Throughout the test I was concentrating on solving complex maths problems in order to avoid any such complications. I think as a result they decided I was impotent but considering the alternatives I wasn't too bothered."

"The test is bad enough, but the so called treatments are even worse. They are using prisoners as guinea pigs to try out potentially deadly cocktails of drugs or some deranged professor's new theory about aversion therapy. Add to that the hundreds of cases of neglect and abuse and you get twenty-three deaths in the last year alone. It makes me feel sick."

"I understand, my love, but you have to let go. If you make yourself ill with stress and worry you won't be able to help anyone. You have to take care of yourself. You are too important to the Liberation Party, you can't burn yourself out on this one issue. Promise me over the next few days you will take a break."

"All right I promise."

"Right, so if Karen calls I have your permission to tell her where to go?"

Rebecca laughed and answered, "You may."

By the time they reached home the rain was falling more heavily and was whisked about by strong gusts of wind. They parked the car and dashed to the doorway. The corridors were little warmer than outside but their flat at least was cosy. Rebecca pulled off her shoes and her damp jacket and collapsed on the sofa. David checked their messages.

"Oh crap!" he exclaimed.

"What's the matter?"

"Nothing. It's just that my dad has called again. It is about the fourth time this week and I still haven't got round to calling him back. I'll do it after dinner."

"Do it now," Rebecca suggested. "If you leave it until later something else will come up or you'll be too tired and before you know it next week has arrived and you still haven't called him."

"Wise words," David agreed. "I'll call him now and then fix us something to eat."

"I'll be right here when you are done. I haven't got the energy to move."

David went into the spare room to make the call but did not shut the door completely so Rebecca could hear his side of the conversation. After the first exchange of greetings and apologies for not calling they were discussing the inquiry and Rebecca's achievements. She allowed her eyes to close and tried to empty her head of the whirring mass of thoughts circulating there. She was sinking into a stupor when a change in David's tone roused her.

"I do know that Dad," he said impatiently then raising his voice slightly, "That is my job… Yes I'm not stupid I realise that… Of course we discussed this. We aren't complete idiots… Oh for goodness sake do you honestly think we haven't thought of that?"

Then David was quiet and when he spoke again it was more softly, "Yes Dad I understand… I worry about that too… No one can be sure how long they will have together, that's why I'm trying to take your advice and make the most of every moment we do have." Then he laughed and said, "I haven't even asked her yet… I will but things have been so hectic I haven't managed to find an appropriate moment… Soon, very soon… Yes well I'd better go and make us some dinner. I'll call you again sometime over the weekend… I don't know, we'll see… Perhaps tomorrow but I'm not promising anything… Yes I will… No really I am going to I just want to do it properly… You'll be the first to know, I'll talk to you again soon… Bye."

As he re-entered the living-room Rebecca asked, "Asked me what?"

"What?"

"You said 'I haven't even asked her yet.' What haven't you asked me?"

"Oh nothing, not you. It was something Dad wanted me to talk to Alicia about, some of her medical policies. It wasn't important."

"Medical policies? Which ones?"

"It doesn't matter. It really isn't important. Is pasta OK? I know we always seems to be having pasta these days but it's quick."

"Pasta is fine."

She followed him through to the kitchen and watched him retrieving onions and garlic from the cupboard. She offered to chop them while he picked some herbs from the pots on the windowsill.

"What were you arguing about?" she asked.

"We weren't arguing."

"It sounded like you were."

"Well, perhaps it was a slight disagreement. Dad was worried that your recent dealings with the Department of Care and Welfare will have created more enemies among the Phoenix Party. I was trying to explain that we were already aware of this and that my primary concern is your safety, but he still insisted on lecturing me."

"Perhaps you should have thanked him for his concern instead of immediately getting on the defensive; after all I expect he is as anxious for your safety as he is mine. He knows that in order to protect me you will be putting yourself in harm's way."

"I know, he is just trying to help, I shouldn't be so ungrateful. I just wish he wouldn't talk to me as though I am a complete imbecile."

"He probably finds it hard to accept that you are grown up and capable of thinking for yourself."

"Yes, well it was only a slight quarrel. I will call him again soon, when I'm less tired and irritable, then hopefully we can talk sensibly. Why don't you pour some wine then go and put your feet up? I've got dinner under control."

She did as he suggested and resumed her former attitude on the sofa. Although David had dismissed the quarrel with his father as unimportant she suspected there was something on his mind, as he was neither singing nor whistling while he cooked, as was his usual habit. This impression was reinforced once dinner was ready and they sat down to eat. When deep in thought David always fiddled with his hair; first straightening out the curls, then twisting them around his fingers, then pulling them taut again.

"Is there something troubling you darling?" she asked.

"No, nothing," he lied.

"Yes there is. I know when you pondering imponderables, I've learnt to recognise the signs."

He sighed, "I was just thinking that as one who claims to be a poet there are certain subjects on which I ought to be able to express myself eloquently, but find I cannot."

"Which subject in particular?"

"I was thinking of love and how as yet I have utterly failed to put my own feelings into any original form of words."

"Perhaps because so much verse has already been written on the subject it is hard to add anything new."

"True, but I should like to communicate something of my own love, my own feelings, find my own voice, but all I can ever come up with are the same four words."

"What are they?"

"Will you marry me?"

Rebecca dropped her fork with a clatter.

"I desperately wanted the right words and a romantic setting," he continued, "but the longer I delay the harder it is to find the courage. I was afraid if I did not ask now I never would so, Rebecca, I love you, will you marry me?"

"Yes," she replied simply.

"You will?"

"Yes. As much as I love your poetry sometimes a straightforward question and answer is better. We both love each other and want to spend the rest of our lives together. What more is there to say?"

CAKES
Simon Chandra

Questions about Alicia Cain's sexuality have dogged her throughout her political career. Her refusal to comment on the subject has met with harsh criticism both from gay rights campaigners and anti-gay groups. Few people close to Cain have been prepared to speak on the subject while many more distant acquaintances have volunteered a great deal of conflicting information.

Entertaining though they are, I personally do not believe any of the stories about a sexual relationship between Cain and Rosa. The many hours they spent in each other's company were most likely to be purely work-related and the occasions where Rosa stayed at Cain's house can be easily explained. In those days there was an 11:00 pm curfew. If they conducted late night meetings at Party HQ they would have had to adjourn in plenty of time to travel home. If meetings were conducted at Cain's house they could carry on for as long as was required, then Rosa would remain until morning. Rosa was not the only Liberation Party member to stay at Cain's house and when she did she was always accompanied by O'Brien.

To my mind the most reliable source of information on Cain's personal life is Samantha Richardson, who worked as Alicia Cain's Personal Assistant between 2102 and 2106. Richardson has previously given interviews describing the nature of her close relationship with Cain during that time but I felt it was worth speaking to her myself, particularly about Cain's relationship with Rosa.

Richardson now runs her own business. She owns and manages a small factory in Yorkshire making traditional cakes and biscuits. She gave me a brief tour of the facility before we sat down in her office with tea and several samples of their products. The demand for the kind of old-fashioned, natural and slightly rustic treats and pastries that they are making is far greater than they can at present supply. In a world fed up with artificially flavoured processed algae and GM fungi, consumers are desperate for a good old honest current bun.

"This is rather different from politics," I say as I munch on delicious shortbread.

"I was never a politician though," she answers. "My job was just to keep Alicia organised and if you can handle arranging her schedule, running a small business is easy in comparison."

"Did you ever consider entering political life yourself?"

"No way! I saw what it did to people. The endless meetings, the eight hundred page reports, the stress, the lack of sleep and always a significant number of people violently hating you. That's why I chose this career. No one hates cakes and no one hates bakers."

"So, tell me about your relationship with Alicia Cain?"

"We were close. We were very good friends for a long time and for a while we were lovers."

"Then she was a lesbian?"

"No, bisexual I think. Certainly there were men in her past and I believe there were both men and women after me."

"Were you in love?"

"We were. It was never an easy relationship. We had to be very careful about secrecy and her work was always her top priority. That was why it ended. I couldn't handle always coming second to her career."

"It must have been hurtful that even when it was possible to do so she would not publicly acknowledge the relationship."

"Not really. I understood that she wanted to keep her private life out of the media but it was difficult having to hide my feelings all the time. Other couples could kiss when they met or hold hands in the street but we never could. I would have liked it if among friends we could have been less guarded."

"Don't you feel it is wrong for her to be ashamed of her sexuality?"

"I don't think she is ashamed of it. She has never denied that we were lovers, only refused to talk about it."

"There are many gay rights activists who are angry that she has not done more for their cause. They feel betrayed."

"I believe she personally would like to do more. She would like to tackle discrimination and give more rights to same sex couples, such as restoring our right to marry, but she has to do what is best for the Party and the country as a whole. Attitudes can't just be changed overnight. The Phoenix Party put a lot of work into stirring up hatred towards us, that can't just be undone by snapping your fingers. Now that democracy has been restored the government can't just do what it wants anymore."

"Some campaigners have suggested that if Rosa had lived she would have done more for their cause."

"Who knows! That is pretty pointless speculation."

"Was there rivalry between Rosa and Alicia? Some biographers have described a vicious power struggle."

"That's nonsense. All their achievements were gained through co-operation. They got on extremely well in fact, but not so well that they were sleeping together, as some other of those imaginative biographers have suggested."

"But they must have had disagreements on policies or strategies."

"I'm sure they did but they resolved them professionally without it ever becoming personal."

"Unlike the disagreement she had with Karen Baker?"

"I wouldn't call that a disagreement."

"You wouldn't? It certainly sounded like one from what Brian Phelps described."

"No I'd call that a blazing row or possibly a full-blown fight."

"Was it really that bad?"

"Oh yes. It was probably after the incident Phelps told you about, but for some reason Karen took a strong dislike to David. She was frequently heard complaining about his presence and started calling him Old Scar-Face behind his back. I say behind his back but she wasn't very discreet. He knew what she was saying."

"How did he react?"

"He didn't seem too bothered. I suppose he was prepared to rise above it. I thought it was horribly cruel referring to his disfigurement like that, but he just laughed it off. Then Rebecca found out, or rather I told her. She was furious. She told Karen what she thought of her in no uncertain terms, called her childish, deceitful and malicious. All the things I would have liked to call her but didn't dare. Rebecca demanded that Karen apologise to David. Karen refused and it turned into a massive argument right in the middle of Liberation HQ with both of them hurling abuse. They might have come to blows if David and Sean hadn't interceded.

"After that they continued working together but neither of them ever had a good word to say about the other. Whenever they met the room temperature would drop by several degrees and you could hear the grinding of teeth!"

"It all seems a bit petty and rather childish considering the important issues they were dealing with at the time."

"Absolutely. At the time I couldn't understand Karen's behaviour at all. With hindsight I think perhaps she was jealous of Rebecca's success. Karen had a first class law degree and years of experience campaigning for the Liberation Party. It must have been hard for her to watch someone with little formal education and no political background get into parliament before she did."

"What was your relationship with Rebecca like?"

"We were always on friendly terms but I never had the opportunity to really get to know her well. We rarely met outside of work so it was always just a brief conversation before or after a meeting. David and I were much closer. There were plenty of occasions Rebecca and Alicia were consulting in private and he waited in my office. I made him tea and we would chat."

"What did you talk about?"

"Pretty much all the stuff people usually talk about; the news, the weather, work, family, relationships."

"Then he spoke to you about his relationship with Rebecca?"

"Of course. He was in love, he talked about her most of the time."

"What did he say about her?"

"I'm afraid I'm not going to tell you all the details, these were private conversations. I will say that her safety and well-being were his greatest concerns. He was completely devoted to her and would have done anything to make her happy. I confess I was a little jealous of their relationship. At the time I was equally devoted to Alicia and would have done anything for her, but David's feelings were returned in a way mine never were. Rebecca never spoke of her love but it was evident to anyone not completely stupid. All those little signs were there. The way she looked at him, the way she smiled, the way she took his arm when he walked her to the car."

"Is it true they were married?"

"Oh yes. I was there, Hackney registry on a freezing cold day in January '05. It was what you would call an intimate ceremony. David's father, Alicia and I were the only people there. They wanted to avoid any fuss or media attention so kept the whole thing as secret as possible. They were in a hurry too. It was after the Re-education Centre inquiry had finished and they wanted to tie the knot quickly before the next political calamity arose. They were just in time, the Bradford riots broke out a couple of weeks later."

"Did the bride wear white?"

"No, she wore a dress and jacket in creamy beige with a silk scarf printed with pale pink roses. She looked absolutely beautiful, but then she always did. After the ceremony we all had lunch together, then the happy couple drove off to spend a couple of days in Brighton. It can't have been much of a honeymoon. I think it was either raining or blowing a gale all weekend. But they were newlyweds, what would the weather matter to them? I just remember how utterly, blissfully happy they both looked."

"Her death must have broken his heart. Did you ever see him afterwards?"

"No. Alicia and I were already growing apart by that time and I was left out of most of the major events, confined to the office. Someone had to be there to answer the phone. In the last few months before Rosa's death I hardly saw either her or David. It wasn't long after her death that I decided I'd had enough and quit. I'm so glad I did. Alicia was a wonderful woman but she could never have made me happy. Dianne, my partner for the last six years, makes me very happy. It would be nice if one day we could marry. It would be the icing on the cake!"

BRIGHTON STARLINGS
The Man Behind the Mask

Three subtly different shades of grey,
The conjunction of land, sea and sky.
Heavy expectant, ominous clouds
Hanging over the cold brooding swell
Which stirs the damp shifting stones.

The old pier groans in the wind,
A monument to pleasures past.
A lingering, drawn out death
As it slowly sinks into the sea.

But from its dead heart comes forth
Life on numerous nimble wings.
The upward surge of aerial ecstasy
Embracing newcomers into the flock.

They shift and change like sentient smoke,
Each bird a part of one mind.
A miracle of motion infinitely varied,
But performed with flawless precision.

Holding hands we pause to watch them
For the moment oblivious to the cold.
United in silent wonder and gratitude
For the beauty that remains in our world.
A precious moment of pure joy.

Tuesday 10th February 2105

There was an important meeting Rebecca had to get to and she was very late. The meeting was on the sixteenth floor but she couldn't find the lift. She asked someone but they refused to tell her. She realised it was because the girl she asked had been in her class at school and Rebecca had spilt red paint over her picture. She was arguing with the girl, who had always been a spoilt little brat and gone crying to the teacher whenever she did not get her own way, when she heard the phone ringing. She told Lucy, the bitchy girl, to answer the phone but Lucy refused. The phone was still ringing and she was getting annoyed. Then she heard David swearing and realised it was their phone and Lucy and the meeting were just a dream.

She heard David say, "For God's sake Karen it is four in the morning!"

She forced her eyes open and sat up groggily.

"Oh shit!" David swore, "when did this start… Oh God! How many?…Yes I'll tell her at once. Have you contacted Alicia yet?…OK I guess we'll just have to wait until she calls us. There isn't much we can do until curfew ends anyway… Yes I'm sure she will, I'll wake her now. Thanks Karen, speak to you later."

"What's going on?" Rebecca asked.

"Trouble," he replied. "Police raided a mosque in Bradford in the early hours of this morning. The local Muslim community took to the streets in protest. So far the police have shot at least a dozen people. There is live coverage on RNN. Karen thought you should see it."

He opened the RNN homepage and went to the live footage. The film was being transmitted from a window of a block of flats overlooking the violent clashes between police and protestors below. Though the scene was poorly lit and the camera unsteady the brutality of the police was evident. The protestors were trying to flee but were trapped between two groups of armed officers. Shots could be heard and figures were falling to the ground. There were screams of panic and cries of pain.

Rebecca looked away from the scene, unable to endure the carnage that was happening in front of her eyes. When she looked back a few minutes later the few remaining protestors who were still able to stand had been rounded up and were being dragged away by the police. The fallen were left unaided although the cries of agony revealed many were still alive. The voice of the cameraman was heard to say he was going down to assist the injured and the screen went black.

Moments later the picture returned and a young man covered with blood was addressing the camera.

"They said to return to our homes or they would shoot," he was saying, "and we tried to do as they said but then they started firing anyway. I got hit in the shoulder. I fell and people were trampling on me as they tried to get away. My brother was next to me. He was shot in the head."

Then there were sirens and a voice off camera cried, "Shit! They're coming back!"

There were violently shaking images as the cameraman fled and the screen went blank once more.

From the rest of the site they learned some more details of the night's events. Police had forced entry into the mosque and community centre just after two o'clock in the morning. Police alleged that the premises, one of three remaining mosques which served the entire city and suburbs, were being used by terrorist groups. This reason had been used in the past for shutting down many other mosques and places of worship. When neighbouring residents had come to investigate the disturbance violence broke out. One man, believed to be the property's caretaker, had been badly beaten by the police.

After removing computers and paperwork from the community centre offices, the police had sealed off the building and stuck up signs forbidding access. As the news spread rapidly through the surrounding high-rise flats, many came out to protest. The police summoned reinforcements and soon had the demonstrators surrounded. Unlike the previous protests at the Re-education Centres the police did not hesitate to shoot. They claimed some of the protestors had been armed but none of the RNN footage substantiated this.

The police cordoned off the area, not even allowing ambulances in. The wounded were left bleeding to death on the streets. As the live pictures David and Rebecca had just been watching revealed, anyone out of doors was likely to be killed. The residents were left with a horrendous choice, either to stay in their homes while people lay dying in the streets, or go to their aid and risk being shot.

The live link-up was showing more pictures filmed from the window of a tower block when the phone rang. Rebecca answered it. It was Alicia.

"Hi, did I wake you?" she asked.

"No, we are already up. Karen called a few minutes ago."

"Good, so you've heard what is happening."

"We're watching it on RNN now."

"I'm on my way to IMC studios. I've got special permission to be out early. Both Grant and Bryant will be making statements shortly and they want me to make one too. Unfortunately this isn't like the Re-ed. Centres, we don't have time to negotiate. I've said I will appeal for calm and ask people to remain in their homes provided I came make some criticism of the police. I'm not certain how far they will let me go."

"Anything is better than nothing."

"True. The reason I'm calling Becky is because I want you to go to Bradford as soon as possible. I want you to talk to people. Let them know Liberation is on their side and wants to stop atrocities like this from ever happening again."

"Of course, I'll get dressed. We'll leave as soon as curfew is up."

"Great, I have to go now. I'll call you again once I'm done here."

As she hung up the phone David said, "So are we off to Bradford?"

"Got it in one. Has my black suit been cleaned?"

"It's in the wardrobe. Do you want breakfast now or shall I fix you something to eat on the way?"

"I'm not hungry."

"I'll make some sandwiches. Pack plenty of warm clothes, the forecast is not good for the next few days."

They both hurried off to attend to their preparations for the journey. They were ready before six and risked going down to the car a few minutes early. David had looked into the possibility of going by train but there were only three trains that day and the first would not depart until nine and was already fully booked. They would have to drive despite the cost of fuel. The roads leaving the city were deserted. They passed through the Watford checkpoint without delay as their papers and vehicle were in good order and it was too cold for the officials to leave their booth for long. The M1 stretched out before them; a vast, potholed, empty stretch of concrete and tarmac.

The condition of the surface made it unwise to travel much above fifty miles per hour. They had been travelling for twenty minutes before they saw another vehicle, then they passed a couple of lorries on the southbound carriageway. After an hour they met their first patrol vehicle and were pulled over. Once their papers were found to be in order they were allowed to continue, although the patrol officer warned them that traffic into Bradford was being strictly controlled and they might not be allowed into the city.

Numerous phone calls to Bradford Constabulary during the journey produced no further information on the situation in the city and none of the minor officials Rebecca spoke to were prepared to say whether she would be allowed into the area. She eventually managed to make contact with representatives of Bradford South's MP, the leader of the Muslim Democrat Party, Mohammed Anwar, who agreed to help but could promise nothing.

Three hours into their journey they were stopped by a second patrol. This time the delay was longer as the officer had to consult with his superiors before they were allowed to continue. At twenty to eleven they reached the junction with the M62. The traffic was heavier; a long tailback of vehicles was waiting to pass through the checkpoint and onto the M1, but there were also several cars in the westbound queue. After half an hour they were permitted to pass only to be stopped again at the M606. This time they were refused permission to proceed as only residents were being allowed into the city.

Eventually, after a number of phone calls between Anwar and the Chief Constable it was agreed that Rebecca was allowed into the city. As Anwar was at St Luke's hospital meeting survivors of the previous night's violence, David and Rebecca were escorted there to meet him.

Thursday 12th February 2105

Rebecca had remained in Bradford for three days. Though her movements were rigorously supervised she was able to speak to many of the witnesses to and victims of the vicious and brutal actions of the police. What she was not able to do was talk about events to the licensed media. After initially reporting on the riots and broadcasting various appeals for calm, IMC rapidly dropped the subject. As far as they were concerned the riots had been started by violent extremists and had been successfully ended by the police; no further discussion was necessary. RNN took a much greater interest in the story, as did the Muslim Press with whom Anwar had his own secret contacts.

During this time Rebecca was able to establish a good working relationship with the Muslim Democrat Party and particularly with Mohammed Anwar, though they achieved very little. The police had the full support of the government and could ignore any criticism from the opposition. Though more than twenty people had been killed during the violence, not a single police officer was to face disciplinary action. Nor had they been able to secure the release of any of the alleged perpetrators in custody. Fifty-six people were still being held, twelve on terrorism charges, with, in most cases, the only evidence against them being that they were out of doors after curfew.

"We have done our best to ensure they have legal representation," Anwar told Rebecca, "but of course those facing terrorism charges aren't allowed a lawyer."

"We may be able to provide some financial assistance," said Rebecca. "The Liberation Party itself doesn't have much cash but I might be able to raise some from my constituents."

"That would be helpful. Most of the lawyers we've mustered are our own supporters and are prepared to waive the fee but they still have expenses and their own families to feed. There are also the medical costs of the injured to think about. I know many people are going to have difficulty finding the money for the care they need."

It was ten past nine in the evening and the headquarters of the Muslim Democrat Party were almost deserted. Rebecca sank wearily into a chair in Anwar's office. As most of Anwar's staff had already departed he made some tea. Rebecca accepted a cup gratefully. Anwar was a slightly built, bald man of about average height. The stress and fatigue of the past few days was evident in the dark circles beneath his eyes.

"I think it is pretty safe to say," said Anwar, "that we will be very grateful for any money you can raise."

"I can't promise much, Hackney being a bit short of wealthy philanthropists, but I will see what I can do."

"Thank you, and thank you for coming as well. It has meant a lot to us to have such high profile support from the Liberation Party. It shows that this isn't just something that affects Muslims."

"Unfortunately not high profile enough. I didn't even get a mention on the IMC News channel."

"You did; there was a brief piece in the regional news, not entirely complimentary but they were less scathing about you than they were me. Anyway, you said there was something else you wanted to talk about."

"That's right. I feel we have established quite a lot of common ground over the last couple of days and I was wondering if it would be possible for our two parties to work closer together in future."

"I'm not sure that will be possible. There are a number of major issues on which we disagree. For example, your party supports the legalisation of homosexuality, which is something the majority of my party is against. Of course we are opposed to the present treatment of homosexuals but we don't want to return to the days of moral degeneracy which led to the spread of disease and the breakdown of society."

"The links between homosexuality, disease and the social problems of the mid twenty-first century are frequently exaggerated, but I don't want to debate that now. There are plenty of other issues where we are in agreement. Firstly the mosques, we would reopen them. Secondly, we would permit the wearing of veils by Muslim women. Thirdly, we would end the censorship which has banned so much of your literature. Fourthly, we would end the media prejudice against Islam. Fifthly, we would not only allow but positively encourage teaching about different cultures and religions in schools. Need I go on?"

"No, you have made your point. Obviously it would be better for Muslims if Liberation was in power but even if we were to form some sort of coalition that isn't going to happen."

"Not if we carry on fighting amongst ourselves the way we do at present. We are too daunted by the might of the Phoenix Party to take them on so we seek easier opponents, which is precisely what Bryant and his kind want."

"What exactly are you suggesting?"

"For a start, your party could stop using the Muslim press to attack the Christian Alliance and Gay Rights and focus on the real enemy."

"That is easy for you to say, but the Christian underground media is constantly attacking us."

"Perhaps you and Williams could negotiate a truce. I had a number of meetings with him during the Re-ed. Centre investigation and found him to be a perfectly reasonable man."

"But even if some sort of Muslim, Christian, Liberal alliance were possible, and it sounds very unlikely, we still wouldn't have the power to take on Phoenix."

"Not just at present but Phoenix themselves have problems. Bryant's popularity among the members of his own party has dwindled of late. The Re-ed. Centre affair made him look weak. It is only a matter of time before someone challenges him for the leadership. If they become distracted by their own internal battles that will be our opportunity to put up a united front against them. If we use the combined power of the whole of the underground press and every opportunity we get to address the licensed media to highlight the tyranny of this government, then people will eventually start to listen. Then come the next general election they might even bother to vote."

"There is some truth in what you say. I will certainly talk the matter over with my party colleagues."

"Perhaps you could do more than that. Perhaps you could contact Richard Williams and agree to bury the hatchet."

"I can't promise anything but I'm willing to co-operate if he is. You are returning to London tomorrow?"

"I am. The events here have had repercussions all over the country and the police are responding in their usual heavy-handed manner. I'm told there have been a number of arrests in Hackney."

"I will be down next week. I expect I shall see you at the House."

"You will; I'll be sure to find an opportunity to introduce you to Williams in person. In the meantime I wish you the best of luck. I will say goodnight now. I know you have a home to go to."

"Goodnight Miss Clayton."

Wednesday 18th March 2105

Since his promotion to Chancellor, many interesting rumours had been circulating about Philip Graysby. There were whispers that he planned to challenge Bryant for the leadership and conflicting reports that Bryant planned to retire and wished Graysby to succeed him. Some accounts suggested that Graysby and Freeman were allied against Bryant, while others implied the Chancellor and former Chancellor were rivals. Rebecca had not spoken to Graysby since his promotion and finding out the truth of all this through gossip and hearsay was impossible. As she wanted to know the facts she took the bold step of inviting him out to dinner.

They met at the main restaurant of the Newman Grand. Rebecca had chosen the venue. She knew it was impossible to keep her meeting with Graysby secret and by choosing a private and discreet location she would arouse suspicion. Instead she selected the most prestigious restaurant in the city where photographers were always hanging around the doors and a significant percentage of the patrons were employed by IMC.

Rebecca had chosen her outfit with the intention of being conspicuous. She wore a low cut, pale gold dress with a split up the side of the skirt revealing her shapely legs. With gold stiletto heels and her trademark bright red lipstick there was little chance of her entering the restaurant unnoticed.

David drove her to the door where she paused and posed for the photographers. Graysby was already inside waiting for her. He wore his usual well tailored suit, today in dark grey. She greeted him with a kiss on each cheek. A significant number of the other diners were looking in their direction. Already the arrival of the Chancellor had aroused interest and people were curious to know who he was dining with. Rebecca's arrival had them open-mouthed and staring. For the benefit of their audience Rebecca spoke slightly louder than was necessary.

"It is great to see you again," she said, "I so wanted to catch up. How are you?"

"I am very well, thank you. I was rather intrigued when I received your invitation. I don't often get asked out to dinner by members of the opposition."

"But we were friends before we were opponents weren't we?"

"True, but I find it hard to believe you would go to this much trouble for a chat with an old friend."

"It is no trouble. I wanted to see what the Grand is like now all the work is complete. I haven't been here since before the bombing. I love the new décor but I'm not sure about the artwork. I find some of those dingy old paintings rather depressing."

"Newman tells me that some of them are extremely valuable. Fine art is a new passion of his. He has plans to open a gallery."

The waiter took their orders for drinks and Rebecca studied the menu.

"I'm glad to see they still have the crab salad," she remarked. "That was always a favourite of mine."

"I've never liked shellfish," Graysby replied. "I'm afraid I'm quite boring when it comes to food. I shall have the tomato soup and the stuffed chicken breast."

"I shall have the garlic roast lamb as I haven't had red meat in ages. Have you looked at the wine list yet?"

"Won't your colleagues in the Liberation Party object to such indulgence as this? I thought you disapproved of such decadence as haute cuisine and wine."

"We don't disapprove of such things at all, what we object to is that so few people get to enjoy them. Even you must think it is wrong that only the very rich can afford real food while the majority of the population are eating toxic junk grown in vats."

"At least they are not starving, unlike many other parts of the world."

They paused while the waiter took their order then Rebecca began a new topic of conversation.

"Newman can't be pleased about Bryant's curfew proposal," she remarked. "It can't be good for the entertainment and leisure industry."

"The proposal is something Grant and Bryant are working on. It isn't anything to do with me."

"It will have economic repercussions surely?"

"IMC is in favour of course. As are the energy companies. They want everyone home by ten using electricity and watching TV."

"So you intend to vote in favour of the bill?"

"I suppose you will be voting against."

"We will all be voting against, not just Liberation but Christian Alliance, Muslim Democrats, Gay Rights and all the minor parties and independent candidates, apart from Moral Justice."

"You are very well informed!"

"I try to be. I have even had a quiet word with a few of your back-benchers and some of them feel this is going too far and will be voting against. In fact I heard Geoff Hanes and Tony Freeman were stirring up a little resistance to Bryant's regime."

"Really, and from whom did you hear this?"

"Sources within the Department of Care and Welfare. Naturally I cannot be more specific. You realise this new curfew is just a desperate attempt by Grant and Bryant to look like they are in control. First there was the Re-education

Centre scandal then the massacre in Bradford. It is obvious Bryant is losing his grip. He's got complacent, that is the problem. He is too used to having no real opposition."

"Do you really think your collection of loony lefties and religious nuts constitute a real opposition?"

"No, but if Hanes and Freeman were to unite enough of the Phoenix Party against Bryant, that would."

"Bryant has already dealt with Freeman once. He can do so again."

"How exactly did Bryant prevent the challenge from Freeman?"

"What makes you so sure Freeman intended to challenge?"

"Oh come on Phil! I promise anything you tell me in confidence will remain so."

"All right. Freeman was canvassing support for a potential challenge but Bryant had a quiet word with him and suggested it would be unwise to do so. He said that should Freeman make such a challenge, certain details of the former Chancellor's financial irregularities may be revealed, along with a few facts regarding his personal life."

"His personal life?"

"Yes, in particular his fondness for wearing women's clothing."

"Really? What sort of women's clothing? Are we talking dresses or undergarments?"

"I really couldn't say."

"John always had a fascination with women's underwear. Not wearing it himself of course, but he was partial to buying it. I dare say he still is. I only hope he has got better at selecting the right size."

"I somehow doubt he buys underwear for Caroline. She does not strike me as the kind of lady who would appreciate such a gift."

"I'm sure she isn't, but I expect he has bought some small frilly items for Sophie Andrews by now. They are still together aren't they?"

"I'm not sure they are. I haven't seen Miss Andrews in some weeks and I had dinner with Bryant and another young actress a few nights ago. Her name was Annabel. I have to say, although both she and Sophie are very attractive women, neither have your charm or intelligence. I always found Sophie's conversation somewhat limited and Annabel's is even more so."

They discussed Bryant and his latest paramour until the first course arrived. Rebecca ate a few forkfuls of her salad then returned to an earlier topic of conversation.

"It would be disastrous for Bryant if he was defeated in the ten o'clock curfew vote," she remarked casually.

"It would," Graysby agreed.

"I suppose it would make a leadership challenge even more likely, especially if the potential challenger had fewer skeletons in his cupboard than Freeman."

257

"Do you have someone particular in mind?"

"Let us just say it could be someone who is not at present very far from this table. How is the soup?"

"Very nice. How is the salad?"

"Delicious. I believe the greatest risk in any challenge to the Phoenix leadership would be creating division in the party. After all, there are still some members who are very loyal to Bryant."

"What about Liberation? I hear there are two distinct factions forming; the Cainites and the Rosarians."

"That's rubbish."

Graysby turned his attention to his soup and said nothing until his bowl was empty. He looked thoughtful.

After the plates had been cleared he asked, "You are quite sure the opposition are united against the new curfew?"

"Absolutely certain," she answered confidently. "I realise that does not mean very much so long as the majority of the government is in favour, but I don't know that it is. Do you?"

Graysby did not reply but sipped his glass of water slowly. Rebecca could see plots and ambitions forming behind his furrowed brow. She felt she had given him enough to contemplate so changed the subject once more.

"How are things in Henley?" she asked. "I hear there has been yet more flooding."

"Well if people choose to live so close to the river they should expect floods," Graysby replied unsympathetically. "There are plenty of other places they could live, there's no housing shortage anymore."

"No, quite the opposite. I know of plenty of empty flats where flooding wouldn't be a problem. There are some lovely single bedroom apartments with wonderful views over Hackney Marshes. The only disadvantage being the block has been condemned and is liable to collapse in a strong wind."

Rebecca continued making small talk until they had finished their meal. Although Graysby replied and tried to take an interest in what she was saying, she knew she did not have his full attention. No doubt he was contemplating greater things. After coffee she said goodnight and kissed him on the cheek.

"I shall be watching developments in the upper echelons of the Phoenix Party very carefully over the next few weeks," she remarked before she departed.

Thursday 9th April 2105

There was a mood of jubilation at Liberation Head Offices. For the first time since the Phoenix Party came to power the government had been defeated in the House. The President had been forced to reject his proposals for a new curfew. Rebecca would have given anything to know what was going on in Ten Downing Street at present, as according to RNN, Graysby had arrived there a little over an hour ago and was in a meeting with the President.

IMC was playing down the government's defeat. It received only the briefest mention on the main evening news bulletin.

"The government has put aside plans to change the evening curfew time," announced the newsreader towards the end of the programme. "Although intended to reduce crime and protect the public, the suggested ten pm curfew proved unpopular so will not be instigated at present."

The programme went straight on to the sport without any mention of the lost vote, rebellion by Cabinet ministers or what it meant for Bryant's leadership. The Liberation Party members gathered around the screen jeered loudly.

"Switch it over to the Real News," suggested Sean, "I want to know if Graysby has been hung, drawn and quartered yet."

"Good old Phil!" said Rebecca as she poured herself a drink, "I knew he wouldn't be able to resist this opportunity to kick Bryant in the arse."

"Which isn't exactly a small target!" remarked Samantha Richardson, who was handing round crisps and nuts.

"Just why are you all rooting for Graysby?" asked Giles Summers, MP for Leeds South. "Would he really be a better President?"

Most of the MPs from outside the greater London area had returned to their constituencies after the vote in order to make it home before curfew, but a few had stayed to enjoy the celebrations.

"I believe so," Rebecca answered. "Graysby is a capitalist. He doesn't care about our morality and religion. He just wants wealth. I'm not saying he will do wonderful things, but I think he will give us more freedom, so long as it is of benefit to the economy."

"We are fortunate that you are so intimate with the President and his Cabinet," remarked Karen, with more than a hint of sarcasm.

"It is good to know your enemy," Rebecca replied.

"But not necessarily carnally," Karen retorted.

A number of embarrassed and anxious glances were exchanged by the others listening but Rebecca just laughed and responded, "What's the matter? Are you jealous?"

"Hardly, just looking at Bryant makes me feel ill."

"Good job you aren't in parliament then. We have to look at him all the time!"

Sean intervened with an excuse to drag Karen away before the conversation became any more heated. Rebecca continued chatting with Summers.

They were interrupted by a cry of, "He's come out! Graysby has just left Downing Street."

An expectant silence descended on the room and everyone gathered around computer screens. A fresh bulletin headline had materialised across the top of the RNN homepage, "Graysby leaves Downing Street after meeting with the President." But there was no further information.

"Is that it?" Stacey Barnes demanded.

"I guess so," replied Sean, "until either Bryant or Graysby makes a statement we won't know what is going on."

"Graysby has to issue a challenge," said Alicia who had just emerged from her office. She had been making numerous phone calls to the other opposition parties, thanking them for their support.

They waited but no fresh announcement came. Gradually people began to drift away from the screen, conversations resumed and more drink was consumed. As curfew approached there was still no news. Rebecca took her leave and she and David departed.

"Were you and Karen arguing again?" David asked as they got into the car.

"Not exactly arguing," Rebecca replied, "just a bit of verbal sparring."

"Who won?"

"I think I did. It's hard to say as Sean broke it up just as we were getting started."

"Good man."

"I don't know how the poor guy puts up with her."

"I believe they are in love. People are prepared to put up with a great deal when they are in love."

"You do. But at least I know that I treat you appallingly. Karen thinks it's OK to go around bullying everyone the way she does."

David laughed and replied, "You don't treat me appallingly."

"Yes I do, I've hardly spoken to you all day."

"You've been busy."

"That is no excuse. I ought to find the time say a few words like, 'Hello darling how was your day?' I always remember just as I'm falling asleep at night that I forgot to ask and then you are already asleep and I feel terrible."

"It's all right, I understand. You needn't feel bad about it."

"But I do, and it always feels wrong introducing you as my bodyguard and not my husband."

"We already agreed we were going to keep our marriage secret."

"I know and for good reasons, but I still don't like not being able to publicly acknowledge how important you are to me."

"As long as you love me Rebecca, that is all that matters. All I want is to make you happy."

"I do love you David. I should say it more often."

"I think you sometimes forget just how alone and miserable I was before I met you. Compared to the emptiness and hopelessness of my old life, being married to you is wonderful. I used to fantasise for hours about what it would be like to have you as my wife."

"I don't expect this is exactly what you imagined. I doubt that spending all day driving me between home, office, Party HQ and parliament featured in your fantasies."

"No in my mind you were still with the circus, but it wasn't so different. I would wait for you backstage while you performed and escort you home, run a bath in the enormous tub which existed in my head but not my flat and rub your back while we soaked in rose scented bubbles."

"It sounds great."

"Yes, but I still prefer reality. Our real life together may involve fewer candlelit dinners and lazy Sunday mornings but helping you with your work gives me much greater satisfaction. I am so proud of what you have achieved."

"I couldn't have done any of it without you."

"I expect you could, but I have helped and I actually feel good about myself. That is far more important than bubble baths and making love on satin sheets."

"True, but making love once in a while would be good."

"Indeed it would," David replied and yawned, "but I'm afraid tonight I'm far too tired."

His yawning caused Rebecca to do likewise.

"Perhaps tomorrow," she suggested.

*

They both slept like logs that night and did not stir until twenty to eight the following morning, when Karen called to say that Graysby was expected to announce his leadership challenge soon. David answered the phone while Rebecca remained in bed with the covers pulled up over her head. His tone of voice clearly suggested he too would rather not have been woken.

"So he hasn't actually made the announcement yet?.. How soon?.. You don't know do you?.. We knew that anyway, there really wasn't any need to wake us up to tell us that!.. What different does it make we don't have any say in who leads the Phoenix Party, do we?..Yes well we're awake now so we will see it as soon as it is on the news… Thank you but I don't think we would have been devastated even if we had missed the announcement, they will be repeating it all day… I'm sure you are but we were quite happy catching up on some sleep… All right but not until after nine… Goodbye Karen… You can talk about it later, goodbye… Later, goodbye!"

As David flopped back into bed Rebecca let out a long groan and asked, "Doesn't that woman ever sleep?"

"I don't think she does. I think she just plugs herself into a recharging socket or something."

"What did she want?"

"She wanted us to know that there are reports of rumours that sources have suggested that Graysby may allegedly announce his leadership challenge this morning, or not."

"Wow! Where does she get her information?"

"I did hint to her that at this precise moment we don't actually give a shit but I think I was too subtle."

"You were much too subtle. 'Go away Karen I'm trying to sleep!' is too subtle for her."

"Well, now I am awake I'm actually rather hungry. How about I do us a proper cooked breakfast? We could always watch the news while we eat it."

"Sounds like a plan; I'll get up and give you a hand in a few minutes."

"No you won't. You'll fall asleep again as soon as I leave the room."

"No I won't. I'm awake now."

As he left the room Rebecca allowed her eyes to close. I'll be up by eight she told herself as she drifted off into sleep. An hour later David brought her a cup of tea.

"This time it is for certain," he said. "Graysby is about to make an announcement."

She threw on a robe and flopped in front of the TV with her tea. The IMC news crew was stationed outside the Chancellor's offices waiting for him to come out. At exactly nine o'clock Graysby emerged, smartly dressed and smiling confidently although his head was a little shiny in the morning sun. His statement was very brief. He began by simply confirming that he intended to challenge Bryant for the leadership.

"Although I have the greatest respect for my friend and colleague John Bryant," he continued, "I feel that he has lost touch with the people. I expressed these views in a meeting I had with the President last night and as he has no intentions of stepping down as Party Leader I have been forced to take this action. President Bryant has been an excellent leader for a number of years but change is a necessary part of government. I am ready to embrace change in a way that my friend is not. I have the courage, determination and enthusiasm to lead Britain into a new age of prosperity. Thank you ladies and gentlemen. Good day."

"Well that wasn't exactly earth shattering!" Rebecca remarked.

"I suppose even Graysby has to be extremely careful about criticising the President. If he said what he really thought, Bryant would probably have him arrested."

"It's all up to the Phoenix Party now. There isn't any more we can do."

Island Nation Magazine
Saturday 17th August 2115

GRAYSBY VS BRYANT
Simon Chandra

Before the Phoenix Party rose to prominence, leadership challenges were a common occurrence for all of the major parties. During the 2060s, contests for the leadership of both Labour and the Conservatives were an almost annual event. However, things changed once Henry Clarkson was elected. During his Presidency there was barely a whisper of any opposition within his own party and on his retirement Bryant assumed the mantle with the unanimous support of the Parliamentary Party.

Although it would be erroneous to suggest that Phoenix had been completely united before Philip Graysby's leadership challenge, no faction had previously gained sufficient size or influence to damage the party unity. Graysby succeeded in splitting Phoenix in two. His most prominent ally was the former Chancellor, Anthony Freeman, who had been demoted to the department of Care and Welfare after allegedly plotting to depose Bryant himself. Freeman was a notable exception as the majority of the Cabinet remained loyal to Bryant, but at least half of the back-benchers wanted a regime change and supported Graysby.

Most importantly, Philip Graysby had powerful supporters outside of parliament. The chief executives of several large corporations were openly backing Graysby. They recognised that the economic growth of the early years of the Phoenix Government was slowing, stifled by Bryant's oppressive rule. Graysby promised businesses greater freedom to expand and grow, in particular by lifting some of the restrictions on international trade. A number of wealthy individuals pledged generous donations to the Phoenix Party should Graysby become the new leader.

For the licensed media this was a very strange time, as while Bryant retained control over the censors, many of the advertisers were supporting Graysby. My father, Rashid Chandra was an IMC employee during this period.

"When Graysby first announced his challenge the news reports were all heavily biased against him," he tells me, "but several advertisers complained and threatened to terminate their contracts, meaning the producers were forced to take a more balanced approach."

We are having lunch together, just the two of us, which is not something we often do. In fact it is extremely rare that my father and I get an opportunity to talk. We see each other regularly but my mother and sister are usually present and tend to dominate the conversation. Dad is naturally a quiet man. Although intelligent and well informed, he seldom offers an opinion without being asked and generally allows debates and arguments to rage around him without getting involved. He is however an excellent moderator and peacemaker. Should one of our discussions get too heated he is the one who will step in and cool things down.

I expect it was while working for IMC that my Dad developed the habit of not expressing his own opinions. He worked as a researcher in the current affairs division and his main responsibility was to collate background material on news stories. At the same time he was also reporting for RNN, frequently using IMC's archives to research articles for the underground press.

"Working for IMC was utterly depressing," he explains. "I would put together a page a text and the editor would cut out half of it, then the censors would remove a bit more until only a few lines remained saying nothing of interest. After a couple of years of this I learned to save all the remotely interesting material for RNN and just give my editor a page of rambling waffle.

"The Graysby challenge was about the only time that some of my work was actually published. I was asked to put together a résumé of Graysby's career, which was easy enough. As usual, by the time it reached the webpage about seventy percent of it had been deleted so that it read as though he had not done anything during his political career. Then the advertisers complained and the original article was published."

"How did Bryant react to the media's sudden change in policy?" I asked.

"Naturally he wasn't happy. He made numerous threats of withdrawing IMC's license, but such tactics were less affective now because if Graysby were to win it would be he who controlled the licensing power. Graysby never openly threatened the way Bryant did but he hinted that if IMC proved too biased he might open the industry up to competition."

"It must have been a very tense time for IMC's senior staff."

"It was. Everyone was stressed and tempers were frayed. The executives took it out on the producers and editors, who in turn shouted at their staff. It was a typical master shouts at servant, servant kicks dog, dog bites cat sort of mentality. It didn't bother me too much though. I was used to being abused and learned to ignore it. I was far too interested in what was actually going to happen, whether or not Graysby would win, to care about all the infighting."

Shortly after Graysby announced his challenge, Harriet Jacobs, the former Minister for Social Reform, announced that she too would stand for the party leadership. Although she had a loyal following among the socially conservative far right of the party, the main battle was still between Graysby and Bryant.

Bryant won the first ballot but only by the slimmest of margins. When Graysby and Bryant went forward to the second ballot the big question was, which of them would the Jacobs faction favour. As Graysby was known to be more liberal in his attitudes towards sex and marriage, this faction mostly favoured Bryant, giving him a modest victory.

"IMC announced Bryant's win as though it were a magnificent triumph when in fact he only defeated Graysby by a pathetically small number of votes," my father says. "The executives were anxious to repair their relationship with Bryant and retain their license so exaggerated his majority and circulated much negative material about Graysby. The upper echelons of IMC naively believed everything would be back to normal. They seriously underestimated the damage Bryant's leadership had sustained. I believe it was IMC's blatantly biased support for Bryant at this time which cost them the last remaining shred of credibility they had retained. Everyone knew that Bryant had only just managed to hold on to the party leadership and it was utterly ridiculous for IMC to attempt to claim otherwise."

In the weeks following the leadership contest it became apparent that Bryant no longer retained the respect of his party. He was jeered by his own back-benchers, some of his ministers dared to openly criticise him and information on his abuses of power not so much leaked as haemorrhaged to the underground press. Graysby and Freeman were both removed from the Cabinet, which angered their supporters even further.

Three weeks after losing the leadership ballot, Graysby announced he was leaving Phoenix and intended to found a new party called 'Prosperity'. His allies deserted Phoenix en masse and signed up.

"IMC performed such a rapid series of u-turns during the next few weeks that everyone working for them got so dizzy they didn't know what they were doing," Dad tells me. "First they tried to dismiss Prosperity as being insignificant but as Graysby still had corporate backing, the advertisers again forced them to change tack. They got Graysby in and interviewed him about his new party and their policies. This made Bryant mad so they cancelled the broadcast just an hour before it was due to be shown, which then caused the advertisers to descend on them in fury.

"A heavily edited version of the interview was broadcast a day later, which they hoped would placate the advertisers while causing the least offence to Bryant. It did neither. The Director General was forced to resign or else lose the company's license. His replacement was approved by Bryant but several of the already enraged advertisers then terminated their contracts, which meant a huge hole in the company's finances and Net UK were threatening to pull the plug on transmission."

On 25th May 2105 Graysby tabled a motion of no confidence. The government lost the vote and the general election should have been called immediately, but Bryant was determined to cling to power. He played for time, making numerous excuses why an election could not be held. He tried to claim national security would be put in jeopardy by holding an election before the end of his term. Graysby issued an ultimatum; call the election at once or his party would boycott parliament. As Bryant still refused, the entire Prosperity Party stood and walked out followed by Liberation, Christian Alliance, Muslim Democrats and every other opposition MP. Even some of those still loyal to the Phoenix Party walked out in protest at their leader's conduct.

I remember that day well. I was sitting a maths exam. There we all were in studious silence when one of the other teachers rushed into the room and told the invigilator in a rather loud, excited whisper. The invigilator, who was head of maths, forgot where he was and swore aloud. The whole class stopped work and began to pass the news around in whispers, not quite understanding what was happening but knowing it was of great importance. The head of maths regained his composure and got us to resume our exam in silence. Mathematics never was one of my strongest subjects and I did particularly badly in that exam, thanks to the distraction.

Parliament remained empty for a whole week until Bryant finally conceded and announced the general election for 2nd July.

"During those days the IMC board of directors had no idea how to act," Dad explains. "They knew they were teetering on the brink of ruin. Bryant still had the power to withdraw their license but Net UK had the ultimate power. Being utter cowards the board cancelled all current affairs programming which meant anyone who wanted to know what was going on turned to RNN. Our audience at least doubled.

"Bryant of course needed IMC in order to run his election campaign but he was without many of the powerful financial supporters who had funded him previously. In order to get IMC running again he had to enter into negotiations with Graysby and his backers. The result was that IMC was able to broadcast and publish news again but only as long as it remained completely neutral. Equal air time was given to both Phoenix and Prosperity campaign broadcasts and an equal proportion of the website was devoted to both parties. Every word either printed or broadcast was under intense scrutiny and the slightest hint of bias was pounced upon by one side or the other."

"I remember how busy you and Mum were that summer," I remarked. "I didn't know about RNN at the time so I didn't realise you were both trying to do two jobs at once. I knew about the election and how important it was, but I particularly couldn't understand what it had to do with Mum. As far as I knew she worked for a women's magazine, writing about clothes and make-up; I was bewildered when her work started keeping her up half the night."

"It must have been a tough time for you and Amira. We sent you away to stay with your aunt and uncle didn't we?"

"It wasn't so bad. We had great fun with our cousins. All the grownups were so distracted we could do whatever we liked."

"I must have hardly spoken to you and your sister for three whole months and the only conversations Monica and I had were about work, and even those were rare. Though we were living in the same house we mostly communicated by email as we were so seldom there at the same time. Even during curfew hours we would be shut in separate rooms working or else we would be asleep. It was stressful and exhausting, but at the same time it was exciting. We knew there was going to be major change and that our work for RNN was vital in bringing it about."

It will not have escaped my readers' notice that in my column this week there has so far been no mention of Rosa at all. For this I apologise but I felt it would be impossible to discuss the next part of her history without first explaining the events which led up to the 2105 general election. Many of my readers will no doubt be familiar with all the events I have described and will send their complaints as they feel appropriate, but for those who are not, particularly my younger readers, I hope this has been informative. I promise that next week's article will prominently feature Rosa and I beg my audience not to desert me.

Monday 1st June 2105

On arriving at Alicia Cain's office, Rebecca was a little flustered and not as neatly turned out as usual. Her hair had been hurriedly tied back but several locks had escaped and fell across her face and her make-up was not applied with quite the usual degree of care. Sam Richardson had called on Cain's behalf early that morning asking her to come at once and she had obeyed. It was rumoured that Bryant was to concede to oppositions' demands and would call the election later that day, so there was no mystery as to the topic Alicia would wish to discuss.

Taking her seat Rebecca tried to look calm and in control.

"You have no doubt heard that Bryant has called a press conference for two o'clock this afternoon."

"Yes Karen told me. She says the word among informed sources is that he will call an election."

"That is what I've heard also. The latest leaks suggest it will be an early July polling day."

"What do you think the chances are of this election being a fair one?" Rebecca asked.

"Both Graysby and Bryant know all the dirty tricks Phoenix have used in the past, so will be scrutinising each other very carefully. It may be that in the end they have no alternative but to hold a free and fair election and see who wins."

"That alone would be a major achievement for British democracy."

"It would indeed, but I should get to the point. I summoned you here to talk about our election strategy. First and foremost I intend to stand down as leader of the party."

"What? Are you crazy?"

"Please listen to me Rebecca. I intend to stand down and for you to take my place."

"No way! I can't do that."

"You can. Before you joined us most of the country had forgotten that Liberation even existed. Your fame got us in the news for the first time in years. Then there was the Re-education Centre scandal and the Bradford riots. It was you that made the headlines, not me. People think you are wonderful. You must have read the comments they leave on our website. Haven't you seen the opinion poll?"

"I think the opinions expressed on the website may be biased towards the demographic who log on purely to look at pictures of me."

"So? Their votes still count. If we win a constituency solely because a large number of the voters would like to sleep with you, that isn't going to bother me. Of course I would rather the electorate focused on our policies rather than the length of your skirts, but it's votes that count not the reasons for them."

"Do you seriously believe Liberation would achieve a better result in the election with me as leader?"

"I do."

"And have you consulted other members of the party?"

"I have and the vast majority are in agreement."

"They must know you are a better leader than I could ever be."

"Perhaps, but they also know how popular you are."

"Maybe we could agree that I will be the face of the party provided you remain the brains."

"There are many more brains than mine running Liberation, but I understand what you mean. You officially take over the leadership but I will advise you."

"I want to speak to our other MPs before I give you a definite answer, but provided I have their support I will do it."

"You do realise the risks? To yourself I mean."

"Yes, I comprehend that my personal safety decreases as my popularity increases. I can only hope that Bryant and Graysby are too concerned with each other to take action against me."

David was waiting outside the office, drinking tea with Samantha.

"What's the news?" he asked as she emerged.

"I'll tell you in the car."

"OK, where to?"

"My office. I have some calls to make."

On the way down to the car he asked, "Is everything all right? You look worried."

"Not worried exactly but I have rather a lot to think about. Alicia has asked me to take over leadership of the party."

She had expected David to be surprised but he just nodded and asked, "Did you agree?"

"I want to talk with our colleagues first but if I have their support I will."

They drove back to Rebecca's Hackney offices where she set to work calling and emailing her fellow MPs. By lunchtime forty-two of her colleagues had responded, all in favour of her taking over the leadership. Karen and Sean arrived at one o'clock with a draft of a campaign leaflet.

"This is excellent work," Rebecca commented, "but you may have to make a few changes."

"Such as?" Karen demanded impatiently.

"It isn't certain yet but it is likely there will soon be a change in the party leadership."

"With the election just weeks away!" Karen protested. "That is ridiculous."

"Alicia and I discussed the matter this morning. She intends to stand down."

"She can't! Not now. Who is to take her place?"

"I am."

Karen laughed and replied, "I don't wish to be unkind Rebecca but the fact is you have very little political experience. You wouldn't know how to lead the party."

"This is true, which is why Alicia has promised to advise me. She will in fact be continuing as leader in all but name."

"Then why stand down?" asked Karen.

"She feels, as do many other party members, that we will do better in the election with me as leader."

"That is quite likely judging from the opinion polls," Sean agreed. "Rebecca may not have experience but she is extremely popular."

Karen shot him a look of pure fury then turned to Rebecca and demanded, "Why were we not told of this sooner?"

"Because I knew nothing of it myself until this morning."

"It is bad enough that we have to pull together an election campaign with such short notice without having to deal with this as well," Karen complained.

They were interrupted by a phone call from Giles Summers. He had received Rebecca's email and wished to express his support. She thanked him and made a tick on the list of MPs which was lying on her desk. After hanging up the phone she made a quick count of those names which did not yet have a tick beside them. There were only fourteen.

"It looks like we are going ahead," she remarked.

"Then we had better change this leaflet," said Sean. "It won't take long. We can just add 'New leader of the Liberation Party' in big letters at the top and remove the section about Alicia and replace it with a short history of the party."

"That sounds fine," Rebecca agreed.

Karen did not answer, as she was still studying the list of names on Rebecca's desk.

"I'll have another draft done in about an hour," said Sean. "Are you coming Karen?"

"I'll be with you in a minute," Karen replied.

After Sean had left them Karen asked, "Do you really think you can do this? Do you actually think you have what it takes to even appear to lead the party?"

"Why are you asking me this Karen? You obviously don't believe that I can do it and it won't make any difference to you if I tell you otherwise."

"Listen Rebecca, I know we have had our differences but I'm not saying this out of spite, I'm saying it because it is true. I do not believe that you are the right person for this job. Politics is a hard and ruthless business and I don't think you possess a sufficient measure of either quality. You are an intelligent and caring person and you are extremely popular because of your charm and looks, but you haven't the strength, ambition and sheer stubbornness that a political leader needs."

"I understand what you are saying and I fear you may be right, but the party needs my fame and popularity to win votes. I may not be the right person to lead Liberation but if the voters believe I am then that is all that matters."

"You know that if we do badly in the election everyone will blame you? You could end up being the most hated woman since Margaret Thatcher."

"I think I have better legs though."

"I'm serious. If you ruin everything we have achieved over the past few years then all the people who profess to support you now will be baying for blood."

"Exactly what have you achieved? I know you and many others have worked your guts out for this party but your successes have been very few. Before I joined you, Sean and David were the Hackney Liberation Party, less than half the population actually knew who Alicia Cain was and even fewer had any idea what our party stands for. We occupy a tiny proportion of the Commons and we are duly ignored. Do we want to carry on being the token opposition, part of Bryant's charade taken seriously by no one?"

"I know the situation thank you! What makes you think you can change everything? Why do you think you will succeed in improving Liberation's prospects when so many experienced politicians have failed?"

"Simply because I am famous. People listen to me. In the past I never said anything of interest and yet people have still listened. If I talk about what colour socks I'm wearing someone will write about it. Alicia Cain has always had plenty of interesting things to say but she has been ignored, but if I say them I won't be."

"You could still be silenced though. It is only because Alicia has been ignored that she has survived for so long as party leader."

"I know, but we are all going to have to take risks. If it all goes wrong then go ahead and say 'I told you so', but this election campaign is going to need your experience and dedication. Can I count on you?"

"Yes of course. I'm no quitter. We'd better call a press conference for this evening. If my information is correct then Bryant will be announcing the election very soon and we want to look like we're ready to fight it. If we reveal your takeover as leader and our manifesto at the same time that should make the most impact. I heard Graysby is still in talks with Freeman over finalising their manifesto so we can get in first."

"Right, I'll call Alicia and tell her we are going ahead. There is no point in waiting for an answer from the last few MPs. They must have got the message and if they were strongly against they would have said something by now. I suppose they are still making their minds up."

"They probably don't want to commit themselves in case you fuck up. Bloody cowards! I'll be back with details of the press conference. See you later."

Part 7

The Price

ROSA'S CAMPAIGN
Simon Chandra

I have been reviewing recordings of some of the speeches Rosa made during her election campaign. If you only saw those which were shown on the IMC News channel you would be forgiven for thinking she was not a very good orator. The press conference she and Alicia Cain gave the evening after Bryant called the election is a prime example. It was held in the foyer of Liberation Party HQ and filmed by an IMC News crew. Cain opens the conference by announcing that she will stand down as Party Leader and that Rebecca Clayton will be her successor. Clayton then makes a very brief statement of the Party's election pledges. She lists what Liberation intends to do without any attempt at elaboration or explanation. She speaks clearly and confidently but it is such bland, unembellished, staccato prose that it contains no passion. Compared with great speeches from history it is positively dull, about as inspirational as a shopping list.

The speech she made the following day in Hyde Park could not be more different. Although the content is similar, in that she lays out the ten key points of their manifesto, the style is not remotely like the previous day. This speech was not filmed by the licensed media but many of the large crowd had cameras, including representatives of the underground press. The quality of recording is poorer than the IMC material but the speech itself is many times superior. She speaks with passion and conviction on the subject of freedom, the language is poetic and the delivery dynamic.

I talked with Stacey Barnes about this variation in her mode of public speaking.

"She was a brilliant orator," she agreed. "Far superior to Bryant or Graysby and at least the equal of Clarkson. Alicia always gave a good speech but she had none of Rebecca's flare."

"But why were some of her speeches so poor compared with others?" I asked. "Did she need a sympathetic audience to perform at her best?"

"No it wasn't that, we just couldn't trust the licensed media. IMC was constantly revising its policy towards covering the election and we never knew whether what it recorded would actually be broadcast or not. It was extremely likely any press conferences or interviews it did show would be heavily edited, so Rebecca had to take great care to keep her message as brief as possible and avoid saying anything which could be used out of context. That is why she so often spoke in that rather unnatural way. Each point had to be made in a single short sentence."

"So that is why that first press conference sounds so awkward."

"Yes, that was probably one of the worst because she had so much to say in so little time."

"She sounds like a robot."

"It isn't a good speech but in a way it worked. IMC did screen some of the press conference during the main evening news bulletin, but as only five minutes of the whole programme was given over to Liberation's election campaign only about two minutes of the ten minute press conference were shown. Though as you say she sounds like a robot, the brief excerpt of her speech which was broadcast included several of the party's key philosophies.

"There were a significant number of citizens who never accessed the underground media. Those people knew very little about Liberation except for whatever misinformation Bryant had allowed to circulate. Though it was just a couple of minutes and not particularly well delivered, that press conference would be the first accurate summary of our policies that many people would have heard. It was enough to get people to take an interest and want to find out more."

"Who wrote her speeches?"

"I believe she wrote most of the material herself. I know O'Brien contributed a lot of the more elegant passages and that both Karen Baker and Sean Nichols advised her on the content, but she usually did the first draft herself. She had an incredible memory. She could deliver long speeches without a script or autocue, just a single sheet of paper with a few notes to prompt her. I expect that was why she always sounded so genuine and sincere, because it came from within rather than reading from a page."

"She was very good in interviews and debates too," I remarked, having reviewed much footage which was not broadcast at the time. "She always had the answers ready and was never lost for words."

"She was brilliant. Of course the debate with Graysby was a defining point in the election campaign."

Philip Graysby had originally suggested a live televised debate between himself and Bryant. The President refused but consented to appear in a pre-recorded debate provided he could approve it before broadcast. Everything was arranged ready for the recording when Bryant pulled out at the last minute, objecting that he had not agreed to a live audience in the studio. Though the producers offered to send the audience away, Bryant still would not take part and they were left with an expensive problem. Then someone suggested they ask

Rosa to take part in the debate. Graysby agreed as television air time was just as vital to him as it was to the Liberation Party.

The debate was filmed over two hours with a brief interval in the middle. Though Graysby is on magnificent form, it is Rosa who argues the most convincingly. The recording was edited down to one hour and shown after the evening bulletin on the news channel. That there was renewed interest in politics is clear from the viewing figures for the debate, which were the highest ever recorded for the IMC News. Viewing figures dropped dramatically however during the hour long promotional film for the Phoenix Party which was shown afterwards. You can view the complete recording of the debate by following the links at the bottom of the page but here are a few illustrative examples of Rosa at her best.

After a brief introduction by Peter Sheridan, Graysby was first to speak. He talked about his plans to reshape the economy. He criticised Phoenix for allowing the nation's industry to be controlled by just a few companies and for its isolationist policies which prevented further growth. His policies were all based on sound principles and he knew his subject, whereas Rosa did not have the same academic background. She chose not to tackle him on fiscal matters immediately but changed the subject to one in which she knew she would have the upper hand.

"Although I have no doubt of the Prosperity Party's ability to make this country richer," she said, "I know from personal experience that money does not buy happiness. At present many people are desperately unhappy because they have been deprived of the most basic freedoms. They have been prevented from having children, oppressed because of their religion or imprisoned because of their sexuality. We in the Liberation Party promise to restore fundamental human rights to the people. We will change this country for the better not by increased wealth but by giving back civil liberties. Under our government there will be free speech, a free press, freedom of movement within the country and the freedom to make your own choices."

"These idealistic promises are all very well," Graysby responded, "but are not practical in the modern world. This country has the resources to support a finite population and by removing government controls on procreation you will ensure that the limit is soon exceeded. How do you propose to feed the hundreds of children born as a result of your policies?"

"I agree that this country's resources are limited, but the fact is we could support a population at least double that of the present if the resources were more evenly distributed. There is plenty of land available which could be used for food production but at currently it is occupied by derelict buildings, many of which are owned by the government."

"I am aware of the large number of derelict buildings in all our cities, and urban regeneration is one of my Party's top priorities, but considerable investment will be required. It is not as simple as bulldozing a few buildings and planting crops. The sites must be properly cleared, decontaminated, and prepared if they are to be used for food production. How does Liberation propose to fund this?"

"I believe the funds for a significant amount of work could be made available. For example, we would redirect the public money which is at present being put aside to restore the royal palaces and convert them to Presidential residences."

"The Palace Restoration Fund does not contain anything like the sum required for such an undertaking."

"Then my information must be at fault. Perhaps as former Chancellor you could tell the taxpayers exactly how much money has been set aside for the President's palace fund, since the whole project has been kept secret."

"I cannot reveal the exact sum."

"Perhaps you could give us an approximation. I understand it is more than three billion pounds."

"I believe the figure of three billion to which you refer is the total budget for the preservation of the nation's cultural heritage, not purely as you allege for the President's residence. However, under the Prosperity Party this money would be put to use immediately for projects which would allow art and culture to be accessible to a wider audience."

"Then you have no desire for a palace of your own Mr Graysby?"

"None at all."

"Then why is there no mention of these arts and cultural projects in your manifesto?"

"I think Prosperity's commitment to our artistic and cultural heritage is clearly stated on the first page."

"But there is no specific mention of the three billion pounds to which I just referred and the use to which you intend to put it. Could it be that you were hoping to hold on to that money for your own comfort and gratification just as Bryant was?"

"Certainly not. We believe in using public money to boost the economy, not in holding on to it as President Bryant does."

"In that case I find it interesting that you have never mentioned this subject before in you criticisms of the government. Is it that three billion pounds is such a small sum to you Mr Graysby that you managed to completely overlook it?"

This time it was Graysby who was forced to change the subject and he spoke in detail about his plans for the National Health Service. Though at first he appeared a little flustered after the unexpected attack concerning the Palace Restoration Fund he soon became more relaxed and confident. He described in detail how he would improve the NHS and there were many nods of agreement and murmurs of support from the studio audience. When he finished speaking there was applause, but then Rosa trumped him.

"We would do all this and much more," she promised. "We will do more, as once we have shut down the so called Re-education Centres, the facilities, staff and budget can be used to treat the sick instead of torturing innocent young people."

Once the rapturous applause died down Graysby attempted to argue that by permitting homosexuality and not discouraging promiscuity, Liberation would be promoting the spread of disease.

"Sex is a fact of life whether vaginal, oral or anal," she replied with characteristic candour. "No amount of government interference will prevent people from copulating. We are all well aware that even President Bryant's sexual morals are not those which his party preaches. By allowing people to have sex by mutual consent and without shame we make it easier for them to take the necessary precautions. If any man or woman can walk into a shop and purchase condoms without the stigma then we need not fear disease. Besides, it was not New Aids which decimated our population, it was Black Flu, an airborne virus, not a sexually transmitted disease."

Graysby's next words were undoubtedly a mistake.

"We are all well aware of your expertise and experience on the subject of sex but…"

The audience did not respond well to this snide remark and his argument was lost amongst booing.

"Perhaps your policies in this area would be improved if you had a better knowledge of the subject yourself," Rosa suggested, fighting fire with fire and receiving loud applause.

Later in the recording Graysby attacked Liberation policies on national security, warning that increased civil liberties would mean a greater danger from terrorists.

"The terrorist threat is a subject of which I have much personal experience," Rosa replied. "I lost several friends in the Newman Grand Theatre bombing and only narrowly escaped with my own life. I also knew the perpetrator of that attack extremely well so I can tell you that terrorists don't just appear. People are not born terrorists nor do they suddenly transform into them overnight. In the case of Martin Ashdown, it was oppression because of his sexuality that made him so desperately unhappy that he was prepared to kill. I am not promising to completely remove the terrorist threat but I firmly believe that by allowing people greater freedom to live according to their own ideals and values we remove the sense of hopelessness which drives people to violence."

Graysby argued, "I fear that Liberation's policies are based on the naïve belief that everyone is a good and decent person deep down. Sadly this is not the case. There are bad people. People who are prepared to slaughter hundreds of innocent victims just to make a point. It is from these people that our country must be protected."

"But it is the oppressive measures the Phoenix Party took to protect the country which have created the problems. We saw this recently in Bradford. In order to protect us from alleged terrorists more than twenty unarmed citizens were killed, including women and children. As a result there is understandably a strong and violent hatred of the government among the survivors."

"I have never supported firing on unarmed civilians."

"Yet in all your time in government you never spoke out against it."

"Not publicly, but I assure you I expressed my disapproval to the President and the Minister for Justice on several occasions."

"How exactly would a Prosperity government deal with a similar situation?"

"We would instruct the police to use non-lethal means to break up the riots. What would you do? Stand back and allow the riots to spread until violence consumed the entire city?"

"We would do exactly what we did. Talk to people. I did not see you or President Bryant or any other member of your respective parties in Bradford in the days following the massacre. Had any of you been there and spoken to the community you would have a much better understanding of the situation. You accuse my party of being naïve, but I believe it is you who is naïve if you think that national security is simply a matter of protecting us from these so called bad people. Have you ever met any of these bad people? Do they have little horns growing out of their heads?"

"Although greater freedoms may seem appealing now, should they be granted there will be crime, violence and anarchy. If the Liberation Party were to gain power, after a matter of months the honest citizens of Great Britain would be begging for curfew patrols and check points to be restored."

"I say to the voters let us test your theory. If abolishing curfew does result in the dire situation Mr Graysby prophesises, then gladly we will admit we were wrong and restore it, but I believe he is wrong. I believe the people of this country can be trusted to go out after eleven without rioting. I believe we are not all criminals and should not be imprisoned in our own homes."

Of course much of this was not broadcast as the censors ruthlessly edited the recording. All mention of the President's Palace Fund was deleted as the government did not want the taxpayers to know what it did with their money. Most of Rosa's remarks on sex and sexuality were considered obscene and discussion of the Bradford riots was deemed too sensitive and liable to cause civil unrest. As more of Rosa's words were cut by the censors than Graysby's the broadcast version gives far more air time to Prosperity than to Liberation. Strangely though this worked in Rosa's favour as the longer Graysby appeared on screen the more the audience became bored by him. Although deprived of some of her best arguments Rosa was still the more interesting to listen to and naturally the fact that she was significantly more attractive cannot be dismissed.

Many commentators suggested that refusing to take part in the debate was Bryant's biggest mistake; however it should be remembered that John Bryant had absolutely no experience of trying to sell his ideals. He had been chosen unopposed as Clarkson's successor and never had to face a hostile media or a credible opposition. Whenever he had campaigned in the past he had relied entirely on his personal charm and charisma. His policies had never before been the subject of scrutiny. I believe that if Bryant had chosen to take part in the debate he would have made a complete fool of himself and been utterly humiliated.

Wednesday 10th June 2105

The recording over Graysby mopped his brow with a handkerchief.

"Don't you ever perspire, Miss Clayton?" he asked.

"Occasionally," she replied. "Perhaps you should wear more make-up."

"Sadly there isn't enough make-up in the world to make me look as good as you. Next to you I look old, bald and sweaty. I wish Bryant hadn't cancelled, I'm at least slimmer than him."

"I rather hope the audience will be paying some attention to our policies and not just how we look," suggested Rebecca.

"That is another reason why I wish Bryant could have been here. You know he's hopeless without his team of speech-writers."

"I'm sure a few of his favourite metaphors would have improved the discussion greatly!"

"It is a great shame the President pulled out so suddenly," remarked Peter Sheridan while removing his microphone. "We are extremely grateful to you Miss Clayton for standing in at such short notice."

"Not at all," she replied shaking his hand. "This has been a great opportunity."

"I only hope the censor's will permit us to broadcast it," said Sheridan.

"There are bound to be some cuts," warned Graysby, "especially since Miss Clayton referred to both oral and anal sex. There is no way that sort of filth will go out. I always thought you were a lady!"

"Really! A little earlier you alluded to my expertise and experience on the subject of sex in a manner which suggested you held a quite contrary opinion."

"That was a mistake and I apologise."

"No need, I am not so easily offended."

"Nevertheless it was wrong of me to make personal remarks."

"Perhaps you would be less repentant had the audience appreciated it more."

"That is unfair. I believe your retort was not entirely without reproach."

"You struck the first blow, I merely responded in kind."

"But I have admitted my mistake and apologised, are you not going to do likewise?"

"No, because I am not sorry and if you were honest neither are you!"

"You can stop sparring now," suggested Sheridan, "the recording is finished."

"Yes, perhaps we should save our energy for our next battle," agreed Graysby.

"But I'm just getting started," protested Rebecca, "I must have more stamina than you!"

"More stamina and more venom," Graysby replied. "It is true what they say about the female of the species." He shook hands with Sheridan saying, "Thank you very much for an exemplary job as an impartial chair. I'm sure we will be seeing each other again very soon."

As he left the studio Rebecca followed not far behind.

"Phil, can I have a quiet word?" she requested.

"Not if you wish to trade insults," he replied.

"No I promise I've finished that for the present. I wanted to ask you about the actual election process."

Both Graysby and Rebecca had been provided with a dressing-room to prepare for the recording. Graysby allowed her into his, which was closest to the studio, so that they could talk in private.

"All right what do you want to know?"

"I would like to know what you think the chances are of this being a free and fair election."

Graysby's brow furrowed and he took a moment to contemplate before he answered.

"I can't promise anything, but my colleagues and I have plenty of insider knowledge of how results have been manipulated in the past. I know which officials have previously taken bribes so know who to watch."

"Or who to bribe with a larger sum than Bryant has offered."

"That would be a very foolish game to play. If I double Bryant's bribe what is to stop him from tripling it? We both have powerful supporters and are too evenly matched to fight that kind of campaign. I honestly believe that our only option is to let the voters choose between us. I intend to fight fair and try my damnedest to see that he does too."

"Do you think you can win?"

"I know I can win, but what worries me is whether or not he will concede defeat. I have many of the big names in finance and industry on my side but the police and military answer to him. I can only hope he still retains enough of a shred of decency to know when he is beaten. The last thing I want to do is start a civil war. That is no good to anyone."

"I doubt Bryant wants civil war but he cannot bear to lose face. He is so utterly ruled by his pride and his ego that he is incapable of admitting he is wrong. We can only hope that others close to him will persuade him to stand down when the time comes."

"Incidentally Rebecca, did anyone see you come in here?"

"I don't think so, why?"

"I was just wondering if it is wise being alone together like this, considering some of the articles which have been published about the two of us during the last week. For myself I find the allegations a rather refreshing change from the usual accusations of homosexuality but I wouldn't wish to harm your reputation."

"My reputation! Bryant must be getting desperate if he thinks spreading rumours about my sex life will affect my popularity. The number of men, and some women, who I have supposedly slept with is already in the hundreds. Does he really think any more sleazy gossip will make a difference?"

"I heard one rumour that you were married."

"Exactly my point. What are a few more rumours to me? Just another drop in the ocean."

"Then you aren't married?"

"It has been very pleasant talking to you Philip but I must go. There is a general election coming up you know and I have a campaign to run."

"What a coincidence! So have I!"

"Goodbye then. No doubt we shall meet again soon."

"Goodbye Rebecca and good luck."

They shook hands and she left the room. David was waiting for her outside.

"I hope you haven't been misbehaving," he remarked as he took her arm and escorted her to the car.

"Sorry darling, you know I find powerful men irresistible."

"What were you up to?"

"Are you sure you want to know? I wouldn't want to drive you mad with jealousy!"

"I'll take that risk."

"We were discussing the lengths Bryant will go to in order to win the election. Graysby thinks he can prevent him from rigging the vote but he is not certain he will concede defeat."

"You're right I am mad with jealousy. I hate it when you talk politics with other men."

Once inside the car Rebecca removed her wedding ring from the gold chain she wore around her neck and put it back on her finger.

"Why don't you just keep it on the chain?" David asked. "Then there's less risk of forgetting."

"Because it is my wedding ring and it belongs on my finger," she replied crossly.

"Sorry, I just meant that I don't mind if you don't wear it. It is only a bit of gold."

"I mind. It is a bit of gold which means I am married to you. I want to wear it."

He was silent for a while, concentrating on driving. Once they had crossed over Waterloo Bridge he spoke again.

"I thought the debate went pretty well."

She didn't answer.

"I'm afraid Graysby is probably right about the censors," he said.

She still made no remark.

"I'm glad you wore that suit. It's a really good colour for you."

Still no response.

"What's the matter?"

"Nothing, I'm just a bit tired."

"You need a hot bath and an early night. We are off to Birmingham tomorrow."

"Birmingham? I thought it was Bristol."

"No they are definitely expecting us in Birmingham."

"Shit! I was sure my diary said Bristol."

"It doesn't matter. I'll see that you get to the right place at the right time. I usually do."

They did not talk any more until they were back at their apartment, then David asked, "What do you fancy for dinner?"

"I don't know."

"Shall I do a vegetable curry?"

"Yeah fine."

"Are you in the mood for slightly spicy or insanely hot?"

"For God's sake David will you stop asking me questions, my brain is going to explode!"

"Sorry my love."

"And don't keep apologising all the time, it's really irritating!"

"OK then, would you rather I didn't say anything?"

"Yes please, give me some peace."

She collapsed onto the sofa with a loud sigh and David went through to the kitchen. He came back a few minutes later and put a cup of tea on the table in front of her without saying a word.

She instantly felt terrible for snapping at him. She followed him back through to the kitchen.

"I'm really sorry," she said. "I'm tired and stressed and being a complete bitch."

He hugged her and said "It's OK. Are you sure you're just tired or is something else bothering you?"

"Oh David, there are so many things bothering me right now it would take me all night to tell you them all. The main thing I'm afraid of is that we are going to make things worse. What if Bryant wins and becomes stronger? What if he loses but resorts to violence to hold on to power? What if he decides to punish the people for not supporting him? If people die because of me I couldn't bear that. I would rather shoot myself in the head than be responsible for that."

"If this election ends in violence it will be Bryant's fault and not yours."

287

"I will still be partly to blame. I have promised the people an alternative to Bryant. I have encouraged them to hope for something better. If the only alternative is war then I will have helped to bring it about."

"Even if there is a war it may be that in the end democracy wins."

"But at a cost I cannot bring myself to contemplate. And suppose democracy doesn't win? I'm not the sort of person who is prepared to take that kind of chance. I'm not comfortable gambling with people's lives."

"We can't stand aside and let Bryant rule this country exactly as he pleases. Someone has to stand against him."

"I know, but I desperately wish that someone wasn't me."

"But if not you then who will do it? Who else could speak about freedom in the eloquent and passionate way that you did today?"

"Using your words."

"They weren't my words!"

"Are you sure? You usually provide the eloquence and passion."

"How about I provide the dinner? That is what I'm best at."

He started chopping onions and peppers.

"The whole section about human rights and freedom was yours I'm sure."

"Maybe but 'No amount of government interference will prevent people from copulating' was entirely your own."

"Yes that was mine. I just wish I had the time and energy to do some copulating myself rather than just talking about it!"

"Was this all a mistake? Should I never have suggested you stand for the Hackney by-election?"

"I don't know. There is no point in agonising over it now. It is too late to back out. If I quit now I let too many people down. I suppose I will just have to put all my doubts and fears to the back of my mind and keep going."

"Are you angry with me? I pushed you into this, it is my fault."

"No that's rubbish. I chose to stand for the by-election and it was my decision to take over the party leadership. Of course I'm not blaming you. It is true I could not have done any of this without you, but it was my choice. If it turns out badly then it will be my fault alone."

"At least you know that everything you have tried to do has been to make things better for the people of this country."

"Isn't the road to hell paved with good intentions?"

"I don't believe that. I believe that if you really, truly strive to do good, no matter how little you actually achieve, you will be welcomed into heaven. Do you think that is enough chillies?"

"Probably, those are the hot ones. Since I don't believe in either heaven or hell I'm only concerned by what happens in this world. I fear that here on earth it is results and not intention by which we are judged."

"You have achieved a great deal already. Whatever happens in the future the country will remember how you fought for the young people in Re-education Centres and how you united the opposition against Phoenix. Could you pick some coriander?"

"I hope you are right. Is that enough?"

"A bit more. Yes that's fine thanks."

"Karen was right. I'm not the sort of person who is suited to this job."

"Perhaps not, and yet you have done it so well."

THE ELECTION
Simon Chandra

Liberation fought a very different kind of election campaign to either Phoenix or Prosperity. While the other two parties had wealthy backers and influence over the licensed media, Rosa's party had to use other tactics to get its message across. Rosa travelled far more than either of her rivals. From the time the election was announced until the moment the polls closed she was touring the country making speeches in every major city. Rosa was also far more dependent on volunteers than Bryant or Graysby. While they fought for control of the News Channel, Liberation had people on street corners and going from door to door, canvassing the way elections were fought in the old days. Rosa's fame and popularity meant there was no shortage of people prepared to help the party.

I remember the way that people who had never shown any interest in politics before were suddenly excited by the forthcoming election. Pubs and cafes started switching their televisions to the news channel instead of music or sport. Even kids my age were talking about it. All the girls wanted Rosa to win because she was their role model, while the boys wanted her to win because they fancied her. It was the first time in my life I had heard people discussing politics in public. One evening when I was round my friend Andrew's house his mum and dad got into a blazing row. His mum was determined to vote for Rosa while his dad supported Graysby.

The opinion polls leading up to the election fluctuated wildly. Each of the three main parties had its own poll which put them ahead. RNN showed that Graysby had a small lead with Liberation close behind, while IMC always had Rosa in third place with sometimes Phoenix and sometimes Prosperity as the winner. As polling day drew closer, Liberation pulled ahead of Prosperity according to RNN, while IMC had Prosperity as the victor with Phoenix a close second.

Although he publicly declared he was confident of victory throughout his campaign, Bryant undoubtedly realised he was in real danger of losing the Presidency. As the election drew closer he instated several emergency measures which he claimed were to keep the peace. A temporary 22:00 curfew was put in place and gatherings in the streets were prohibited. This meant Rosa had to change her tactic. Whereas previously she would have set up a platform in a public place and amassed a crowd of hundreds she now needed to find a sports field or other suitable venue. However by this time people were so keen to see and hear her that they were prepared to come to her if she could to come to them.

In the last week before the election Bryant gave several dire warnings of the chaos that would follow if he was defeated. He claimed that Britain would be vulnerable without his strong leadership and that enemy nations were poised to take advantage and invade. He promised that without his authority the country would lapse into anarchy. He did his best to remind the voters of the situation before Phoenix had risen to power and promised that without him those troubled days would instantly return. Had there been any violence or rioting in the run-up to the election, Bryant's warning might have been taken more seriously. As it was both Rosa and Graysby urged the people to be patient and to tolerate the President's oppressive emergency measures as they would soon have the opportunity to be rid of him.

Looking at pictures of the three of them you can see what a hard campaign it was that they were fighting. Even Bryant, who probably put the least physical effort into the battle, seems to age several years after those few weeks. I've been looking at the footage of him casting his vote and as he waves to the cameras his trademark broad smile looks rather stiffer than usual. Later in the day when he is being interviewed by Peter Sheridan, his shoulders are clearly drooping with fatigue and his voice lacks its normal strength.

Although still looking beautiful, by the time Rosa made her final speech on Election Day she had almost lost her voice. Addressing a loud and enthusiastic crowd at Homerton Football Ground she is barely audible. She is forced to cut the speech short as her vocal chords give out completely, but her audience still cheers wildly. As she leaves the stage she leans heavily on O'Brien's arm and he looks exhausted too.

Thursday 2nd July 2105

Rebecca was greeted by a huge cheer as she arrived at Liberation Party Headquarters. Alicia Cain was first to greet her, hugging her and thumping her on the back.

"Both the RNN and our exit polls suggest we've done it!" Alicia announced triumphantly.

Rebecca's throat was still too sore to answer so she just shrugged. She collapsed in a chair as people gathered around to congratulate her. She shook hands, smiled and nodded but refrained from speaking. David prepared a soothing honey and lemon drink and politely persuaded some of the well wishers to disperse.

"How long until the results start coming in?" David asked Alicia.

"I'm not sure but I doubt we will hear anything until midnight."

"It is too late for us to get home before curfew now. Perhaps Becky could catch a couple of hours sleep in her office until then?"

"Good idea. I got stuck here after curfew several times so I started keeping a folding bed in the cleaners' cupboard. Becky is welcome to borrow it. Come on, I'll get it."

"Thanks Alicia, I should have known you'd be prepared. Come on Becky, bedtime."

Not long after Rebecca was fast asleep on Alicia's folding bed while David dozed in the chair. It was not until nearly two o'clock that Alicia called to wake them.

"The results are being announced now," she said. "So far three to Graysby, one to Bryant and one to us."

Rebecca dressed, combed her hair and fixed her make-up and she and David went to join the others gathered around the TV in the reception area.

"They are coming in fast now," Alicia said when she saw them. "Two more for Prosperity and another for us."

"It's looking good for Graysby then," Rebecca replied hoarsely.

"It can all change."

The room went quiet as Peter Sheridan announced the first victory of the night for the Muslim Democrat Party. Mohammed Anwar had retained his South Bradford seat.

"Shall I make some tea and coffee?" David suggested.

"It's all right, Sam has the drinks under control. Quiet everyone! It's the results from Leeds."

Giles Summers won by a huge margin, earning loud cheers from the assembled party members. Cheers quickly turned to boos when the next seat went to Phoenix. The results began to arrive more quickly with Prosperity winning five in a row, then Liberation gaining three. After half an hour a pattern began to emerge, Prosperity in the lead with Liberation a close second and Phoenix some way behind them. This continued until almost three in the morning when Sheridan announced that a technical fault meant he could not announce any more results at present.

For the next ten minutes he filled air time by recounting the results already in and discussing them with his studio guests. As time dragged by Sheridan began looking increasingly uncomfortable. Eventually he made an announcement.

"We have to apologise as it seems we won't be able to bring you any further results tonight. Some irregularities in the counting of the votes have come to light and no more results are to be announced until these have been fully investigated. The President is expected to make a statement tomorrow morning; in the meantime we have been asked to end this broadcast. We can only apologise again and hope that we will be able to bring you the election results soon. Thank you for watching, goodnight."

The programme was replaced by advertisements and Alicia switched the TV off.

"This is Bryant," she said. "He knows he has lost so now he is trying to cover it up."

"I will call Downing Street at once," said Rebecca, "tell him that we know what he is up to."

"Yes and try to contact Graysby too," agreed Alicia. "He won't take this lightly."

Rebecca made the call to Downing Street from her office. The President was apparently unavailable but she left her message of protest with his secretary. She then called Prosperity's central offices and was eventually put through to Graysby himself.

"Of course we were watching," he replied to her initial enquiry. "We feared something like this might happen."

"I have just tried to call Bryant but he wouldn't answer," Rebecca told him.

"Yes we have tried too but we only got various receptionists and secretaries. I would try going to Downing Street in person but there are rather a lot of police around here at present."

"Yes we have several patrol cars outside too. I expect Bryant would like us to break curfew, then he would have an excuse to arrest us."

"I'm going to call IMC and insist they broadcast a statement from me. If they don't I'll have Net UK pull the plug on them."

"Send me a draft of your statement and I will issue one in support."

"Thank you Rebecca, I will do that."

"What do you think Bryant's next move will be? Do you think he will declare the election void?"

"I suspect he will delay making any definite statement for as long as possible. Fortunately I have a plan to prevent that. I'm afraid I can't talk about it over the phone but I believe I can put some serious pressure on Phoenix."

"I hope so. You will have my party's full support. If the people of this country have duly elected you as their President we will do whatever we can to see that their wishes are respected."

"Thank you. Now if you will excuse me I had better get to work. No doubt we will speak again soon."

For the next hour she was occupied calling members of Liberation and the leaders of the other opposition parties. She passed on what Graysby had told her and did her best to reassure them that the battle was not lost. Graysby's office sent through a recording of his statement in which he condemned the President's actions and demanded that the results be released. She asked Sean to come up and together they drafted a short speech echoing what he had said, then recorded it in her office. They sent one copy to Graysby and another to the IMC News offices.

Since the election results broadcast had gone off air the IMC News channel had been showing only adverts and a regular but brief news bulletin explaining the situation. At five am Peter Sheridan returned and Graysby's statement was broadcast followed by Rebecca's. Sheridan then informed viewers that the President would make his own statement shortly.

At six Bryant appeared before an IMC film crew and repeated his allegation of irregularities in the counting and promised that a full investigation was taking place.

"I urge you to be patient while these inquiries are taking place," he said. "Certain factions will no doubt try to take advantage of this period of uncertainty to promote their own violent agendas. For this reason the emergency measures put in place in the run up to the election will remain until the results have been announced. As a further precaution public gatherings of more than fifty people will be prohibited at the present time. This government is dedicated to democracy and to the security of the nation. We ask that you help us to keep you safe until the problems have been resolved. Thank you."

Graysby already had a film crew of his own at the Prosperity Headquarters and was prepared to answer Bryant immediately. Within a few minutes of Bryant's statement ending, the news channel went live to Graysby.

"This has been a very bad night for democracy," he began, "There has been an election and yet the people are forbidden from knowing the results. The President claims there have been irregularities in the counting but has offered no evidence of this. He says there will be an investigation but has given us no assurance of when the results will be made known. I refuse to tolerate this and I know that the British people feel the same. I demand full publication of the results and complete disclosure of all the evidence for these alleged irregularities. I demand that this happens within forty-eight hours or sanctions will be taken against the government.

"Throughout my election campaign I have shown that I have the support of several influential corporations. Among my supporters is the board of the telecommunications company Net UK. Should the government not agree to what I ask within the time specified, Net UK will stop transmission of IMC and will cut off all government departments from its network. I believe the government will find the daily running of the country extremely difficult without telephone, email or access to the media. Should the government take any action against me, Net UK will carry out this threat immediately."

Everyone at Liberation Party HQ was gathered around the television when Graysby made his statement. A huge cheer went up.

"Nice one Phil!" Rebecca exclaimed. "Sean, get me a film crew. We may not have Graysby's friends in high places but we can add our voice of support."

"That is pure genius." remarked Alicia, "Bryant will be paralysed without Net UK. He will have to give in."

"Who knows about telecommunications?" Rebecca asked, addressing the whole room. "Someone tell me the facts. Is there any way he can get around this?"

"There's no way around it," Stacey Barnes answered. "Net UK control everything. The only way he could stop Net UK from cutting him off would be to have the army invade their offices and commandeer the network."

"This is Bryant we are talking about," Rosa replied, "can we rule that out?"

"If he uses the army against one major corporation others won't be happy," responded Karen. "The big companies own Bryant. If he turns on them he is really sunk."

"Then we are confident Graysby's threat will work?" Rebecca asked.

"It will certainly produce a reaction though exactly what we must wait and see," said Alicia.

Sean returned to the reception area with a mobile phone clasped to his ear.

"IMC have a crew outside already," he informed them. "They assumed you would want to say something so sent their people out before Bryant even made his statement."

"That's great," replied Rebecca. "Tell them I will be out in a few minutes. OK what am I saying? We condemn Bryant's attempts to derail democracy and fully support Graysby's efforts to restore power to the voters?"

"Talk directly to the voters," Sean suggested. "They're going to broadcast live so make the most of it. Get angry, lay into Bryant, but be confident and reassuring. Don't refer to Bryant as the President because as far as we are concerned he isn't any more."

"OK, what do I say about Graysby? Are we assuming he is the new President?"

"Not until the results have been disclosed," Alicia replied. "Perhaps throw in some praise for him, but not too much."

"I will stress my respect for him as an opponent but refrain from calling him my friend. How is my hair?"

"A mess and your eyes are all puffy," replied Karen, without any attempt at tact.

"Where's my bag? Emergency make-up needed."

David produced her handbag and she set to work with comb and powder.

"How is anyone supposed to look presentable at this time in the morning?" she grumbled as she inspected the results. "That will have to do. Please tell me it isn't raining."

"It is quite sunny at the moment," Sean answered.

"Even worse! I'll be squinting and looking shifty. OK Sean. Tell them I'm coming."

After giving her brief statement for the film crew Rebecca returned with Sean and David to the reception area. The rest of the party were still gathered around the television.

"How was it?" she asked.

"Good," replied Alicia, "I think you made it clear we weren't going to take any more crap from Bryant."

"The light was bad," remarked Karen. "Your face was half in shadow and I think you should have indicated that we are taking action of our own and not just leaving it to Graysby."

"Why? What action are we taking?"

"None as yet, but you should have tried to make it appear that we are."

"I thought we were supposed to be the honest ones!"

"You know what I mean. Graysby hasn't won yet. We shouldn't just hand power over to him."

"Well hopefully in two days time we will know who has won the election; in the meantime I don't see there is much that we can do. David, will you take me home?"

"Sure, are you ready to go now?"

"You're going?" exclaimed Karen.

"Yes, I can wait for Bryant's next move just as easily at home as I can here."

"Good idea," Alicia agreed, "we should all get some rest while we can."

Karen opened her mouth to protest but saw that everyone else was in agreement.

"Come on honey," said Sean taking her by the arm, "let's go and have some breakfast, I'm starving."

She acquiesced, perhaps feeling that having something to eat would not be such a bad prospect.

*

Their car was spotted as David and Rebecca pulled into the parking area behind their block. Many of their neighbours had been up all night as the story of the election unfolded and when the news spread of Rebecca's return, a small crowd gathered to greet her, bombarding her with questions.

She held up her hands for quiet then replied, "I'm sorry but at the present I don't know anything more than what you have already heard on the news. It is up to Bryant now and we will just have to wait and see."

"But who won?"

"Was it rigged?"

"What if Bryant doesn't release the results?"

These and many more questions were repeated from all sides and David was forced to push a path through the crowd to the lift. When they eventually made it to the safety of their flat they both collapsed onto the sofa and let out sighs of relief.

After lying inert for several minutes David asked, "Right, what do you want to do first, eat or sleep?"

"I'd like something to eat first, then some sleep, after that I'll have a bath and after that who knows, maybe I'll even have sex with my husband."

"Sounds like a good plan. Would you like me to tell him?"

"If you find him. You'll know him if you see him. He looks a lot like you."

"Poor bastard!"

"At least he doesn't have puffy eyes!"

"God! Karen can be such a bitch."

They partook of some tea and toast before retiring to bed. Later, after sleeping all morning and making love for most of the afternoon, they were talking about not much in particular and the conversation returned to Karen Baker.

"Do you think she is as domineering in the bedroom as she is at work?" Rebecca asked.

"How do you mean?" David replied.

"I was wondering if she regularly has Sean handcuffed to the headboard while she whips him."

"Now there is an image I really didn't want! Thanks for that!"

"I thought you liked that kind of thing. I read your poem about bondage."

"It was a metaphor."

"That's what they all say!"

Before David could defend his work they were interrupted by the phone.

"Speak of the devil!" said Rebecca as she got up to answer it. "I bet that is Karen."

It was.

"What's the news?" Rebecca asked.

"It's not good I'm afraid. Graysby is at Downing Street meeting with Bryant."

"Is that bad?"

"Probably. It means that Graysby is doing a deal with Bryant and leaving us out of it. We won't know how bad until one of them makes a statement."

"What sort of deal?"

"I'm afraid I don't know. I've been calling everyone and anyone who might be able to shed some light on it but either no one knows anything or they are scared to talk."

"I'll call Graysby's office. I doubt they will tell me anything but I can remind them how much they owe us and let them know I'm not happy."

"Right do that, keep pestering them all night if necessary."

"I will. I'm glad I got some sleep when I did."

"I'll call back as soon as I know anything. Good luck."

"You too. Bye for now."

Rebecca immediately called Prosperity's head offices but was fobbed off with promises that Graysby would contact her later. Eventually, just after six that evening, Graysby emerged from Downing Street and made a statement live on IMC News.

"After lengthy discussions with President Bryant we have reached a compromise which we feel is in the best interests of the country."

"Compromise! I don't like that word!" Rebecca complained to David as they watched.

"The President has shared all the evidence of electoral fraud and we are in agreement that the results of yesterday's polling cannot be considered valid."

"Shit! What is he playing at?" exclaimed Rebecca, grasping hold of David's hand and squeezing it hard.

"Therefore I withdraw my demands that the results be made public. They are to be declared null and void. A fresh election will be called, which my party is determined to contest fairly and honestly. In the meantime it is of great importance that the perpetrators of the fraud are caught and punished. I will be doing everything in my power to co-operate with the criminal investigation and ask that the representatives of all other parties do likewise."

Another statement from Bryant followed in which he tried to reassure voters that their wishes would be respected and urged them to be patient. Rebecca did not even listen to the whole of his speech. She was already on the phone to Graysby's office demanding to know the truth. As Karen advised she continued to call repeatedly for the rest of the evening, but Graysby's staff soon stopped answering and she got tired of leaving messages. She called Downing Street but no one there was prepared to speak to her either.

At nine o'clock Karen called again but she had no further information.

"I've got no idea what kind of deal they have struck but we can guarantee it is going to involve stabbing us in the back," she warned.

"I don't doubt it, but what can we do?"

"Perhaps tomorrow you should go to Graysby in person. We could try to get a news crew to go with you, then he will look bad if he attempts to avoid you."

"It is worth a try. Get Sean to contact IMC and see if they will agree. I assume Stacey has been in touch with her friends in the media?"

"Yes, they don't like this either."

"How are the public reacting?"

"Hard to say as yet. There were some protests against Phoenix today but the police broke them up without much violence. I think in general people are as confused as we are. Our supporters don't trust Bryant or Graysby but until they know exactly what they are up to they don't know how to react."

"I'll keep an eye on the news channel and RNN for the next few hours as I don't think I'll be able to sleep. I'll be ready to call on Graysby first thing in the morning with or without a film crew but there isn't anything else I can do tonight."

"Not tonight. We will just have to hope things stay calm until morning."

"It's going to be another long one."

"Yes, good job we're used to it. I'll call you at five unless I have any news before then."

"OK, goodnight."

"Goodnight Becky."

After flicking between IMC News and RNN for the next three hours and learning nothing, Rebecca eventually decided to retire to bed. For some time she lay awake but finally began to doze off. An alarm sounded, jolting her awake. David sat up beside her.

"It's the intruder alarm on the front entrance," he said. "Stay here while I investigate."

The clock showed it was eight minutes past three. David threw on a robe and retrieved the cricket bat he had recently started keeping under the bed.

"It's times like this I wish I had a gun," he complained.

As he opened the apartment door the sounds of panic from the other residents reached Rebecca.

"It's the police!" she heard someone say.

She got out of bed and put on her own robe. David discarded the useless cricket bat as several armed police officers entered their flat.

"Miss Rebecca Clayton," said the officer in charge, "I am placing you under arrest for treason and crimes against democracy. You are obliged to answer all questions or face further charges."

"May I get dressed first?" she requested.

"Sorry miss, you are to come with us immediately."

They patted her down, checking for weapons then cuffed her hands behind her back.

"Where are you taking her?" David demanded.

"I'm sorry I can't answer that," replied the officer. "I suggest you remain here sir as if you try to follow you will be breaking curfew."

"But I need to contact a solicitor," David protested.

"I'm afraid the severity of the charges does not permit legal counsel."

As she was escorted down to the waiting car many of her neighbours came out to observe. Officers cleared the onlookers roughly aside and held them back as she was pushed into the vehicle. She felt vaguely reassured by their cries of support and anger but she knew public opinion would do her little good now. This was what she had most feared since she first stood as a parliamentary candidate. She was alone and at the mercy of the police. Her innocence was completely irrelevant.

She did not bother trying to ask any questions of the officers escorting her as she knew they would not answer. She remained silent throughout the journey into central London. She guessed they were destined for the headquarters of the Metropolitan Anti-Terror Police.

As the car pulled up at the rear entrance her stomach lurched, as she knew that from now on things could only get worse. More officers were awaiting their arrival. She was dragged roughly from the car and into the barren and forbidding corridors of the building. She was taken to room which was labelled Suspect Processing. Inside she was searched again, photographed, fingerprints and DNA taken and her retina scanned. After this the male officers left the room leaving her with a female officer who was putting on rubber gloves.

"Oh god!" Rebecca exclaimed. "Is all this really necessary?"

"Remove your clothes please," replied the policewoman.

"What are you expecting to find?"

"A full search is standard procedure, now remove your clothes."

Rebecca obeyed, knowing the purpose of the search was to subject her to as much discomfort and indignity as possible and her only option was to tolerate it. Any attempts to resist would result in far worse treatment. That the men had left the room was little comfort as there was a two way mirror on one wall and a CCTV camera in the corner.

After every part of her anatomy had been prodded and thoroughly investigated she was permitted to dress, but the only clothing she was given was a thin, hospital-style gown smelling strongly of disinfectant. She was escorted to a cold and comfortless interview room. The walls were bare and painted a dirty off-white and there was no window. The floor was an institutional blue-green, non-slip rubber and the metal table and two chairs were bolted into it. There was a camera in the corner by the door and directly above the table a vent blew chilled air into the room. Sitting facing the door Rebecca found she was shivering in the full force of the icy blast, so stood and paced about.

The room was perfectly square, exactly four paces in both directions. Eventually she grew tired and leant up against the wall in the corner. She had no idea what the time was but it felt as though she had been in that room for hours. Her bare feet were going numb. The hum of the air-conditioning fell silent and she sighed with relief. A few minutes later a familiar person entered the room. It was Detective Superintendent Patrick Hunter.

"Sit down please," he instructed, taking the chair closest to the door.

She obeyed without speaking. Hunter's usually grim expression was even more so.

"These are very serious charges against you," he said. "However, if you confess immediately you will escape the death penalty."

"What exactly are the charges?" she enquired.

"We have evidence that you bribed the returning officers of eleven constituencies to wrongfully claim Liberation candidates were victorious, and we believe this is only the tip of the iceberg."

"The Liberation Party does not have the funds for bribing anyone," Rebecca replied coolly.

"We understand you used your personal wealth in this."

"My personal wealth was exhausted some time ago. I spent the vast majority of my savings on my initial by-election campaign and most of my salary I use on transport."

"There is no point in denying these charges. We have sufficient evidence to prove your guilt and if you do not confess you will hang. I should also warn you that the President has given me the authority to use any means necessary to acquire the full facts of this case."

"Would that be President Bryant or President Graysby?"

"This is no joke Miss Clayton."

"I am quite serious. When I went to bed last night the results of the election had not been revealed, so I think there is some cause for uncertainty as to who actually is the President."

"Since the election was unfairly influenced by you and your party and has been declared null and void, John Bryant is still President. Mr Graysby is content with that as the alternative would be to allow you to steal the election."

"You mean we won?"

"As a result of your fraudulent activities your party did indeed win."

Rebecca laughed aloud in triumph. She had defeated Graysby and Bryant; unfortunately they were now both her enemies.

"I would not open the champagne just yet Miss Clayton. Once the public know that you tried to deceive them and to rob them of their democratic rights, I don't think they will be applauding your victory. You won't be moving into Number Ten any time soon. The best you can hope for is a comfortable cell and if you don't co-operate you won't even get that. You're still a young woman Miss Clayton. I don't think you are ready to die yet. Do the sensible thing and confess."

"I will not be confessing to something you know that I haven't done. Do you honestly think the public are going to swallow this crap? Whatever evidence you have fabricated against me is not going to convince my supporters. They will know that Bryant and Graysby cooked this up because they couldn't take defeat."

"I am disappointed by your attitude Miss Clayton. From my past dealings with you I believed you to have more sense than this. If necessary I can get the information I require from other members of your party. Your stubbornness will gain nothing but disgrace and death."

They were interrupted by a knock at the door. A uniformed police constable entered and said something into Hunter's ear.

"Oh shit!" Hunter swore. "I'll come at once. Hopefully Miss Clayton will be a little more co-operative when she has had time to think over the alternative."

He departed, slamming and locking the door behind him.

Island Nation Magazine
Saturday 7th September 2115

AFTER THE ELECTION
Simon Chandra

My sister and I were not happy about being sent to bed on election night. Even though we were not old enough to vote we desperately wanted to know if Rosa had won, but it was a school night and Mum insisted. She and Dad had no intention of going to bed themselves however. They each had an office at home. Dad's was upstairs in the spare room while Mum's was downstairs at the back of the house. Both were at their desks when Amira and I finally gave up our protests and went to our rooms. I turned out the light but was watching IMC News on my mobile until well after midnight when I must have dozed off.

I was woken by a great commotion at around 3:00 am. As soon as Sheridan announced that no more results would be released that night, Dad went running down the stairs whilst still trying to hold a phone conversation with someone from IMC. This lead to him tripping and almost breaking his neck. Meanwhile Mum was calling anyone who might know anything and cursing loudly when they could tell her nothing. They made a few feeble attempts to send Amira and me back to bed but we refused and remained watching TV in the living-room until Graysby delivered his ultimatum. We cheered wildly when he threatened to pull the plug on the government's telecommunications.

We did go to school that day but the teachers had their minds on other things than our lessons. Many classes were cancelled and we spent much of the day assembled in the hall watching the news. I fell asleep several times after my disturbed night's rest. When I arrived home I found Mum and Dad slumped together on the sofa, both completely exhausted. Amira and I cooked dinner. I can't remember what we made but I think it was just about edible.

Later that evening Dad learned that Graysby and Bryant were going to meet. Mum was furious when he told her as she knew that it meant Graysby was planning to betray Rosa. When Graysby left his meeting at Number 10 and declared the election results null and void, we all screamed at the television in futile rage. I put on my shoes and announced I was going to Westminster immediately to protest.

"Don't be an idiot," Mum replied, "you're just a kid. Do you really think they will listen to you? You'll just get yourself arrested."

"We have to do something!" I argued, feeling all the helpless anger of an adolescent.

"If you want to do something you can make some calls for me," she answered.

Mum had decided that since the government was attempting to suppress the election results she would do her best to get them published. On behalf of RNN she began collating the results. Even though only a few of the results had been announced, the counting had been completed for the vast majority of constituencies and several officials knew who had won. We pretended we were collecting the information for IMC, giving my father's name and saying we worked for him. The combined efforts of the four of us and several other RNN volunteers gained ninety-five percent of the results by morning.

It was in the early hours that the rumours of Rosa's arrest were officially confirmed. A large number of people broke curfew and gathered outside parliament and along Victoria Street between Scotland Yard and MAT Force Headquarters to demand her release.

At six am Mum picked up her bag and said, "Right I'm going where the action is. I'm heading into the city to get some footage of the protests."

I said I would go too and an argument followed but as she was impatient to go she permitted me to accompany her, provided I ran at the first signs of trouble.

We set off towards Hampstead tube station but on the way we learned that all public transport had been shut down. So we joined the throng of others who were headed on foot towards the city centre. Straggling groups coalesced into a protest march and we began chanting "Release Rosa", which was nicely alliterative. As we approached Regents Park, several police cars blocked our way and a voice over a megaphone ordered us to return to our homes. They threatened that anyone found out of doors would be arrested.

At first it appeared as though the threat was to be heeded and the crowd began to break up, but soon we reformed and continued our march along another route. This was repeated several times until we encountered an army roadblock. A helicopter flew low over us, spraying us with tear gas. This was the point my Mum ordered me to go home. My eyes were streaming and I was terrified so I obeyed without question. By the time I reached home the shooting had begun and Dad was frantically worried. Mum called to say she was all right but ignored Dad's instructions to come home at once. When she finally did stumble in through our front door she was half blinded, her eyes red raw. Her clothes were filthy and her hands were bleeding from when she had fallen in the panicked stampede which resulted when the army opened fire. However she did have extensive footage of the whole event.

From the reports sent to RNN it was clear that the situation was the same in every major city. While IMC was trying to assure viewers that the police and army had the situation under control, it became increasingly evident that this was not the case. By lunch-time there were unsubstantiated rumours that several police officers had been killed. When both Bryant and Graysby appeared on television appealing for calm they had the opposite effect, causing more people to take to the streets to vent their anger.

At the time we knew nothing of the divisions and conflict within the police and armed forces. Months later it emerged that senior officers held very different views as to how the demonstrations should have been dealt with. Although the Ministry of Justice and Security had given clear instructions that live rounds were to be used if CS gas failed, some senior officers had contradicted these orders, forbidding their forces to fire on civilians.

Some of my readers may feel it is rather self-indulgent to give this account of my family in the days following the election. They are probably correct, but as almost everyone has a story to tell about that time I found it very difficult to choose whose story to tell. I therefore chose to tell my own, not out of egotism or because I thought it the most interesting but simply because it is the one I know best. I did not give an account of Rosa's personal story during this time because no new information is available. Her own report of the treatment she suffered has already been published and since she is dead she can add nothing to it. Only the police officers who were present during her interrogation could yield any further details, but none of them are available to comment.

PROTEST SONG
Anon

I am – though you choose not to see me
One of so many with good reason to hate
Beware, like an army we're marching
Your downfall approaches, we're scaling your fate

I am – though you choose not to hear me
One of a choir that's singing a new song
We've torn up the old score of fear and of hatred
The ballad of Phoenix we've sung for too long

I am – though you choose not to know me
One of the legions who sees through your lies
No longer fooled by your threats or your promises
We will never surrender for hope never dies

Saturday 4th July 2105

After pacing the room until she was exhausted, Rebecca had returned to her partially sheltered corner. She recited snatches of poetry in her head to keep her calm while the minutes dragged by. She wished she had learnt more of David's verses by heart. When her legs grew too weary to support her she sank down on the cold floor and tried to restore circulation to her numb feet. Her mouth was parched but her bladder was uncomfortably full.

She called out, "Hello! Is anyone there? I need to use the toilet."

She repeated this request several times but there was no response. She crossed over to the door, banged on it and shouted. After doing this for a number of minutes the door finally opened and a uniformed policeman consented to escort her to the toilet. Holding her firmly by the arm he led her down the corridor to where there were toilets and showers. She relieved herself and drank from the tap, fearing it might be a long time before she was offered any food or water.

On returning to the interrogation room another policeman was outside the door. He exchanged a few whispered words with the first while looking her up and down. Then he pushed Rebecca roughly back into the room and forced her to sit on the metal chair opposite the door. Snatching her wrists and pulling them behind the chair back, he handcuffed her so she could not move. He left without a word.

Now unable to escape the icy blast from the air conditioning vent her discomfort was greatly increased. She rubbed her legs together trying to warm them and she fidgeted in her seat, trying to ease the aches in her neck and shoulders but nothing helped. Eventually she sank into a kind of stupor, unable to think of anything but the cold and pain.

Finally Superintendent Hunter returned, accompanied by Detective Sergeant Dale whom she had met the last time she had visited the MAT Force headquarters. Hunter took a seat while Dale remained standing.

"I don't suppose you have any idea of the trouble you have caused," Hunter began. "The rabble rousers at RNN have published your so-called election victory and incited the people to riot. Twelve people have died so far, four of them just outside this building."

He unfolded a portable screen and placed it on the table in front of her. On it were photographs of four bodies each with visible gunshot wounds. One was a woman shot through the head, another a young man hit in the neck, the last two were older men shot in the chest. They were all naked and lying on trolleys, presumably in a police mortuary somewhere close by.

"You are directly responsible for these deaths," said Hunter.

"I didn't shoot them," she replied.

"They were protesting on your behalf, like hundreds of others. No doubt many more will be killed before the day is over. The sooner you confess and put an end to these riots the more lives you will save."

"Do you really believe that a false confession will end these protests?" Rebecca asked.

"We believe you are an evil, lying bitch," replied Dale.

"Even if I were to confess no one will believe I was not coerced into doing so."

"We wish you to convince them," Hunter explained. "You are to make a statement to the media confessing your guilt and asking your supporters to end the violence. Your co-operation will be taken into account when it comes to sentencing."

"Suppose I would rather hang than co-operate. Surely Bryant doesn't want to make a martyr of me?"

"You won't be a martyr, just another corrupt Liberation politician," answered Dale.

"That isn't what the public believed though is it?"

"It will be once they learn the truth," said Hunter.

"I would be careful using words like truth. The truth is that if you had any real evidence against me you would not be so desperate to extract a confession. If Bryant wants to end the protests he will have to negotiate. Let me speak to him."

"The President does not negotiate with terrorists or traitors," stated Hunter.

"Since he knows I am neither he will speak to me."

"This is a waste of time," Dale complained.

"I agree," Hunter concurred, "let's leave her to reflect on the trouble she has caused."

He switched the screen on the desk to display footage of the riots happening all over the country, turning the volume up so that it was painfully loud, then he and the sergeant departed. She watched MAT Force police open fire on the protestors, the noise of the gunshots hurting her ears. The crowd tried to run, some falling and being trampled in the panic. Then the pictures showed the police rounding up the stragglers, hitting out with batons. They loaded their injured and bleeding victims into vans like cattle bound for the slaughterhouse.

Similar scenes from all over the country passed before her eyes, then the whole sequence repeated. She closed her eyes but could not shut out the sound of the screams, the sirens, and the shooting. She asked herself if confessing to the charges would put an end to all this. She feared not, but if she were to hang for treason the violence would surely escalate. To confess would be letting down her supporters and yet might save lives.

If she were to confess it would destroy the Liberation Party. There would be a fresh election, a two horse race between Bryant and Graysby. By declaring the election null and void Graysby had proved himself no more a democrat than his opponent. Even if he were to win the Presidency he would be little better than Bryant. The battle for freedom would continue. There would be more protests, more shootings, more bombs. More innocent people would be imprisoned.

She was committed now, and must continue her course until the end, even if that meant death. Now that the people had been offered democracy she could not have any part in destroying that ideal, even if it meant the civil war that she had most feared. It was too late to undo what had been done. She had made her choice and now she must see it through, even if ultimately that choice proved to be the wrong one.

While contemplating her fate she drifted into an uncomfortable doze. She no longer felt the cold and the noise from the screen on the table had receded into the background and become part of the pounding ache in her head. She was roused when the door opened and one of the uniformed men entered. He shook her roughly, shouting into her ear.

"Oi! Wake up bitch! It isn't bedtime for you yet."

"I am awake thank you. Since you're here I need the toilet."

"Tough luck!"

He left without another word. Now roused to full consciousness she was aware that she was very much in need of the toilet. She called out several times but there was no response. She tried not to think about it but there was no way she could hold it in indefinitely. Eventually she had no choice but to let go and feel the tingling warmth running down her numb legs. It soaked through the thin gown and cooled, the gown clinging to her. Soon she was shivering uncontrollably.

The reality of the situation came crashing in on her. They could do whatever they wanted to her. No one would stop them. She was freezing cold, soaked in piss and unable to move but she knew things could get far worse. She tried to prevent her mind from wondering and contemplating all the terrible things her immediate future might hold. Overwhelmed by fear she began to cry.

She recalled the camera in the corner of the room. They were watching her. They were waiting for her to break down. If she showed weakness they would use it. She fought back her sobs and dried her eyes by rubbing her face against her shoulder. She remembered some of the accounts she had read of young people held in Re-Education Centres. Innocent youths who had endured years of appalling treatment rather than the hours of discomfort she had so far suffered. Thinking of them gave her strength.

Numbness had spread throughout her body and the blaring noise from the screen sounded distorted, as though she were hearing it underwater. She tried to estimate how long she had been there. Though she felt no hunger she did feel an ache in her stomach which suggested she had not eaten in many hours. She was desperately thirsty, her lips so dry she could feel the skin cracking.

As her eyes began to close she was again shaken awake. DS Dale had returned but not with Hunter, with another man in a dark grey suit. They stood either side of her, studying her critically.

"Well?" demanded Dale. "There must be something you can do."

"Yes but we must take into account the risks," the other man replied.

The screen had been switched off and folded closed. The second man placed a black bag on the desk and removed several items which looked like medical instruments.

"I had better check her over before we do anything. Could you remove the handcuffs?"

The doctor, as she assumed the man to be, took her temperature, pulse and blood pressure and looked in her eyes and mouth.

"I will have to be careful as she is dehydrated and her blood pressure is quite low," the doctor said. "I can give her a small dose of something which may help, but it may just make her sick."

He took a syringe from his bag and injected Rebecca's arm.

"That will make her disoriented and may cause minor hallucinations. Hopefully that will be enough to weaken her resistance but anything else could kill her."

"All right Doctor. Thanks for your help."

As the doctor left, the room began to spin and Rebecca could feel a tickling sensation like hundreds of ants crawling over her skin. The tickling turned to itching, then to stinging. She could see the ants all over her arm and legs. They were biting. She tried franticly to brush them off but more appeared. They were inside her gown and crawling up her back. They began to burrow under her skin. She tried to stand up and shake them off but Dale shoved her back in the chair and replaced the handcuffs.

She closed her eyes tight and tried to concentrate on where she was. She was in the interrogation room and there were no ants, only Dale and the effects of whatever drug the doctor had given her. When she opened her eyes she could no longer see the insects although she still felt the crawling sensation on her skin.

"You know you are guilty," Dale was saying. "Spare yourself and confess. If you think this is bad you have no idea what else I have planned for you."

"Go to hell!"

Now the room was swaying like a ship at sea. There was water trickling down the walls and forming pools on the floor.

"All you have to do is sign a confession and we'll leave you alone."

She shut her eyes again but she could feel the freezing cold water rising around her feet and ankles.

"Come on Becky. You know Bryant will never allow you to be President. The idea is ludicrous. What is the point in suffering like this?"

Now the water was around her knees and rising fast.

"Oh God we're going to drown!"

"Just confess and we'll save you."

But they were not going to drown. There was no water. Dale was standing on firm dry floor; the water was only in her mind. Gradually the sensation of wetness began to disappear but the swaying continued. She felt increasingly nauseous. She bit her lip and swallowed hard. A cold sweat broke out on her face. She retched and could taste bile in her mouth. It burned her throat and threatened to choke her so she was forced to cough it up over the table in front of her.

"You're disgusting!" complained Dale. "I used to think you were attractive but look at you, shaking with fear and stinking of piss and sick. Perhaps I ought to fuck you anyway, just so I have something to tell the lads."

He slid his hand down the front of her gown and roughly grasped her breast.

"Or maybe I should get all the lads in here and let them each have a turn. You would probably like that wouldn't you? Dirty slut like you would take them two at a time, one up the cunt and one up the arse!"

He squeezed until she cried out with pain, then he grabbed her neck, digging his fingers into her throat.

"I'm running out of patience with you. Some of our boys have been killed because of you and your gang of queers, Pakies and slags. Either you confess now or I'll make you really suffer."

"Screw you, bastard!"

He slapped her across the face.

"No bitch, it is you that is going to be screwed!"

He unfastened the handcuffs from the chair and twisting her arm behind her back he pulled her to her feet. Then he forced her forward, slamming her face down on the table. She struggled desperately and kicked, aiming for his groin. She only succeeded in striking his leg but he still cried in pain and anger. He pulled her up by her hair and flung her against the wall. He punched her in the stomach and as she doubled over, shoved her to the floor and kicked her three times.

She was winded and as she tried to catch her breath and get back up he placed his boot on the side of her head and forced her back down. She saw with revulsion and dread that he was unfastening his flies.

"I'll fight," she told herself. "I'll make him beat me unconscious before he does it then at least I won't feel it."

Then in utter horror she felt something wet falling on her face and in her hair. She covered her face with her hands while he urinated over her.

When he had finished he threatened, "Next time I'll make you swallow it!"

He left her. At first she could not move. Then she tried to wipe away the piss with the gown. The stench of it made her retch, but as her stomach was empty she could not vomit. Now she could not stop herself from crying. She gave way to despair and curled herself into a ball, hugging her cold limbs and weeping. Worse than the pain and the humiliation was not knowing when he would return and whether he would carry out his threats.

Consumed by fear she knew she would yield. When that terrible man returned she would confess. If only she could die now before she could betray her supporters. Why had no one thought to provide her with a cyanide capsule or some other means of blissful release? Perhaps if she bit into her wrists she could open a vein and bleed to death. But no, the camera was watching her. They would not let her die without the confession they were taking so much trouble to secure. She must try to find more strength within herself. Perhaps in his impatient rage Dale would go too far and smash her skull before she confessed.

Island Nation Magazine
Saturday 14th September 2115

PHILIP GRAYSBY
Simon Chandra

Although he has always denied it, the general consensus is that Philip Graysby betrayed Rosa. He has repeatedly stated that President Bryant presented him with sufficient evidence to convince him that the election results had been tampered with by the Liberation Party and that he had good reason to declare them void. As this evidence was the testimony of eleven electoral officials who later revealed they were bribed, blackmailed and threatened into making false statements, Graysby was very easily persuaded.

He has always laid the blame for Rosa's arrest and subsequent treatment firmly on Bryant. He denies any knowledge of the pain and humiliation Rosa endured at the hands of the police. He also denies that any kind of bargain was struck between himself and Bryant. He insists that the announcement he made on the day after the election was the truth, that there was to be another election which would be contested honestly and fairly.

That many commentators have expressed doubts about Graysby's assertions is hardly surprising. Throughout his political career Philip Graysby showed himself to be an ambitious man, who forged and broke alliances whenever it suited his purposes. Some sources have suggested that Graysby and Bryant had plans to reunite the Phoenix Party and that Bryant would retire gracefully after a couple of years, allowing Graysby to become President. Other sources allege a second election would have been held but the two of them would predetermine the result so that Bryant would only lose by a very narrow margin. Either way, Graysby's claims to be acting in the best interests of the country would be utterly false.

I find the former leader of Prosperity a difficult man to understand, a much more complex character than John Bryant. Bryant sought wealth and power, they were his dominant motivations. He was not especially intelligent and had no serious ideals or convictions. He pursued policies which were in the interests of the party's financial backers and those which kept power in his hands and not those of the people. Graysby also desired wealth and power, but was this his only goal? His policies were intended to boost the economy and benefit the nation as a whole. He was prepared to allow the people more freedoms at the expense of the President's absolute power.

It could be that had he made it to power, all these pledges would have been forgotten, but I believe that too much work went into Prosperity's manifesto for it just to be empty promises. I believe that Graysby truly desired to be a good President and was so sure that he would be better for the country than either Bryant or Rosa that he was prepared to go against the wishes of the people. Although the arrogance of this is overwhelming, I think that Graysby betrayed Rosa and the electorate because he felt it was for the benefit of Britain. When he spoke of the best interest of the country this was not an empty lie as when Bryant used such phrases, but what he sincerely believed.

This is just my opinion and no doubt many of you are violently disagreeing with me while you read this. On this matter we are decidedly short of facts. We have only Graysby's words. No one close to Graysby has ever spoken out. In fact it seems there were very few people close to Philip Graysby. He was never married and although he had brief relationships with a number of women he never cohabited. In researching this column I have contacted many of his former employees but he never confided his personal feelings to any of them. It is hard to imagine that anyone could go through life without sharing their thoughts and emotions, but this does seem to be the case with Graysby.

According to his memoirs, Graysby had an extremely high regard for Rosa herself even though he did not agree with her party's policies. Her feelings about him are unknown. Prior to her arrest there does appear to have been some sort of understanding between them, perhaps even a friendship of sorts. If she did have genuine esteem for him, his actions must have hurt her greatly. He claims that she did not blame him and that they remained friends until her death. He writes a very moving account of their final conversation on the day of her death. However, although they did meet on that day, other sources including Karen Baker and Alicia Cain have stated that their time together was far too brief for this lengthy and emotional exchange to have occurred. Perhaps these poignant words are what he would have wished to say had he had the opportunity, or maybe they are just some good PR composed with the benefit of hindsight.

I have been unable to discuss any of this with Mr Graysby himself as there has been no response to any of my attempts to contact him. After retiring from politics just over five years ago he moved abroad. His last known address was in southern Spain where he is believed to be living a comfortable but secluded life on the profits from his memoirs. I did consider travelling to Spain in search of him but the cost of such a trip with no guarantee of success prohibited it.

Sunday 5th July 2105

The door opened and two people entered. From where she still lay on the floor, Rebecca could only see their feet. Her first fear was that Dale had returned to carry out his threats but as they approached she saw they were uniformed officers.

"God what a stink!" one complained.

He bent over and shook her.

"Wake up miss," he said. "Come on, on your feet."

The two of them pulled her up with greater care than she had become accustomed to of late.

"We need to get you cleaned up," one said. "We are expecting an important visitor."

Rebecca hardly heard his words and it was only later that she understood the significance of what he had said. As they led her down the corridor, the only thing that registered through the fog in her mind was a slight feeling of relief at being out of that room, even if it was only for a little while. Suddenly she found herself alone in a shower cubicle. There was a towel and a clean gown on a bench opposite. The sight of these two simple items filled her with utter joy. She stripped off the stinking gown and washed thoroughly, even though the water was cold.

As she dried herself vigorously on the thin, rough towel, her head began to clear a little as though she had washed away some of the confusion of drugs and fatigue along with the vomit and urine. Was it possible that the important visitor was John Bryant? If he was coming then he must be prepared to negotiate. She would need to gather her wits and be ready for him.

There was banging on the shower room door and a shout of, "Hurry up, we haven't got all day."

She pulled on the clean gown and ran her fingers through her hair to straighten some of the tangles, then she went out to meet her escort. They took her back to another room, which was so like the first she would have thought it was the same one if it had not been for the variation in the pattern of stains on the table. She felt weak and dizzy, so sat on the chair which was just as hard and uncomfortable as the other but at least they did not handcuff her again. Also this room was much warmer. No arctic gales came from the vent above her head.

One of the policemen fetched a small plastic cup of water, which she drained in a single gulp.

"I don't suppose there is any chance of a cup of tea?" she asked.

"Don't push your luck," he replied.

They left her to enjoy the luxury of being clean and comparatively warm. She struggled to stay awake but her eyelids drooped continually. Eventually the door opened and her illustrious guest arrived, accompanied by Superintendent Hunter. It was indeed John Bryant.

"Dear God Becky!" he exclaimed. "It is terrible seeing you like this."

"If you think this is bad you should have seen me a little while ago."

"Thank you Hunter. You may go now."

"Are you sure sir?" asked the Superintendent. "Perhaps someone ought to stay in the room. For your safety."

"I will be quite safe. Rebecca and I are old friends."

Reluctantly Hunter left and Bryant sat for some time just staring at Rebecca, his eyes displaying a mixture of pity and disappointment. She stared back, her face expressionless. It was the first time they had met face to face since Rebecca had won her seat. He had lost weight since then but the looseness of his skin had caused his wrinkles to deepen. His hair was still dark but she knew that was dye and it was thinner about the temples than previously. He was not dressed with his usual care. His expensive suit was crumpled and his tie was slightly askew. He looked tired and old.

"I thought you and I understood each other Rebecca. When we discussed your political career you seemed so rational and sensible. I thought you were going to be my voice of reason within the Liberation Party."

"I lied."

"Now look at the mess you have made. The whole country is descending into anarchy because of you."

"Because of me or because you and Graysby will not accept the decision of the electorate?"

"Listen Rebecca, people are being killed out there. I want to stop the violence and I am prepared to compromise. Here is the deal. You don't have to confess to being personally responsible for the fraud; just admit that the bribing of officials did occur. Then you name a few people in your party, who you don't like, a few rivals you would like to be rid of, and say they were responsible. We drop the charges against you in return for your help. Then you resign as Liberation leader and have a nice life away from all this. I'll even throw in a sum of money as an extra incentive. Let's say half a million so you can buy a nice place in the country."

"You really are getting desperate aren't you?"

"Come on Becky, I'm offering you the chance to end the violence and not only save your own life but live in peace and comfort."

"Ending the violence is my priority too. Why don't you release the election results and declare me President? That will work."

"You know I am never going to do that."

"All right then, a compromise, but not yours. Here is my offer. I will make a statement saying that electoral officials were bribed and threatened but not by members of my party. I will concede that the election is void and ask my supporters to end their protests. We will then contest a fresh election before the end of the year and I will stand for Liberation. This time there will be no dirty tricks. You can see the people are losing patience with you John. Contest a fair election and lose gracefully or be forced from power in a revolution. Perhaps *you* would like to retire to the country. Surely that would be better than having your naked dismembered corpse dragged through the streets."

"There will be no revolution."

"Are you certain? I don't know what deal you have made with Graysby but he is bound to stab you in the back. He's been sharpening his knife since you first promoted him to the Cabinet and I doubt he is the only one. If one of you has to face the wrath of the public, he will ensure that it is you and not him."

Bryant smiled, but Rebecca knew him well enough to recognise the falsely confident smile, which hid a million anxieties.

"I have the situation under control, I merely wished to spare the country further bloodshed. I will give you an hour to think over my offer, then if you still refuse I will resort to the military option. Tell you what, I'll make it a million pounds, I'm feeling generous."

"Whether it is a million or a billion the answer will still be no. Why don't *you* use the hour to give my proposal some serious consideration? If you were really that confident in your military option you wouldn't be here."

"You underestimate me Rebecca. I am reluctant to use force if I can avoid it. I have been extremely kind to you in spite of your duplicity and malice. I am a compassionate man."

"And how compassionate were you feeling when you ordered Hunter and his men to beat me into confessing?"

He flinched slightly, his broad smile momentarily becoming a grimace but he soon resumed his former expression.

"Do you even know what they have been doing to me John? I dare say it is nothing compared to how they treat other prisoners."

"I loved you. I made you rich and famous but you repaid me with treachery. Did you expect to escape without any punishment? You are fortunate to be alive. Remember that when you think over my offer."

He was no longer smiling as he stood and left the room. As she sat drumming her fingers on the table and waiting for the hour to pass, Rebecca gave no thought at all to the President's proposal. She was only concerned with her own. Bryant's visit had given her hope, but not the lifeline he had offered. Though she believed his promises of freedom and money were in earnest she never, even for a moment, contemplated accepting them. Her own death was still a very possible outcome, but at least the confession was no longer of such great importance and she would be spared Dale's attentions. Compared with what he had threatened, hanging was a welcome alternative.

Though there was no way in which she could judge the amount of time that had passed, she felt certain she had waited for over an hour. If this was so, what was the cause of the delay? Was he seriously considering her bargain or had something occurred to distract his attention? Perhaps the violence had escalated. If only she had some way of knowing what was really going on outside. How many people had actually been injured or killed? What was the mood among her supporters? How far were they prepared to go to resist Bryant?

Finally President Bryant returned. He placed a document on the table in front of her.

"I'm sorry to keep you waiting but you know what lawyers are like," he said. "I believe this agreement should be a satisfactory compromise, so I suggest you sign it."

He spoke without smiling and the tone of his voice revealed he was trying to contain his anger. Evidently things were not going well for him. She made no reply but carefully read the document he had given her. She tried to keep her face impassive but it appeared from the first paragraph that he was agreeing to her terms. Naturally he was not giving in completely and as she read on she saw that Bryant and his advisers had added several conditions of their own.

"If I understand this correctly," she said calmly, "I am to be under house arrest until after the second election. I am to contest the election without being permitted to campaign."

"You will be allowed to campaign using the licensed media once the date for the election has been fixed, but you understand that I wish to avoid any large gatherings which could lead to further violence."

"And when will the election be?"

"The date will be set as soon as the present violence has ceased."

"But it will be before the end of the year?"

"Unless continued violence makes that impossible."

"Very well, I will sign, but you must understand I will only keep to the terms of this agreement as long as you do. If I am not given equal opportunities to campaign through IMC or if I find you are attempting to rig the election in any way, I will ensure that the people are told, even if that means more violence."

"I understand," he replied taking out his pen. "There are two copies so I shall sign one for you. There, are you satisfied?"

"Reasonably; may I borrow your pen?"

He handed it to her. It was the gold one he always used for signing documents. It had been a gift from his wife when he became President and was engraved, "To my dearest John with all my love."

"How is Caroline?" Rebecca asked.

"She is fine. Now sign please, you have wasted enough of my time already."

She signed and gave him back the pen asking, "And how is Annabel? Poor Sophie didn't last very long did she?"

"What is it to you? Are you jealous?"

"No, I pity them."

"So long as neither of them treat me as badly as you have done you will have no cause to pity them. I will have someone call your office to arrange your release. You will be making that statement on your way out so I hope whoever writes your speeches is a fast worker. Goodbye Rebecca."

"See you later John."

As he departed she was overwhelmed with relief. She felt no triumph or elation at securing this compromise as she knew she had much more hard work ahead of her keeping him to his side of the bargain, but it was a temporary reprieve. She wondered just how narrow her escape had been. How close to death had she actually come? Had Bryant honestly intended that she should face the noose or had it just been a threat to secure her confession? There had been something in the way he had avoided looking her in the eye during their conversation which suggested his conscience was troubled. As Bryant's conscience was not easily awakened she feared he must have seriously contemplated her death.

Utterly exhausted, Rebecca flopped forward and rested her head on the table. She closed her eyes and before she realised how tired she was, she was drifting into a dream. She was woken when the door opened and David entered, closely followed by Karen. She leapt from her chair and flung herself into her husband's arms. She was so weak her legs could hardly support her, but it did not matter as he held her tightly and would not let her fall. When she kissed him, his face was wet with tears and she was crying too.

Feeling how weak she was he helped her back to her chair. Brushing her hair back with his fingers he examined the bruises on her face.

"Are you hurt?" he asked. "What have they done to you?"

"I am not seriously harmed, I will be all right. How long have I been here? What has been going on outside?"

"There have been riots everywhere," answered Karen. "The government can't cope. The violence is too widespread for the police or the army to contain it. Several police have been killed and there are rumours of soldiers deserting their posts. The people know they elected you as President and know that Bryant has cheated them. No amount of threats will stop them. But what about you? You have made a deal with him, right?"

"I have, it is the only way to stop the violence."

"What is the deal?"

Rebecca did her best to explain but she was so tired she found it difficult to be coherent.

"Then you haven't confessed?" asked Karen.

"No."

"And you haven't conceded defeat?"

"No, not exactly."

"That is fantastic!" Karen exclaimed. "We are still fighting! Right, we need to work on this speech. We have to make it clear that we intend to win the second election."

"Slow down Karen," said David, "Becky is hurt and exhausted. We need to take care of her before anything else."

"I'll be fine," Rebecca replied. "I just need some fluid and some sugar to get me back on my feet, then if I'm going to talk to the media I'll need something a little more respectable to wear."

"We brought clothes," said Karen, indicating the bag she carried. "There were some vending machines on the way in, I'll get you a drink and some chocolate."

"Thanks. David, will you help me get dressed? Don't worry about the camera, they've seen everything already."

Part 8

Endings and Beginnings

THE FIRST ATTEMPT
Simon Chandra

So where were you at 10:12 am on Sunday 5th July 2105? Like most of the population I was watching television. If you weren't glued to the TV, was it because you were out protesting for Rosa's release, or were you one of the police or soldiers trying to break up the demonstrations? Perhaps you were working in a hospital, treating victims of the riots. At any rate if you were not watching the news channel that morning there must have been a good reason.

The rumours that Rosa was to be released began to circulate at around 7:00 am. The protests subsided and most people returned to their homes to await further news. Only around the MAT Force building where she was believed, but not confirmed, to be held was there still a large crowd, kept back by a cordon of police. At 9:21 Superintendent Patrick Hunter addressed the crowd and an IMC news crew, announcing that the charges had been dropped and that Rosa had been released and would make a statement shortly. Twenty-five minutes later she appeared, accompanied by David O'Brien and Karen Baker. She was smartly dressed in navy blue and cream, her hair tied up and her lips painted their usual deep red.

At the time I don't remember observing the bruises on her face and neck but watching the recording now, the injuries are clearly visible beneath her make-up. She smiled and waved to her supporters before approaching the microphone and beginning her statement. She spoke clearly and confidently giving no impression of having recently been through such a horrendous ordeal. When she firmly stated her intention to fight a second election there was cheering from the crowd. She finished her speech by asking her supporters to return to their homes and end the violence. By the time she had finished speaking, her audience was chanting her name and shouting out messages of support.

A police car was positioned a short distance from the door. This vehicle was to drive her back to Hackney. The crowd had been held back so there was a clear space between the main entrance and the car. Two policemen escorted Rosa and O'Brien to the car while Karen remained behind. Her supporters were still cheering wildly but above the noise of the crowd, two gunshots resounded. Cheering turned to screaming. Watching the IMC footage you see the scene whirl around sickeningly as the cameraman dives for cover. On reaching the safety of the doorway he turns the lens back towards Rosa. She is on the ground. I remember leaping to my feet and screaming as I watched this.

Slowly the police escorts get to their feet and draw their weapons. More police barge past the film crew, shoving them aside. The sound goes dead but the pictures continue. O'Brien is helping Rosa up. Neither appears to be hurt. Keeping low they dash for the car. O'Brien shoves her inside, follows behind, and slams the door. The sound returns and the siren begins to wail. Police force the crowd aside as the car pulls away.

Within an hour Superintendent Hunter again appeared on IMC News announcing that the gunman had been arrested. He is described as a Christian extremist who opposed Liberation's policies on Muslim rights. Since the case never made it to trial as the suspect died in police custody, there has always been a great deal of doubt about this. Although it has never been proved that Bryant had any part in the assassination attempt, there are many suspicious circumstances.

From watching the news report the first question that comes to my mind is, why was the car parked so far from the door? Why did they not bring the car right up to the steps rather than clearing a path through the crowd? Also if you observe the group as they walk to the car you will see that while O'Brien remains very close to Rosa, her police escorts do not. One officer walks ahead while the other lags behind by a significant distance. It is as though they are trying to allow the gunman a clear shot of his target.

The speed and ease with which the police caught the culprit is also rather dubious. The shots were fired from a third floor window of the office block across the street, and the suspect was arrested while attempting to leave the building with the gun still in his possession. If the man were capable of obtaining and using a rifle accurately (ballistics evidence shows the shots only missed by a matter of centimetres), would he really be stupid enough to leave the scene of the crime with the weapon?

Some commentators have suggested that if Bryant had really been intent on killing Rosa he would have been successful. It has been said that with the resources at his disposal, Bryant could have found an assassin who would not have missed. I do not agree with this as it was not a lack of skill by the gunman which saved Rosa's life that day. Her escape was entirely thanks to David O'Brien. I have been studying much footage of the incident, not only the IMC recording but film from CCTV cameras and several members of the crowd who were recording events. From this I have been able to put together a precise picture of what occurred.

Firstly, from the IMC film it is clear that during Rosa's speech, O'Brien's attention is not on her but on their surroundings. As they leave the MAT Force building steps and are escorted toward the car he is looking across the street towards the gunman's location. He must have seen something as he pushes Rosa to the ground a fraction of a second before the first shot is fired. I have watched the recording in slow motion. He is walking holding her arm and repeatedly glancing across the street. He pauses, he says something, then he pushes Rosa to the ground.

CCTV footage shows how he dives down on top of her to protect her. While everyone else is still in confusion he is looking around, getting to his feet and helping Rosa to the car whilst keeping his body between her and the source of the gunshots. His military training was put to good use on that day. Though they are surrounded by armed police officers no one else demonstrates the same presence of mind. There is a definite hesitation before the police react and their first action is to reach for their guns and their radios, not rush to Rosa's aid. There is no doubt in my mind that as her bodyguard and as her husband O'Brien was dedicated to Rosa's protection while the police were at best incompetent and at worst accessories to an attempted murder.

Sunday 5th July 2105

As they reached the safety of the patrol car David slammed the door and addressed the driver.

"If you value your life drive and don't stop for anything; not red lights, not orders from the President, not even a martian invasion."

The policeman turned on the sirens and revved the engine. Slowly the path before the car began to clear and they inched forward. The radio crackled into life.

"446 respond, what is your status, over?"

"This is 446, I'm getting out of here, move these people out of the way."

"Understood, proceed to destination, we will clear the road and send an escort as soon as possible."

"Tell them the gunman was in the building opposite," David instructed. "Third floor, third or maybe fourth window from the right."

The policeman relayed the information while his colleagues parted the crowd and allowed them out onto the road. David's mobile rang.

"We're OK Karen," he said as he answered it. "I don't know, I just want to get Becky to safety... Don't worry, just meet us at our place as soon as you can... I hope so... I'm doing my best... I'll talk to you later."

As soon as he hung up it rang again.

"Hi Sean... No, she's OK... We're on our way now... She should be following... Right see you soon."

This time he switched it off. They reached Parliament Square and were joined by two police motorcycles. Along Whitehall there was no other traffic and they could pick up speed.

"Fasten your seatbelt," David advised, securing his own.

"Just how close was that?" Rebecca asked. "I'm sure I heard the bullet whistle past my ear."

"You did. Are you all right?"

"I don't know, I don't feel too good."

"You need to see a doctor. Fortunately my Dad is in town. He left Peterborough as soon as he heard about your arrest but they closed most of the roads so he didn't make it into the city until this morning."

They were joined by another car and several more motorcycles as they turned down Hackney Road. As the motorcade entered their street they saw there were many more blue flashing lights ahead. The tower block was completely surrounded by police but their car was allowed through and pulled up by the main door.

Uniformed men surrounded the car, waiting to escort Rebecca inside.

"Don't move!" David instructed.

She remained seated in spite of their obvious impatience until David had got out of the car and crossed around to her door. He pushed the policemen aside and helped her out of the car. He led her into the lobby, where yet more police were stationed, and towards the lift. The doors opened and he pushed Rebecca inside but remained in the doorway to prevent the two police officers who were attempting to follow from entering the lift.

"Thank you gentlemen, but we will be fine now," he said firmly.

"Our orders are to escort Miss Clayton to her flat," replied one officer, positioning his hand ready to draw his gun.

David stepped back, allowing them to enter the lift but kept himself between them and Rebecca. The lift ascended slowly, rattled to a halt and the doors opened. Two more armed men were ready to receive them. The police officer smirked at David, confident in his superior man and gun power.

"Follow me please Miss Clayton," he said.

"Thank you but I do know where I live," she replied.

"These precautions are for your safety."

Flanked by their armed escort they followed the officer to their door. David unlocked it and allowed Rebecca inside but stopped the police officer from following.

"Mr O'Brien, are you obstructing me in my duty?" demanded the officer.

"You said your instructions were to escort Miss Clayton to her flat. You have done so."

"I would like to check the security of the interior, for her safety."

"I will see to that."

"It would be better done by professionals."

"I am a professional."

There was a stand-off as the police officer attempted to intimidate David into backing down. They stared at each other until eventually the officer decided it was not worth the effort and he turned away. David slammed the door and bolted it, sighing with relief.

Sean Nichols, Stacey Barnes and Nathaniel O'Brien were all assembled in the flat awaiting their return.

"No one opens this door without my permission," David instructed. "Becky, I want you to stay away from the windows and don't eat or drink anything I haven't prepared for you."

Rebecca sat down on the sofa feeling dizzy and nauseous. Around her everyone was talking at once and she could not make out what anyone was saying. The phone was ringing and Sean was asking her a question but she felt too weak to even raise her head to look at him. Then she heard David's reassuring voice cutting through the confusion.

"That's enough people!" he shouted. "Dad, take Becky into the bedroom and check her over. I want you to photograph any bruises or injuries so we have evidence against those bastards. Becky, when you are feeling well enough I want you to tell me exactly what they did to you, every detail. I know you don't want to talk about it now but the sooner you get it over with the easier it will be."

"I don't mind talking about it," she replied faintly, "but not to you."

"Not to me! Becky, I'm your husband!"

"Precisely, it will upset you too much."

"Upset me! Someone just tried to kill you! I'm already upset!"

Nathaniel intervened, "You can talk about this later. Becky is exhausted."

"OK," David agreed, "you see to her. I'd better make some calls."

Rebecca allowed the doctor to take her arm and lead her through to the bedroom. He closed the door, muffling the sounds of discussions and arguments still continuing in the living-room. She sat down on the edge of the bed and he checked her temperature, pulse and blood pressure.

"It is fortunate you're here," she remarked. "What made you come?"

"I was worried about you. When I heard you had been arrested I was afraid of what would happen to you and I just wanted to be with my son. The trains weren't running so I borrowed a friend's car and hit the road. I met a load of road blocks around Barnet and had to turn back. I ended up driving around in circles for most of Saturday until I was forced to pull into an old service area off the M25 by a police patrol.

"There were quite a few cars trying to get into the city. More than I have seen on the roads since I was a kid. They were all forced to stop for the night. The hotel and restaurants had been closed for years so we all had to sleep in our cars but there was at least a garage selling coffee and some food. The police let us back onto the road early this morning but advised us not to go into the city. I ignored them, taking a very tortuous route across country and then through the back streets until I eventually got here."

"I'm glad you did."

"I see there is some bruising on your face and neck, is it painful?"

"Not very, but my wrists are quite sore."

She showed him the marks where the handcuffs had rubbed her skin raw.

"That does look rather tender. I'd better take some pictures as instructed. Can you show me where else you are hurt?"

After he had photographed her wrists, cheek and neck, she undressed and allowed him to inspect the bruises on her arms, legs, stomach, back and around her right breast. As he touched and examined her, pressing on the tender spots and checking the severity of the injuries, it occurred to her that his hands were exactly like David's. Both men had large, strong hands with broad fingers but their touch was surprising gentle.

"Did David never consider being a doctor?" she asked.

"I don't think so. He spent most of his childhood listening to me complaining about the NHS so I expect that put him off at an early age. Why do you ask?"

"I was just thinking that he would have made a very good doctor."

"I believe he would have. He was certainly smart enough to study medicine. One of the reasons I was so annoyed with him for joining the army was that I felt he was wasting his intellect."

"If he had been a GP like you, things would have been very different and I doubt I would have ever met him, so I suppose I'm glad he made the choices he did, in spite of everything."

"I never did understand how exactly the two of you got together. The way David tells the story it sounds like he was stalking you."

"He sort of was. At first I thought he was a nutcase."

"What changed your mind?"

"You know, I'm not exactly sure. He was just there when I needed him, like he was today. You know in dumb romantic stories when the heroine says she can't live without the man she loves, that she would die without him, in my case it is probably true. He has already saved my life twice."

"Well, in spite of all these injuries you still seem to be in one piece. I haven't found any broken bones or signs of internal bleeding. I would recommend some painkillers and a topical gel or lotion to tackle the inflammation. I'll have a look what David has in his cupboard and perhaps pop out to the chemist if you need anything else. In the meantime the best thing you could do is get some rest."

"I intend to. I don't think I have ever felt so tired."

"I will try to persuade them to keep the noise down out there."

Rebecca retrieved a nightgown from her bottom drawer and pulled it on. The one she had been wearing at the time of her arrest had not been returned to her. Nathaniel plumped up the pillows and pulled the covers over her as she lay down, like a loving father tucking his child up for the night. She felt a strange longing for something she had never had. She had never known her father and could not remember her mother ever putting her to bed. He smoothed her hair and kissed her on the forehead before leaving the room.

As she lay drifting into sleep she felt envious of David for having such a father and almost angry with him for not appreciating what he had. Although the quarrel between them had been patched up and they now spoke regularly there was still a residual tension. David was always defensive when conversing with his father and quick to interpret every remark as a criticism.

Nathan had always been a little awkward with Rebecca also. He talked to her rather formally and never seemed to be quite at ease. When they met there was usually that uncomfortable moment when he never quite knew whether he should hug and kiss her or not. He would embrace her briefly and perhaps place a tentative kiss on her cheek, but the gesture was more one of obligation than affection. It was as though as her father in law he knew he ought to greet her with a kiss but was embarrassed about doing so.

That last kiss though had been different. It had been all affection and no awkwardness. Perhaps seeing her naked and hurt had made him love her. She hoped so. He was a good man and she wanted his love. He had always expressed his admiration and respect for her but she already had the respect and admiration of many. Love she had only from David. She found love was rather like olives. Once she had discovered how good it was she wanted more.

*

When Rebecca awoke, she felt as though she had only just closed her eyes but the clock told her she had been asleep for over three hours. David was sitting on the edge of the bed, watching her for signs of consciousness.

Once her eyes were open he said, "I hate having to wake you, you looked so peaceful and snug. I've brought you a cup of tea by way of consolation. I would have let you sleep but there are some people here I want you to meet."

"Who?"

"They're in the living-room. Come and see."

There was something slightly impatient and excited about David's manner which aroused Rebecca's curiosity. She took a sip of tea and put on David's robe; her own, like her nightdress, was still in police custody. She followed David through to the living-room and was both surprised and alarmed to see three soldiers standing there.

"Rebecca, I would like you to meet Major Thomas Stanford, Captain Oliver Jenkins and Lieutenant Aaron Pierce of Seventh Interior Division."

All three soldiers were wearing grey and black urban combat fatigues but Rebecca was relieved that they did not appear to be carrying weapons. She was rather bewildered but shook hands with each of the men in turn.

"It is a great honour to meet you Miss Clayton," said Major Stanford, who was a tall sandy haired man with a broad neck and square jaw.

"Tom and I served together when I was in the army," David explained.

"Indeed, you were a damn good officer and sorely missed," Stanford replied, "but we aren't here to reminisce. Things are getting a little tense outside. Your supporters have ignored all the threats and warnings and are still protesting. There is a huge mob gathered just down the street, desperate to see you and to know you are all right. The Ministry of Defence is concerned that the police can't cope and has requested that the military take over responsibility for the security of this building."

"I understand," Rebecca replied although she did not really see why any of this was particularly significant as it made little difference to her whether it was the police or army which was guarding her; she was still under house arrest.

Stanford continued, "What I want you to know is that my own personal priority is ensuring your safety. When I joined the army I swore to defend the democratic government of this country. I do not believe that oath binds me to the Phoenix Party when they are no longer the democratically elected government. At present I am here under orders from the Ministry of Defence but if I should receive any orders which I feel would endanger your life or compromise the forthcoming election, I will disobey. I have discussed this with my fellow officers and I have their support."

Captain Jenkins and Lieutenant Pierce both nodded their heads in agreement.

"While you were asleep, Tom and I have been discussing how best to keep you safe," said David. "The police thugs have withdrawn and Seventh Interior is now surrounding the building, guarding the doors, the lifts and the stairs. There is even a man out on the balcony and three more on the roof."

"One of my boys will check any mail that comes for you and we will bring in any provisions you need," said the Major. "We've been round the rest of the flats in the block and warned your neighbours that they might wish to move out for a while. Most have agreed to go to friends or family as life is going to be a bit difficult for any who stay. They won't like having to pass through three security checks each time they pop out to buy a pint of milk."

"I was only asleep for a few hours," remarked Rebecca. "You seem to have got all this organised very quickly."

"We've done our best," Stanford responded. "Captain Jenkins is our communications man. The police will be monitoring your computer and phone so he will set up a secure line for you."

"I can't promise it will be completely safe from eavesdroppers," said Jenkins, "but it will take some time and effort for them to hack into it. I recommend you conduct your most important conversations in person. We will ensure that anyone you need to talk to can get in through the police cordon."

"Thank you gentlemen," Rebecca replied. "I see your help is going to be extremely valuable."

"Damn right," David agreed. "You have no idea what a relief it is having you on our side. At least now we stand some chance of defending ourselves against whatever the bastards throw at us."

KEEPING THE PEACE
Simon Chandra

It is rather too easy for us in the media to cast the police and armed forces as the villains in the drama of the country's fight for democracy. Certainly a great many atrocities were committed by those who were supposed to be defending us and keeping the peace. There were countless incidents of police brutality and innumerable examples of the use of excessive force against unarmed civilians. Taking the security forces as a whole, regarding them as a single organism, they did indeed deserve to be branded as evil, but the reality is far more complex. Both the police and military consisted then, as always, of diverse individuals. Most of these men and women in their own way were striving to do what was right, whether that meant serving their country out of a sense of patriotic duty or just earning a living and feeding their families.

Many police and military personnel have spoken about their experiences during those weeks of political unrest, but I feel that journalists have been too focused on the major figures and have paid too little attention to the PCs and privates who made up the majority of the front line. Most of these people were constantly treading a fine line between obeying orders and obeying their consciences. One of these was former Police Constable Mark Bainbridge. Mr Bainbridge left the police force in 2106 and has worked in insurance ever since. He contacted me by email several weeks ago and described some of his experiences following the general election in July 2105. We exchanged several emails and phone calls and finally met for a coffee a couple of days ago.

Bainbridge joined the Metropolitan Police after leaving college at eighteen.

"I didn't know much about politics at the time," he told me. "I just wanted a secure job with a decent wage and prospects for promotion. My mother had cancer so my family was pretty hard up. I knew every penny my parents had was needed for my mum's treatment so I had to take care of myself. I wasn't particularly ambitious. I spent the first year or so on curfew patrol, railway security, road side check points and the usual routine stuff. I was happy enough. I never worried about civil liberties or whether all this security was really necessary. I believed what I was told, that we were there to protect London from terrorists.

"I was aware of the protests over Re-education Centres and of various disturbances in the wake of the Bradford riots but I wasn't involved in any of that. My rather dull life only changed after the election. I was on curfew patrol in Hackney the night Rosa was arrested. Of course I wasn't told anything about the arrest before it happened. My partner on patrol, Joe Evans and I were just ordered to go to her tower block and ensure no one left the building.

"After the MAT Force men had taken Rosa away Evans and I helped to quieten things down and get the rest of the residents to return to their flats. I was pretty naïve. Although I had voted for Rosa I actually believed that she must have done something to warrant her arrest. I remember telling Evans how disappointed I was. He was a couple of years older than me and a little less green. He laughed and called me an idiot so we argued. We had been working long hours and were both tired and short-tempered. By the time we were eventually relieved and were able to go home to our beds we were no longer on speaking terms.

"The following evening we were both back on duty at Rosa's block. It was a very long, tedious, uneventful night and as Evans and I still weren't speaking we didn't even have much conversation to pass the time. Most of the other officers on duty there were MAT Force and they looked down on us regular bobbies. They took all the easy jobs like watching the lifts and the stairs, while we had to do all the legwork, patrolling the streets in the rain. I tried making conversation with one of the MAT sergeants to find out more about what was going on but he just told me to mind my own business.

"By the early hours of Sunday morning I was fed up. I was soaking wet, tired and longing to be home, but when the time came when I should have been relieved I was told I had to stay as more manpower would be needed. They didn't explain why, just issued the orders. When a load more Special Forces thugs arrived I guessed Rosa was going to return. I wish I had seen her arrive, that would have given me something to tell my kids about, but I was sent around the back to watch the fire exit. After pissing down all night it then turned into one of the hottest days of the year and I was roasting under my flak jacket and sweating buckets. I was stuck out in the sun for hours until the army arrived.

"When an armoured car turned up and one of the soldiers said he was taking over the watch I didn't question it. I went to find Evans and the others from our station hoping this meant I could go home. When I returned to the front of the building I found the MAT Force Chief Inspector having a blazing row with one of the army officers. From what I overheard they both seemed to be under the impression that they were in charge. The Seventh Interior chap must have won because we were given orders to withdraw to the end of the street and set up a roadblock. The end result was that the police were manning an outer cordon about fifty metres from the Rosa's building while the army had jurisdiction within.

"That was how the situation remained for weeks. I spent every shift manning the roadblock and patrolling the neighbourhood in a circuit centred on the tower block. It was unbelievably dull. The hostility between the police and army was utterly ridiculous. It was easy to forget we were supposed to be on the same side. Whenever army vehicles passed through our checkpoint we had to verify the identities of everyone on board. After a few days I began to recognise most of the soldiers but my superiors insisted I had to check their name, rank and serial number against the computer records every time.

"Frequently one of the MAT Force morons would find some pathetic excuse to delay the soldiers, like finding a fault with their brake lights or insisting someone did not look like their photograph and demanding further proof of identity. The soldiers started to get their own back by demanding to see our warrant cards before they would deal with us. There were frequent exchanges of insults. I think some of my colleagues actually enjoyed these puerile games and childish name-calling. I suppose it was one way to pass the time. I just found it pointless and depressing.

"All this time we were waiting for Bryant to announce when the second election was to be held. After Rosa's release the riots had subsided but there were still some protests. We often had Liberation supporters gathering at our cordon demanding to see Rosa. Bryant used these incidents as an excuse not to call the election. After a fortnight the people began to lose patience. There were more demonstrations and some violence. Bryant made the situation worse by announcing that because of this disorder he would not name the date of the election for at least another week.

"One day, about the beginning of August I think, the protestors broke through our cordon in spite of our efforts to hold them back. We were ordered to open fire. I obeyed but I only fired above the heads of the demonstrators. I knew I would never be able to live with the guilt of killing someone, no matter what the orders were. The soldiers held them back from entering the building but could not or perhaps would not break up the mob. Eventually Rosa appeared on her balcony and addressed the crowd. I deserted my position and went to hear what she had to say.

"From where I stood at the back of the crowd I could barely see her and although she used a megaphone I could only just hear her above the other noise around me. She begged her supporters to be patient and to return to their homes but she promised that the date for the election would be announced before the end of the month. She said that Bryant had given his word and that she was determined to see that he did not break it.

"Most of the crowd dispersed after she had given these assurances, but I wondered how she was going to force Bryant to keep his promise and I was afraid of what would happen when he broke it. It took us nearly three hours to move on or arrest the remaining protestors. Several put up violent resistance.

The army helped us with the most belligerent troublemakers and eventually peace was restored. Lieutenant Pierce helped me to load the last of the demonstrators into the van. I thanked him for his assistance.

"'No problem,' he replied. 'Are you going to have enough cells for that lot?'

"'I doubt it, but that is someone else's problem,' I answered.

"By this time I was really starting to hate my job. The abuse from the protestors and the insults from the soldiers were getting to me as well as the heat and the long hours, and I was finding it hard to see the point in what I was doing. If Bryant wanted to keep the peace he should have held the election he had promised and stopped making excuses. In the meantime, the woman the vast majority of people wanted to see as President was being imprisoned in the tower block down the street for reasons which were utterly beyond me.

"'How is Rosa?' I asked the Lieutenant.

"'She is OK. This is a pretty stressful time for her, as you can imagine, but she seems to be holding up pretty well.'

"'Do you think Bryant will call the election?' I enquired.

"'I doubt it. Even if he does he will find some excuse to cancel it or delay it further, and then there will be trouble.'

"'What can Rosa do?" I asked.

"'She will have to do something,' he replied. 'She can't carry on like this indefinitely. The last thing she wants is more violence but she can't keep appealing for calm and promising the election will be soon. Her supporters will lose patience. If Bryant breaks his promise again I fear there will be the worst riots this country has seen in years and we may be right in the middle of it!'

"'This is just shit!' I complained.

"'I know," replied the Lieutenant sympathetically. 'This isn't what you joined the police for, shooting unarmed civilians. It isn't why I joined the army either. A word of advice; if Hunter sends in his goons to arrest Rosa again stay well away.'

"'Why? What is going to happen?' I asked.

"'I'm afraid I can't talk about it,' he answered, 'but you seem like a decent sort of guy, so when the shit hits the fan be as far away as possible.'

"I guessed from this warning that the soldiers intended to resist any future attempt to arrest Rosa. I was pleased they were taking her side but I was also apprehensive. So far during the riots the police had only come up against unarmed civilians. Once faced with armed soldiers there were bound to be many more casualties, hence the Lieutenant's warning.

"I took the Lieutenant's advice. A couple of weeks later I was in an altercation with a protestor trying to get past our cordon. I was only slightly injured but I chose to remain off work for the next seven days, claiming to be more seriously hurt. This probably seems very cowardly. I don't pretend to be particularly brave, but I believe I would have been prepared to risk my life and done my duty had I not felt I was on the wrong side. There are causes worth fighting for but Bryant's government was not one of them. I suppose if I had been a heroic young man I would have joined the soldiers and fought to defend Rosa, but I was no hero. I was just an ignorant young man who wanted to stay alive."

Wednesday 2nd September 2105

The seconds ticked by with agonising slowness as Rebecca sat watching the clock. She used to love this room filled with all David's books and plants but after spending nearly two months confined to the block she had begun to loathe the sight of those four walls. The pain in her stomach made sitting uncomfortable but she felt dizzy and nauseous when she stood and was too restless with anxiety to lie down.

She took a sip of water, her hands trembling as she held the glass. Still the second hand had not completed its full circuit. Every minute seemed to be passing slower than the last. Though the clock on the wall and her watch both confirmed it had only been twenty-three minutes since David had left the flat she felt he had been gone for hours.

At least she was not alone. Corporal Lee was standing by the door exactly as David had asked him to do. With perfect military discipline the young man had barely moved a muscle or made a sound during the entire time. An occasional cough or the movement of the shadow against the blinds betrayed the presence of the other man on the balcony.

Rebecca opened her laptop and glanced at the paragraph which was all she had succeeded in writing that morning. It was supposed to be a statement for the media, both legal and unlicensed, but she was having difficulty concentrating. What she was trying to say was that she no longer recognised Bryant's authority as President, but while the police were still acting on his orders it was hard to dispute that he was still in power. Her protests that he had no right to that power seemed feeble and irrelevant.

Early that morning Superintendent Hunter had arrived with several squad cars and a warrant for her arrest. Major Stanford had refused to allow him entry to the building. Threats had been exchanged but as yet no shots had been fired. It was a stand-off which had so far lasted for over three hours.

At least this time she was guilty of the crimes of which she was accused. The warrant was for providing information to the unlicensed media. When the end of August deadline had passed and Bryant had still refused to set the date for the election, Rebecca had sent a statement to IMC News saying she considered the President to have broken his agreement with her, therefore she was no longer bound by it and could communicate with the media. IMC naturally refused to broadcast this statement so she sent it to the underground media, which released it immediately.

Finally David returned. Corporal Lee changed position to outside the living-room door, closing it behind him.

"What news?" Rebecca demanded as her husband took a seat beside her.

"No change, just a lot of very nervous people staring at each other with their fingers on triggers. Sooner or later someone's nerves will crack and the shooting will start. Tom's men have the advantage at the moment. Hunter has slightly more men but our guys are in a better position as they have the building for cover and elevation."

"Do you think Hunter is waiting for reinforcements?"

"Probably. More men wouldn't improve Hunter's position but if he had helicopters or heavy artillery… "

David tailed off, not wanting to finish.

"When it comes to that I will give myself up," replied Rebecca. "There is no point in us all dying."

"The Major won't let you do that, nor will I."

"For God's sake David, you know this is exactly what I most wanted to avoid. I don't want people throwing their lives away because of me."

"I know, but it is too late now. Tom and his men have chosen to fight for you. You have to respect their decision."

"Are you saying that if I attempt to give myself up they will physically stop me?"

"Probably, I certainly will."

"What about the other residents of this block? Are you going to let them be killed in the crossfire?"

"No of course not. They have all been evacuated."

They sat in silence as more slow seconds ticked by, Rebecca contemplating the hopelessness of the situation and desperately trying to think of a solution while David faced their inevitable defeat with stoic resignation.

Eventually David broke the silence with his usual pragmatism.

"Would you like a cup of tea?"

"No thanks, I still feel sick."

"How about ginger tea then? That is supposed to be good for nausea."

"No thanks."

"Try it, it can't hurt."

"All right."

While David was busy in the kitchen there was a knock at the door. Corporal Lee answered it and announced Major Stanford.

"Good timing!" David called from the kitchen as the Major entered the living-room, "I've just put the kettle on, do you want tea?"

"No thanks, I just came to inform you of some news," Stanford replied.

His face was grim so Rebecca knew the news was not good.

"Are you all right ma'am?" he enquired, "You look rather pale."

"My nerves are getting the better of me," she replied. "I haven't had much sleep the past few nights and I'm feeling a little sick, but it is nothing serious."

"Well I'm afraid what I have to say isn't going to make you feel any better."

David joined them, anxious to hear the news.

The Major began, "I have heard a report that the 12th Coastal Defence Unit has been mobilised. They are heading into the city. That means tanks, helicopters, rocket launchers, the lot. I don't know for sure but I am willing to bet they will be coming here. The way things are at present it may take a while to get a tank through the streets of Hackney but I expect they will be here before the day is out."

"Shit!" David swore, then he sighed and said, "We knew it would happen sooner or later. The question is how best to defend Rebecca. Where in the building is she going to be safest?"

"Sadly nowhere in this crumbling mass of concrete and chipboard is going to be particularly safe. There isn't a basement but the storage cupboard beneath the stairs on the ground floor is probably the most structurally sound place."

"I'm going to need a gun," said David, "there is no way I'm going out without a fight."

"Sure," replied Stanford. "You still remember how to use one?"

"It will come back to me. I'm probably still a better shot than you at any rate."

Their exchange of bravado was interrupted by the phone ringing. Rebecca answered it and was surprised to hear the voice of Philip Graysby.

"Good morning Mr Graysby," she said, forcing herself to sound calm and businesslike. "I assume you received my letter concerning the election."

"I did," he replied, "and I am calling to tell you that I share your concern over Bryant's refusal to set a date."

"I see, and what, if anything, do you intend to do about it?"

"As Bryant appears to have no intention of keeping his promise of holding a free and fair election I will shortly be releasing a statement in which I will renounce my objections to the results of the previous election and ask that they be regarded as valid."

Rebecca almost dropped the phone. "Would that not mean recognising me as the President of the United Kingdom?"

"Exactly so, on the condition that you acknowledge there is some doubt over the validity of the result and agree to hold another ballot within a year. In the meantime I will assume the role of leader of the opposition."

"I will gladly agree to that condition, but I have a rather pressing problem at present. The police and military are still taking their orders from Bryant."

"I am aware of this and have been in contact with several senior officers. General Wallace of Interior Defence has expressed concern about Bryant's abuses of power and is anxious to talk to you. Also Commissioner Brown has contacted me. He believes that Bryant's policy of delaying the election is contributing to the violence and unrest."

"What about Coastal Defence? I understand they are still loyal to Bryant."

"I have not been able to speak with General Stewart yet. I believe if Brown and Wallace are prepared to accept your authority, he will also."

"Then perhaps you would tell me how I may contact those gentlemen."

"You can expect a call from both very soon. I have taken the liberty of giving them this number."

"Why this sudden change of heart Graysby?"

"I have not changed. I have always wanted what is best for the country. I do not believe that Bryant has the country's interests at heart any longer and am hoping that you do."

"You can trust me to keep my promises. You cannot say that I have ever dealt dishonestly or unfairly with you."

"No, you have not. Good luck Rebecca. I hope we shall meet again very soon, perhaps in parliament."

"I hope so. Goodbye Mr Graysby and thank you."

After putting down the phone it took Rebecca some time to absorb the full impact of what this meant. Both David and the Major were standing expectantly waiting for her to explain, but she had to compose herself before she could speak to them. Her legs felt weak so she resumed her seat on the sofa.

"That was good news I think," she said hesitantly. "According to Graysby, General Wallace and Commissioner Brown are beginning to question Bryant's authority. It would appear that Graysby has also lost patience with Bryant's refusal to relinquish the Presidency and is again prepared to bargain with me. He says both Wallace and Brown will contact me shortly. It would seem everything now depends on persuading them to support me."

Before either David or Stanford could respond the phone was ringing.

THE NEW PRESIDENT
Simon Chandra

At 10:45 am on Wednesday 2nd September, Philip Graysby made a statement live on the IMC News channel in which he stated his support for Rosa as President of the United Kingdom. Bryant immediately responded with a written statement condemning Graysby's actions and accusing him and Rosa of conspiring to destroy democracy and create a state of anarchy. Peter Sheridan had only just finished reading this statement when they switched to another live broadcast, a statement from the Commissioner of the Metropolitan Police, Anthony Brown. Brown announced that he too recognised Rosa's authority as President. The warrant for her arrest was cancelled and the police would ultimately take their orders from her government.

11:07 am: General George Wallace of Interior Defence issued his statement of allegiance to Rosa's government. He warned that his units would defend Rosa with all necessary force even if that meant firing on fellow soldiers. Though he mentioned no names, this advice was obviously intended for General Stewart, whose Coastal Defence Units were en route to the capital at that time.

11:22 am: Rosa herself addressed the nation live from her flat in Hackney. She thanked the people for their support and promised to serve them faithfully as their President. She announced that she and her fellow MPs would be travelling immediately to Westminster to take their seats in the Commons. A few minutes later, escorted by 7th Interior soldiers, she left the tower block where she had been a prisoner for the past two months, climbed into the back of an armoured car and began her journey. Several police cars and motorcycles joined the convoy, which progressed extremely slowly as huge crowds choked the route, desperate to catch a glimpse of their new President.

While all this was happening Bryant had not left Downing Street. In spite of Commissioner Brown's statement, Bryant's protection officers remained loyal to him. Neither the police nor the military made any attempts to enter Downing Street at that time, as their attention was focused on Parliament and attempting to clear a route in expectation of Rosa's triumphant arrival. There were many angry citizens gathered at the railings however, protesting at Bryant's continued presence in what was now Rosa's official residence.

Alicia Cain was one of the first to reach St James' Palace, shortly followed by Philip Graysby. A brief conference was held between them while IMC and RNN cameras observed. They agreed not to enter the building until Rosa arrived as she ought to lead the way. Afterwards Graysby insisted this was entirely Cain's idea and that he wanted to wait in Westminster Hall to welcome Rosa on her arrival, but Cain does not recall him making any such suggestion.

12:37 pm: a procession of vehicles festooned with Liberation Party banners entered Parliament Square, which by this time was packed with onlookers who greeted Rosa's motorcade with rapturous cheers. The armoured car pulled up close to the main entrance. Rosa got out flanked, by O'Brien and Major Stanford of 7th Interior Division. She greeted Alicia Cain, embracing her warmly, shaking hands and exchanging a few words with Graysby. Then Rosa waved to the crowd, turned and led the way up the steps and into the Houses of Parliament.

She had one foot over the threshold when the gunshots rang out. She was hit and fell. Several soldiers, including Major Stanford, rushed forward through the open doorway while O'Brien remained with Rosa. He and the driver lifted Rosa into the back of the armoured car. The crowd begin pushing forward desperately trying to catch a glimpse inside the vehicle. More soldiers tried to clear a path to allow the car through and slowly Rebecca was conveyed away.

There was no further shooting. At 12:52 pm Major Stanford declared the interior secure and Alicia Cain led her fellow Liberation MPs into Parliament, followed by Graysby and the Prosperity Party, then the Christian Alliance, Muslim Democrats, Gay Rights and all the rest. There was muted cheering from the crowd but without Rosa leading the way the triumph was greatly diminished.

The atmosphere in Parliament Square grew tense and restless while the people waited for news of their President. At 2:04 pm Alicia Cain addressed the crowd and the media from the steps of St James' Palace. She announced that Rosa had been killed instantly by a single shot to the chest. Many of those hearing this news cried out in rage or broke down and wept. Cain herself was dry eyed as she climbed into an armoured car and was carried away to an unspecified location.

*

In the days that followed, grief rapidly turned to confusion. First it emerged that Rosa had never arrived at St Thomas' Hospital, the closest A&E department to Parliament. There was also the fact that Rosa had been wearing a military flak jacket, so a single shot to the chest should not have proved instantly fatal. The moments after Rosa fell were not recorded by the IMC or RNN crews as after she was hit the crowd surged forward obscuring their view, but the following day, film of those moments was released.

Several people in the crowd had cameras and had been recording the incident, one piece of footage clearly showing Rosa bleeding from a wound to the left shoulder and still very much alive as she clings to O'Brien's arm with her right hand. This sequence is only a few seconds long as the camerawoman lost her position in the jostling crowd and Rosa's face cannot be clearly seen, but when broadcast it was enough to cast serious doubt on Cain's account.

Then there was the question of Rosa's body. Where was it? Who had signed the death certificate? When would the post mortem examination be carried out and by whom? It was at this time that the first conspiracy theories began to emerge.

Alicia Cain had issued no further statements concerning Rosa's death but had assumed leadership of the Party on returning to Parliament at around four o'clock on the afternoon of the shooting. She immediately convened a meeting with police and army chiefs. This meeting precipitated the arrest of several prominent figures, including Superintendent Hunter of MAT Force.

Prior to Hunter's arrest, MAT Force had ignored Commissioner Brown's statement and continued to act on Bryant's orders but had been powerless without the support of the regular police force. They had been prevented from arresting Rosa that morning by Major Stanford's men and had been awaiting reinforcements from the 12th Coastal Division based at Sheerness, when Brown had issued his statement and ordered them to stand down. With the whole of the Interior Defence Force against them, rather than just Stanford's Division, and without the support of the local police, they were obliged to withdraw to their Headquarters. 12th Coastal advanced as far as the M25 where their progress was halted by 5th Interior Regiment. Although the Coastal Defence Division had superior fire power they were reluctant to open fire on fellow soldiers. They held their position, awaiting developments.

Bryant remained under siege in Downing Street until noon on Friday, when General Wallace dispatched heavy artillery to aid the police in his arrest. For a few tense hours it looked as though Number 10 would be reduced to a pile of rubble, but Bryant eventually chose surrender rather than a glorious death. After Bryant's arrest, General Stewart finally stated his allegiance to the new government and recalled his Coastal Defence troops. Bryant's trial and sentence are of course still a major source of controversy, but I personally feel that Cain was right to abolish capital punishment for all crimes, including his.

By Saturday, Cain could no longer ignore the questions about Rosa's death. She made a statement to the Commons which was broadcast live to the nation in which she explained that she had been misinformed of some of the circumstances and apologised for misleading the public. She promised that the doctor who treated Rosa would make a full statement later that day, answering all the questions and explaining the irregularities.

The full statement when it was made was not short on bombshells. The doctor who had treated Rosa was Nathaniel O'Brien, David O'Brien's father. Dr O'Brien had been staying with his son and Rosa during her period of confinement. He had accompanied them in the armoured car on the journey to Westminster so was at the scene to administer first aid immediately after the shooting. They had intended to take Rosa straight to St Thomas' but the crowds on Westminster Bridge made the direct route completely impassable.

They took a detour via Waterloo Bridge, a journey which took over half an hour because of the dense throngs of people on the embankment and blocking the bridge. While en route they learnt that the A&E department was so overloaded with casualties after days of violence that it had been forced to close its doors to incoming patients. Crawling through the vast crowds surging towards Westminster, it would have taken hours for them to reach the Royal London Hospital. Instead Dr O'Brien instructed the driver to take them to a small private clinic off Blackfriars Road which was owned and run by a friend of his.

The clinic specialised in minor surgery and elective procedures. It had been closed during the recent unrest following the election so there were currently no staff or patients present. Dr O'Brien was able to contact his friend, who was out of town, and get the security codes to enter the building. Dr O'Brien believed that with the drugs and equipment available at the clinic he would be able to stabilise her condition and make her comfortable until she could be conveyed to hospital.

Unfortunately, shortly after arriving at the clinic the bullet dislodged from the muscle tissue of Rosa's shoulder and entered the aorta, restricting blood flow to her heart and causing cardiac arrest. All efforts at resuscitation failed and she died. Distraught with grief, David O'Brien had been unable to face the glare of publicity which would follow. He could not bear the media frenzy over the post mortem and funeral arrangements. In order to protect his son, Nathaniel O'Brien took actions which were both illegal and unethical. Using a combination of bribery and forged documents he arranged to have Rosa's remains cremated the following morning. David left the city and was not seen or heard of again for more than two years.

Although Dr O'Brien's behaviour was met with intense criticism, no charges were ever brought against him. President Cain, as she was officially by then, defended him against accusations that his negligence or incompetence were to blame for her death and the unauthorised disposal of her body was a cover-up. She insisted he had done everything possible to save Rosa and that the rapid, discreet cremation was what she would have wanted rather than a public funeral.

The gunman who fired the fatal bullet was shot dead by Major Stanford's men seconds after Rosa fell. He was eventually identified as Alistair Cartwright, one of the Special Forces police officers responsible for the security of the Houses of Parliament. In the subsequent investigations Cartwright's colleagues revealed he had an extreme hatred of homosexuals. It is generally accepted that he chose to kill Rosa out of personal motives, violent opposition to her policies on gay rights, rather than on the orders from Bryant or anyone else. His death however means there will always be some room for doubt.

In fact, ten years afterwards, there is still a great deal of doubt about the circumstances of Rosa's death. There are an immense number of different conspiracy theories, ranging from the plausible to the just about possible to the completely bizarre. I will begin exploring some of these in my column next week but for now I wish to close with a few of my own feelings.

In researching these articles over the past few weeks I feel I have got to know Rosa. I believe she was intelligent, courageous and truly cared about the British people. I do not think she was either the ambitious, self-serving manipulator or the innocent, helpless victim others have made her out to be. Though she began her life just trying to make things better for herself, she ended it trying to improve this country for everyone. Without her the Liberation Party may have never come to power. Without her Phoenix could still be controlling the country and we would have none of the freedoms we enjoy today.

Like many people I often wonder what things would have been like had she lived. Would she have made a better President than Cain? Would she have been more progressive, making more changes and at a greater rate? I'm certain the world would be a different place if she had crossed that threshold and taken her rightful place as our leader, but in what ways I cannot say. The fact that she died when she was so close to triumph is the greatest tragedy. She achieved so much and yet one man and one bullet brought it all to an end.

KNOW THIS
The Man Behind the Mask

Of all who loved her,
I did love her best.

I loved her in the night
When she was scared and couldn't sleep.
When she was drained by care,
Cross and tired and sick.

I loved her feet which hurt
From not wearing sensible shoes,
And her hands which were callused,
Worn rough by ropes and bars.

I loved her unfailing courage,
Her dogged refusal to give in,
Her quick sharp mind and ready wit.
I even loved her often short temper.

Of all who loved her,
I did love her best.

Island Nation Magazine
Saturday 12th October 2115

CONSPIRACY THEORIES
Simon Chandra

Some of the theories concerning Rosa's death are so wonderfully imaginative I find myself almost wishing they were true. I have been inundated with them ever since I began writing this column and I confess I am not entirely sure which ones I am intended to take seriously. Among the most ludicrous I have two personal favourites.

The first is that Rosa was actually an alien sent from another planet to restore democracy to Britain. When she was injured, the mother ship beamed her up so they could treat her with their advanced alien medicine before any human doctors could discover that she had two hearts.

The second is that the real Rosa, the circus performer, was killed in the Newman Grand bombing. The Rosa elected as President was a genetically engineered clone created by the Liberation Party to fight their campaign. Once Liberation had achieved power and the Rosa-clone had served her purpose, they killed her and disposed of her remains to prevent anyone from discovering that she was not the real Rosa.

There are many more equally outlandish theories but some are much harder to dismiss, especially those originating from people close to Rosa at the time of her death. Former 7th Interior Division officer Lieutenant Aaron Pierce is one of many people convinced that the official version of events is not true. Pierce was Rosa's driver on the day of her death. It was he who drove the armoured car to the clinic where she died. Pierce's scepticism comes not only from the unorthodox way in which Rosa's remains were disposed of but several other suspicious circumstances.

Since leaving the military Pierce has resided in the West Country, working mainly in agriculture. He lives a rather reclusive life and would not reveal his current address even to me. He fears his knowledge about Rosa's death could put his own life in danger. I had of course read Pierce's account of events before and had not been convinced. I thought he was either paranoid or had made the story up in order to sell it. I had regarded his claims that he feared for his life as self aggrandisement, but after meeting him in person I was less certain of these opinions.

We met in a small pub near Warminster station. For an ex-soldier Pierce looks decidedly bohemian these days. With his dark hair hanging down past his shoulders and his ragged clothing, he had an artfully dishevelled appearance which at first served to reinforce my doubts about the veracity of his story. He heartily recommended the local cider and I agreed to try it out of politeness but I confess I was rather alarmed when I was presented with a pint glass filled with murky liquid which could have come from the bottom of the nearest pond. I reluctantly took a sip and discovered it was not half as bad as I was expecting, in fact quite pleasant.

"It's the real thing this," Pierce assured me. "No chemicals, no sugar, no algae or genetically modified organisms, just fermented apple juice."

"It's not bad," I replied, "though I think it would look more appealing without the layer of sludge at the bottom of the glass."

"The sludge is the best part! It proves it is authentic West Country cider."

"So you have grown fond of this part of the country then?"

"I always was. I was born not far from here you know."

"You are rather dark for a Somerset lad."

"That's pretty racist coming from you. My parents were British and so were my grandparents."

"My apologies, I just meant that judging from your appearance you must have some Asian roots, as I do."

"Yes I have Asian roots, as many of my fellow officers liked to remind me."

"You mean you suffered discrimination?"

"I mean they called me a Paki and told me to fuck off back where I came from. You must know the score. Anyway I thought you came here to talk about Rosa, not racism in the army."

"I did, I was just trying to find out more about you."

"It isn't me you should be trying to investigate, it's David O'Brien."

"I have tried to contact Mr O'Brien but he has declined to be interviewed."

"I bet he has! He's kept a very low profile since Rosa's death hasn't he."

"I understand he lives a rather solitary life somewhere in the Scottish Highlands."

"Solitary! That's where you are wrong. He has a family."

"A family?"

"Yes. I did a bit of investigating of my own. I found out roughly whereabouts he lived from Tom Stanford, but even Tom had never been invited to visit. I went up to Kyle of Lochalsh, which is the nearest town of any sort. It is where the bridge over to Skye is so it used to be a reasonable sized town for that part of the world, but now it is like everywhere else out in the sticks, all empty houses, half falling down and most the residents over seventy. There are still a few shops there and most importantly there is a school.

"I asked around, at the shops, in pubs and at the school gates and quite a few people there knew O'Brien. They were reluctant to speak about him much as they have had quite a few journalists sniffing around in the past, but several people confirmed that O'Brien has two children who go to the primary school. Their mother seemed to be a bit of a mystery. No one knows where she came from or even if she and O'Brien are married. All I could find out about her is that her name is Eleanor.

"I never saw either her or O'Brien while I was there and the descriptions of the mysterious Eleanor I got were all rather vague. Most people estimated her as mid-thirties, average height and having either dark blonde or mousy brown hair. Some people said she was about average build and quite pretty, others said she was plump and plain, but I guess that is in the eye of the beholder."

"You didn't actually find out where they lived then?"

"No. I understand it is an old farmhouse out in the middle of nowhere, but there are so many empty buildings and deserted hamlets in that part of the world I didn't know where to start looking. I only spent a couple of days in Kyle anyway, as people started to get suspicious. They are rather protective, these isolated communities. They didn't want anyone poking into O'Brien's business."

"Are you sure it was the right David O'Brien? It's a fairly common name after all."

"How many David O'Brien's with a severely scarred face are there?"

"OK, fair point."

"Here is another good point. If O'Brien and this woman have two school-aged children they must have got together within a few years of Rosa's death. Now since he was supposed to be utterly devastated at losing her, he appears to have recovered fairly quickly."

"Just how old are these children? Are you certain they are O'Brien's? Might they not be this woman's children from a previous relationship?"

"I suppose it is possible, but I don't believe O'Brien ever loved Rosa at all. I believe he used her and manipulated her. Think about it. He must have known the dangers she would face as Liberation leader. If he really loved her he would have tried to stop her facing such risks, not encouraged her."

"He did his best to protect her. He saved her from the first assassination attempt."

"I'm certain he could have saved her from the second also had he wanted to. I was there. He let her go ahead into the building. More importantly I saw the wound when we lifted her into the car. I'm no doctor but I had seen a few bullet wounds during my army career. This wasn't life threatening. There was quite a lot of blood but she was conscious throughout the journey to the clinic. I heard her and the doctor talking. I heard him say she was going to be fine."

"Doctors generally say that, even to critically injured patients."

"True, but it was the way he said it. He sounded completely calm. Even when we realised that we weren't going to be able to get her to hospital he wasn't the least bit alarmed. He suggested the clinic and directed me there. O'Brien carried her into one of the examination rooms and stayed with her and his father. I was sent outside.

"I was standing by the door and I could hear their voices. Although I could not make out what they were saying, never at any point did they sound panicked or stressed and I am certain I heard Rosa's voice too. From what I heard I am convinced they were not fighting to save her life. After a while it went very quiet. Dr O'Brien came out and told me to take the car back to Westminster and fetch Cain. I asked how Rosa was but he refused to answer, just insisted that I fetch Cain immediately. I was on my way back when I heard over the radio that Rosa was dead."

"What do you believe happened?"

"I believe the O'Brien's murdered her. I believe it had been planned all along. David O'Brien seduced her with his love poems, convinced her to stand in the Hackney by-election, then encouraged her to take over the party leadership. Alicia Cain stood aside as she knew she would never lead Liberation to victory. She allowed Rosa to do the difficult and dangerous work then had her killed so she could resume her position and take over the Presidency. Unfortunately their assassin inside Parliament missed so David and his father had to finish the job off themselves, which was why they had me take her to the deserted clinic and why I was sent away."

"You have no evidence of this."

"Of course not. Dr O'Brien saw to that when he illegally disposed of Rosa's remains. While most people were demanding he face prosecution, Cain refused to have him charged. Meanwhile David O'Brien conveniently disappears completely and is living quite happily with another woman in the Highlands, no doubt with a large sum of money given to him by Cain."

From listening to Pierce talk it is clear that he is sane, rational and firmly believes in the truth of his story. He speaks about Rosa with great tenderness and there is genuine anger in his voice when he refers to Alicia Cain and the O'Brien's. Although I find it difficult to imagine O'Brien and President Cain as co-conspirators in a murder, Pierce's story fits the facts alarmingly well. I have always regarded the manner in which Dr O'Brien disposed of Rosa's remains and the fact that the President was so eager to defend him as highly suspicious. Like Pierce, I am now convinced there is more to it than the official account suggests, but unlike Pierce I am not ready to believe our President complicit in her murder.

What I found most unsettling about my interview with Pierce was the revelation that O'Brien has a family. From everything about him which I have learnt so far I believed him to be completely in love with Rosa. That he should be living a reclusive grief-stricken life in the Highlands seemed to fit with the picture I had built up of his character. A partner and children do not fit at all.

I am now facing a dilemma as to how I should proceed. Uncovering any evidence to either prove or disprove Pierce's claims is extremely unlikely ten years after Rosa's death, especially considering the absence of a body. President Cain has refused to enter into any discussion of so called conspiracy theories so no new information is likely to originate from her. This only leaves one avenue of investigation, the O'Brien's. I contacted Dr Nathaniel O'Brien but received only a brief reply saying that he had nothing to add to his previous statements. David O'Brien has not responded to any of my attempts to communicate.

Though I seem to be at a dead end I refuse to accept defeat. I appeal to you, my readers, for help. Someone must know some small detail, though it may seem insignificant, which could be the key to the whole case. Contact me please. Let us work together and finally discover the whole truth.

ROSA'S ILLNESS
Simon Chandra

I must begin by thanking you for your responses to my appeal for help. I have been completely inundated with emails and have had to enlist several colleagues to help me sift through them all for valuable information. To my great surprise my mother actually volunteered to assist me in this task. It would seem she is no longer convinced that this column is a selfish indulgence on my part. I have gained many little insights into Rosa and O'Brien and could easily fill this page for several weeks with interesting anecdotes about them, but I feel I ought to concentrate on the final part of Rosa's story, on her death.

The most promising lead came from another 7th Interior officer, Lieutenant Alexander Lee, who had been a corporal in Major Stanford's unit at the time when they were responsible for Rosa's protection. I was fascinated by what Lt Lee had to say so arranged to meet him in person at the first possible opportunity. Our rendezvous was at a pub in South Bermondsey near to the Interior Defence Barracks. Lt Lee is rather short and slight for an army officer but his collection of medal ribbons suggests he is an extremely capable soldier in spite of his stature. His hair is chestnut brown, his eyes blue and he appears much younger than his thirty-one years.

Lt Lee was very anxious to tell me that Aaron Pierce's story was complete rubbish.

"I was with Rosa and O'Brien a great deal during those last weeks and I can tell you with absolute certainty that he would never do anything to harm her. He adored her. He was utterly devoted and would have done anything to protect her."

"Why have you never spoken about the time you spent with them before now?"

"Because it was private. I have only chosen to talk about it now because I am tired of hearing all these lies about them. I don't know why Pierce has nominated himself as expert on the subject of O'Brien and Rebecca when he didn't spend anything like as much time with them as I did. I spent nearly two months guarding that flat, sometimes at the door, sometimes on the balcony and often in the living-room with them. I saw what was going on. I couldn't help knowing about it."

"What was going on?"

"Rebecca was sick."

"That is hardly surprising considering the stress she was under."

"No it was more than that. I mean she was seriously ill. She wasn't well when we first arrived on the scene but I assumed that was because of her ordeal with the police. She recovered and seemed OK for a couple of weeks but then she started complaining of headaches and feeling sick."

"That just sounds like nerves to me."

"I thought that at first but O'Brien was getting worried about her. His dad had moved into one of the empty flats, as had Karen Baker, Sean Nichols and several others of Rosa's staff. O'Brien insisted that she let his dad examine her. Dr O'Brien came while David O'Brien was out on patrol with Major Stanford. David had told me that when he wasn't there I should keep a constant watch on Rebecca but obviously I made some exceptions, like when she was in the bathroom. I remained in the living-room while she and the doctor went into the bedroom. They were in there for a good twenty minutes before the doctor came out and asked me to call David on the radio and tell him to come back immediately. Rebecca was crying.

"Once David arrived the doctor left. David asked me to wait in the hallway. He shut the living-room door but I still heard some of what they were saying.

"At first she was speaking softly then I heard him exclaim, 'Jesus Christ! When? How long?' I heard him repeat her answer, 'Six months,' and I think he was crying too. There can be no doubt about what those words meant. She must have been terminally ill and the six months were how long the doctor thought she had left."

"You can't be certain of that. You didn't hear the whole conversation."

"I heard what followed so I am certain. He was begging her to stand down as party leader but she insisted that she had to carry on. I clearly heard her say, 'Afterwards Alicia will have to take over, but not yet. I have to keep going for as long as I can.' When they had finished talking I went with them up onto the roof as Rebecca needed some fresh air. She could hardly walk. She almost fainted in the lift and David and I had to support her."

"Have you any idea what her illness was?"

"No, I'm not a doctor. I remember Dr O'Brien coming to see her a few days later. She had been vomiting all morning. She complained, 'Those pills you gave me are no bloody good at all.' He said he was sorry and I recall his exact words were, 'You would think we would have a cure by now but sometimes nothing works.' He gave her some advice about trying to eat and making sure she didn't get dehydrated. Before he left she said, 'I just hope this is over soon, I'm not sure how much more I can take.' He replied, 'I wish I had better news for you but I'm afraid there is nothing more I can do.' Then he hugged her and kissed her on the cheek. She went back to the bedroom to lie down so I asked the doctor what was wrong. He said that he couldn't tell me but he patted me on the back and asked me to take good care of her. I promised that I would."

"Why do you think they were so anxious to keep Rosa's illness secret?"

"I suppose they didn't want her enemies to know about it. Or perhaps they just wanted to keep it private."

"Do you think Dr O'Brien arranged the disposal of her body to prevent her illness being discovered?"

"No I think there is more to it than that. Although I don't believe Aaron Pierce knew the whole story I believe his account of the day she was shot is the truth. The bullet wound probably wasn't that serious and Dr O'Brien could have treated it. I believe he lied. He announced her death when she was still alive, although very sick. David then took her away to Scotland or wherever, so she could die in peace. I don't think they planned it, as such. I think they just took advantage of circumstances as they happened. As soon as she was shot there were rumours going around that she had been killed. David and his father took the opportunity to protect her from the frenzy of publicity her illness and death would have produced. I expect Alicia Cain knows all this which is why she defended Dr O'Brien from those who wanted him prosecuted."

"What about this woman Pierce talked about? Where do she and her children fit into the story?"

"I don't know anything about them. Perhaps they exist or perhaps Pierce was mistaken. It isn't impossible that David could have met another woman, although after seeing him with Rebecca I find it hard to imagine."

On leaving Captain Lee I was completely convinced of the truth of his theory. It fitted perfectly with all I had learned about Rosa and O'Brien so far. My only doubt was regarding the exact nature of her illness. From the symptoms Lee described New Aids seemed likely, and would also fit with their desire for secrecy. As soon as I returned home I began to research various medical reference sites, hoping to add more backing to my supposition but the results had the opposite effect.

Although the headaches, vomiting and faintness Lee described fit the diagnosis of New Aids, he did not mention skin lesions or symptoms of respiratory disease which, are typical. My next idea was that she was suffering from some kind of cancer but it is usually the treatment for cancer which causes vomiting and not the cancer itself. Nothing Captain Lee told me seemed to suggest she was undergoing chemotherapy.

You are probably ahead of me, but whenever I entered Rosa's symptoms into a medical database one diagnosis repeatedly came up, pregnancy. Then I got thinking about the exact wording of what Lee had overheard. Perhaps the six months referred to was not how long she had to live but how long until the baby arrived. If she were pregnant of course O'Brien would beg her to give up her campaign. The words "Afterwards Alicia will have to take over," could have meant after the birth, not after Rosa's death.

Does this mean that Rosa did die of the bullet wound after all and that Dr O'Brien disposed of her body to conceal her condition? Why would he take such extreme measures to conceal a pregnancy, especially when David and Rosa were married? Was it just to preserve their privacy?

I believe, or rather I want to believe, that part of Lee's story is true. The weight of responsibility on Rosa's shoulders was immense. So much was expected of her. People believed in her. They were prepared to die for her. She could not simply quit and walk away. Only her death allowed her to hand over the leadership of the party to Cain without any shame or recriminations. Is it possible that rather than lying about her death so that she could end her life in peace, David and Nathaniel O'Brien lied so she could *live* in peace?

Which brings me to the woman and two children in Scotland. Eleanor was Rebecca Clayton's middle name. It is true the description of the woman Pierce gave me was not much like Rosa but it is ten years since anyone saw her. Ten years, some hair dye and the birth of two children could easily change the beautiful, slim, raven haired Rosa into plain, mousey haired Eleanor.

Perhaps it is just a childish desire for a happy ending that makes me so desperately want this to be true. Maybe I am wrong and Rosa is dead, but I intend to do whatever it takes to find out the truth one way or another. I shall bombard both Dr O'Brien and his son with emails and calls and if necessary I will bang on every door in the Highlands. My mother is now convinced that I have become one of the paranoid, delusional, obsessive maniacs whose conspiracy theories I ridiculed only a week ago. A small part of me fears she may be right but I intend to pursue this investigation either until I have the truth or they lock me up.

THE TRUTH AT LAST
Simon Chandra

After all the rash promises I made last week, finding the conclusion to Rosa's story turned out to be much easier than I expected. Shortly after my column went to press I received the following email:

> Dear Mr Chandra,
>
> I apologise for not responding to your many emails sooner but I was interested to see how your narrative would progress without my contribution. I have been reading your column with interest and congratulate you on your thorough and unbiased investigation. However since your line of inquiry now threatens to disturb the peace of my neighbours I thought I would save you a journey.
> I will be coming down to London on Wednesday for a meeting with the President. If you wish to speak with me in person I will meet with you then.
>
> Yours sincerely
> David O'Brien

I responded immediately agreeing to meet with him. At first we were going to meet in Portcullis House, but on Wednesday morning I received another message from him suggesting that since the weather was so good we ought to meet at Duck Island in St James's Park. At this point I began to fear I was being set up. Perhaps I was about to go on a wild goose (or possibly tame duck) chase.

With more hope than expectation I went to the agreed location and was immensely relieved to find my suspicions were ill-founded. There, sitting on a bench tossing scraps of bread to the assembled birds was David O'Brien. His face was exactly as it appeared in all the pictures from ten years ago. The mass of scars completely hides any evidence of aging. His hair is now flecked with grey, but otherwise he is exactly the same as the man in the news footage, the man who lifted Rosa into the back of the armoured car the last time we saw her.

He recognised me from the pictures on my website and stood to shake my hand.

"It is good to finally meet you," I said.

"Yes, here we are at last," he replied and invited me to sit down beside him.

He offered me some of the bread which I accepted out of politeness and tossed it half-heartedly towards the water. The ducks did not seem to be interested but the pigeons and gulls pecked at it eagerly. After our initial greeting he seemed reluctant to say anything more and I had so many questions I didn't know which to ask first. I went for the most important one.

"Was I right?"

"You were wrong about one thing. A few weeks ago you speculated as to why I haven't had surgery to get rid of these scars. You came up with several romantic suggestions but I'm afraid the truth is much more mundane. I just couldn't be bothered. I didn't want the pain, the days in hospital, the poking and prodding. It was just too much trouble."

"But what about Rosa? Is she alive?"

"No, Rosa died shortly after Alistair Cartwright's bullet hit."

My stomach sank in disappointment. I was wrong after all. She was gone. Then I thought about his words.

"What about Rebecca?" I asked.

"Rebecca Eleanor O'Brien is alive and well."

I literally jumped for joy. I leapt to my feet and scattered the pigeons as I cried out in elation. Several of the passing joggers and dog walkers turned to stare but I didn't care.

I sat down again and said, "She was pregnant wasn't she?"

"She was."

"But how?"

He smiled a crooked half smile and replied, "Well, when a man and a woman love each other there is this thing that they do—"

I interrupted his sarcasm, "Yes I know that part, I mean why wasn't she using a contraceptive? It can't have been planned."

"It certainly wasn't planned. You see when Becky first moved in with me she cut off all ties with her old life to stop Bryant's people from hounding her. She changed her email and phone number and never gave her new contact details to the Family Planning Authority. The whole system being automated when her next appointment was due, the letter just went to her old address, then the reminder, then the warning, then the fixed penalty notice.

"By the time anyone actually bothered to look into it and try to contact Rebecca we were in the run up to the election so you can understand how she could forget about it completely. It was only after my dad examined her and asked when she last had her contraceptive injection that she actually realised she hadn't had it. Even when she started throwing up it hadn't occurred to either of us that she could be pregnant. It seems really dumb now but with all that was going on we had sex so rarely and she had assumed the absence of her periods was just because of stress and had never even mentioned it."

"So she had the baby?"

"Yes, a little boy. His name is Daniel."

"And you have both been living in Scotland all this time without anyone knowing! Surely someone would have recognised her. I mean everyone knows what Rosa looks like. She was the most famous woman in the country."

"It is because everyone knows what Rosa looks like which made it so easy for Rebecca to go unnoticed. When people think of Rosa they see dark hair, pale skin and red lips but none of that is real."

"You realise that people are going to be furious when they find out they have been lied to all these years? Everyone was devastated by Rosa's death. People were weeping in the streets. How are they going to respond when they learn she has been alive and well all this time?"

"I don't know. I only hope that when you explain all the circumstances they will forgive us. I can't pretend it has been easy. We have both felt the guilt for our deception and living with such an immense secret is a constant struggle. Daniel is just getting to the age when he realises something is not right. He sees how other families live and knows how different it is to our reclusive lifestyle. Once you uncovered the truth we felt it was time to come clean and hopefully start rebuilding some sort of normal life."

"Who knew about this?"

"Other than Rebecca and me, only my dad and Alicia. It wasn't planned beforehand. When the bullet hit I was terrified. I thought I was going to lose her and our child. My dad was in the car because from the moment we first knew she was pregnant I insisted he stayed close the whole time. He examined her and said that she would be all right but I was still afraid she would lose the baby. I vividly remember every moment of that journey. After we had finally managed to cross Waterloo Bridge, Lt Pierce was on the radio and I heard someone tell him not to go to St Thomas' but to proceed to the Royal London instead. I started to panic. I knew it would take hours to get through the crowds. Dad was perfectly calm and thinking far more clearly. He directed Pierce to the clinic in Southwark.

"When we arrived at the clinic, Dad examined the wound under local anaesthetic. The bullet wasn't in very deep so he extracted it and stitched her up in a matter of minutes. I was still panicking about the baby but a quick check up revealed he was fine too. Not that we knew he was a he then, it was too soon. Of course by this time Alicia, Tom, Karen and everyone were calling trying to find out what was going on.

"I spoke to Alicia first and I remember her saying, 'What the hell is going on? People are saying she's dead.' I thought I replied that she wasn't dead but afterwards Alicia told me I was completely incoherent. You see I suddenly felt terrible. The room was spinning and I thought I was going to be sick. I hung up on Alicia without answering her questions and sat down before I fell. Dad was talking to me, asking if I was OK but it was like being drunk. I knew what I wanted to say but just couldn't articulate the words.

"It was Dad who had the idea of announcing Rebecca's death. He sent Pierce away then he called Alicia. He hadn't time to work out the details so he told her to say that Rebecca had died instantly from a shot to the chest. Of course he had to revise this story later as you know. I wasn't really thinking straight at the time. I just wanted to protect my wife and child. I wanted to take her far away from the people who were trying to kill her, so when Dad gave me the keys to one of the clinic's patient transport cars and told me take her and go, I did. It wasn't until days later I realised the enormity of what we had done."

"Do you think if you had had time to consider you would have done the same?"

"Probably, but who can say? I think Rebecca might have been more reluctant to go along with it if she hadn't been recovering from shock and woozy with loss of blood. There were several times in the months afterwards when she called Alicia and asked her to come clean, but Alicia always advised her against it."

"I suppose it would have been political suicide for Alicia to admit one of her first acts as President was to lie to her people."

"Yes, but it wasn't just that. Alicia does actually care about Rebecca. She felt bad about handing her the Party leadership and putting her literally in the firing line. Between us we agreed to wait until the baby was born and then reconsider our position. Then when Daniel arrived everything changed. To be perfectly honest Rebecca and I didn't give a shit about anything else anymore."

"I still find it hard to believe that no one recognised her. Surely people must have thought it was odd that you were living with another woman so soon after Rebecca's death? People must have asked questions."

"We didn't go straight up to Scotland. My Dad still owned a house in North Norfolk. It used to belong to my Gran and it is impossible to sell because it is in one of those half flooded villages which won't be there for much longer. It still has running water but no electricity, phone or internet. There are a few other old folks still living in the village, desperately clinging to the mouldering remains of what were their homes. There is a bus service into Norwich once a week but otherwise it is totally isolated. It certainly isn't the sort of house I would recommend for a couple expecting a child but we were fugitives and didn't have much choice.

"My Dad visited us regularly and looked after Rebecca throughout the pregnancy. We were most worried that something would go wrong with the delivery and she would have to go into hospital. Then she would surely be recognised and our deception revealed. As it was the birth went without a hitch. We stayed in Norfolk for about eighteen months after Dan was born but the isolation and rising damp started to depress us. When we found out we were expecting another child, planned this time, we decided to make a fresh start.

"We chose the Highlands pretty much on a whim. Rebecca had never been there and I had fond memories of going on hiking holidays with Dad. We bought our cottage for less than the price of my flat and set about doing it up. It has a wood-burning stove which supplies heating and hot water, that was a vast improvement on my Gran's place. After I sold my book we had solar panels and a wind generator fitted. We grow our own food and we keep chickens."

"It sounds idyllic."

"It is, but also it's lonely. We don't have friends over for dinner, go out to the pub or do any of the things normal people do. Obviously we see people in Kyle; other parents, our kids' teachers, the doctor, the shopkeepers, but we have not been able to form friendships."

"How do you suppose all your old friends will react when they hear this? How do you think they will feel when they learn she is alive?"

"It is hard to say. The fact is we didn't have many close friends. Apart from each other there were very few people who we confided it and I've been a loner since I left the army."

"Is there any chance I could talk to Rebecca herself?" I asked hopefully.

"Sure, come on."

"Where are we going?"

"To the hotel. Rebecca and the kids have been out sightseeing but they are probably back in the room by now."

"She's here in London!"

"Yes, we thought it was time Dan and Martha saw Big Ben and Nelson's Column."

"You mean I am actually going to meet her? After all these weeks writing about her I'm actually going to speak to her?"

"Of course. She's been as fascinated by your articles as I have and is very curious to meet you."

O'Brien and his family were staying in one of the new hotels near Elephant & Castle. Though smaller and with fewer facilities than the major chains such as Newman's, they are friendlier and more suited to families. It was only a short walk from the tube station to the hotel but by the time we got there my heart was hammering. As we entered the foyer my knees were trembling. O'Brien made a quick call on his mobile and informed me they were coming down to join us.

We took a seat in the lounge area and O'Brien ordered tea. A few minutes later the lift doors opened and a pair of curly haired children came tearing across the foyer towards us, shouting. They threw themselves on their father, excitedly telling him about their day. I was almost trampled in the stampede and by the time I had recovered my composure she was standing next to me.

"You must be Simon," she said.

I'm afraid I just stared. It was definitely her, but she was so different from all the pictures I had seen. She was older, her hair was lighter and she had perhaps put on a little weight. Certainly her face was softer and more rounded than the face I knew. She was wearing no make-up and dressed in jeans and a baggy jumper. I could see why the other mums at the school gate wouldn't give her a second glance. And yet she was still incredibly beautiful. As I stared she smiled, and suddenly I was an adolescent boy again. All my youthful desire was suddenly reborn. I tried desperately to say something, anything.

"How is your mother?" she asked while I was still struggling with my thirteen year old self.

I replied that my Mum was well.

"She must be really proud of you. I understand your articles about me are extremely popular."

"Even she won't be able to say that this column was a waste of time now."

There were so many questions I should have asked but my mind was a blur. While I was struggling to put my thoughts into some kind of order the children were describing some of the statues they had seen at the British Museum in anatomical detail.

"Do you plan on returning to politics?" I asked.

"Hell no!" she replied.

"Perhaps you regret ever getting involved in the first place?"

"No, I don't really have any regrets. Alicia is a much better President than I would have been but she needed my fame and popularity to get the party noticed. I'm sorry that we deceived my supporters but when I consider the alternatives I think we made the right choice. We have led a rather sheltered and lonely life up in Scotland but at least we were safe and had our privacy. I would have hated raising my children under the scrutiny of the press and surrounded by bodyguards. I can only hope that people will understand that and will forgive me."

"I think most will," I answered. "I believe the majority of people will be so glad that you are alive they would gladly forgive you for far worse than wanting to protect your children."

"And what do you think? Do you think what we did was right?"

"I do," I replied honestly, "and not just because it gives me a fantastic story."

"You've earned your exclusive. You have worked hard and uncovered far more truth than any of the other journalists who have written about me."

"But there is so much more I want to know. If I had known I was going to meet you today I would have written a list of questions. There are still so many things I don't understand. I feel like I have only scratched the surface."

"Perhaps we can arrange an interview some other time. I expect the kids are getting hungry and we promised them pizza tonight."

At the word "pizza", cheers rose from the children followed by a discussion about favourite toppings.

"I doubt one interview will do justice to your remarkable story."

"Then we'll do several, but you may be disappointed. I'm actually a lot less interesting than people seem to think. The times in my life when I have been the happiest have generally been the dullest so perhaps I'm actually quite a boring person."

"Oh no, you are a most remarkable person."

"If you insist, but I'm taking my husband and my kids for pizza. We'll talk some other time."

"You realise that once I break this story there will be a complete media frenzy?"

"I do. We'll be back in the Highlands by then so I fully expect to find reporters hiding in the heather and crawling out of peat bogs. It will be hell for a while but I dare say they will go away eventually when they realise we're only going to talk to you."

"I'm honoured. You are handing me the biggest scoop of the decade. I feel like the man who wondered why his mattress was so uncomfortable then found it was because it was stuffed full of money. I'm forever going to be known as the man who broke the Rosa story. I feel quite giddy."

"Goodbye Simon, we'll talk again soon."

"Goodbye Rebecca, I look forward to getting to know you."

We shook hands and I left the hotel with a floating feeling of elation. I was excited about breaking this story. I was anxious to tell my colleagues the news, especially my Mum. I knew that this would be a huge leap forward for my career. Now every editor in the country would know my name and would regard me as a journalist in my own right and not Monica Chandra's son. Yet in spite of all this the thing that gave me the most joy was the simple knowledge that she was alive and happy.

As I walked back towards the tube station I realised that had she asked me not to break the story, to lie and say that she had died, I would have done so gladly. I could easily have sacrificed the biggest break of my life for her happiness. It would be a small recompense for all that she had done for this country. My mum will be furious when she reads this but perhaps journalism is not really in my blood afterall.

The tube was packed with commuters wearing the usual weary, vacant expressions on their faces. Several gave me strange looks, no doubt wondering why I was grinning so much. I wanted to yell out "Rosa is alive" but thought it best to save the news for my readers. As we rattled along I thought of the family eating pizza together. Such a simple thing, but somehow so wonderful. Perhaps it was the contrast between the glamorous Rosa of my youth and the wife and mother I had just met which made the image seem so extraordinary, or perhaps it was the children's delight over this small treat that made me realise how much we have to be thankful for.

Thanks to the Liberation Party and thanks to Rosa we live in a country where we are free to fall in love, to have as many children as we want, when we want, to travel, to live wherever we choose and to watch, read, write and think what we like. Though the wealth and luxuries of the previous century are long gone we have weathered the storm of poverty and disease and come through it. As I left the tube station and ascended into the sunshine I was overflowing with optimism and longed to share it. I called my parents and invited myself around for dinner.